Jenny's Dream

Victoria Morrow

POCKET BOOKS

New York   London   Toronto   Sydney   Tokyo   Singapore

For Jennifer Shanno, my sister and my friend,
who taught me the true meaning
of courage many years ago. I love you, Jeni.

Vicky

An *Original* Publication of POCKET BOOKS

POCKET BOOKS, a division of Simon & Schuster Inc.
1230 Avenue of the Americas, New York, NY 10020

ISBN: 0-671-70163-0

First Pocket Books printing May 1990

10 9 8 7 6 5 4 3 2 1

POCKET and colophon are registered trademarks of Simon & Schuster Inc.

Printed in the U.S.A.

ACKNOWLEDGMENTS

A book is a child—*JENNY'S DREAM* is my first, and I know she will not be my last. But, like all children, she came into being with the help of more than one person; in this case, quite a few more. Joan Diamond and Sherry Newman of DMS, carefully screened and typed each raw page, always letting me know what they liked and what they didn't. They were my "secretarial support," and more—they were my friends. Then I was extraordinarily blessed with a wonderful agent, who found my manuscript in a mountain of others, and most importantly, liked what she read. It was a rough, untutored child, crude and disorganized; but she saw something there that my inexperienced eyes couldn't perceive, and she drew out all the bits of beauty hiding there until *JENNY'S DREAM* seemed to shine. She had confidence in me—a new writer who didn't even know what SASE stood for—and she patiently taught me as I stumbled my way through this new world. Her name is Irene Goodman, and no aspiring writer could be as lucky or as blessed as I was to have found her. I can never repay what she has done for me, not in a million years or a hundred manuscripts. She gave me a chance to fulfill my dream. Thank you, Irene, from the bottom of my heart.

Also, I would like to take this opportunity to recognize John Scognamiglio, my editor, and a wonderfully talented writer, whose enthusiasm for my work brought it to the attention of some very important people. After prying a few doors open for me, he then proceeded to painstakingly use his journalistic expertise in crafting a neat manuscript out of an awkward pile of papers. Metaphorically speaking: I gave him an uncut stone; he gave me a diamond. Thank you, John. I couldn't have asked for a better teacher, or a more considerate friend.

And last but not least, my husband, Dan, and our son Dan Christopher. They have had a great deal to put up with these last few years, but they loved me enough to let me follow my heart, encouraging me to continue, when I was ready to give up. They gave me the gift of hope, and nothing I could say could possibly express how much I love them for that.

Here's to *JENNY'S DREAM*. She belongs to us all.

I thank you.

Vicky Morrow

CANTO 120

I have tried to write paradise

Do not move
Let the wind speak
That is paradise

Ezra Pound

ALASKA

Is not all dark night and cold wind
It is the bluest of blue skies
And the longest of long days
It is the immortal dance
Of life and death
Into eternity
It is

Paradise

M.

PROLOGUE

Kansas City, Missouri,
Winter of 1847

Hey! Stop, you lil' bastard—that's my bread!"

The dirty little boy with the runny nose pistoned his legs faster, hitting the ground hard with his small, uncovered feet. Slush lay on the boards, gray and cold, in the late October day, and it burned his skin like fire as he ran, clutching the loaf of bread to his chest.

He was so hungry. His stomach kept contracting painfully as he thought of the still warm bread in his arms . . . but, it wasn't for him.

He could hear the fat man coming closer now, and he glanced quickly over his shoulder. The man, whom he had stolen the bread from, was gaining on him. His huge body swayed as he ran, puffing, along the boards.

No one paid them any mind as the chase continued, and the boy seemed less than a ghost as he ran with his stolen treasure, weaving through the people as expertly and quickly as a thief, which is what he had become. A small, ragged boy with flaming hair.

He knew the streets well and felt a sense of relief as he recognized the alley ahead. If he could make it down there, past the doors to the old broken fence and squeeze through . . .

"Gotcha!" screamed the fat man jubilantly. The boy felt thick fingers pressing into his shoulders, turning him around. He looked up into the man's face, his green eyes burning coldly with a fierce hatred too old for one so young. He didn't flinch or struggle to get away. He just looked at him without fear, and this made the fat man furious.

"You stole my bread!" he spluttered. The fat man tensed, startled to see such fury in the eyes of a child and shook him violently.

The boy just stared, knowing what was coming. He'd been beaten before, many times, and he knew he was too small to do anything about it now, but someday . . .

"Oh!" the fat man sneered. "Yer a tough one, ain't ya?" He twisted his fingers cruelly into the boy's wasted shoulder. "Well, we'll just see how tough, boy, 'cause I'm gonna thrash you within an inch of yer life!" He pulled back his arm, curling his hand into a fist.

The boy swallowed and slowly raised his eyes to the face above him. They were dry, green and intense, and as if the fat man had read his mind, he flinched, as the boy waited helplessly.

"Don't look at me that way, boy!" he snarled. The fist came down, crashing into the side of the boy's head, rocking him backward.

He would have fallen if the man hadn't been holding him up. The pain was numbing, he was dizzy, and he wanted to cry, but he couldn't. His tears were all used up. They had been spent and flowing along the deck of the ship that had brought him and his mother to this place from Ireland, spent on the dirty floors where he had slept, and on the fists of the other boys who stole his food and called him a "dirty mick." No, he wouldn't cry, not now, especially not in front of this man, but someday they would pay . . .

Another blow caught him squarely in the nose and he felt a lightning bolt of pain in his head. His vision blurred as he struggled to retain consciousness. He shook his head weakly from side to side, trying to focus on the face above him. A great roaring began in his ears, and he felt strangely disconnected from his tiny body, as the fat man, his face contorted with rage, began to beat the boy in earnest.

Later, much later, the man took his bread and walked away, leaving what looked like a pile of rags in the snow.

The boy looked up slowly, one eye already swelling shut. He hurt all over, but he still managed a small, weak smile to himself. Reaching into the tattered rags covering his skinny body, he pulled out a piece of bread, a part of the crust he had managed to save. He swallowed hard, his mouth watering so much it made him weak. Slowly he stood up, every muscle in his battered body screaming in protest, as he turned into the long, low alley. Filthy rags lay strewn about, with broken boxes and bottles scattered randomly around them. Water dripped and ran down the center, creating a dirty little stream where garbage floated freely. He walked unsteadily along it, following it until he came to a broken fence and squeezed through, into a courtyard of broken windows where people lay like scattered ruins. He didn't seem to see them as he picked his way along, searching for the low, dark window that was his door. He found it at the bottom of a building, its glass long since gone, and he slipped easily between the jambs into the darkened room. He stood still for a moment, waiting for his eyes to adjust to the gloom. It stank in here, in spite of the cold. Sweat and urine, dirt, and a dark, sick smell—all mixed together, surrounded him.

"Mum?" he whispered, and tiptoed softly to the far wall. Down in a corner was a lumpy brown blanket, so threadbare in spots you could see through it. His mother lay wrapped and shivering within.

"Mum?" he asked softly. The once beautiful eyes opened slowly. She tried to smile and reach for him, but she was too weak.

"Child!" she cried happily, her fever giving her voice a dreamlike and faraway quality that made the boy afraid. He knelt down beside her, picking up her wasted hand in his.

"I brung sumtin' to eat, Mum," he said eagerly. He stretched out his free hand with the crusty bread to her mouth.

"No, son . . . I'm naught a bit hungery." She pushed the crust away from her, toward him, and smiled a little sadly.

"Eat it, son . . . eat it an' gro' strong for yer Mum."

Her breathing was becoming rapid and shallow, and her skin had taken on an ashen hue, but in the dim light, the boy couldn't see.

"Eat it," she repeated. The command was weak and filled with sorrow, but he obeyed, shoving the crust into his dry mouth. He barely chewed, swallowing the bread and wanting more, but knowing there wasn't any. He heard his mother sigh, and he felt her thin arm reach for his and the soft rustle of the blanket being drawn away.

"Cum here, lad . . . yer so cold. Cum lay down beside me and sleep."

He was weary and submitted quickly, stretching out beside her. She felt dry and hot against his skin, but she warmed him, and soon he fell asleep.

"Child," she whispered, stroking his soft hair. She held him tight, while hot tears rolled down her cheeks. She knew she was dying, but it didn't frighten her. Death seemed like a kindness to her now, but what about her son? Who would look after him when she was gone? She shuddered violently.

"Be strong," she murmured. "Be strong, an' gro' . . . Oh God!" she pleaded. "I do no' want to leave him!" The boy stirred restlessly against her, moaning in his sleep.

"Shhh . . . child," she soothed. "Shhh . . . now . . . I'm here . . ." She wrapped her arms tighter around him and prayed.

He was cold. Opening his eyes to the sunlight streaming through the window, he shivered. He had moved in his sleep, and when he sat up he noticed that the blanket had been wrapped securely around him.

"Mum!" he cried in terror, and stood up quickly, looking around the room until he spotted her. Then he ran, dropping to his knees even before he stopped, nearly falling on top of her. She was lying against the far wall, a small, sad smile frozen on her face. He reached out to touch her, and drew back in horror at her coldness. "Mum!" he screamed, and wrapped his arms about her, willing his warmth to her, wanting to make her well. "No . . . Mum! Do-o-n't le-leave me!" The dam he thought was dry burst open. Great wrenching sobs filled him, and a great wound was torn open in his soul.

The people in the courtyard looked up, each pausing for a second at the sound of the intense, painful cries they heard. Pity and a knowing light filled some of their eyes, but they were used up, too. Their lives had been battered and tossed about by a seemingly uncaring fate, and the feelings that would have shown they were human were quickly replaced by their own desires to survive for at least one more day.

Later, much later, when the light had changed, and only poked feebly into his room, he stood up. With old, tired steps he walked around the room, searching for a sharp stick. When he found one, he fell to the earth and began digging with hard, violent strokes. He wanted her to rest in the earth, comforted by its cool walls and protected from the rats and prying eyes of people. But after an hour of furious digging only an inch of soil would move. Exhausted, he gave up. Even the cursed ground of this country refused to open for her!

He was dazed and nothing seemed real. He moved as if he were in a dream and headed for the window, unable to look back, as he pulled himself through it. Some of the people scattered around looked up guiltily, but he knew they wouldn't help him. He was a dirty mick, a potato eater and worth less then spit. He was an Irishman.

He stared at them, bright anger in his eyes.

"What're ya lookin' at?" he screamed. "Ain't ya never seen an Irishmun b'fore?"

Slowly, he turned and walked toward the broken fence, gulping great chunks of air to hold back the tears as he went. When he reached the fence he didn't try to squeeze through. He gripped a loose board and pulled back sharply. It creaked and snapped and he dropped it to the ground. With his head held high, he walked through it, a lonely, angry boy with flaming hair.

CHAPTER

1

"Gannon! Mr. Gannon! Time's a-wasting!"

Dugan's lighthearted voice rang out, followed by a heavy fist beating a staccato rhythm against the old, oak door.

"Are you planning to sleep all day?"

"What if I am?" Aaron growled imperiously. "It would be a definite improvement over looking at your ugly face all day!"

Laughter rang out from the other side of the door.

"That may be true, my young friend, but I don't think lying in there will pay your mortgage. Besides," he added, "Mr. Addison's here to, ah, pay his respects."

Aaron sighed. "Fine, Dugan," he said gruffly. "I'm coming."

He rolled away from the young girl sleeping peacefully in his bed, and shouted at the door.

"Have Joshua bring some strong tea and eggs to the study."

He stood up, reaching for the brown, silk pants he had worn last night to the Governor's dinner. It had been a boring affair, with moderately good food and plenty to drink. The only thing which had kept him from sliding into total oblivion was the bevy of young ladies who regularly

6

attended these affairs, hoping for a "match." There were dozens of eager, young debutantes, who decorated the halls and drawing rooms like rare pastel flowers in their brightly colored silks, and the lovely, blond creature curled up sweetly in his quilts had been one of these rare flowers who had danced and fluttered her eyelashes and smiled sweetly at him from the moment he had entered the room.

He had been late because of a business meeting. When he was finally ushered into the hall, a moment of silence fell upon the crowd of people who had been animatedly talking and eating.

He was not the elected Governor, though he could have been, or a king of a foreign country or a prince, but he ruled Kansas City, and everyone knew it.

Pride and power were in his every movement, as his long, lean legs carried him into the hall, where the gas lights' flickering glow caused his hair to shimmer like golden-red fire around his noble face. His wide-set green eyes gave him a feline appearance like that of a majestic cat. He looked like a lion, king of the beasts, and he knew it. Women longed to stroke him and hear him purr and men were in awe of his legendary temper and iron fists.

He had accepted their silence as his tribute before he had entered the hall and was immediately surrounded by the women.

He smiled as he remembered the story the young girl had concocted in order to go home with him. She had told her parents that she was going to spend the night with her cousin. Since the cousin was newly married, and testified that the invitation was legitimate, swearing wholeheartedly that her younger cousin would be appropriately chaperoned, the girl's parents had agreed. Aaron had repaid the subterfuge with a night of memorable loving, expertly fulfilling all the physical needs they had felt with sensuous abandon and unbelievable stamina. He gave and gave with almost Herculean strength, and took all that she so willingly offered with a driving, obsessive hunger which left her weak and spent and confident of her own charms; and him, sadly empty.

This time had been just like all the rest, physically satisfying, mechanically perfect, but the act had lacked the thing he feared and desired most, *love.* His past had taught him many things he could never have learned in books, such as how to survive the streets by being faster, smarter, or stronger than your opponent, while the subtle art of camouflage had let him become nothing more than an observant shadow at will when the odds were too great; learning, always learning, and never forgetting anything no matter how insignificant it seemed at the time. He had been born in a time of famine, grown up with pale death a constant companion, been baptized to nearly drowning in the murkiest rivers of life, and yet he had somehow survived. Like the warrior Achilles he had grown into maturity, invincible and ready to do battle, except for one fatal flaw . . . his heart. He did his best to conceal its overtender condition in corded muscles and sinews of iron, isolating it from the world by a will of steel, which let no one in. To do so, he felt, would be certain suicide, because loving someone made you vulnerable and weak, promised you only pain, suffering and loss. For him it was the tortured memories of a desperate seven-year-old boy who stood helplessly by in filthy, threadbare rags as his beloved mother wasted away before his eyes. She had been the only good thing he had ever known in his short life; the very sun around which his small world revolved. Nothing within her power to give had been denied him, her only payment exacted in hugs, or sticky, honey-wet kisses placed eagerly on dry cheeks while his chubby, sweaty hands had reverently offered her fragrant bouquets of wilted dandelions and wild pink roses.

Catherine of the blue eyes and soft, heather-brown hair had given her love unconditionally to her little russet-headed son with the mischievous cat-green eyes. It was only natural that his forceful soul, which felt everything so keenly, with such fervent intensity and depth, could never respond to her devotion with tepid mediocrity. It was with fire and a fierce loyalty that he returned his mother's love, magnifying it a thousandfold. When she had died on that dismal winter's morning, his child's mind had expected the earth to shatter from the pain, the mountains to collapse in grief over their loss and the seas to boil over in anger. Yet, the thunder didn't roll and the earth didn't crack. Voices continued their chattering banter in the courtyard, the sun continued to shine, and the wind to blow indifferently through every crack and crevice in the room. Even his own traitorous heart continued to beat . . . da-dumm . . . da-dumm . . . slow and regular as always. The world had ignored her passing as if she had never existed. *Nothing happened.* Nothing . . . except deep inside himself Armageddon raged in cataclysmic horror, destroying his world forever. "Don't leave me, Mum!" he had cried, his tears falling, his small hands working feverishly, willing her to return.

But she was beyond his hearing, beyond his touch, and a deep, primitive wailing cry issued from his bowed head, echoing forlornly through the courtyard. His universe had collapsed, and he was left abandoned and alone with a void in his soul he could never hope to fill. Never again would he let anyone that close; the pain was too consuming, the price too high. He had loved many women in his time, but he had never given his heart to anyone and that was a prize that many coveted.

Sighing, he pushed his memories back once more, feeling so empty and alone that he ached inside. He buttoned the last button of his trousers, and raised his arms high above his head, the muscles of his back rippling with the slightest movement.

His socks came next, followed by a pair of glossy, black boots. He felt a hand touch him lightly, but didn't turn around as he reached for his shirt and slipped it on.

"Aaron?" asked the girl sweetly. "Will I be seeing you again?" She played with the sheet, pretending to study it with great interest as he turned halfway around, his hand already resting on the latch of the door. He gave her a warm and intimate smile.

"If you have no way to spend your day, perhaps you can

remain at your 'cousin's' for a while. I'll be finished with my business by noon, and I do enjoy a warm bed to climb into." He grinned at the blushing girl.

She swung her white legs over the bed and came quickly toward him. Hesitating, she looked up into his face and slid her arms up his chest as she pulled him gently forward to place a sweet kiss on his lips.

He responded to her kiss and the sight of her warmly. When she pulled away he was smiling at her in such a way that it made her blush. He winked impishly and placed a feather light kiss on her forehead before he opened the door. A moment later he was gone.

The study was quiet and soothing. The drapes had not been pulled, so it was dim, and for that Aaron was grateful.

His head was pounding dully, and he wished for his tea. But, headache or not, he wouldn't allow it to interfere with his business.

A single rap was made at his study door before Dugan's old and weathered face appeared from behind it.

Aaron looked up from the sheaf of papers he'd been studying and motioned him in. Joshua, his cook, trailed behind, loaded down with a tray and the morning paper.

"Well?" asked Aaron irritably. "What does Addison want *this* time?" His eyebrow shot up quizzically, giving his face a cynical look.

"He says that a boy who's been working for him has been skimmin' . . . and he wants you to do something about it."

Aaron nodded quietly. "Send him in." He looked back down at his papers as he rounded his desk and settled into his chair.

Joshua quickly placed Aaron's tray nearby and left without so much as a word, knowing that it was better to see little and talk less.

The door swished open again, whispering across the thick, Persian carpets. This time a red-faced Addison stormed through. His gray suit looked as if he'd slept in it and his belly threatened to pour over his belt. Aaron disliked him intensely, but it had nothing to do with business. He smiled a little to himself as he noticed how meticulously Addison had combed what was left of his hair. He had pulled the long strands from the back forward across his forehead and plastered them in place with dressing. They were salt-and-pepper gray and the comb had left furrows exposing his white scalp beneath.

Aaron's attention was drawn to the boy who had followed Addison in. He was young and stoop shouldered. His hair hung down past his neck in lifeless clumps and he refused to look up. Dugan stood behind him and gently closed the door.

"Gannon!" Addison burst out, stalking forward. "I demand that you do something with this boy! He's been stealing me blind!"

"Demand?" Aaron asked softly. "You *demand* I do something? He looked pointedly into Addison's watery-blue eyes.

"I mean . . . Mr. Gannon," Addison said nervously, dropping his eyes. "That I hired this boy on *your* recommendation . . . and as of this date, he has filched five cases of whiskey from me! See!" He shouted excitedly, waving a sheaf of papers at Aaron. "It's all here . . . in black and white, and I . . ."

He had been coming forward, but a look from Gannon froze him to the spot. He lowered the sheaf of papers and waited quietly while Aaron transferred his gaze to the miserable boy behind him.

"Danny," he said softly. "Is this true? Have you been stealing from me?"

The boy looked up, crimson roses in his cheeks, his eyes brilliant with tears. His skin was swollen tightly around his eyes and bruised nasty shades of black and blue.

"Yes!" he cried vehemently. "I stole the whiskey . . . but Mr. Add'son's owed me money and would'na pay me!"

His face was a mixture of fear and defiance as he turned to face the man he accused.

"I would'na have stolen, if you'd paid me what ya *owed* me!"

Addison started to sputter, spittle flying. "You lying, sneaking thief! I don't owe you a damn thing!" he screamed.

"You don't owe me? You've naught paid me now on two months . . . I've got lil' brothers and sisters to feed . . . I needed the money!"

His pleas were wasted on Addison, who had come to this country from England a wealthy man. He had never known want, nor shame, or lugged cases until his back felt ready to break. But Gannon knew.

"Is that true, Addison? Do you owe him money?"

"No!" he shouted. "He owed *me* for things. I deducted them from his wages!"

"Things!" shouted Danny indignantly. "I was late on deliveries because you made me run errands for your wife . . . and I broke a dish last week because you hit me for not being quick enough! And if I stop to eat during the day . . . you take all my wages!"

The boy was nearly in tears as Addison came toward him.

"Why you . . . no-good, Irish hooligan! I give you a job and this is how I'm repaid?"

He raised his walking cane and started for the boy, his face livid with rage. Danny made a small whimpering sound and instinctively raised his hands to cover his face, but before Addison could bring the cane forward, powerful hands gripped his arm.

"I wouldn't do that if I were you."

Addison turned in surprise and stood staring into the glittering, green eyes of Gannon.

He plucked the cane easily from Addison's hand and shoved the tip roughly into his stomach in one deft movement. Addison groaned loudly and bent over, clutching his sides.

Gannon's voice was soft and deadly quiet when he spoke. "How much do you owe the boy?" He punctuated his words with a vicious jab.

"Nineteen dollars . . . oh! . . ." groaned Addison, who couldn't stand upright without a great deal of pain.

"Pay him," Gannon ordered softly. He stood beside Addison, waiting to be obeyed.

Addison nodded and tried to stand up, but it was an effort. He reached for the desk and placed one hand against it, forcing himself upright as he reached into his jacket with the other.

Danny stood gaping dumbfounded, his gaze ping-ponging back and forth between Gannon and Mr. Addison as Gannon walked back around his desk and sat down, an unreadable expression on his face.

Addison had pulled his purse out and began counting out dollar bills. When he had nineteen, he looked at Aaron expectantly. Gannon only nodded coolly and gestured with a quick jerk of his head toward Danny.

Addison sighed heavily and walked back toward the boy. All he wanted to do was strangle the sniveling, Irish runt. Now he was forced to walk over to him and pay him money he didn't deserve.

"Say you're sorry, Mr. Addison," Aaron commanded softly.

"Sorry?!" Addison said, startled. "I'm not a bit sor . . ." He started to tell Aaron that he wasn't sorry for the way he had treated the boy, and if you asked him, he had been too good to him in the first place, but when he turned toward Gannon and saw the look on his face, he thought better of what he had been going to say. After all, he still had to do business with Gannon once this unpleasant mess was over. Gannon was the only whiskey supplier in the area. He not only determined how much you sold, but if you sold any at all. If he were cut off from Gannon, he'd have no way to supply the liquor he needed to run his taverns. In short, he'd be out of business.

He grudgingly stuffed the bills into Danny's outstretched hands and muttered, "Sorry," before turning abruptly and heading for the door.

"Mr. Addison?" Gannon asked softly. He turned around to face Gannon. He didn't trust himself to speak. He just looked at Gannon, trying to hide his fear and anger.

"I've noticed that you've been a trifle pale as of late . . . perhaps the climate here in Kansas City is bad for you. Might I suggest a warmer climate? Something more southerly would perhaps be a great deal healthier for you."

It had sounded like a question, but it had really been a

statement, a veiled threat. Addison didn't know what to say or do. When he looked across the wide, shining desk at the elegantly dressed man, with the pleasing manners and deadly eyes, he knew that the threat hadn't been idle. He had been told to leave Kansas City.

His flesh was prickling beneath his clothes, and his heart was pounding. He swallowed hard, and nodded to show he understood before he turned and quickly left the room.

Meanwhile Gannon had resumed the study of his books which showed everything running at a healthy profit.

Dugan stood quietly by, waiting for his next order. He had known Aaron since he was a small, orphaned boy running the streets. He had caught him one day as he was arrogantly stealing an apple pie his wife had placed out on the windowsill to cool. When he had grabbed the little vagrant by the scruff of the neck, the boy had held the pie next to him and stared defiantly into his eyes. Dugan had felt pity for the skinny waif and a little respect too for the lack of fear he had shown when he had been caught, so he had let him go. Several weeks later, he had stumbled on the same boy in a street fight. He had been fighting like a demon against boys much older and larger than himself, even though it looked as if he had no chance of winning. Dugan had broken it up, scattering the older boys, and catching the smaller red-haired boy as gently as he could by the shoulder.

"Do ya need a place to stay, lad?" he had asked gently.

The boy only continued to stare angrily at him.

"Mad at the whole world, is that it then? Well, you can come home with me, if you'd like. I've got half a dozen of my own running about, and I don't think one more will make much difference."

He had already spoken about the boy to his wife, whose heart was nearly as large as her girth and whose laugh could easily match both. She had agreed quickly with her husband when he suggested bringing the boy home if he ever saw him again. Maggie would mother the entire world if she could, and Dugan loved her dearly.

"Can ya speak, boy?" he asked kindly. "Where do ya live?"

For a moment the boy's expression had changed. The anger had been drawn aside from his eyes like a green curtain to reveal the deep sorrow that lived inside.

Dugan had started to say something more, and released his grip. That was all that had been needed. Aaron shot past him like a shadow and was gone.

Dugan had suspected all along that he was one of the many abandoned or orphaned children who lived off the streets, and he felt such a sadness for him that he called out, asking him to come back, but it had been no use.

He had looked for him, after that, every day, on his way to work in the dark mornings and when he wearily dragged himself home in the late evenings. But he never saw a sign of him for a long time.

When the months began to roll by and the dark, cold rains came, he had nearly forgotten about the boy, until one night while he was on his way home after a particularly hard day of shoveling coal. It was raining, and every muscle in his body ached as he walked along the streets. They had just bricked all the roads, and the rain pattering against them made them shine as if they had just been waxed. He walked along, methodically dodging puddles and debris, not really thinking, until a large, dark object caught his eye. It looked like a bundle of rags with papers thrown on top and the rain had caused the ink to run until none of the words could be discerned. But the papers trembled, and it wasn't the wind, because there wasn't any. Just the gray, pitter-pattering of the rain falling straight down.

He approached the bundle cautiously, fearing a dog or some other dangerous thing, and gingerly bent forward to pull the papers away.

Everything underneath was brown and gray and soaked, except for the brilliant red curls which had not quite been hidden. Dugan frantically pulled the soggy rags away until the poor, shivering child was exposed. It was the angry, red-haired boy from before, who now looked nearer to death than life.

"Oh, lad," Dugan whispered in sorrow, pulling off his own brown coat. He picked him up and wrapped the coat around him, holding him securely to his chest. Dugan felt no weariness in his bones now as he made his way quickly to his house.

Maggie had taken one look at the boy and flew into action, boiling water and making poultices of strong mustard seed. Her arms quickly took the soggy rags covering him away, and warm, thick quilts were thrown over him by the other children. Camphor was poured into steaming water and laid beside him, and the little ones were admonished to say prayers for the sick boy. But even with all her ministrations, Maggie doubted that the boy could be saved. His pneumonia was deep, and even for a healthy, well-fed child, it would have been a struggle to survive. But this poor, wasted thing! She shook her head sadly.

"Will the lad make it?" Dugan asked softly. He looked at the large bed where the thin boy barely made a dent, and wished he could shut out the sound of his labored breathing.

"God only knows," she said sorrowfully, looking at the beautiful child. "His fever is so high, and he's so pitifully thin."

Together they sat down, knowing the night would be long. But their vigil had been rewarded, because Aaron was a fighter. He struggled with his death that night and won. His fever broke and he opened his eyes with the first rays of the morning sun.

Dugan and Maggie had been delighted, as well as all of their children, who took turns bringing him soup and covering a foot that had slipped from beneath a quilt.

Aaron had grown strong under their care, and his anger had slowly dissolved, replaced by love for these people who had taken him in as if he were one of their own.

He wanted to give them something, to repay them for what they had given him, but he was small, and the only thing he had was himself. He watched the little ones at school, and protected them from bullies. He did chores nightly, getting them done in record time so that he could rush down the street and meet Dugan as he was coming home. Together they would walk each evening, usually silent, or occasionally making small talk about the day's events. But Aaron never spoke of his beginnings. Dugan felt as if the boy had a score to settle with life—a score that he would someday settle and win. Matilda and he had talked about Aaron many times. Like a great many others they had come to America from Ireland in 1846. It had been a great exodus of starving people fleeing from a land that could no longer feed them. Thousands had died when the blight had taken their potatoes—the only source of food many had—and even the ruling British government's repeal of the Corn Laws had come too late. The Irish had nothing to sell to buy the corn they could now import, and so they perished or fled. Dugan knew that Aaron had been one of these immigrants, like himself, but his luck had not been as good. Dugan did not know if Aaron's family still remained in Ireland, or had died coming here. All he knew was that the boy was alone and something terrible had happened to him.

Aaron had a boundless curiosity and a way with numbers. After he had learned to read there had not been one book or newspaper that had escaped his attention. Dugan would find him reading the labels on cans or boxes, anything just to satisfy his craving to learn.

Aaron discovered to his great delight, that if you were lucky enough to possess something that someone else wanted, you could usually get them to pay you for it at a profit. Then taking that, you could invest it into something else, make it better, turn around and sell it, and make more. He had learned about business and saw it as a great game and a wonderful challenge. The key was to find something that someone else was willing to pay for. Aaron did so, saving each penny and investing it over and over again, so that as he grew, so did his wealth.

He was honest in all his dealings, even if they were not all entirely legal, and his reputation as an honorable man grew. But so did the knowledge that he was a man to be feared if he were crossed.

He rose quickly, staking out his territory as he matured, until by the age of thirty, there was not one business deal in all of Kansas City he did not know about or control.

Dugan had risen with him. Aaron had kept him affectionately by his side, taking care of him and his family as he aged. So when Aaron had reacted to the way Addison had treated Danny so violently, Dugan had not been in the least surprised. Aaron saw his own suffering in the lad, and his own tormentors in Addison. He had meant to protect Danny as he himself had been protected by Dugan many years ago.

With a deep sigh, Aaron looked up from his work. Danny had stood by as quietly as a condemned man, a mixture of fear and confusion on his face. Dugan stood silently by as well, waiting for a word from Aaron.

"Clean the boy up a bit, and put him to work."

Dugan smiled, and Aaron grinned at Danny.

"You're working for me now, Danny, so don't worry. Just do what Dugan tells you. Never, never steal so much as a penny from me and we'll get along fine. Understand?"

Danny nodded quickly, a smile so broad spreading over his face that Dugan feared it might crack.

"Dugan . . . give Danny an advance and take some of the kitchen stock to his family, too."

The boy's smile had begun to tremble slightly. Aaron looked quickly away as he saw a glimmering tear slide down the boy's face.

"Come on boy, we've got work to do," Dugan said gently as he led the boy out of the room.

Moments later he returned, smiling with satisfaction. Aaron looked at him when he entered. There was not a trace of any emotion on his face. Whatever he had felt had been pushed to the depths and his surface was as calm and unfathomable as a still pool.

"Today is the day you set aside for hiring new people," Dugan reminded him.

Aaron nodded absently. He had nearly forgotten. Their bartender had quit unexpectedly and he was always in need of new waitresses and barmaids for his many establishments.

He sighed. "Start sending them in and tell Josh to bring me a tray at noon. And send the lady upstairs my sincerest regrets," he said as an afterthought.

He brushed aside his bookkeeping as Dugan nodded and hurried out.

Soon after, the first one came in. A woman, about forty, huge and dirty-looking with the air of the streets about her. Her appearance was rough, but Aaron couldn't help but notice the gentle, good humor in her eyes.

Bravely she stepped forward. The elegant trappings of the room did not intimidate her.

"I seen yer sign, an' I need work," she stated matter-of-factly.

"What kind of work, woman?"

"Well, most anything there is. I been a barmaid for now going on twenty years. The only time I was idle is when my babes was born. I'm good at it, and I don't mind putting up with the foolishness of men, or long hours. My kids need taking care of, so's I gotta find me a job."

He nodded in understanding and mentally ran through his list of openings. He could use her down at the wharf, but she wouldn't fit in here, not even in the kitchen or scrubbing floors.

"Would you mind working the wharf? It can get pretty rough there at times."

She chuckled good-naturedly.

"I was *born* there—and half my babes got sailors for pa's . . . why would I mind?"

He nodded sagely, and smiled.

"Start tonight—Journey's End. You'll have six days of work and your Sundays off for church. One dollar and fifty cents a week, plus all the whiskey you can drink, and tips of course."

Her eyes brightened and she nodded happily.

Gannon looked down at his sheet and began to write. It was his way of dismissing people.

He heard her steps retreating and the opening and clicking shut of the door. Dugan had come back in.

"Well, Aaron, did you hire her?"

"Yes," he said. "For the Journey's End . . . perhaps them great breasts of hers will give some lonesome sailor solace for a time . . . and her as well. Send me the next."

Dugan felt the sadness in Aaron's words and knew that the street woman was not the only one who felt alone. All these long years, since that rainy October night, he and Maggie had tried desperately to heal his hurt, but all their attempts had been in vain. Aaron always remained the silent observer, the outsider gazing longingly through a locked window with his wistful, wanting eyes; a prisoner of his own past. Maggie had shamelessly used every trick she knew to bring him around, but even her buoyant, blithe spirit and rollicking laughter seemed to have no effect. Still, she persisted, using every weapon in her arsenal of kindness, hugging him as he passed, kissing his shining locks as frequently as she did her own well-adjusted brood, but all she received in return was a frozen stance, a sharp intake of breath and carefully hooded eyes in a wary face. Cautious, courteous behavior, so controlled . . . so *old;* except at night when shadows grew long, and reason seemed to flee with the setting sun.

Tucked beside Kevin and Kelly, Dugan's boisterous twins, Aaron would feign sleep until he could hear their soft and rhythmic breathing, knowing they had entered the Land of Dreams. But it was here that he didn't want to go, feared to go. Stubbornly he willed his eyes to stay open, until he felt as if hot needles laced his lids, and he could "see" the different shades of black within the room. But he mustn't sleep! He mustn't dream! Stay awake! his mind warned. But the warmth of the quilts and the soft settling sounds of the house caused him to drift, while the soothing breeze became a song in his ears, singing him to sleep, and then he would dream . . . his screams shattering the silence, his cries bringing Dugan running. He would find him sitting up in bed, rigid as a statue, drenched in sweat.

"What is it, lad?" he would ask, his concern for the boy growing daily. Aaron would shake his head, slowly, wearily, refusing to look up while Kevin and Kelly stared apprehensively at their bedmate. "Can't you tell me, boy? What were you dreaming about?"

"I don't remember," he would say, and then look guiltily away.

"Aye," Dugan would sigh. "One of those kind . . . Will you be all right now?" he asked.

Aaron would nod, and quietly, obediently, lie down, looking as exhausted as a marathon runner who had lost the race. Then Maggie would cluck and soothe, tucking the covers around his neck, and smooth his still damp hair away from his forehead, watching skeptically as his eyes would close and he seemed to drift back into sleep. But in the morning, when the first rays of the sun had cleared the horizon, and Dugan made his way down to the kitchen, with Maggie trailing behind, there he would find Aaron, perched on the high stool by the warm stove, leaning against the wall, with a cold mug of coffee clenched in his hands and every light in the room lit.

"We have to do something," Maggie urged. "He can't continue this way for much longer . . ."

Dugan nodded, knowing he would have to take a chance and confront him before long. That night, when the dreams overtook the boy and his cries rang out, Dugan was ready. He sent Kelly and Kevin out of the room with Maggie. Each boy glanced back anxiously, wondering if bad dreams were grounds for thrashing, but Maggie shut the door on their curious gazes, leaving her husband to do battle with Aaron's ghosts.

"Listen to me, lad," he started. "Something's wrong here, and I want to know what it is . . ."

Aaron just stared at him.

"What were you dreaming about?"

"Nothing!" he said angrily, because as always, after he had awakened, the dreams had fled like the shadows they were, and he really couldn't remember what they were about. The only thing that lingered was the persistent fear . . .

" 'Nothin'' don't make a boy cry out in the night, wakin' the whole house . . . 'nothin'' don't cover you with sweat, and make you afraid of the dark!" Dugan's voice rose and thundered strongly around the room. He knew he had to break through, or there would be a good chance that they would lose him . . . "I want you to tell me some things, boy.

21

I want to know *where* your mum is, and what happened to your dad, and I want to know *now!"*

The carefully guarded expression left Aaron's eyes in a flash, leaving them livid with pain and hate and so much hurt that Dugan flinched. Then Aaron flew at him, kicking and hitting, while hot tears raced down his cheeks. But Dugan was prepared, catching him by the wrists, wrapping his arms securely around him, holding him as tight as he could, till he felt his fury weaken, and finally subside until all he had left was a sobbing boy in his arms.

"Shhh, lad . . . it's all right . . . I'm here . . ." he crooned, sitting down on the bed beside him. The street lamp's golden glow partially filled the room through the open window. Aaron looked at it for a long time, and suddenly it seemed as if he could see his mother in the distance, suffused in glowing light, coming toward him. She was smiling and happy, dressed in homespun blue cloth, with flowers he had picked adorning her soft brown hair. "Aaron . . ." she called, her arms outstretched, reaching for him . . . Suddenly a groan escaped his lips, and a trembling sob shook his tiny frame . . . "Mum . . ." he whispered, and turned and gazed up imploringly into the compassionate eyes of his friend.

"Dugan . . ." he cried, clasping his hand to his chest, as his voice trembled. "My . . . heart . . . hurts . . ." and then more tears fell, tears unlike any Dugan had seen before, great painful, glittering drops that must have issued from his soul.

"Laddy . . . cum here . . ." Dugan said softly, his voice filled with pity as he gathered him up as if he weighed less than a feather.

"She's gone, Dugan!" he wailed, taking comfort from the sound of his beating heart. "And I miss her *so* much . . ." Broken words fell from a broken heart, and then he cried until Dugan's nightshirt was soaked, letting his story unfold far into the night, ending with a plea that Dugan tell no one. "Not even Maggie?" he asked. The boy with the serious green eyes shook his head slowly. "No one then," Dugan agreed, "just you and me." The boy sighed in relief, his demons exorcised. He snuggled wearily against Dugan and fell into the first deep sleep he'd known in months, with his arms wrapped possessively around Dugan.

And now, a grown man with power and success, more money than he could ever spend in a lifetime, and all the women he could want, he still had never found the person whom he could love. Someone who could understand and accept all that he was, and make up for the pieces in him that he no longer possessed. His lovers had never understood that he hungered not only for a union with the body, but with the mind and soul as well. His lovemaking had always been intense, but it was only the tip of what he actually wanted to share with someone. When it was over and the physical ache had been satisfied, the emptiness inside of him grew larger, and his longing for a love he had never known became more intense. So he had married his business a long time ago, condemning his passionate soul to thirst forever for something he felt he could never attain: a true and lasting love.

Outside, in the hallway, stood a double line of people stretching all the way out to the street. The sign in the window had simply read, "Help Needed," and these people had flocked here, hopeful and needing.

There were old ones and young ones, sick ones, and healthy ones. It was a small slice of humanity, some pretty and some not, but all desperate for a chance.

In the corner, still far from the study door, stood a girl. She was young and pretty, and her worn, tattered dress said she was poor. Her name was Jenny.

She looked around at all the faces patiently waiting. It had been days since she'd last eaten, and just as many days since she'd seen her parents. They were gone now, forever, consumed in a tenement fire. Vivid scenes danced in front of her eyes. She could see the building, brown against a blue sky, orange flames bursting through the windows like some obscene flower, devouring those inside. Those who had been trapped screamed for help, their cries mixing with the clanging of the fire engine bells and the "oohs" and "ahs" of the spectators, creating a hellish symphony that presented itself nightly to her in her dreams. People burning like torches jumped from the upper floors, flailing their arms, shrieking as they fell to the ground below.

"Mamma! Pappa!" she screamed, and ran toward the burning building, but the circle of people prevented her from entering, holding her back, telling her there was nothing she could do, until their cries and the snapping of the fire began to blur, and the world began to spin crazily, as darkness mercifully enveloped her.

Later, much later, she had awakened. Someone had propped her in a doorway, out of the way, and far from the ruined building.

Just hours before, her mother had teased her about becoming a young lady, and had laughingly sent her to the market for the dark bread her father loved, and now . . . now there was nothing, nothing at all. Not even a trace of who she was in the smoking, black ruins.

She had wandered aimlessly along the streets, desperate, weak and hungry and so hurt inside that she tried not to remember what her life had been like just five short days ago.

Nights had come and gone barely noticed. Temperatures dropped and the sun had risen with only the barest impression on her mind, until the gnawing in her stomach and the painful ache of her limbs tugged her back toward reality. She began to notice the streets she walked upon and the people she passed. Ahead of her, in front of a huge and grand hotel, stood long lines of people, standing in orderly rows, patiently waiting, for what she didn't know. She walked forward until she saw the sign propped against the large, front window. "Help Needed" it read, and like a magnet it drew her obediently toward the end of a line, as hopeful and needing as the rest of the people who were there.

Each person who passed through the great, oaken doors ahead of her was just one small drop in a trickling stream, until the line began to shrink. Minutes had passed, or maybe hours . . . time had lost its meaning . . . until she found herself standing inside the hallway, wearily resting against the polished walls, praying she'd get a chance.

Inside, Aaron had nearly filled all his vacancies. He had his bartenders and waitresses and even a couple of cooks. Satisfied that he had what he wanted, he looked over at Dugan, who had been lounging on one of his chairs, sipping brandy.

"I think that is all . . . you can send the rest away." He resumed his writing.

Dugan nodded and stretched, standing up with a yawn. Aaron watched the old man affectionately from beneath his lids, and nearly smiled. Dugan had been the first person to give him a break, much like the one he'd given Danny today. He'd never forgotten it.

A soft click of the door, and a muffled "damn" from Dugan told Aaron that the next applicant had been let in. He looked toward the door as Dugan scuttled forward, ready to send her away . . . and stared in surprise. Meanwhile, Dugan had stopped in his tracks, openly gaping at the girl who had entered.

She seemed less then a will-o'-the-wisp as she stood before them, small and fragile with huge, blue eyes and pale, ivory skin. There were dirty smudges on her cheeks and her golden hair had been bound in a large and hurried knot. She held her head high, with no fear showing on her features. Yet she trembled.

Aaron thought she was a child, with her pure and innocent face, until a sweeping glance took in the flowing curves her worn, brown dress could barely conceal.

She didn't speak.

Dugan blinked and came to his senses. She was a beautiful little thing, but Aaron had said there was no more work. He moved forward, ready to send her away, when Aaron's words stopped him.

"What can I do for you?" he asked. His voice had noticeably fallen to a gentle timbre with the faintest trace of his Irish burr softening the words into a caress. She looked like a shy, soft doe, and he was afraid the slightest movement or loud word would cause her to bolt. He didn't want that.

"What can I do for you?" he asked again quietly.

"I saw your sign," she started timidly. "About needing help, and I came to apply."

Dugan started to tell her that all the positions were filled when Aaron raised his hand to silence him.

"What is your name, lass?"

"Jenny, sir. Jenny Bydalek."

"Bydalek? What sort of a name is 'Bydalek'?"

"It's," and she licked her lips nervously, not knowing what to expect. "It's Polish. My family came here from Poland."

Aaron nodded his head. Most of the people who made Kansas City their home had been immigrants at one time or another. No one seemed to have always been from here.

"Well, Jenny," and he smiled brightly. "Just what is it that you can do for me?" He couldn't quite hide the twinkle in his eyes as he said this. It was easy to see that if she were cleaned up a bit, and put in some lovely silks, she would be breathtaking. If the streets had educated her enough by now, judging from her ragged appearance, she would understand the double meaning in his words. Strangely, he wished this little angel had escaped the lessons most young girls learned when poverty forced them to survive any way they could.

Jenny looked thoughtful. She didn't appear to understand what he had implied as she began to list her accomplishments.

"I can cook, sew, clean, read, and write, and I can also play the piano . . . I'm not afraid of work, sir . . . all I ask for is a chance."

"Piano? You can play the piano?" Aaron looked surprised. Those sorts of talents were possessions of the rich. Most people who were not born to money had neither the time nor the energy to pursue those things. He frowned slightly when he looked at her. Her clothes and generally rough appearance said she was poor, but her voice and manners said otherwise. She even claimed to read and write.

26

Jenny saw him frown and felt a sinking feeling in her stomach. She didn't know how much longer she could go on.

"In Warsaw," she explained. "We had a piano and many books. My parents had a small store and my father also did carpentry work. They taught me to read and write, and we all loved music. In the winter, when the nights were very long, we spent most of our time singing and playing the piano."

She had a wispy, dreamlike appearance as she described her life. Aaron couldn't imagine what had happened to her. There were dark circles beneath her eyes as if she hadn't slept for a very long time, and her skin was so pale, it was nearly translucent.

"My Uncle John went to America when he was very young, to a place called Alaska, and he would write to my father, telling him how wonderful this land was, how new and fresh. My Uncle John is rich. He wrote that in Alaska, everyone is rich because there's so much gold there. All you have to do is bend over and pick it up . . ."

Aaron saw the tears welling up in her eyes as she continued. She spoke as if they were no longer in the room and she was all alone.

"He asked my father to be his partner. To come to Alaska and work with him . . . he said we would be wealthy beyond our wildest dreams. My father sold the store and withdrew our money from the bank . . . but it wasn't enough. When John had come here, prices were lower. We didn't have enough money to continue, so we rented a room here, and my father found a job shoveling coal . . . we were going to continue west as soon as we saved enough money . . ."

Her voice trailed off, and Dugan and Aaron watched as a single tear slid down her cheek, leaving a white trail through the black smudge.

"Where are your folks, Jenny?" Aaron asked softly.

Jenny struggled with herself before she could reply. She could still see the flames and smell the burning bricks and timber.

"There was a fire . . ." she began, and she let the tears roll from her eyes. "In the building where we lived . . . I wasn't home. My mother had sent me to the market for some bread and when I returned there were fire wagons all around and people carrying buckets of water down long lines . . . I couldn't find my parents. I looked and I looked. I ran and tried to go inside . . . but they wouldn't let me!" She began to cry. She tried to muffle the sounds of her sobbing by placing a hand in front of her mouth, frantically wiping her tears away with the other. She fought courageously to control herself.

Aaron glanced quickly at Dugan and saw the old man sniffle and rub his red nose quickly. He was about to speak when the door clicked softly and Joshua entered. It was noon and Aaron had instructed him earlier to bring a tray.

Jenny quickly looked at the floor, embarrassed by her outburst and not wanting to further humiliate herself by having someone else see her like this.

Joshua walked silently past her. His tray was heavily laden with meat and steaming potatoes and the perfume of the fresh baked bread was all around her.

Jenny's stomach gave an involuntary lurch and began to growl hungrily. She felt the blood go quickly to her head and the room began to buzz as a rush of warmth washed over her and her knees began to buckle. The room began to blur and spin and the edges began to smudge and darken as the floor rushed up to meet her.

"Easy, lass," came a warm breath in her ear. She felt strong arms move beneath her, supporting her and lifting her up. The dizziness refused to leave and she was unable to hold herself upright. Gratefully she laid her head against Aaron's strong shoulder as he carried her to a chair.

He was moved by this woman-child, who seemed to weigh less than the air about her. She appeared fragile as china, but the way she fought to control herself said she was strong.

Dugan appeared quickly by her side, shoving a glass of strong brandy toward her lips.

"Here, now," he crooned softly. "Sip on this a bit and let your head clear." He soothed her, and clucked about like an old hen. Dugan had had many children in his long life, and

28

some of them had been girls, so the vapors was something he was well acquainted with.

She sipped the brandy quickly, and the liquid burned like fire as it passed her parched lips and trickled down her throat.

She choked a little and Dugan patted her shoulder comfortingly.

"Here, here lassie . . . easy does it."

Aaron had walked to his bar and poured himself a stiff drink, deep in thought. Without turning around, he spoke to her quietly, but in a voice that carried like one much louder.

"How long has it been since you've eaten?" he asked.

She studied her glass, now nearly empty, and didn't speak or look up, even when she heard him approach. She felt so ashamed and embarrassed. Why would they hire her now after she had made such a spectacle of herself?

He stood in front of her and placed his hands on each arm rest, looking hard into her downcast face.

"Jenny . . . how many?"

She looked up, expecting to see contempt on his face and was surprised at the intensity of his gaze. For a moment she was lost in shimmering pools of green jade that nearly took her breath away.

"How many?" he repeated. "A day? Two? Five?"

Something flickered in Jenny's eyes at the mention of five. A memory momentarily flitted by and Aaron caught its passing. Five days would put it right at the time the great brownstone on 1st and Elm had burned, that had to be the one. Which meant that she had been lost and alone on the streets since then.

There was no need to say anymore. He moved quickly and deliberately placed his tray in front of her.

Her mouth began to water in spite of her shame.

"Eat," he commanded and began to turn around to go toward his desk.

"No," she answered.

He stopped in surprise and turned quickly around, staring in disbelief at the small woman there. He was not used to being disobeyed, especially by someone of the opposite sex.

"What?" he asked.

"No," she answered again, shaking her head weakly. "I didn't come here for charity . . . I came for work. If you have work, I'll do it, and then I'll eat. I'm not a beggar."

Her pale cheeks had begun to become pink, and he wasn't sure if it was from anger or shame.

"It isn't charity," he explained. "I can't have my *employees* passing out on me. It wouldn't be very *efficient*. Now eat, so Dugan can find some work for you."

"I don't *want* Dugan to *find* me any work," she said angrily. The food had been forgotten in spite of her hunger and with every ounce of self-respect she had left she protested. "I just want to work, if there *is* work . . . and I will work *hard,* too!"

A kaleidoscope of emotions flitted across Aaron's face. Compassion changed to confusion which flickered briefly into anger before settling on apparent indifference. He shrugged his shoulders to show his lack of concern, and replied a little more gruffly then he had intended.

"All of my *employees* eat here . . . I'm not giving you any charity. I *expect* you to work hard for me, that is until we decide what to do with you . . . but I can't have you fainting in my kitchen, or out on the floor . . . it would be bad for business!"

He reached over and picked up a fork and placed it in her hand.

"Now . . . *eat!"*

She stared at him in disbelief. So did Dugan.

"But, Aaron . . . you told me . . ." Dugan began and stopped.

"I'm the *boss* here!" Aaron roared. "Or has everyone forgotten that?" His eyes glittered dangerously.

That damned look, thought Dugan. The boy could shoot daggers at you with those eyes. He became quiet, wondering what was next.

Aaron grabbed his papers from his desk.

"And when you're done *eating,* Jenny, Dugan will take you to meet my housekeeper, Mrs. Merit. You can sleep in her room. Ask if she has an extra dress or two to fit, then in the morning, Dugan will take you to the kitchen where you'll meet Joshua, my cook. He'll put you to work." He stopped, a thoughtful expression on his face. "And if he can't keep you busy through the day, you can teach me to play the piano after dinner." He smiled brightly.

"Piano?" said Dugan, clearly puzzled. "We don't have no piano!"

"Find one," Aaron hissed flatly. He laid his papers down on his desk and threw back his head to swallow the last of his drink.

He turned to face Jenny.

"When you see Mrs. Merit, have her help you post a letter to your uncle and explain your situation. If he is as wealthy as you suggest, he will be able to help you. This city is no place for an innocent, even one with as bad a temper as yours. Until your uncle comes, I will see to your protection."

He had given his orders, and like a man used to being obeyed, he had no doubt that they would be carried through to the last detail.

He walked to the door without so much as a backward glance, and opened it. A second later, he was gone, leaving Jenny and Dugan staring dumbfounded at each other.

"Go ahead, there lass . . ." Dugan said slowly. "Soon as you're finished, I'll take you to see the housekeeper."

Jenny nodded and woodenly jabbed the fork into a cold potato.

Dugan was used to some strange and impulsive orders from Gannon, and he had gotten used to his temper long ago, but he had never, never, in the twenty years he'd known him, seen him loose it at a lady . . . but then, he mused, very few ladies had ever defied him as she had. He shook his head slowly, an amused grin beginning to crinkle his worn features as he gazed down at the little girl eating Aaron's cold dinner. The next few weeks promised to be very interesting indeed, of that he had no doubt.

Outside in the hall, Aaron had gained the steps, still angry and not sure why. He bolted upstairs, mentally listing what he had left to do this afternoon. It was no use, though. He couldn't stop thinking about Jenny. How could someone who appeared so fragile and broken, and totally vulnerable one minute, turn into a spitting hellcat the next, especially when someone was only trying to help her? "Women!" he snorted. Would he ever understand them?

He reached his room and threw open the door. A slow smile began to spread across his handsome features at the surprised "Oh!" that greeted him from his bed. It was still unmade; a wild tapestry of different colored silks was strewn about, and resting demurely in the center of his soft nest was the girl he had left that morning. She was still waiting for him, every bit as inviting as before, with one of his pale blue sheets pulled up innocently past her breasts.

Well, he reasoned, women did have their strong points as well! He grinned as he walked in, quickly shutting the door behind him.

The afternoon promised to be a good one after all.

CHAPTER

2

The steam from the heavy pots rolled and boiled upward, forming tiny drops on the ceiling and walls in the noisy Kansas City kitchen. Curses and laughter intermingled within the noisy room, which buzzed with life and the powerful aroma of sizzling fats and baking breads. Steadily, with dreadful purpose, Jenny beat and pounded the rising dough. Her hands thudded rhythmically against the white mass which seemed to utter little "umphs" and "ahs" of protest with each resounding whack.

"Jen? Jen! Aren't those rolls ready yet? The men'll be in to eat in just an hour or so. You'd best hurry now, else we'll be short for the supper table."

Joshua's hands and whirling tea towels created quite a breeze as he blustered and scolded his way about the kitchen. Jenny smiled when she watched him, because his hands and legs would sometimes seem confused, one part flying north while the other half was determined to go south. He never stood still, the huge mass of his body defying the laws of natural science by moving and twisting with a speed and grace which should have been alien for his size.

She had been here a week now, and she liked him, knowing that his scolding was only meant to hurry, not hurt, and that when the meals were over, and it was time to clean up, his mood would change. He would laugh and tease and make the time fly by.

"Well, Jenny . . . are they going to be ready or not?"

"Yes, Joshua . . . they'll be ready shortly."

Her reply was short and polite, if not spoken a little too quickly. It was accepted with a deep sigh and a "very well . . . see that they are" before Joshua turned and scolded a scullery maid for leaving spots on the glasses.

Jenny smiled. Joshua acted as if each meal he prepared were for kings instead of the common men who ate here. Everything had to be perfect. As he had explained to her, cooking was all he knew, it was everything he was, it was his life.

Jenny liked working for him, and cooking came as naturally to her as breathing. But from the first day she had walked through the doors, she had had nothing but trouble from everyone else.

Her natural beauty and voluptuous figure had caused instantaneous jealousy in the women and unabashed lust in the men. It might not have been so bad for her, had she been like the others, but she was not. She would have no part in their games or vulgar talk and her aloofness from their ways made them hate her.

Daily they taunted her, becoming more bold each time. The boys would grab at her until she swatted at them or pushed them away, then everyone would laugh, and say she was "stuck-up" and thought she was better than they were. At first she tried to explain that she loved to laugh and joke about, but no man would touch her until she was married. When Jenny had revealed her feelings, this admission had sent most of the girls into peals of laughter. She could still remember the sting of their laughter.

Jenny was shaken from her thoughts when Kevin, the worst of the men, appeared before her. He doffed his cap and bowed low while winking at his friends.

"Miss Jenny . . . I beg yer pardon for my ungentlemanly ways."

Jenny stood very still, not knowing what to say, but sure

that he was teasing her as well, not meaning a word of what he had just said.

He stood upright, his gaze lingering hungrily on her breasts.

"You can be sure, lass, that if you ever need saving, that is, saving from your *virginity,* I'll be happy to help!"

Everyone roared as she stood there.

"Oh, look, gents! I've made the *lady* blush!"

But he was wrong, Jenny was not blushing, she was angry. She started to move toward him, ready to slap his face.

"Look, gents, she wants to be saved now, she's coming to meet me!" He laughed until Jenny's hand connected sharply with his cheek, leaving a perfectly red handprint behind.

"Why you . . ." He reached up to rub the sore patch of skin as he walked toward her.

She didn't move, too mad to read the message in his eyes. She had slapped him and that hurt, but not half as much as his pride.

"Kevin," said a voice that Jenny instantly recognized as Aaron's. He had told Joshua that if she had any trouble to come and get him. When Joshua had seen the look in Kevin's eyes, especially after Jenny had struck him, he had rushed from the room to find Aaron.

Kevin stopped, his gaze riveted to Aaron's. Jenny turned abruptly, relieved when he stepped through the door. She hadn't seen him since the day he had hired her.

He strode through the room in his elegant pin-striped suit, his eyes flashing fire as he came toward them. He knew that she had been having trouble, and was sure it would eventually come to this. He stopped in front of them. Jenny was surprised at how her heart quickened when he approached.

"Don't you *like* working here, Kevin?" he asked.

"Well . . . yes!"

"Yes, what, Kevin?"

"Yes, Mr. Gannon . . . we were just havin' us a little fun with the new girl . . . that's all."

Gannon saw the handprint still slightly red on his cheek and nodded his head.

"Just a little fun . . . is that right?"

"Yeah . . . we didn't mean nothin' by it."

"See . . . that . . . you . . . don't . . ." With every word he jabbed his finger into Kevin's chest. "You're a good lugger. I'd hate to have to let you go."

The two men stared fixedly at one another, as though sizing each other up. Kevin was the first to drop his eyes and take a shuffling step backward.

Aaron seemed satisfied and turned to address the rest of his help.

"Miss Bydalek is waiting here for her uncle. Until he comes, she is under my protection. I will not allow any harm to come to her. Do I make myself clear?"

There were nods and murmurs of "Yes, sir" by the people present. When he was sure that everyone understood him, he turned back to Jenny with a smile.

Her heart skipped a beat as he spoke to her.

"I've purchased a piano . . . a Steinway, they call it. I've instructed Joshua to dismiss you after dinner so that you can teach me to play. We will start tomorrow, Jenny." He patted her gently on the head as if she were a small child, before leaving.

After he had gone, the kitchen became noticeably quieter. For Jenny, it seemed quite empty.

"All right, party's over . . . back to work now. And Jenny, I *still* need those rolls," Joshua said.

She nodded her head and turned around, bending over the still heaving mass of white, and sighed. She wondered how many days it would take before her uncle received the letter she had posted. It had been hard to write to someone she had never met. The worst had been telling him that the brother he had asked to join him in America was dead, along with his wife. Knowing that her father's dream would never be fulfilled . . . to see Alaska . . . had brought tears to her eyes. He had described it to her so often from the letters he had received from John that she felt as if she could see Alaska in her dreams. High mountainous peaks carpeted in sparkling snow glittered in the sun like jewels cast upon the ground by some careless, giant child. Ice like jewels, water so blue and pure and colors as glowing and intense as the rainbows she had seen and painted as a child had filled her mind. Her hours had been filled with dreams and pictures, real and imagined, of birds and flowers and anything else she would see to paint. She knew that someday she would draw Alaska's ancient mountains and paint pictures of its valleys carpeted in snow while listening to the music of the waterfalls. She felt this deep in her heart.

She thrust her fist deep into the dough, which sighed and rolled up to enclose her wrist. Softly she spoke out loud, wanting the words to reach only her ears.

"Please, Uncle John . . . please, come for me," she whispered as she drew back her hand and thrust again.

It was nearly noon, and with each passing second, the kitchen's activity increased along with its noise. The morning's incident had been all but forgotten by everyone . . . everyone that is except Kevin, whose eyes never left Jenny as he lugged heavy sides of beef and boxes from the storage rooms to the kitchen. He wanted her, in spite of her uppity ways. He'd find a way to have her *and* even the score with Gannon. He'd never forgive him for embarrassing him in front of his friends. He intended to pay him back . . . or die trying.

Somewhere, far away, a train rattled and bounced along its track, heading west. In one of its anonymous looking cars rode the United States mail sacks, bound for the coast.

There were dozens of sacks in the car, rubbing against each other and there were thousands of letters and packages inside destined for someone's eagerly waiting hands. And somewhere, in those dark, brown burlap sacks tied with twine, rode Jenny's letter. Its final destination: Alaska, where her uncle sat, patiently waiting for news of the arrival of his family . . . patiently waiting for his brother who would never come.

CHAPTER

3

Autumn is a brilliant flash in Alaska. Summer's green meadows and warm days filled with sunshine are threatened by the first kiss of frost at night. Knowing her days are numbered, nature puts on her brightest dress to do one last dance before the long sleep comes.

John felt the change. He looked up at the blue sky rolling with huge white clouds and the meadows and trees gone red and gold in the fading autumn light and knew that the snows would come soon.

He wanted to be back at his mine. Even Anchorage made him nervous. People everywhere. He yearned for the solitude of the mountains, to watch the changing face of the seasons through the windows of the house he had built. Everyone who saw his cabin thought it was too big, and couldn't understand his need to have windows, large windows, everywhere. How could you explain to someone the feeling you had when looking at the land? It was true that the glass had cost him dearly, more fox skins than most men trap in a lifetime; but to him, it had been worth it.

The land, he thought, is like a woman. A woman could be so beautiful, she'd break your heart, and cruel enough to let you freeze.

He loved the land.

Sitting at the table, waiting for the mail to come in, he watched the people scurrying about their business through the squared panes of the leaded glass in The Miner.

His brother was supposed to come to help him work his claim and he had warned him to come before the snows. The thought of seeing Stephen and Theresa again made him smile. It had been too long. Then there was his niece Jenny. He had never seen her, but Stephen had written him so many letters about her that he felt he had known her all her life. He liked the idea of sharing his home with his family. He had never married, although the thought had crossed his mind once, long ago, in Poland. She had been a beauty, tall and statuesque, with raven hair and ebony eyes, but she had been a town girl. Even though her passion for John had been achingly hot, the thought of following him to some remote, ice-covered region had terrified her. So she had traded her body and mind to a local merchant for a ring and a secure future in Warsaw, and he had left, taking her heart with him. But he was getting old now, in his sixties, and dreams of gold were no longer enough. He had spent every last dime he possessed to purchase the deed to an old, lost mine he had stumbled upon. He'd sent to Seattle for the claim. When he had received it he rolled it into the leather throng around his neck, along with a reminder of what he had found dangling beneath it. His dream was close to being realized and now he longed for someone to share it with. He had begged Stephen to come and to bring his family with him. John had learned the hard way that solitude and loneliness were two different things. He was tired of being alone.

"More coffee, John?"

Emily, the owner of The Miner, hovered over him, her width effectively blocking any view he had of the room behind her.

"No-o-o . . . I reckon there's only so much of this can fit in a feller, and I jest got this here seat a comfortable temperature. I'd sure hate to get it cold again on account I got to run out back." He winked.

Emily smiled good-naturedly and moved on. He liked her. She'd seen her share of hard times and come through like a trooper.

His gaze wondered back toward the window and he didn't appear to hear the tall, dark young man, wrapped in fur, who sat down next to him. Both men continued to stare at the sky, quietly content in each other's company.

As the minutes continued to tick slowly by, the sun began to move and the sky to darken. There were faint bands of color beginning to glow overhead. Kaiuga, the young, Nunivak Eskimo became restless as the lights continued to grow brighter.

The sun had moved, and farther away, deeper north, its light played upon the icy tundra which stretched past the huge Baird and Endicott mountains into the frigid Arctic Ocean. The freeze had begun early, and the Brooks Range reflected the sun's light like a mirror, sending shimmering, rainbow colors soaring into the sky.

The Lights seemed to be alive as they danced across the heavens. John watched as Kaiuga nervously fingered his hunting knife as their colors continued to grow bolder.

"Lights is early," John stated matter-of-factly.

Kaiuga nodded, watching as most of the gold and yellows turned to shimmering shades of red.

"Not good," he muttered, pointing to the ruby color.

John nodded silently. The Nunivaks believed the Lights were alive; real beings who came down to the earth to take the people. They saw signs in the Lights, both good and bad, but mostly bad. When the Lights cavorted early in the day, turning a bloody, gleeful, shimmering red, the people believed it to be a bad sign, a frightening sign, of evil days ahead.

John didn't laugh at what would seem foolish to most. He had lived here too long and seen too many strange things to laugh.

"There is a pack of wolves," Kaiuga offered. "My people think they are demons."

"That so?" John asked quietly. He knew Kaiuga well

enough to know that he had something important to tell him. He waited patiently for him to continue.

"These wolves," he said. "They do that which is not natural . . . they follow men and their dogs instead of the caribou . . . and their leader, he is old and wickedly wise. We have tried to kill him many times and have failed. My people say he has the spirit of a man inside. Now the Lights burn red, too . . . it is not good." Kaiuga shook his head sadly.

John was about to ask him more about the renegade pack of wolves when the door to The Miner opened. Tanith McGree stepped through lugging a bag of mail behind him.

John smiled when he noticed Emily fidget with her hair as she came forward and Tanith smiled broadly when he saw her. He was a ship's captain who made the run from Seattle to Anchorage every four to six weeks. He had a large crew under him and any one of them could've run the mail sack to The Miner. But Emily was his woman and had been for nearly twenty years. He was always anxious to see her.

"Mail's in!" he hollered. People in the bar moved closer to him, most out of curiosity but some because they expected something. John stood up and stretched, walking toward Tanith too, half expecting to receive his letter today. He had waited now nearly three weeks. He was starting to get anxious.

"Seattle newspaper here," Tannith muttered. He started pulling the letters and packages out as quickly as he could, handing them out as he went. He knew nearly everyone there, and knew which ones had something coming.

"Pat, looks like your wife sent a little note!" He laughed as he dug out a ten-pound package, crudely wrapped in brown paper, from the bottom. "I think she done put some of her cookies in it, too . . . it weighs a bleedin' ton!" Everyone laughed uproariously as Pat sheepishly accepted his package.

Slowly, the people began to drift away, to read their cherished letters or hoard the sweets that had been sent to them. Tanith had reached the bottom of the sack and felt around inside. He noticed that John still waited patiently. "Damn!" he muttered, frowning. He turned the burlap sack inside out. Nothing. He looked at John with a sympathetic expression. John shrugged and smiled back a little sadly.

"Maybe next time, John," Emily said kindly. She had watched him wait daily, sipping coffee and staring out her window. She knew how lonely he was.

"Maybe so," he sighed, walking away with shoulders now visibly sagging.

The Lights had grown redder and Kaiuga had slipped away while Tanith had handed out the mail. John had a nagging feeling, a tug somewhere below his ribs, that made him feel uneasy, like something bad was going to happen. He didn't know if it was the changing of the seasons or Kaiuga's strange talk. Maybe it was just the edgy feeling you got from drinking too much coffee. But it was there. Something was wrong, only he didn't know what.

Slowly he settled back into his chair and stared vacantly out the window, ready for another long wait.

CHAPTER

4

Worked thoroughly and bone weary, Jenny should have slept easily that night. Yet somehow, a peaceful sleep eluded her. She had been tired enough, and when she lay down on the soft feather tick and plumped her pillow thoughtfully beneath her head, she was confident that sleep would soon follow. But it didn't. The moment her head touched the pillow and her lids closed over her eyes, she became fully alert, with confusing thoughts buzzing around in her brain like a hive full of bees. Seconds measured in heartbeats ticked by, and grew into hours punctuated by fitful turnings and tired yawns until, exhausted, she began to doze as the night began to slow and shift into dawn.

"Jenny, Jenny, dear . . . it's time to get up."

Mrs. Merit shook her gently and Jenny wearily pried her eyes apart.

The light was dim, but it *was* morning, and she could have sworn she had just closed her eyes.

Mrs. Merit frowned and studied her face.

"You look tired, Jenny. Have they been working you too hard?"

Jenny shook her head and licked her dry lips.

"No . . ." A great, bone-splitting yawn silenced her. "I

43

didn't sleep well last night," she explained, starting to stretch and push away her covers.

"That's understandable." Mrs. Merit nodded her head in sympathy. "You've been through a great deal these past weeks, losing your parents and all." She handed Jenny the dress she held in her hand.

Jenny couldn't explain to Mrs. Merit that she didn't understand what exactly *had* kept her awake last night. She hadn't been thinking about her parents. That was something she wouldn't allow herself to do—it hurt too much. Sometimes while she worked, or even when she wasn't doing anything in particular, their faces would float unbidden across her mind's eye and the numbness would slide away to reveal the wound in her soul. Thinking about them caused it to fester and ache, and she would hurt, oh, so badly, until she chased their faces away and scattered the specters of their memories from the corners of her mind. She wouldn't think about them, she told herself fiercely, no matter what. It always hurt too much. So then, she reasoned, what *had* kept her awake? She really couldn't remember and sighed.

Mrs. Merit took Jenny's sigh to mean she was displeased with the dress she had handed her. It was understandable as it was a dark and dreary gray. But it was all she had left, except for her best Sunday dress of light green muslin. Perhaps the soft, spring color would cheer her. A little self-consciously, she offered it to Jenny.

"Jenny, why don't we try on my green instead? This old thing is so cheerless and large. Would you like to wear my green?"

Jenny realized what Mrs. Merit had been thinking and she smiled a little sadly. Ever since Mr. Gannon had placed her in Mrs. Merit's room, the old woman had tried her best to take care of her, lending her clothing and hairpins, brushes and petticoats. Late at night, she would rise and tuck the covers over her, checking to see if she was warm. Jenny reached over on impulse and placed a soft kiss on the old wrinkled cheek. Mrs. Merit had been a widow now for twenty years and had no children of her own. Yet instead of letting her barrenness make her bitter, she loved others as if they all belonged to her.

"Thank you, Mrs. Merit, but this one is fine. Besides, I like gray."

The old woman blushed and smiled, happy to be of help.

"You best hurry, Jenny, if you want something to eat before work." She hurried toward the door, pleased with herself, as Jenny began to dress.

Jenny quickly pulled the tired looking gray dress over her head and walked toward the basin on the bureau. She filled it full of water and washed her face carefully. Then she combed her hair, pulling it straight back and twisting it into a knot that she pinned at the nape of her neck. Done with that, she turned and ran back to her bed, pulling up the covers and smoothing them neatly into place. The room was small, but cheery. It was on the top floor of the hotel and the trusses of the roof gave the room variation, while the dormer style window gave it ample light. The chairs and beds were overstuffed and treated with elaborate doilies and intricately patterned needlepoints. Mrs. Merit loved to sew and her handicrafts overflowed in the tiny room, adorning walls and windows alike. The room was warm and livable and Jenny liked it very much. A short, cursory glance showed her that everything was in its place. Satisfied, she hurried out the door for breakfast.

This morning went like most others with a short, quick breakfast in the kitchen with Mrs. Merit and Joshua before the others came. Then she would begin to prepare the rolls and chop the vegetables for dinner.

It always went the same with her. She didn't mind the work in the kitchen and she received only friendship and kindness from Joshua and Mrs. Merit. But the others who worked there took turns mocking her or snubbing her. No matter how hard she tried, she could not make friends with them.

One scullery girl who lived outside the hotel, and who always seemed on particularly friendly terms with Kevin, gave her the worst time. Jenny was small and petite, whereas

Angie was tall and angular with bony ribs where soft flesh should have been. Her face was not unpleasant, but it was set in a constant sneer that gave her a hard and cold expression. She had made fun of Jenny from the first day, when she noticed Mrs. Merit's work dress on her. Jenny's breasts were ample and Mrs. Merit's dresses fit her well there. But her waist, in contrast, was so tiny that the dress hung sharply and she had to tie her apron securely around her to keep from tripping over the hem.

She was a breathtakingly beautiful girl with an hourglass shape who affected others by simply being in the room. If she knew that she was beautiful, she kept the secret well hidden and never appeared to flaunt her charms. She simply *was* beautiful, and that was enough.

The other girls in the kitchen had lived a good many years in the area. The hardness of their lives had chipped away much of their hopes and dreams, making them coarse and harsh. Jenny was a constant reminder of what they had lost. To see their shattered illusions living in her was more then they could bear. They were jealous. Mrs. Merit had told Jenny not to worry. Jenny had recognized the signs for what they were, but knowing what was wrong and having to face the constant problems it created were two different things. Ladylike though she was, her patience was running out and her temper was bubbling closer to the surface every day.

"Look girls . . . 'ere she comes, *'Queen'* Jenny with the BIG BOSOMS!"

Angie held her hands out in front of her at arm's length, cupping extraordinarily large, imaginary breasts in front of her.

The others began to titter and finally laugh and the boys grinned and winked lustfully at her.

Jenny was kneading a large pan of dough and refused to look up. She didn't have enough flour in it and every time she'd pull her hand away, stringy masses of gooey dough clung to her fingers. She gritted her teeth and sprinkled in another cupful of flour, pretending not to hear what Angie had said.

Kevin had just walked in lugging a huge sack of potatoes.

When he heard everyone laughing and carrying on, he demanded to know what had happened.

"What is it?" he asked, starting to grin. He'd seen the stormy expression building on Jenny's face and knew it had something to do with her.

"Never mind what's goin' on Kevin—just get to the storeroom and pick me up a sack of onions, white or red . . . it don't matter."

Joshua had seen the trouble brewing and was doing his best to diffuse the situation before it became worse.

Angie saw Kevin and walked toward him, giving him her very best imitation of a sexy walk by thrusting her hips out as far as they would go. She looked like an arthritic crab who had scraped its bottom on a sandy beach as she scuttled across the room with a side-to-side motion. Kevin dropped his potatoes to the floor and patted her backside appreciatively, winking as she leaned against him. Her smile broadened.

"What's going on?" he asked her.

"Huh!" she snorted. *"Queen* Jenny here thinks she *owns* this bleedin' place!"

"That so?" he asked, a malicious grin spreading over his face. "You mean, 'Miss-innocent-and-wide-eyed' there thinks she *owns* this place? Well, just what do you suppose her and ole' Gannon *do* that makes her think that?"

Angie snickered. "Lord only knows!" she said sarcastically, thrusting her bony chest forward. "She's probably sneaking around with him . . . you know, doing it on the sly. *I've* heard the stories about Gannon, and *Lord* knows, *I've* tried to get 'im to *my* bed . . . supposed to be something pretty special . . . and he's rich too!"

She pushed away from Kevin and walked toward Jenny.

"Probably getting it all along, ain't ya?" she sneered. "And then you come strutting in here, with them big bosoms poking out, acting like 'lil-miss-innocent' "!

Jenny's head was still bent over the bowl and she silently pummeled the dough. Angie reached out and pinched her sharply on the breast.

Jenny looked up, shocked and angry.

"You think *these* are fair trade for the grandest hotel in Kansas City? Huh! He'll *use* you, like he does all the others. Lord knows he'll never *marry* no poor girl. He'll just use you till he gets tired of you, then—poof!" She snapped her fingers rudely in Jenny's face. "You're *gone!*" She looked at the other girls for confirmation. None had ever slept with him *personally,* but they *had* all heard stories, so some of them nodded in agreement. "See, I'm right!" She started to reach forward to deliver another cruel pinch, but Jenny had had enough. Quickly, before Angie had time to react, she grabbed her outstretched hand and twisted it hard. Surprised by the pain, Angie bent forward, trying to relieve the pressure. It was just what Jenny had been waiting for. She instinctively turned around slightly and brought her other hand around, placing it on the back of Angie's head. Then she pushed with all her might, shoving Angie's face into the bowl full of gooey dough.

The entire room exploded in laughter. Even Josh managed a grin.

Jenny's face was set in fierce determination as she struggled to hold Angie down. She didn't care what was going on in the room around her. All she cared about was keeping Angie's head in the dough and giving it an occasional twist for good measure for as long as she could.

"Let her up, Jenny," came a soft voice from behind her.

Startled, she turned around quickly as she recognized who spoke. Her eyes grew wide in horror as she saw Gannon standing in the doorway, casually resting against the post. He appeared stern as he looked at her, but his eyes were twinkling merrily.

Angie sprang back from the bowl the minute the pressure was gone. Dough dripped from her nose and hung from her hair in loose strings. The sight of her scooping the gooey mess away from her eyes caused the entire room to burst into fresh peals of laughter.

"Oh! Mr. Gannon . . . I'm sorry!" Jenny blurted out. "I didn't mean to hurt her . . ." She hurried to explain. "She said some things to me. I guess I just forgot myself and I . . ." She motioned to the bowl and Angie's dripping face before she sighed and stopped speaking, a dismal expression on her face.

Gannon nodded his head and pretended to study the tips of his fingers with great interest as he tried to retain his composure. But he was losing control and his lips were twitching slightly as he tried not to laugh out loud. Here she was, a little slip of a thing who looked at times as if she would jump if you yelled "boo," surprising him again with a display of her temper.

"I have some time this afternoon, Jenny." He looked up, a calm and unruffled expression on his face. "Meet me in the study for my piano lesson after dinner. We will keep the door *wide* open." He looked around the room pointedly to see if everyone got his message. Some looked down or turned away guiltily. Kevin just continued to stare fixedly at him, until Gannon's steady gaze forced him to drop his eyes. Satisfied, he turned to leave. In midstride and nearly out of the room, he stopped and turned halfway around to peer over his shoulder at Angie.

"Please wash that glop off your face, Angie—you're ruining my appetite," he said lightly. Then he turned and left the room with a broad smile on his face as the cooks and maids and delivery boys doubled over in laughter, leaving Jenny to stare miserably at the empty door.

Sometime later, after dinner, Jenny washed her hands and face and tidied her hair. She had gone back to her room for a moment before going on to the study. Mrs. Merit had insisted she wear her best Sunday dress for the piano lessons. Jenny looked at herself in the large, oval mirror which hung against one of the walls. The midday sun shone like golden fire through the garret window, illuminating the glass as Jenny ran her hand appreciatively over the soft material of the pale green dress. It reminded her of the colors of early spring, when the leaves are just born and their color is fragile and nearly translucent. It was as soft and pale as a new meadow of hay. She closed her eyes dreamily as she remembered the hills of rolling green grass outside the city of Warsaw in the fresh, early days of spring. The air would be laced with the scent of new beginnings; the promise of hope after winter's cruel hardships. Perhaps that is what Mrs. Merit had intuitively wished for Jenny when she had offered her this dress of green. A wish for a new beginning.

Jenny sighed and opened her eyes, a heavy sadness filling her. She wished that spring would never have to end, and that there would never be another winter to remind her of her loss. She wished that things had always stayed the same and never changed, and that new beginnings didn't always mean that something had to end. Wishes, she thought, and dreams. How different they are from reality! The image in the mirror wavered and blurred. She self-consciously wiped away a tear as memories of her parents flooded back into her mind, escaping from the dark corner in which she had locked them.

"Jenny!" Mrs. Merit's voice and a gentle tap at the door drove her to quickly wipe away her tears. "Mr. Gannon will be a few minutes late. He asks that you wait for him in the study."

"Yes, Mrs. Merit . . . thank you." Her voice trembled a bit and broke.

"Jenny?" Mrs. Merit's voice was filled with concern. "Can I come in? Are you all right?"

"Yes, yes . . . I'm fine!" She forced her voice to be cheerful. She didn't want Mrs. Merit to see her like this, but it was too late. The latch began to move, and the door opened.

Mrs. Merit entered frowning slightly until she noticed the tearstained cheeks and swollen eyes. Her expression became soft and filled with pity, as Jenny looked away in embarrassment.

"I'm almost ready, Mrs. Merit. I'll be just another minute." She smiled and looked into the mirror, pretending to arrange an unruly curl.

Mrs. Merit studied her face quietly for a moment before backing out of the door and shutting it slowly.

She resolved to forget as much of the pain as she could and go on with her life, if only in some way to fulfill her parents' dream.

Jenny gave one last glance at herself before leaving the

room. Mr. Gannon's piano lessons started today and she didn't want to be late.

The doors were open wide, as Mr. Gannon had instructed. He hadn't arrived as of yet. Jenny walked across the thick, Persian carpets to the elegant Steinway resting by the window. The drapes had been pulled and sunlight shined brightly against its ebony finish. It was a grand piano and, somehow, so well suited to this room as it waited for someone to coax the music from its rich and secret soul. Its keys beckoned to be touched, so much so that her fingers tingled in anticipation as she sat down.

A sheaf of music had been placed on the bench, and she ruffled through the pages, seeing everything from beginner's repetitious scales to complicated and beautiful concertos. She stopped and stared at the music sheets labeled "Mozart" and nearly cried out in delight. It was his complete works, and her favorite pieces. She paged through his *Symphony No. 25*, and the first movements of the *Marriage of Figaro*, until she found his *Concerto No. 20 in D Minor*. It was a piece which moved her by turns from joy to tears and she always felt as though she could almost conjure up Mozart himself when she played this piece. It was as if his soul had been translated into little black dots and squiggly lines. If you were clever enough, and your fingers nimble, you could resurrect the melody from the thin, white pages until the sounds flowed through you and became pure and elemental feelings.

Tentatively she touched a key. The tone was clear and resonated deep within the belly of the piano. She smiled and ran her hands lovingly up and down the board. Art and music, the same thing, she thought, just different languages. She laughed out loud as she tickled the highest octaves on the board, turning the huge piano into a tiny music box filled with tinkling glass. She paused and breathed deeply, looking at the music spread before her. It was there, securely in front of her if she needed it, but she didn't think she would and began to play.

She lightly touched the keys with a fast and happy rhythm, drawing out the first few measures of the concerto, which were deceptively simple and carefree and gave no hint at the dark and Dionysian quality at the heart of the piece. She knew the first few measures were a facade, covering up its passionate, turbulant depths. Steadily she worked, playing intently, caught up so completely as she built toward the crescendo that she did not notice the audience she had attracted.

Gannon stood in the doorway, flanked by Dugan and Mrs. Merit. Down the corridor, standing silently in the hall, was half of the kitchen staff with Joshua in the lead. Dugan was clearly amazed and delighted and Mrs. Merit looked at Jenny with motherly pride. Gannon, however, gave no hint as to what he felt as he gazed intently at her bent head.

Unaware that they watched, she played. On and on, losing herself in the building chords until the piece reached its peak and the emotion inside of her broke and flew away with the dying chords. She felt drained and sad inside. She finished the concerto with the same whimsical, carefree notes as the notes she had started with. Yet for a few moments Mozart's genius had translated her most secret and hidden emotions into a song and she had been a part of it.

Softly she inhaled and smiled until the sound of clapping hands caused her to turn around sharply.

Dugan and Mrs. Merit were clapping loudly.

"Wonderful, Jen! Wonderful!" Dugan enthusiastically praised. He walked in with Mrs. Merit. She nodded in agreement and smiled.

"It was the most beautiful thing I've ever heard, Jenny!" She beamed in delight.

Jenny smiled and began to feel the color rise to her cheeks. She had played for her family often and for any visiting relative, but never for anyone else. Embarrassed, she looked quickly at Gannon, who still stood in the doorway. She couldn't read his expression and wondered vaguely if she had offended him in any way.

When he realized that she was looking at him, he strode forward, until he stood nearly in front of her. Her cheeks were flaming and she couldn't look at him.

"It *was* beautiful, Jenny. You play with a great deal of feeling . . . you play very well."

Encouraged, she looked up at him and smiled happily.

"May I?" he asked, and gestured to the bench.

"Yes . . . of course." She moved toward one end, tucking her skirt in neatly around her to make room.

Quietly he sat down. There was a long and awkward silence while Dugan and Mrs. Merit stood behind them, smiling. Jenny stared self-consciously down at the keys.

"How long will it take me to learn to play as well as you?" he asked softly. He couldn't help but notice how incredibly blue her eyes were.

"Well," Jenny started. "It all depends on you . . . how much time you'll have to practice, and so on."

"I see." He nodded. "Well . . . shall we begin? I think I have all the necessary equipment." He held his hands out in front of her and wiggled his fingers.

Jenny smiled and Dugan laughed heartily, striking Gannon good-naturedly on the back. But he didn't make any move to leave.

"That will be all, Dugan. Thank you also, Mrs. Merit."

"Hmmm?" Dugan acted as if he didn't understand.

Gannon turned until he faced the old man and gave a sharp jerk of his head toward the door. "Unless I'm mistaken, I do not need a chaperon as I have left the connecting door open and I do not think I am ready for an audience yet." He gave another sharp jerk of his head toward the door.

"Oh. Oh-h-h! Yes, of course, Mr. Gannon . . . I was just . . . hmmm . . . leaving. Come along, Mrs. Merit," he said sharply. "Let's leave them to their lesson." Dugan and Mrs. Merit hurried from the room, only to pause at the doorway and look back briefly at the couple seated on the bench.

Gannon's broad shoulders seemed immense next to the petite and tiny form next to him. Her head barely met his shoulder and her blond hair shone with a silvery cast next to his flaming curls. Dugan wondered if they knew how beautiful they looked together, how right. His old heart yearned for a miracle to happen which would heal Aaron's old wounds and make his loneliness nothing but a bad memory.

Mrs. Merit tugged gently at his sleeve and the two of them backed away as the first scale was played. Murmuring voices filled the air. One was light and soft and fairly high, the other, deep and masculine with just the barest trace of an Irish burr. Together the two created a harmony that was more than sound which filled the early afternoon air.

Later, after dinner, when all her work was done, and Jenny lay snuggled into the soft quilts, her mind would not be still. Images floated in her thoughts, and always they ended with pictures of Gannon. She felt restless when she thought of him and no matter how she tried, she could not stop. When he had sat down beside her, her heart had quickened and a nervousness had filled her. It was not an unpleasant feeling, but oh . . . so different than any she had known before! When she had been able to concentrate on the music, she was amazed at how fast he learned. He devoured her words and played with an intensity that was almost frightening. She made herself stare at the keys, but her eyes refused to remain fixed. Slowly, hypnotically, they would be drawn to his long, slender hands. They were well muscled and calloused, but possessed a beautiful elegance in their shape and the way they moved that nearly mesmerized her. His nearness drew her like a magnet and his eyes threatened to consume her in their flickering, green depths. Her feelings were new and intense, but she tried to reason them away, telling herself that friendship and gratitude were the only emotions he aroused. But a still, small voice deep inside of her whispered other thoughts, secret thoughts of a hunger deep inside of her that he had awakened and longed to be fulfilled. But she refused to listen. Impatiently she pounded her pillow, treating the soft, goose-down as if it were bricks beneath her head which would not let her rest.

Somewhere, in another room, on the other side of the hotel, Gannon tossed about in his large, empty bed as well.

His muscles felt stiff and wired, filled with a crazy energy. No matter how he turned, or whether he was covered or uncovered, sleep would not come.

"Damn!" he muttered, slamming his pillow down on the bed. He couldn't sleep and there was no point in trying. He rose from his bed and poured himself a stiff drink. He swirled the brandy around in his glass and stared moodily at its amber color. She was only a child, and innocent as well. He must remember that. But still, she was so beautiful . . .

"Damn!" he muttered again, grabbing his trousers. He began to dress, quickly pulling them on as he reached for his shirt. He knew what he needed, the restlessness refused to leave. He pulled on his boots and reached for his coat as he headed toward the door. As he passed the mirror, he caught a glimpse of his reflection. The shirt he'd put on was a shimmering blue. The color reminded him of the innocent eyes which had looked up at him all afternoon. So innocent . . . so blue . . .

"Damn!" he said in annoyance, slamming the door behind him.

CHAPTER
5

The study was bright and filled with light. Aaron and Jenny sat beside each other on the piano's slender bench.

"Listen to him, Joshua! Laughing and talking as if he were a carefree young boy!" Dugan whispered excitedly.

Joshua nodded and smiled as he and Dugan peeked carefully around the polished, oak door frame. The connecting door had been left wide open as Gannon had instructed. Dugan didn't want him to think he was spying on him, yet, he couldn't help it. He had known Gannon ever since he was a boy, and he had never seen him act as he did now. In the past two weeks he had barely lost his temper and his smiles had come freely and quickly without the air of cynicism they usually bore.

"I think the boy's fallen in love, I do!" he announced happily.

"No! Do you really think so?" Joshua asked incredulously. As long as he'd worked here, he had come to know and respect his employer, admiring the smooth and easy way he had with the ladies. But Joshua, like everyone else, sensed that Gannon held something back, that there was a part of him he would never reveal to anyone, least of all to a woman. Yet he, too, had to admit that the last two weeks Gannon had been different. Once or twice he'd even heard him humming one of the tunes Jenny would play. "Dugan, I'm just an old cook, and I can see that he's different, but what makes you think he's in love?"

"Because," he said, "I do! I really do!" he whispered and started to explain. "He's in love all right, though I doubt as *he* knows it! I've seen it all before, with my own lads. First they meet someone they think needs protecting or help or something of the like, though I'll tell ya truly, I don't believe any of the lassies my boys married needed too much help . . . same as her . . . but that's not my point. You see, it's natural. Pretty soon, a man starts feeling protective toward a certain woman, like he's got to look out for her. My Maggie used to say that God put that there, that feeling, for a reason. Maybe so, I never did understand it myself, but I know it's true.

"Sooner or later, he starts feeling like he needs to have her around him, all the time, or else he gets nervous, wondering what she's up to. The whole lot of them seem to be scatterbrained and full of mischief, and Lord knows they usually are up to something. Then, after a while, he starts thinking that all the other men in the whole world feel exactly the same way as him about her, but he can hardly blame them for it, because this girl of his is the grandest girl of them all! It's about then he starts feeling like maybe she belongs to him. Mind you, not like a cow or horse or a piece of land, but he still feels she's his, or ought to be, even though he's not once said out loud or admitted to himself that he loves her. No, that would be giving away too much and no man I've ever known enjoyed making that sort of a commitment, unless of course, they didn't mean it. It's then that them bonny, sweet, helpless creatures have us at their mercy. And they know it. All it takes then is the proper moment. You're a little tight from too much to drink or maybe the moon is awfully bright that night as you drive her home and she's looking especially sweet. We're done for: hook, line, and sinker for the rest of our harrassed and worrysome lives . . ."

His eyes softened as he remembered Maggie, gone now for some time. "Aye, they've got us then, and all we get in return is a house full of lusty, screaming babes and a bed full of a warm, sweet woman who knows your thoughts before you speak and fills all your lonely nights . . . that's all we get."

Dugan stared misty-eyed into space and Joshua nodded, understanding the truth in his words. He'd been in love, too, once long ago, when he had first started to cook for the previous owner of the hotel. He remembered her as though it had been yesterday instead of twenty odd years ago. She was a fine lady, with porcelain skin and eyes the color of sweet, brown sugar. Her husband was a wealthy merchant and took her everywhere he went. Joshua had been a fine, strapping youth, with masses of wavy brown hair and a rugged build. In contrast, the lady's husband was small and frail-looking, with mousy brown hair and wire-rimmed spectacles that slid down his nose and rode at half-mast most of the time. But he loved his wife dearly and denied her nothing, even when her greedy eyes had burned with lust for Joshua. They would come every so often and stay at the hotel, until he and the beautiful lady became lovers. Their affair was wild and filled with delight, but the love was only one-sided. Joshua tried to convince her to run away with him. Over and over again he would beg her, and each time she would refuse to give him an answer, which only made it worse as Joshua's love grew into obsession. Days wore on until his pleas turned to impassioned threats which only drove her to stormy tears. But still, she refused to give him an answer. Then one day, driven half mad with jealousy and love, he threatened to tell her little husband about their affair. At first she laughed, thinking it only a ploy to get her to agree to run away with him. When he refused to recant his decision, she knew that he had meant it. Angrily, she accused him of seducing her, blaming the whole affair on him. When he laughed and reminded her of their first night together, how she had cleverly dropped her key in front of him, telling him as he bent over to pick up the key that her husband had a business meeting that night and he would be *very* late, she fell into a rage and began to pound him with her tiny fists. He held her gently, knowing her little blows could not hurt him. But when he had urgently whispered to her, "Marry me, run away with me and be my wife . . . I need you!" she had stopped hitting him and started to laugh.

"Marry you? You're nothing . . . nothing but a cook! How could I marry you? What could you give me but poverty? How could I marry you?"

Her little fists had not even raised a bruise, but her words had broken his heart into little pieces that not even time could mend.

"Joshua! Didn't you hear me, move back!" Dugan hissed.

"Hmmm? Oh . . . oh, yes!" Joshua quickly moved back down the hall as he glimpsed Gannon start to turn around.

"Did you hear something?" Gannon asked, as his eyes searched the empty doorway.

"No!" Jenny laughed. "Just you hitting a sharp when it's supposed to be a flat. Are you trying to distract me from your error?" she teased.

He turned toward her and grinned, feeling warm and alive as she looked up at him with laughter in her blue eyes.

"No, I'm not trying to *distract* you from my error. I don't think anything could do that. However, I thought I heard someone speak. As far as me hitting the wrong key, how in the devil do you expect me to stretch my fingers halfway across the board without moving my hand?"

She laughed, reaching for his hand. "Like this," she instructed, placing his thumb on middle C and pulling his littlest finger until he thought it would come off, trying to stretch it to the key designated by the music.

"Just . . . stretch . . . them . . . apart . . . see!" she said happily while she held his hand over the keys with her own. She turned to look at him, wanting to tease him into laughter again, amused by his frustration at being unable to reach the keys easily. That would come in time. He was very close, so close that she could smell the faint odor of soap on his skin mixed with some pleasant, spicy aroma she was not familiar with. Every time she bent forward, toward the keys, she could feel the touch of his breath, warm and soft, on the back of her neck.

As she held his hand across her lap with both of hers she could feel the faintest touch of his arm against her breast. It was warm where they touched and she started to blush as she looked at him. He seemed unaware of the contact as he smiled impishly at her. His eyes glowed warm as a cat's, bright green. She began to lose her smile as she became lost in their brilliance, following the outline of black created by the heavy fringe of sooty lashes to the corner of his eyes where his brows seemed to start as shadows, climbing higher and higher to form arrogant peaks above them. She couldn't stop studying the lines of his face, tracing the brows until they connected with his nose. It seemed like one long, thin line as she followed it down to the corner of his crooked smile, where she lingered.

The room became quite warm as she watched his smile slowly fade, until the hand she held on the keys turned upright and curled ever so slowly around both of hers. She dared not look up, afraid of what she would see in his eyes, wondering if it would only be a reflection of what was in hers.

The front door slammed and the magic was shattered. Gannon cleared his throat nervously and gave a small imitation of a laugh. He patted Jenny's hand with his other and released them as Dugan's head poked around the corner.

"Mayor Kenton's wife here to see you, Mr. Gannon . . . and her daughter."

Gannon nodded and stood up, giving Jenny a remote, polite smile and a semblance of a bow.

"Lesson over, Miss Bydalek," he said formally.

His expression had changed so rapidly that Jenny doubted the moment before had even been real. She felt embarrassed and a little confused at the feelings he had aroused. She had friends before who were boys, some she had liked very much. But the feelings Gannon stirred inside her were like none she had ever known before. One minute he was treating her as an equal and a friend, and the next he was patting her hand as if she were a small child.

She watched as he made his way to the door, and couldn't help but notice how tall and handsome he was. Or the way he moved as he crossed the floor. She wished her mother were here. She needed someone to talk to, and there wasn't anyone. Once, when she was young and a boy in class had grabbed her and kissed her hard, she had run home as fast as she could. The kiss had bothered her, not because she didn't know what it meant, but because she and the boy had just been friends, and now, after he had kissed her, that had changed. She couldn't feel comfortable around him again, no matter how hard she tried. Her mother had laughed, telling her to expect many such moments in her life, and that someday, someone's kiss would be special, like something she had never known before. And it would be right, and good, and would change her life forever. She thought again of Gannon's crooked smile, and wondered, just for a second, as she gathered the music together and prepared to leave the room, what it would be like if he kissed her.

Out in the hall, Mayor Kenton's wife waited with her daughter. Gannon was surprised when he noticed that the blond girl who accompanied the mayor's wife was the same eager, young lady who had concocted the brilliant story about staying with her cousin so that she could spend the night in his bed. He was even more surprised when he saw Mrs. Kenton. Her hair had obviously been blond like her daughter's at one time, but it was there that the resemblance ended. She was small and round with a cherubic face. Bright, blue marbles peered out from beneath scraggly brows that seemed to connect over her nose. Her face was powdered in the fashion of the day and bright, perfectly round, red cherry rouge adorned her cheeks. She floated toward him, her diminutive feet in direct contrast to her ample figure, which was magnified by the volumes of purple silk she wore. The odor of lilacs filled the room. He vaguely wondered how many gallons she had used as he tried not to breath too deeply.

"Mayor Kenton's wife," she gushed, extending a heavily ringed hand toward him. Gannon choked back a smile as one of the large peacock feathers nesting on her hat came forward, trying to tuck itself neatly into her open mouth.

"Mrs. Kenton?" Gannon stretched out his hand to take hers. "It's a pleasure to meet you."

"Oh, yes . . . pfff!" she said, as she tried to blow the feather out of her mouth.

Her daughter smiled brightly at Gannon, her blue eyes gleaming at him with their secret knowledge. But the gaze he returned to her was merely polite and not intimate; her self-assured expression began to waver and she started to look confused.

"Mr. Gannon," Mrs. Kenton began. She gave an elaborate curtsy, tipping forward unsteadily until her peacock feathers fell forward, covering her face, and she nearly lost her balance.

Gannon reached for her arm to steady her as he suppressed a smile.

"Thank you," she responded, giggling like a schoolgirl. Then, with all the pomp and ceremony she could muster, she waved her arm in a wide and elaborate arc, drawing attention to the lovely young woman beside her. "May I introduce you to my beautiful daughter, Penelope?"

"Charmed," Gannon said lightly, touching her hand as he bowed. Penelope lost her perplexed expression immediately and regained her self-confidence as she smiled her most brilliant smile at him.

"Is there something that I can do for you ladies? Some refreshment perhaps?" He motioned toward the study.

"Oh, no. We don't have time to stay. We're on a shopping expedition to buy some new silk for Penelope, something quite special for a very special occasion . . . speaking of which . . ." She stopped in midsentence as she and Penelope stared, openmouthed, as Jenny walked through the door into the hall.

Gannon saw the women gaping at her, noticing how they stared at her dress. Their dresses were of the finest, tailored to fit their every curve or hide their tiny flaws. It was obvious to them that Jenny's dress was at best second-rate, and at worst? Ruefully, Gannon had to admit that Jenny would have looked wonderful dressed in a flour sack tied with twine. Even the borrowed dress couldn't hide her exquisite figure.

Mrs. Kenton was the first to regain her composure. Not hesitating for a moment, she took a step forward and introduced herself.

"Mrs. Kenton . . . Mayor Kenton's wife, and my daughter, Penelope." She extended her hand. "And whom do we have the pleasure of meeting?" Her voice was pure saccharine, oozingly sweet, and each word rose higher and higher until "meeting" sounded like a squeak.

"Jenny, ma'am . . . Jenny . . ."

She tried to finish when Gannon abruptly cut her off.

"Jennifer Bates," he finished smoothly and went on as casually as if it weren't a lie. "Mrs. Kenton, Penelope . . . I'd like to introduce you to my cousin, Jenny, just newly arrived from England."

Jenny stared at him in astonishment.

"England?" Mrs. Kenton squeaked. "Cousin? I wasn't aware of the arrival of any of your relatives. In fact, I do believe she is the *only* relative I've ever known you to have. Please correct me if I'm wrong, Mr. Gannon, but I was under the impression that you were, ah, how does one put it . . . of Irish descent?"

"You are, of course, quite right in the assumption that I am Irish by birth, but some of my relatives were *fortunate* enough to marry those of English descent. As for not knowing my relatives . . . I do not mean to be rude," Gannon said coolly. "But, surely you do not expect to know everything about someone, whom, as you have said, you've only just met?"

"Well, of course not! I just meant that at tea I heard, well, you know what gossips some people are. I really had no idea that you had any *living* relatives!"

"To be sure, Madam, Jenny is quite alive," he pointed out dryly.

"Well, yes, of course she is. Forgive me . . . I was just a little surprised."

"No more so than I," murmured Jenny.

As always Gannon remained unreadable except for his merrily twinkling eyes.

"What did you say, my dear?" asked a bewildered looking Mrs. Kenton. Gannon was sure that after this meeting, Mrs. Kenton would check her sources much more thoroughly.

"Just that I'm very pleased to meet you, and your daughter."

"Yes, well how nice, how very, very nice. But now, Mr. Gannon, I would like to tell you why we've come. My husband, Mayor Kenton, is having a birthday celebration August 15. Since we were in the neighborhood, we thought we would extend the invitation to you in person. A more formal one has already been sent, but since you are one of Kansas City's leading citizens, we wanted to issue the invitation in a personal and more meaningful way. Isn't that right, Penelope?"

Penelope, who had stood nearly motionless and mute for the past five minutes, failed to answer her mother.

"Penelope?" She nudged her daughter a little ungently with her elbow. "Pen—el—op—ee! Isn't that correct?"

Her worldly ways had been forgotten and her facade of sophistication had melted away as she continued to stare at Jenny.

"Yes, Mama . . . quite correct," she managed.

"And Jenny, since you are Mr. Gannon's *cousin,* I would like to extend the invitation to you as well. I'm quite sure there would be a great many people in this town who would be very eager to meet a piece of Mr. Gannon's somewhat mysterious past."

Down, but not out, Mrs. Kenton's wheels continued to turn, as she thought how she might yet get Gannon to escort her daughter to the ball.

"There will be many fine, young gentlemen there who I am sure would be quite pleased to escort you. I see that you wear no wedding ring. As a matter of fact," she gushed. "I know someone who would be absolutely *perfect!*"

"That won't be necessary, Mrs. Kenton," Gannon injected softly. "Since my cousin is just newly arrived, and this is her first journey so far from her homeland, I feel it is my responsibility, and my pleasure, to escort her. But it was very kind of you to offer."

"Yes, wasn't it though? Well, you *both* must come. It will be the grandest event of the entire season!" She went on gayly. "But we really must be running along now. We have a mountain of shopping to do . . . ta!" She chirped and waved her hand as she headed for the door, until she realized Penelope was still standing in the same spot, gaping and looking nearly comatose.

"Hah!" Mrs. Kenton forced out a fraudulent laugh, as she hurried back to her daughter. "Come Penelope, dear, it's time to *leave.*" She grasped her arm tightly and tugged her toward the door.

"But, Mama! I told all my friends Mr. Gannon would be my escort. Ouch, Mama! Don't pull so hard! Ma-ma-a! Ouch!"

"Ta!" said Mrs. Kenton gayly, as she ignored Penelope, pulling her outside and shutting the door behind them with a resounding thud.

Gannon burst into laughter as Jenny stood staring at him in horror. With Mrs. Kenton safely out of earshot, she could wait no longer. The only true thing Gannon had said during their entire visit was the first part of her name and that this was her first visit away from her homeland. Everything else had been a gigantic fairy tale, and she, the primary character in it.

"Mr. Gannon," she begged. "Stop laughing! Mr. Gannon, it really isn't that funny! Why did you say those things?" she pleaded, tugging at his sleeve. He still hadn't stopped laughing. She thought that he might be in danger of splitting his sides and just for a second, she wished that he would.

"I'm not your cousin. And I'm certainly not a 'Bates' or English. I'm Polish! And I can't possibly go to some ball with you. I've nothing to wear!"

The absurdity of the situation amused Gannon and he smiled deeply as he tried to explain.

"Jenny, I had to tell them you were a relative of mine. My reputation in certain circles is, how would one say it . . . well-known. A young, unmarried woman living under my roof, even though she is a working and paid employee, would have her reputation severely tarnished, to say the least, by being here."

He guided her to a settee resting against the wall, and pulled her down beside him. His smile had faded and his features darkened with concern as he spoke.

"I have been wanting to speak to you about something for quite a while. Perhaps now is the right time. Jenny, have you ever given any thought to the possibility that your uncle may not come for you?"

That thought had never occurred to her. She shook her head adamantly.

"He *will* come, Mr. Gannon. I know he will!"

Her words were said with such force that Gannon knew speaking to her in such a way would only bring back a lot of the pain she seemed to have been forgetting about these past few weeks. But she must be made to face her situation realistically. He talked on, as gently as he could.

"Jenny, sometimes things happen over which we have no control and we are left to deal with only a handful of options at best. Many times what we have to choose from does not seem to be what we want, but circumstances sometimes force us to decide what we will do. If, for some reason, your uncle does not come, you have to begin to think about your future and what you will do."

"You needn't speak to me as if I were a child, or an idiot!" she cried fiercely. She stood up, trembling. "My uncle *will* come for me! And even if he doesn't come . . . I'm going to *Alaska*. There isn't anything you can do about it. It was my parents' dream and since they cannot fulfill it themselves, then it shall be fulfilled through *me!*"

"You tell me not to treat you like a child, or an idiot . . . but when you *act* like one, how can I treat you any differently?" he roared. "You are being foolish, Jenny! You have no idea what that wilderness is like, or the people you will be forced to deal with. All your life your parents have looked out for you. Now I am looking out for you . . . but that cannot continue indefinitely. People will talk, especially now that Mayor Kenton's wife has seen you. Right now, she's probably putting it on the front page of the *Tribune!*"

He tried to reason with her, but he could see that her mind was made up. He'd already come to know how stubborn she could be when provoked.

"We have to think about your future," he went on through gritted teeth. "In that light, I have decided to escort you to local functions masquerading as my cousin. There, perhaps, we may be able to find a suitable match for you."

"A suitable match!" she raged. "Taken care of all my life? What am I, a side of beef to be auctioned off? Is that what you want? Me, *married,* so that you no longer need to *protect* me?!"

He stood up facing her. No one had ever made him this furious, no one had ever dared. But the idea of marrying Jenny off to someone else didn't feel right to him, either. Yet he could think of no other way.

His voice was icy.

"It's either marriage to someone who can provide a decent life for you, or you can spend the rest of yours working in kitchens like mine and being pawed by men like Kevin, who only want one thing from you. It's your choice."

They stared angrily at each other for a long time, neither moving nor speaking, until, quite to Gannon's surprise, a big, glittering tear slid from Jenny's eye and rolled slowly down her cheek.

He sighed, softly reaching out to touch the tear. It must have been a magic tear, because the feel of it against his skin dissolved all the anger he had felt. Gently, he spoke.

"Jenny, come to the ball with me . . . as my cousin. I promise I will do everything in my power to contact your uncle, but until we know for certain whether or not he's coming, do as I ask. I want only the best for you. I don't want to see your life quickly burned out, tied to the wrong man, with hungry babes to feed and nothing to feed them.

I . . . I care about you . . ." he said softly. "We *are* friends, aren't we?"

The last words broke her and she began to weep. Gannon stepped forward and gathered her into his arms, holding her tightly as she cried. He soothed her like a baby, stroking her hair and murmuring soft words. He didn't notice Dugan leave or hear Mrs. Merit come in.

"Oh, poor child!" she cried out and rushed toward them.

Gannon carefully pulled away from Jenny and placed a stray lock of hair, wet with tears, back into place.

"He *will* come," she whispered fiercely. Gannon nodded silently as he turned his attention to the worried Mrs. Merit.

"Mrs. Merit, I would like to introduce you to my cousin, Jenny. She will be accompanying me to the Mayor's birthday party, and possibly other functions as well. Call in the dressmaker and see that she is suitably attired."

Mrs. Merit was confused, but she smiled happily, going off to do what had been ordered. The situation at the hotel was becoming quite interesting. Confusing, that was true, but interesting, nevertheless.

"Better?" Gannon asked softly. Jenny nodded. "You needn't work tonight . . . or ever again in the kitchen, if you like. Since you are to be my 'cousin,' it would perhaps make me seem very cruel to make my little immigrant work so hard."

"No," she flatly refused. "You are doing so much already. Please let me work. At least I'll feel as though I'm helping too." Sadly she turned around, heading for the kitchen, unaware that Gannon watched her every step, until she stopped and turned to face him once again.

"He will come, Mr. Gannon . . . I know he will." She swallowed hard as she turned and left the room.

The ship's main sail was being unfurled and John looked up and watched as the huge canvas came billowing slowly down, filling with wind as it came.

The ocean was choppy and gray with foam-crusted waves. He swayed unsteadily on his feet as the ship moved through the water. Ropes were creaking constantly as the waves slapped in rhythm against the prow of the ship as it lunged forward. John felt as if he were on a giant rocking horse as the ship pitched and rolled endlessly in perfect time.

He would have found the ocean beautiful, and the scent of the salted air fresh and clean, if he had not ached so inside. The pain he felt numbed his senses as he held Jenny's letter tightly in his hand.

It had come thousands of miles, so deceptively white and anonymous. Worst of all was that he had *wanted* it to come, his anticipation rising by degrees daily. He had felt as if some psychic link had existed between him and this piece of paper. He had known it was drawing nearer every day. So sure was he that final time, on that particular morning, in that particularly nondescript, brown burlap mail sack held in Tanith's trustworthy hands . . . so sure was he that its contents had held something for him that he hadn't waited at the old, familiar table by the old, familiar square-paned window, sipping coffee till his bladder felt ready to burst . . . so sure was he, that he had fairly bounded over to the salty old sea captain with his hand thrust out expectantly . . . waiting, as the seconds ticked agonizingly by.

Tanith grinned at his outstretched hand, but the more packages and letters he produced without John's name inscribed upon them, the more difficult it was to retain his smile. But not John. He just *knew* it was in there, believed it wholeheartedly with every fiber of his being, concentrating so hard, he felt he could materialize it out of the very air. And then, with his eyes screwed nearly shut, and his heart, with its tired, old irregular beat, pumping madly, he felt something light and smooth fall into his waiting hand.

"He-heee!" he cackled, proudly displaying *his* letter to the crowd around him. *"See!"* He beamed a most beatific smile. *"Mr.* Jonathan Bydalek, General Delivery, Anchorage, Alaska!" Then, like a grizzled old school teacher tutoring a host of roughnecks and rowdies he dearly loved, he turned the letter over and read aloud the return.

"From 'Miss Jennifer Bydalek' . . ." His mind sounded a soft warning bell with the appearance of his niece's name instead of his brother's, but he shrugged off the feeling and continued anyway.

"The Grand Hotel, Kansas City, Missouri." *Kansas City?* he thought worriedly. They still had a long way to go, and winter would be setting in soon.

"Read it, John!" Emily excitedly urged, exchanging a happy wink with Tanith. "When are they coming?"

"I'm gettin' there!" he argued, opening the letter with all the fuss and flourish of a natural-born showman. "Uh . . . hmmmm!" he began again, clearing his throat loudly, conscious of all the eyes on him and their waiting ears. "Dear . . . why, *she* called *me 'Dear!'* Did you hear that?" He flashed the page in front of everyone, lest anyone doubt his credibility. "She called me *dear!"*

"Get on with it, John!" laughed Tanith, as he casually slipped his arm around Emily. Moments like this were meant to be shared. "We don't have all day, ya know . . . *dear!"* Everyone laughed in a good-natured, comradely way, happy for the old man.

"Oh, ah . . . sure . . ." he started, looking a little embarrassed, his cheeks flushed a merry, cherry pink, but too happy and proud to care. *"Dear* Uncle Jonathan . . . 'magine that, 'dear' and *'Jonathan'* on the very same line . . ." he murmured to himself. His eyes, which always appeared as clear and blue as an Alaskan summer sky, glowed tenderly, humbly wondering how an old rock hound like him rated such fine treatment.

"John?" Emily asked softly as she watched his eyes fill with tears. "Are you all right?"

"Oh, yeah," he replied as her voice broke into the soft, cloudlike feeling that had enveloped him. "Just got a little cinder in my eye . . . that's all." He grinned as he rubbed his eye and then his nose with his free hand before starting in again. "I-have-written-this-letter-over-and-over-again," he read slowly, each word measured and carefully enunciated. ". . . and-no-matter-how-many-ways-or-times-I-write-it, what-I-have-to-tell-you-always-ends-the-same . . ." Two warning bells jangled loudly in his mind. This time he didn't try to ignore them as his smile began to fade and the people around him began to exchange fearful glances. "Let's see here," he said softly, blinking a little to focus while his finger searched the page for his place. "She says, 'Mama-and-Papa-are-gone . . .'" Stunned silence, the only sound the faint hissing of the stove, and the ever-present wind sighing through the town. "Gone?" he repeated, as if he didn't understand the word. It felt as if he had stepped from beside a warm fire and jumped headfirst into an icy bay. He couldn't breathe, his mind remaining locked on those few words, sinking deeper into his brain like stones thrown into powdery snow, deeper and deeper until they finally hit ground. The room began to turn an odd shade of blue around the edges, and a horrid feeling came over him as though some large, dark weight had settled over his chest. "Sedna . . ." he croaked, knowing that the dark mistress of the dead had come to seize him, sucking his breath away, scrambling his senses, as she began her hard dance upon his chest . . . tha-THUMM . . . THA-THUMMM!, knocking him to within a breath of the gates of Adlivun, the Eskimo land of the dead, while the words "Gone! Gone!" followed him, spiraling down, down in the rushing waterfall that filled his ears, until darkness settled in around him and he knew no more.

Much later he had awakened to find himself stretched out in Em's bed, with a downy pillow tucked beneath his head. "Water . . ." he had begged, not recognizing the weak-throated bleating as his own voice as Emily obliged his request.

"Easy, John," she admonished, placing the half full glass near his still blue lips while she rested his tired head on her soft bosom until the water and the beating of her own heart lulled him back to sleep and forgetfulness.

Two days passed in a blur. The fourth he took a rich broth and the fifth he packed his gear, stubbornly refusing to listen to anyone's well-meant advice.

"I'll bring your niece," Tanith offered. "You just rest a bit."

"Nope," he replied obstinately. His Polish mind had been made up and nothing between heaven or hell would change it. "Jen needs me now . . . and I . . . I need her," he admitted softly as his old friend fell silent.

He had sold all the fox furs he possessed to buy a ticket to Sacramento because of this letter. It was one thing not to ever see your own flesh, but as long as you knew it existed, healthy and happy, somewhere, even thousands of miles away, somehow it was bearable. But now, knowing his only brother was gone, along with his beautiful sister-in-law . . . it just seemed too hard somehow. But he still had Jenny. She was all he had left now in the world, except for a huge chunk of frozen ground in Alaska with a hole in it. She was his only remaining family, and he longed to see her.

He had bought return tickets for both of them, and Emily told him not to worry when he returned. There would be room for them both at the hotel and plenty to eat as well. John had smiled and thanked the Lord for his friends, telling her he'd pay her back, someday, because he was going to be rich when he mined his gold in the spring. Rich as old Midas himself, and Jenny too. He'd look after her, see that she wanted for nothing. Give her what he had wanted to give his brother. Deep down inside he felt responsible for Stephen's death. If he had not talked him into coming all the way over to this strange land, he would not have burned to death in a tenement fire in some foreign city.

The wind had picked up, and the sail was as potbellied full as it could be. He turned away from the slowly disappearing coast and stared at the horizon, which seemed so far away. He wondered what Jenny would be like, and he wondered if she would like him. He hoped so, because he needed her to care. He was getting old, and although he didn't like to admit it, he was also getting tired. Someday his old body would up and call it quits. He wanted someone to remember him when he was gone; someone to care that he wasn't around anymore. He sighed.

A voice behind him startled him slightly until he recognized it as Tanith's.

"Why don't you take your gear down below, John, then

come stand beside me on the foredeck for a while. We'll talk and swap some lies. How's that sound?"

"Sounds pretty darn good, Tanith. I reckon a talk'll do me just fine." He smiled a little sadly as he slung his pack over his shoulder and headed carefully down the narrow stairs belowdeck.

CHAPTER

6

Nearly a month had gone by since the mayor's wife had visited Gannon. Nothing had changed at the hotel; it ran as smoothly and as orderly as always with him in control. His plans for introducing Jenny to society had not changed either. In fact, with all the time he had been spending with her these past weeks, his concern over her future had grown stronger with each passing day.

They had still not heard from her uncle. In a way, Gannon was relieved. He did not like the idea of Jenny going off to a wilderness in some obscure, northern country to mine for gold. Kansas City was supposed to be civilized and it was wilderness enough. There was a large hill outside the city which overlooked the entire area for miles. Sometimes, when he was restless and needed to be alone, he would go there at night and watch the lights being lit until the city looked like a giant, shimmering lake with roads running into it like many rivers. The surface seemed calm and lovely, dancing with lights, but beneath the soft and shimmering top, cold currents jigged and capered about like dangerous fingers which tried to drag a man to its murky bottom. Once there, he might never escape. He had started at the bottom, and he knew what it took to swim to the top. You had to be powerful and a titan to stay there, because even when you thought you were safe, every once in a while the currents would change, and you could feel them dangerously close, hungry to pull you down.

Dugan and Mrs. Merit interrupted his musings as they came into the study.

"You wanted to see us, Aaron?" Dugan asked.

"Yes, I did. I will be leaving for about one week to take care of some business in St. Louis. A friend of mine thinks he has come into what he considers a once in a lifetime opportunity and is unable to acquire enough cash to take advantage of it. In his wire he promises me a return on my investment that I just can't ignore." He was not worried about leaving his business in Dugan's capable hands. But he was worried about leaving Jenny. Lately, Kevin had been quiet, and hadn't bothered her. But Gannon wondered just how long that would last if Kevin knew that he was gone. Joshua tried to look after Jenny in the kitchen, but he was old, and Gannon knew he would be no match for Kevin if the situation arose. "My leaving on business is nothing new . . . nothing we have not dealt with before. Just continue to supervise the staff as you always have. But," and he sighed, "I think there is one problem that needs to be addressed . . ."

"Jenny," Dugan said matter-of-factly.

"Exactly."

"Why, Jenny's no problem, Mr. Gannon!" Mrs. Merit exclaimed. "She's a dear!"

Gannon smiled.

"You don't need to defend Jenny to me, Mrs. Merit. I know what she is, and that is precisely the problem. I have made plans to move Kevin down to the wharf permanently, once I get back. I'd fire him right here and now, if it weren't for his family. Dugan, you probably remember his mother, Sara Woods. Last year she lost her husband with the consumption, and she has become dependent on Kevin to bring in a little money to help take care of that mob of kids she's raising. For her sake, I'd like to try and keep him on for

75

as long as possible. But I don't want him around Jenny, not even for a minute. Do you understand?" They both nodded solemnly, each wondering how they would accomplish it. Kevin lugged all day for the kitchen. Keeping him away from Jenny seemed next to impossible. Dugan was about to speak, when Aaron continued. "While I'm gone, I've instructed Joshua to make up a list of things he needs . . . things which will take Kevin away from here for at least a week. Then, when I get back, I'll move him to the wharf with a few of the other luggers; that way, I don't believe there will be too many problems."

"Mr. Gannon, you wanted to speak to me?"

They all turned their attention toward the door as Jenny entered. She wore a soft yellow dress, and her hair was done in lovely curls. Gannon had been about to speak as she walked in, but only stared at her for a very long time. Dugan and Mrs. Merit exchanged a knowing look before Gannon answered her.

"I have to leave on business for a few days, Jenny," he said curtly. "So you needn't worry about giving me piano lessons for a while."

His attitude was arrogant and flip when he spoke to her. Dugan understood what was wrong with him and smiled softly. But Jenny didn't know why he had talked so roughly to her. His words sounded harsh, and she didn't like the idea of him being gone at all. She had the nervous sensation that if he was ever too far away, part of her would begin to die. Her smile slowly faded.

"I don't *worry* about the piano lessons, sir . . . I enjoy them . . ." she explained and paused briefly. She frowned slightly and her forehead wrinkled in reply as she took a tentative step toward him. Mrs. Merit had bought her a bottle of rosewater with the faintest trace of ambergris in it. As she came closer to him, he could smell its delicate scent as it mixed sweetly with her own, and hear the faint rustle of her skirts as she approached. He knew at that moment, should the sun stop shining and the world become cloaked in darkness, or if his own eyes were plucked from his face or gone dim with age, he would always know her, even in a crowd of thousands, by her fragrance. Like a signature or a haunting melody, it belonged only to her, and etched itself forever in his mind.

"Do you have to go?" she asked quietly.

"Yes!" he snapped, looking at her through narrowed lids. "Do you wear that dress when you're in the kitchen?"

Jenny stopped and looked confused as she touched the skirt and looked down. The dress molded perfectly to her figure, and the neckline had been dropped quite low as was the style of the fashionable women of the day. Its daffodil color softened her skin to cream, and contrasted beautifully with her eyes. "Yes, Mr. Gannon . . . it's one of those you had made for me. Is there something wrong with it?" She took another step nearer.

He glared at her, noticing how perfectly white her skin was, and how very, very soft it looked. He couldn't help but follow the delicate line of her neck to her shoulders, before he caught himself and abruptly turned around. Cussing softly, so that only Dugan heard, he reached for papers on the desk.

Jenny had come to think of him as her friend. The idea of him being angry at her made her feel terrible. Thinking that she had done something wrong, she reached out and touched his arm softly. When she did, he jumped as though an electric current had passed between them, and slowly, as though unwilling, but unable to stop himself, he turned around.

"Have I done something wrong?" she asked.

He shook his head wearily and his expression softened. He felt as if he had been fighting a battle for too long, and was losing.

"No . . . I just wanted to tell you that I will be gone for about a week, and not to worry . . . Dugan, Joshua, and Mrs. Merit will look after you until I return."

She nodded, still confused as to why he had reacted so violently a few minutes before. They looked at each other for a moment, before Gannon pulled his gaze away.

"Mrs. Merit, you and Jenny can return to work now." He dismissed them lightly. "I still have a few things I would like to discuss with Dugan."

"Yes, sir," said the old woman. Taking Jenny by the hand, they walked toward the door. For a very brief moment, Gannon had an overpowering urge to run to her and take her in his arms. The idea of being separated from her for even a week seemed more than he could stand. He squeezed his eyes tight against the impulse and slowly shook his head, like a man filled with a drug he could not control.

"How about a drink, lad?" Dugan's voice soothed his jangled nerves and he opened his eyes slowly. Together they walked to the bar and Dugan poured two, very full, very potent glasses of pale amber brandy. Dugan sipped his and watched as Aaron fought to maintain his control.

"Why don't you tell her, Aaron?" he asked softly.

"Tell her? Tell her what?"

"Tell her that you're in love with her," he answered.

"Love?! I'm not in love with her!" he roared.

Dugan was not prepared for the violence of his reaction, as Aaron turned and slammed his glass against the fireplace, shattering it to pieces. The alcohol in the brandy made the flames turn blue and shoot hotly up the chimney.

"Yes, you are," Dugan retorted. "You're in love with her, and *she* is in love with you . . . you do *know* that she loves you, don't you, lad?"

Gannon started to laugh. "Love. Yes, to your first question, or should I say statement, yes, I love her, like a child or a friend. As to your second statement—Jenny's just a child. What would *she* know of love?"

"Enough to make her nearly cry at the thought of you leaving . . . enough to care if she's done something wrong . . . enough . . ."

"Stop it, Dugan," Aaron thickly demanded.

"No, I will not! I've known you all these past years, watched you grow up, taken care of you when you've been sick, and put up with your vile temper. I'd say I've earned the right to speak my mind to you, and I will, by heavens! Even if you open the door and throw me out . . . it's about time someone talked to you. You're like a son to me, boy, and I intend to treat you the same as I would any of them."

Aaron looked at him coldly, but refused to speak. Dugan continued. He knew he was walking on thin ice by provoking Aaron, but he loved him. If he couldn't talk to him, then no one could.

"You've been deceiving yourself these past weeks . . . keeping her at arm's length by telling yourself she's just a baby . . . a child to be watched over. But, lad, open your eyes as well as your heart! She's not a baby . . . she's a fully grown woman . . . a lovely woman, who just happens to be in love with you!"

"All the more reason to find her a *suitable* husband, wouldn't you agree, Dugan?" he said coolly. He poured himself another drink and walked to his chair, where he sat down, slouching so far that his legs stretched clear to the middle of the rug. He cradled his drink between his hands and rested his chin on top of them as he stared moodily off into space.

"Another *man* for Jenny?! Are you mad, boy? Do you really believe another man is the answer? I've seen the way she looks at you . . . and the way you look at her! You can't keep your eyes off of her for a second! How do you suppose you'd feel on the night of her wedding if you knew some other man were taking her to the bridal bed instead of *you?*"

Gannon's eyes flashed fire.

"She doesn't love me . . . she can't!" he said through gritted teeth. "Maybe she thinks she does . . . but it isn't love . . . it's gratitude and nothing more!"

"Aye, lad . . . just keep talking that way, and maybe you'll convince yourself. But you won't convince me! What happened to you as a child is over. Put the past behind you. Your past did two things to you, Aaron, *two things* . . . it made you strong, stronger than anyone I've ever known, but it hurt you too, hurt you so deep, that I don't believe you've ever truly healed. Why can't you let Jenny love you, boy? Let her help you heal . . . why do you find it so damned hard to let anyone love you? Even when you was with Maggie and me, we'd give you a hug, and you'd shovel the walk, or we'd tell you your marks at school were good and you'd do all the washing for a week. You always paid us for giving you our love. Why can't you believe that someone could love you just for yourself and not need to be *paid* to feel that way?"

Gannon still stared into empty space, but when he heard what Dugan had said, he looked up and laughed.

"I don't find it hard to believe someone could love me for myself," he whispered. "No, not at all, Dugan. I'm worth a fortune. Every lass between here and the coast is in *love* with me . . . and my money . . . didn't you know that?"

"Oh, so that's it then? Hit a nerve, did I? You think if you were just another Irishman shoveling coal for a nickel a day, or going out on the boats in the morning, that she wouldn't love you. Am I right? You think . . . for all you've been through and accomplished in this life . . . you still think you're not good enough. Just another mick, right? Or maybe," he added, sure of his feeling, "or maybe the real reason is you're just afraid to love her, afraid she'll hurt you, like your mother did!"

"Damn you, Dugan!" growled Aaron, and came to his feet.

"Your mother died when you were so young, boy. But she didn't *mean* to die, she didn't *want* to leave you. You can't let your fear of being hurt blind you to the truth of the feelings coming from your heart! Most things in life you have to take a chance on . . . *you know that!* . . . and love is one of them!"

"Stop it!" Gannon warned.

"No!" replied the feisty old man. "I'll not stop, because if you succeed in pushing Jen away, you're only going to be cheating yourself, and her, out of a lot of happiness . . . Aye, there may be some hurt, but *real* love is worth the price you pay!"

Dugan knew he preached the gospel truth to the boy, having loved only one woman his entire life. There had been troubles and times when he wouldn't have called her "friend," but never a time when he didn't love her. Always there was the love, always the possibility of pain.

"I'm warning you, Dugan!" he repeated. "Keep it up and

I'll show you just how 'good' a shantytown mick can be!"
His eyes were blazing infernos of pain as he took a threatening step forward, his right hand clenched so tightly that his knuckles were white.

If Dugan had been any other man, he would have been running by now. But he knew Aaron, knew him and trusted him, so he just stood his ground and waited patiently for the storm to pass. He had pushed him further then he ever had. He had opened his wound.

Gannon's face was chiseled stone and he was breathing hard. Seconds ticked by and neither one spoke, until Dugan saw the hurt in Aaron's eyes and went on more gently.

"We're all immigrants, Aaron. You, me, all the fancy folk, and Jenny as well. Everyone here except those Indians I've heard about. They're the only ones what belongs here. If measuring up to the fancy folk is what bothers you so much, let me tell you something. You and Jenny are worth more then ten transplanted lords and all their ladies put together."

The clock in the hall began to chime and Aaron didn't wait any longer. He quickly walked to the door.

"Aaron!" shouted Dugan. "I'm not through! You've got to stop living in the past! Take a chance, lad. Let yourself love her . . . Aaron!"

When Aaron turned to face him Dugan felt as though he was looking back into the face of the ragged little street boy who had fought so furiously, and stared so defiantly at him, so many years ago. And just as briefly, beneath the tough exterior, he glimpsed the same sad, lonely boy who had nearly died in a pile of wet rags, desolate and alone on a rainy, October night twenty years ago.

"Aaron . . . forgive me . . . I . . ."

Aaron raised his hand to silence him, that haunted look still in his eyes.

"Take care of her, Dugan," he whispered. And then he was gone as the chimes in the hallway died.

CHAPTER

7

Tonight was the mayor's ball! Even though Jenny disliked the lies which had been told, she was so excited about going that she could hardly concentrate on her work. Mrs. Merit had told her to quit early so that they would have enough time to get ready for tonight. She still hadn't seen the dress she was going to wear. Gannon had insisted that Mrs. Merit keep it a secret until tonight. He wanted it to be a surprise.

"Hurry up, Jen!" Joshua said happily. "You'll want to look your best tonight!" He smiled. She was so unlike the others. So good.

"Joshua!" she teased. "I think you're more excited than I am!"

"Oh, go on now! I'm just happy for you, that's all. You're a very good worker!"

Jenny smiled. That was probably the highest praise anyone could ever receive from him. She started to wipe the counters down, happily dreaming about tonight.

The back door opened and a swirl of air rushed in. Both Jenny and Joshua turned to see who had come in. As she looked she felt a sinking feeling in the pit of her stomach, recognizing Kevin. He was loaded down with boxes, and from the way he swayed on his feet, she was sure he was drunk.

"Here, now!" Joshua said loudly. "Them goods are to be taken to the wharf!" He rounded his counter and headed for Kevin. But Kevin didn't even look at Joshua. His eyes, bloodshot and half-lidded, were focused on Jenny. He dropped his goods to the floor and started unsteadily toward her.

Joshua rounded the corner, standing in front of him. His huge, wooden spoon was held out like a club. Kevin looked at him and smirked.

"What? *Another* protector for Gannon's *cousin? Cousin.* Is that what they're calling them now?" He hiccuped and laughed drunkenly.

"Just leave her alone, Kevin. She's done you no wrong."

"Wrong? No . . . she's done me no wrong . . . jest made me a laughin' stock is all! Had Gannon send me off on some wild goose chase while he's gone . . . made me a laughin' stock, is all!"

He shoved past Joshua easily. Jenny stared wide-eyed as he approached, screaming as Joshua grabbed Kevin by the collar and tried to turn him around.

"You dumb old man!" Kevin bellowed, savagely clubbing Joshua over the head with a fist.

"No! Kevin, don't . . . you're hurting him!" She looked around frantically, trying to find something to stop him with. Joshua was already unconscious, but Kevin didn't care. He just continued to pound him.

"What's she giving you, huh, protector? Is everyone in this whole damn place getting it, 'cept me?" He held the unconscious man up. "What she giving you!" he roared, hitting him brutally across the face. Suddenly he stopped hitting Joshua as he felt a sharp, needlelike prick at his back. He was drunk, but he'd grown up on these streets, and been around enough to recognize the business end of a knife without seeing it. A sly smile spread over his face as he dropped the senseless old man to the floor.

He raised his arms above his head. With a smirk on his face, he slowly turned around to face Jenny.

Her dress was cranberry red, and she looked pale and frightened as she held the huge butcher knife out in front of her. He looked at her, his eyes lingering hungrily on her breasts. Her hand was trembling so violently that he smiled.

"Now, Jenny, just put that old knife away there, and let's us be friends. What do you say, huh? I don't mean nothing by my teasing. I just want us to be friends."

"You killed Joshua!" she screamed fiercely, starting to cry.

"No, no, you're wrong. Look it here," he said soothingly, bending down and moving Joshua with his hand until the old man moaned and tried to open his eyes.

"Joshua!" she cried, bending to help him.

That was all that Kevin needed. He spun so quickly that Jenny didn't have time to react. He grabbed her wrist and she watched helplessly as the knife clattered to the floor. He pulled her to him, and she started to scream as he lifted her up.

"Shut up," he hissed, covering her mouth with his hand. She could taste tobacco on his fingers, and smell the whiskey he had drunk as he carried her backward to the wall. She tried to bite him, but it was no use. Roughly, he pinned her body against the wall with his until she couldn't breathe and she was afraid that she was going to pass out. Then, as his hands began to roam slowly over her body and touch her secret places, she prayed that she would. Helplessly, she closed her eyes, as he bent his head and began to kiss her cheek. His breath became ragged and his hands brutal as his kisses inched downward slowly. Unable to help herself, she prayed that Gannon would come soon.

In another part of the hotel, Gannon stood waiting, expecting to see Jenny as she passed the study on her way to her room. Letters lay unopened on his desk, his accounting book remained closed, as his thoughts focused, whether or not he consciously cared to admit it, on her. A restlessness seized him, and he paced along the giant Persian carpet, back and forth, back and forth, like a tiger in a cage. The anxious feeling continued to grow as he nervously examined his watch, first every ten minutes, then five, then one . . . Still, he didn't see her tiny, familiar form . . . and still he waited, glancing now more frequently at his watch, wearing a path in the thick pile beneath his feet. She should have been done long ago, he thought, feeling a trace of irritation, which was becoming a very common feeling whenever she was not within his range of vision. "Damn!" he muttered when his patience finally gave out and she still hadn't come. He started to walk toward the kitchen, wondering just what sort of mischief she had gotten into this time, increasing his pace with every step.

Voices reached him through the open door, muffled and masculine, somehow familiar. It wasn't Dugan's light tenor nor was it the deep, booming baritone of Joshua. But it was familiar, and Irish, and thick. The words were slurred. Frowning, he walked into the room.

The lamps had not been turned down for the night and water still boiled briskly on the stove. Joshua, bloody and still, lay quietly in the middle of the floor. Gannon's narrowed gaze missed nothing. His muscles coiled and tensed, ready to explode as a murderous rage began to build inside of him.

Jenny was trapped helplessly against the far wall, her hair loose and falling around her face, her eyes desperate and pleading as the drunk man grunted and fumbled, trying to remove her clothing.

"Bastard!" Gannon roared, knowing without a doubt that he would kill him if he could.

Kevin's eyes flew open in surprise when he heard him, but he had waited too long for what he now held. He wouldn't let her go.

With the agility of a cat, Gannon leaped across the room, grabbing Kevin before his numbed senses had time to react, and threw him hard against the door.

"You son of a bitch!" he whispered, and turned toward him, as his hands automatically curled into fists. He didn't run, he walked, revenge boiling his blood and making his face livid. Kevin's senses had begun to return and seeing the fury in Gannon's face, he decided not to stay. He groped unseeing for the latch, and finding it, pulled the door open and ran out into the night. Gannon lunged, but caught only empty air. For a second he debated whether or not to follow, until a muffled groan from Joshua decided the issue.

Jenny had already run to him. He was bleeding in several places, but he was alive, and he smiled at her.

She tried to lift his head, and wipe away some of the blood with a towel she had found. Gannon came to them, kneeling down beside her as Dugan walked through the door.

"Holy Mother of God!" he cried. "What's happened here?"

"It was Kevin," Gannon breathed in disgust. "Dugan, go get a doctor."

Dugan shouted for a couple of young luggers. When they came in, he instructed them to take Joshua to his room. But, before they could, Joshua opened his eyes and called weakly to Gannon.

"Mr. Gannon," he called as Gannon came closer.

"Don't try to talk, Joshua. The doctor's on his way."

"Listen . . ." he said. "Jenny . . . she saved my life . . . she stopped him from beating me . . ."

Gannon nodded, and couldn't stop himself from thinking about what might've happened if he hadn't been home.

"Jenny . . ." continued Joshua weakly. "I just want to tell you . . . oh!" He swooned and nearly passed out again.

"It's all right, Joshua, Jenny understands. Let the lads here take you to your room and let the doctor take a look at you. You've got some pretty nasty scrapes there."

The boys picked him up very gently, and Gannon spoke softly to them.

"Let me know how he is. We won't leave until I find out." They nodded and left the room. He turned to face Jenny. She still looked pale and shaken, and her hands trembled.

"Are you all right?" he asked. His voice was slightly husky and filled with emotion.

She started to tell him that she was fine until, quite to her surprise, she felt his arms go about her, and he brought her close to him. His breathing was hard, and his arms held her tight, but not in the way that Kevin had. She relaxed against him, comforted by the sound of his heartbeat, safe within his arms.

"Don't worry," he soothed. "I will never . . . never allow him near you again. I promise." His voice was barely above a whisper, but she knew that he meant every word. She felt a brief touch, at the top of her head, and looked up in surprise. It had felt like a kiss, a very, very soft kiss . . .

"Go," he said softly. "Get ready for the ball . . . I'll let you know about Joshua as soon as I find something out."

"I'd like to stay with him," she offered. "He was only trying to protect me."

"I know, Jenny, but right now there isn't anything that we can do. I promise, if he needs us, we won't go tonight. All right?"

She nodded, still seeing Joshua's poor battered face in her mind, and all because of her.

"Now go get ready. Just in case."

She quietly left the room. Gannon felt as if he could have happily murdered Kevin at that moment for what he had done to Joshua and what he had tried to do to Jenny. Tomorrow morning he would instruct the rest of the staff to be on the watch for him. He planned to make certain that Kevin never bothered Jenny again. He walked to the back door and locked it, shaking it to see if it was secure, determined to get even no matter what it would take.

Running until he had come to the wharf, Kevin looked back over his shoulder in fear. That bastard was going to pay for what he did! And he knew just exactly how!

Gannon must have forgotten that his brother-in-law was the sheriff. That was good, because no matter how rich or powerful that son of a bitch thought he was, he still wasn't above the law . . . his law, and he laughed.

The sun had finally set, and the cooling night air blew across the black waters. He could hear the rats as they started to come out, scuttling across the planking, squeaking at each other.

Bloyd owed him . . . owed him good. He'd kept his mouth shut about that whoring bastard all these years . . .

for certain favors, and now he needed another one. He knew what he had to ask him, and he knew how Bloyd would react. It was one thing to pick up a few dollars cash, rolling locals, but it was quite another to take on Kansas City's richest man. But he'd do it . . . oh, yes he would, otherwise he'd have to tell his little sister all about Bloyd and his women. He laughed to himself as the rats scampered and played under the rotting old boards of the pier.

CHAPTER

8

Jenny was breathless as she opened the door to her room and entered. Mrs. Merit was waiting for her, eager to show her the new dress.

"Hurry, Jenny. I've had a bath prepared for you!"

She smiled. Apparently she had not heard about poor Joshua as yet. Jenny didn't know if she should tell her, but before she had a chance to decide, Mrs. Merit went on eagerly about tonight.

"Look, Jenny, I even have some scented bath salts for you. 'Rose of Attar', they call it. Very nice." She sniffed at the opened bottle dreamily, closing her old eyes. Jenny wondered for a second who was going to the ball, Mrs. Merit or her.

"When I was young," she recalled as her eyes sparkled like diamonds, "my Glenn would take me dancing all the time. At church doings, or weddings, barn raisings, and birthings. All he needed was someone to hum a tune . . . Lord! How that man loved to dance! And such a gentleman . . . he'd bow so low . . . he looked just like a prince in one of them stories you read about . . . and he'd say, 'Anna, you're looking mighty lovely tonight . . . may I have this dance?', and I would say, all prim and proper, 'Why sir . . . I'd be pleased to dance with you.' Then he'd take me in his arms . . . he was so strong and tall . . . and he'd hold me real close till I thought we were the only ones in the room, and we'd dance, and dance . . . till the night was clean wore out."

Wistfully she closed her eyes. Her face, though powdered white and wrinkled, seemed beautiful just then, as she held her arms around her Glenn and danced with his ghost around the room.

Silently she stopped, poised on her toes as gracefully as any ballerina in the middle of the room. Jenny imagined that Glenn must have kissed her from the soft, warm glow which spread slowly over her face. The music that only she could hear had ended, taking her Glenn with it as it slowly faded from her mind. She opened her eyes a little heavily now, glistening with salty tears, and smiled self-consciously at Jenny.

"Oh, Lord, how I miss that man!" she said, sighing so deeply that Jenny thought she heard her old heart breaking.

"Well . . . enough of that nonsense . . . don't pay any attention to this old fool, we're wasting time. Don't you even want to see your dress? Mr. Gannon had it made special!"

"You're not a fool, Anna. I could never think of you as that. You must have loved him very much." Mrs. Merit didn't reply at first. Her gaze had shifted to some faraway place, and a half smile, both sad and sweet, lingered on her face, as she spoke.

"Must have," she whispered softly. "Still do . . . and always . . . always will! Now . . . do you want to see your dress or not?"

"Yes . . . yes, I do!"

In the space of a few brief seconds, Mrs. Merit had become Anna to Jenny. The moment they had shared had brought them close and made them friends.

Reverently, Anna laid aside the tissue paper covering the gown.

"Oh!" Jenny proclaimed breathlessly. "It's the most beautiful thing I've ever seen!" Anna had to agree.

The dress was brilliantly white . . . so white, that the folds cast deep, blue shadows across it. The bodice had been cut deep, and tiny, glowing pearls were sewn through it. Its sleeves were full, and captured at the wrists by bands of beaded satin. Gently, Mrs. Merit picked it up and held it out, so that Jenny could see the intricate work, and the beauty of the full skirt. It shimmered in the candlelight, and looked as though it had been spun from dreams and silver moonbeams, and made for a fairy princess instead of for her. She reached out to touch it, fearful that it might vanish.

"This is mine?" she whispered.

Anna laughed, delighted at her reaction. The dress really was magnificent, and on Jenny, it would be breathtakingly beautiful.

"Come on now, Jenny, we'd better hurry. She laid the satin gown gently across the bed. "Mr. Gannon will be expecting you shortly and he doesn't like to be kept waiting."

On the other side of the hotel, Gannon was supposed to be getting ready too. Like Jenny, who had kept her feelings to herself because she didn't want to spoil tonight for Anna, Gannon was worried about Joshua. His black satin suit lay neglected on the bed, as he waited for word about his friend. As if on cue, he heard a brief knock on his door, and turned as Dugan walked into his room. He looked at him expectantly, hoping for the best.

"Doc says he's going to be fine . . . good as new. Says to let him rest a few days, and take it easy for a while."

"Good." Gannon gave a sigh of relief. It would have been difficult to go dancing, if not impossible, knowing that his friend had been hurt while trying to help Jenny. "Until he's better, have Mrs. Merit help in the kitchen. We'll get someone to supervise the housekeeping. Did you tell Jenny?"

"Aye. I've had one of the girls go directly to her room. I knew she would be miserable until she knew something."

"True. Dugan, could you hand me that black case on the dresser?"

"This one?" he asked, pointing to a shiny, rectangular box laid casually on top of it.

"Yes. Bring it to me, please."

"Sure. But what is it?"

"Open it."

Dugan did, letting out a low whistle.

"Can I guess who these are for?" he asked slyly.

"They're obviously not for *me*," he stated sarcastically. "Jenny's birthday is coming up at the end of September. I thought I'd make her an early present." He sounded irritated as he explained, almost guilty.

"Should've been a ring, if you ask me!" Dugan snorted.

"I didn't!" Gannon snapped, taking the box from Dugan and shutting the lid with a loud click.

"Oh, yes, I'd forgotten." Dugan faked a yawn, trying to seem indifferent. "You're planning on auctioning her off or something of the like. That necklace will be good bait. It'll make her look that much more attractive to all the young bucks tonight."

Gannon's eyes flashed. "Is the carriage ready, Dugan?"

"Aye. I personally brushed the horses myself this afternoon."

"Then I'd better get dressed. I don't want to keep all the 'young bucks' waiting."

He reached for his suit and began putting it on.

"You're impossible, Aaron! And exasperating!" Dugan fumed. "You'll never find another like her. Never!"

"What you're saying . . ." Aaron pulled his trousers up over his long legs, "is true." Then he buttoned them over his hard, flat stomach, tucking his white silk shirt in. "She is perhaps the finest young lady I have ever known." He slipped his jacket on, shrugging it easily into place over his wide shoulders. "That is why," and he paused long enough to comb his flaming locks into place, "she should have only the best." He finished by flashing his most brilliant smile at Dugan. "Getting her the best is the whole idea behind this 'auction,' as you put it. Now do you understand?"

"Indeed I do. You're mad!"

Gannon laughed. "At least we agree on one thing." He finished dressing. "Well, what are we waiting for?"

"Not a thing, lad, except some common sense for you, and the girl, of course." Dugan opened the door and bowed low as Gannon walked through.

"Your Highness!" he teased.

Gannon paused long enough to muss the old man's hair as he went out. He was eager to go and felt strangely exhilarated at the thought as he made his way down the hall to Jenny's door.

When he reached it and knocked, an excited Mrs. Merit answered.

"Come in!" she called gaily, her voice rising like a song.

Gannon did, opening the door and stepping through into a brightly lit room filled with the scent of roses. Standing in the center of the candle's golden light was Jenny, statue quiet and as perfect as a goddess. His heart raced as he looked at her and she nearly took his breath away. Seconds ticked by, but he couldn't speak as his gaze swept over her, devouring her with his eyes. The dress fit her perfectly, and his mouth became dry as he saw how low the bodice was cut. Mrs. Merit had dressed her hair high atop her head, placing tiny white roses in it. She needed no rouge, as she glowed and flushed beautifully whenever he looked at her. Mesmerized, he stepped forward, still unable to speak.

"Aren't you going to give her your present?" Dugan prodded jovially, grinning at Mrs. Merit, who did her utmost to wink.

"Oh, yes, of course." He brought the case out in front of him and handed it to Jenny. He was suddenly overcome by a deep fear that she wouldn't like it and nearly drew back. But before he could, she had taken the box, a question in her eyes. He hurried to explain.

"It's an early birthday gift, Jenny." Then he added as an afterthought, "I hope you like it."

Slowly she opened it, and an astonished look spread rapidly across her face.

"Mr. Gannon! I can't possibly accept this! It's much too

valuable. You've already done so much. It's so beautiful! It must be priceless!"

He smiled, suddenly very relieved and very pleased. He strode forward, thinking what a perfect word she had chosen to describe the necklace. It was priceless, one of a kind, completely irreplaceable, as she was beginning to be to him. Quietly he took the sparkling diamonds from the case. They flashed fire when the candle's glow touched them, and Mrs. Merit gasped in surprise.

Gannon opened the clasp and walked behind Jenny. She was acutely aware of his presence. When he placed the necklace around her neck she shivered as his fingers brushed softly against her skin.

He turned her around so that she might see herself in the mirror, and he studied her quietly for a moment, pleased with the effect the necklace made against her skin. She was all fire and ice. A snow princess in glittering white. Behind her, he stood, tall and darkly suited, her opposite, with his smoldering bronze curls and glowing, cat-green eyes.

"Carriage is waiting!" Dugan called gleefully and the moment was gone.

Carefully, Gannon placed Jenny's wrap around her, and gallantly escorted her to the door, leaving a beaming Mrs. Merit and a smiling Dugan gaping fondly after them.

When the couple was out of earshot, the two conspirators, pleased at the progress of the plans, laughed out loud.

"There will be a wedding b'fore spring, and knowing the lad, as I do, there'll be a wee babe not long after!" Dugan confidently predicted.

Mrs. Merit nodded in agreement and they both laughed happily.

Down below the carriage driver held the door as Gannon helped Jenny in. He seated himself cautiously beside her and stared rigidly ahead. Neither one spoke as the carriage pulled away from the hotel and headed at a fast pace toward the mayor's house.

The summer night was beautiful, and the full moon rode high in the sky, peeking through the carriage window like a curious and intimate friend. A gentle breeze stirred the leaves into murmuring song and the crickets danced their wooden dance in the tall, fragrant grasses of August.

Gannon couldn't remember a night as lovely as this and felt as though he was seeing the moon for the very first time. Somehow, this night was different, special, and he knew it was because of Jenny.

They were drawing near to the mayor's house. Carriages were strewn about like carelessly discarded toys and the house itself was ablaze with golden light from every window.

Gannon tried to remember the reason he was doing this. He needed to find someone for Jenny, but with her sitting so close, bathed in the moon's enchanting light, that thought seemed a million miles away.

Abruptly the carriage came to a halt in front of a large, stone stairway which curved ornately upward to the house's main doors. The driver hopped down and opened the door. Gannon leaped out and extended his arm to Jenny. The moonlight must be Jenny's kin, he thought, because wherever she went, it cast its silvery glow about her. Gannon couldn't help but notice the gentle rise and fall of her breasts as she bent forward, gracefully stepping down.

Music filled the warm night air. Soft, sweet violins, accompanied by the deep, mellow sounds of cellos playing waltzes she had never heard, surrounded them as they entered the hall.

The entranceway was Austrian and very baroque. Gold leaf covered everything, elaborate and bright, and a huge open stairway dominated the view. Mrs. Kenton fancied herself American nobility, and had greedily adopted the styles of the old European aristocracy. Lush paintings adorned the walls and crystal chandeliers hung like glittering fruit from the ceiling. Even the people looked like bright ornaments themselves as they stood about. Their shimmering pastel dresses and elegant jewelry created a constantly changing tapestry that was a delight to the eyes.

Mayor Kenton's wife stood with a few guests near the door. The moment she saw them, she rushed over to greet them, towing Penelope along behind her. Most of the guests recognized Gannon, and had already heard about his mysterious cousin, so when Mrs. Kenton approached them, the entire hall became quiet, while dozens of pairs of eyes stared boldly.

"Mr. Gannon!" she gushed, literally pushing Penelope out in front of her so that she stood nearly nose to nose with him. "And Jennifer . . . how lovely that you could come too. Isn't it, Penelope?" she coaxed halfheartedly. Secretly she had hoped that Jenny wouldn't make it, but now that she was here . . .

"Penelope, de-a-r-r . . . isn't it *nice?*"

Penelope only nodded. Her blue eyes had turned positively green when she saw Jenny and she was too busy trying to find something wrong with the way she looked to talk.

Gannon smiled when he noticed her envious staring. Penelope, too, had dressed in white, though he doubted the color choice had much to do with what it was supposed to represent. Chastity was as foreign to Penelope as it would be to a doe in rut. However, he had to admit that with her pure white dress and slippers, and the pale pink roses and baby's breath in her hair, she seemed determined to give it the very best imitation she could. Her mother, on the other hand, had chosen *not* to look pure and innocent. It hurt his eyes to even look at her. He was totally at a loss as to just what color she wore or even if it had a name. It couldn't have been called a pastel, because it was far too bold, and it might've been orange, except for the faintest touch of purple running through it. Rotten oranges or sour grapes might be an apt description of the color. For want of a better word he christened it "rot" and nearly choked as he stifled a laugh. You certainly noticed her. If that was what Mrs. Kenton had wanted, she had gotten her wish. She was painfully bright.

"Come in, come in!" she gushed. She took Gannon's free arm, pulling him into the circle of waiting people.

"You all know our Mr. Gannon? Of course you do! But I'm sure *none* of you has ever met his cousin Jenny," she added confidently. It was so nice to know something that no one else knew about, she thought with satisfaction. Even her best friend, Ida, had nothing compared to this to talk about over tea! "Everyone . . ." she continued, with much pomp and ceremony, "this lovely . . . *unattached* . . . child is Mr. Gannon's cousin, Jennifer Bates, just newly arrived from England!"

There were nods and "charmings" and "pleased to meet you's" from nearly everyone present. Gannon couldn't help but notice how, after Mrs. Kenton had told the crowd of Jenny's marital status, the men had nearly surrounded them, gently shoving and milling about, jockeying for position, trying to get nearer to Jenny. It was obvious from their delighted expressions that they found her *very* attractive.

"Have you a dancing partner for tonight?" one eager young man asked. Gannon shot him a scathing look, but he didn't appear to notice as he continued to stare at Jenny.

"Mr. Gann . . . uhm . . . Aaron is my escort." She replied politely. He had instructed her to call him by his first name in public, as he didn't think it would look quite right if his "cousin" called him, "Mr. Gannon."

Gannon had felt a certain rush of pride when she had said he was her escort . . . and a certain amount of possessiveness, which he shrugged off as simply looking out for her best interests.

A new waltz had begun and Penelope, with no prompting from her mother, grabbed his arm tightly.

"I do so love to dance!" she declared, batting her eyelashes at him. Any other time, this gesture would not have failed to get a suitable reaction from him. But tonight it only seemed like an irritation.

"Yes . . . well." He patted her hand in a fatherly fashion. "I would be happy to dance with you, but my cousin is new here and has made no acquaintances. It would be rude of me to leave her unattended." He deftly unwound Penelope's arm from his.

"Oh, come now, Gannon," insisted one eager young man. "Dance with Penelope, for heaven's sake! I promise you . . . Jennifer will not lack for acquaintances . . . starting most appropriately with me!"

Gannon had always like Jeffrey before, when they played

cards or drank late at night in the company of liberated women. But now he was really getting on his nerves. Gannon wondered if he had ever *really* liked him in the first place. As he was pondering this new possibility, Mrs. Kenton chirped loudly.

"Yes, Mr. Gannon, you needn't worry about Jennifer. There are many fine, suitable young gentlemen here. I and the other ladies will help to see that she does not lack for company." She smiled her most gracious, and what Gannon believed she thought, her most *motherly,* smile at Jenny. He couldn't help but glare at her, wishing she wore her peacock feathers tonight instead of her gaudy tiara. He felt like stuffing them one by one into her mouth.

During this whole time, Jenny stood quietly by, not sure of what to do. Gannon had told her that tonight was the first part of his plan to introduce her to a suitable match. But with the odd way he was acting, she wondered what was wrong. Perhaps she had been too hard on him. He was only trying to help and she still hadn't heard a thing from her uncle. If Mr. Gannon would feel better at least *thinking* that she was looking for a match, then she felt, that with all he had done for her, it was the very least that she could do for him.

Of course, she had no real intention of *marrying* any of these silly young men, but she would put on the grandest show she could in order to set his mind at ease. She was not used to coquettish ways, but after watching Penelope and the others, she didn't think it would be too difficult to do. If she thrust out her chest just so, and tilted her head slightly . . . and she mustn't forget to bat her eyelashes a good deal . . . and if she laughed even if what they said wasn't funny, and talked without saying anything, she was sure she would be indistinguishable from the rest of the young ladies at the ball. Perhaps it would set Gannon's mind at rest, at least until her uncle came . . . and, she mused, it was the very *least* that she could do . . .

"It's all right . . . Aaron. I'm sure these gentlemen will keep me occupied." She tilted her head just so, and smiled sweetly at all the avid young men around her, not forgetting to flutter her eyelashes with every other word.

Gannon's mouth nearly hit the floor. He couldn't believe what he was seeing . . . and less of what he had just heard! He stared hard at her, waiting to see her wink, waiting to see what sort of joke she was playing . . . waiting . . . but she didn't appear to notice.

"Well that settles it then!" Jeffrey pronounced. "Miss Bates, my name is Jeffrey Willshire. Gannon can vouch for both my considerable charm and my lavish bank account. I would be deeply honored if you would consent to dance with me!"

He smiled and gave a gallant bow.

Jenny looked quickly at Gannon for permission, and was startled by the ferocity in his face. He was positively glowering at her. Perhaps she wasn't doing it right . . . wasn't trying hard enough to seem available. That must be it, she thought, and she turned, giving Jeffrey a dazzling smile and a delicate curtsy, which helped to show off her ample bosom before she extended her hand to him.

"Wonderful!" he raved, absolutely delighted at the outcome of the conversation. He accepted her hand and led her off toward the dance floor, imagining that he was the envy of every male present.

Gannon stared after them, with his jaws clenched tightly shut, as he watched them melt into the crowd of slowly moving dancers and fade away on the first few measures of a waltz.

The other men didn't wait for more of an invitation. In a group, like a herd of bachelor lions, they peeled away, forming lines on the edges of the crowd, in hopes of being next.

Gannon watched all this and tried to remain calm, telling himself that this is what he wanted, what he had planned, what was best. Over and over, he recited these words in his mind, until they became almost like a chant. But it was a chant he didn't believe in. He glimpsed Jenny briefly as Jeffrey whirled her around the floor, and noticed at a glance everything about the pair. His eyes automatically measured the distance between Jeffrey's hands and her lovely curves and took into account how animated he seemed. Yet the worst part of all was the way that Jenny *looked* at him. She actually seemed to be *enjoying* the dance and her gaze was so soft and intimate that it hurt. For the first agonizing time in his life, Gannon understood what real jealousy was, and he didn't like it one bit. It wasn't just a word written in some sonnet by a hopelessly lost lover, or anger, or foolish pride. It was pain . . . searing deep, torturous pain that touched your soul and burned like hellfire. For him, it was the sudden realization that he might lose her to some fop like Jeffrey . . . and he simply couldn't bear it. Suddenly he needed a drink.

Gannon made it to the bar with a scowl so deeply embedded on his face, it threatened to be permanent. He looked just like a thunderstorm fast approaching, even to the lightning flashing ominously in his eyes.

"Brandy," he ordered roughly. "No, wait . . . make it a double."

The bartender obeyed quickly, silently setting the drink down in front of him. Gannon swallowed the entire drink in one fluid motion. "Another," he demanded. The bartender looked in surprise at the empty glass, wondering if the 100 proof brandy had mysteriously turned to water. Before he could fully contemplate the mystery of the vanishing brandy, Gannon snapped irritably at him. "Another, man. Are you deaf?" The bartender hastened to obey.

Out on the floor, Jenny was with her third partner. By now her feet had begun to ache, but whenever one set was over, and before another had begun, a new man was already waiting to take his turn. They were even squabbling, flipping quarters to see who would be next and within the brief space of a dance each one attempted to make the very best impression he could. Some were witty and nice, while others chose to rely on their good looks or wealth. Whatever they used, they were trying to sell themselves to her and she didn't like it. She felt like no more than a pretty doll made of

clay which everyone wanted to play with. She knew without
a doubt that, should she choose to be, she could be rude or
mean by turns. Or stupid and shallow. They would still not
see beyond the wrappings. They didn't want what was inside
the box, only the pretty papers that covered it. Her mind
kept drifting back to Gannon, and how he treated her. He
never talked *around* her, but *to* her . . . and he didn't seem
so wrapped up in himself that he couldn't speak of anything
else. She liked the way he was, and was sure no one . . . at
least not here . . . could ever compare to him.

Someone named Roger held her now. He was a pleasant
young man, with straw-colored hair and liquid brown eyes,
who had talked nonstop since they had started. Jenny hadn't
heard a word he had said, as she scanned the crowd on the
dance floor, looking for Gannon. He was nowhere in sight.
For a moment she thought of Penelope and how she had
latched onto him from the moment he had entered the hall.
She wondered briefly if he were with her. That thought felt
ugly in her mind. She tried not to dwell on it, but it refused
to leave. For a moment she wished that Gannon held her
instead of Roger and that Penelope didn't exist.

Gannon was holding his fifth brandy as he made his way
toward the dancers. He searched the floor and spotted Jenny
easily. It was almost as if she were a magnet and he a piece of
steel. He could feel her, even when he couldn't see her. She
was dancing with Roger. That was all right. Good family,
good fellow. Not too notorious with the ladies. As a matter
of fact, if he remembered correctly from all the rumors he
had heard, Roger was still a virgin. Judging by the distance
Roger held Jenny from him, he intended to remain that way
for quite a while. Wonderful fellow, thought Gannon happily, wondering if it would be possible for him to talk Roger
into maintaining that type of relationship, even if he and
Jenny married. He thought about taking him aside, and
telling him about all the virtues of a celibate life . . . only
right now, while he looked at Jenny, he really couldn't think
of any except, perhaps, a long and healthy life—because he
was beginning to feel positively homicidal toward any man

who would think of doing otherwise with her. "Long life, Roger," he muttered under his breath, and saluted him with his drink, before he finished it.

The waltz ended and Roger escorted Jenny safely to the side. Immediately she was surrounded by the men, each one asking her at the same time if they might have a dance. Her feet ached and her ears were numb, but she still smiled politely at them, not sure which way to turn . . . or whose turn it was . . . when suddenly a deep voice from behind her interrupted her thoughts.

"I believe it's my turn," he said. Before she could object, a dark-haired man grabbed her hand, pulling her out onto the floor.

"Hey!" called Roger. "You've only just come!"

"Phillip . . . it's my turn!"

"You rogue! What do you think you're doing?"

The other men were angry, nearly shouting at him, but he only laughed and ignored them, as he began to dance.

It had happened so rapidly that she had not really gotten a good look at him until they had begun their set. When she did, though, she was pleasantly surprised. He was nearly as tall as Gannon, but instead of flaming curls, his were of onyx . . . deep black and silky straight; and his eyes, instead of gleaming green, were dark and smoky brown. He certainly wasn't shy, as he smiled brilliantly at her and confidently tried to pull her closer. Yet she wouldn't let him and her back began to ache with the effort of arching back away from him.

On the edge of the dancers, Gannon was moodily nursing his sixth drink along. When he saw Phillip come in and make a beeline directly toward Jenny. He watched quietly as Phillip stole her from the crowd of angry men and swept her easily out on the dance floor. He and Phillip were not friends; and they never had been. When he saw Phillip try to pull Jenny closer, the hackles on the back of his neck rose in response. Grudgingly he had to admit that Phillip was probably every bit as wealthy as himself, and nearly as good-looking. But that was where the comparison ended. Phillip had acquired his wealth from his parents, and Gannon had sweated every dime. Money wasn't the only difference between them either. Phillip had always had his way. Everything had come easily to him, or been given. He had even inherited his looks and charm, although someone had forgotten to give him a conscience. He also lacked honor. The stories of the women he had used and thrown away were monumental. Now it looked as though he planned on adding Jenny to his list of conquests. Gannon watched her face closely, confident that she would see through Phillip . . . trusting in her judgment.

Out on the dance floor, Jenny was becoming quite irritated. Phillip kept trying to pull her too close, and he never appeared to look above her neck. She started to push him away, meaning to tell him that she *did* have a face above her breasts. Before she got that far, she noticed Gannon at the edge of the floor. He appeared to be watching her. With all the willpower she possessed, she tried to remember why they were here and what Gannon had already done for her. If he knew she wasn't enjoying herself, after all the trouble he went to, it would only hurt him. She didn't want to do that. So, much to Phillip's delight and her disgust, she forced herself to relax in his arms and smile. Immediately, he pulled her closer, till she could feel the sharp, diamond studded buttons on his jacket rub coldly against her skin. His smug, self-assured smile nearly set her into a rage. With all the self-control she had left, she pretended to enjoy his advances.

On the sidelines, Gannon couldn't believe his eyes. All this time he had thought that Jenny was different, somehow smarter and less vulnerable to the pathetic charms of such men. Obviously he was wrong! She not only appeared to understand Phillip's intentions, she was *encouraging* them. She seemed to be *enjoying* it too!

"Women!" he grumbled aloud in disgust. It was then that Phillip appeared to stumble slightly, catching himself by holding onto Jenny and slyly placing a kiss against her ear. That was more than Gannon could stand! He slammed down the rest of his drink and walked angrily through the crowd. People took one look at his livid features and parted quickly for him. They stared at him after he had passed, but he appeared not to notice. His eyes were fixed on only two things . . . Jenny and Phillip.

Out on the floor, Phillip was confident that he had snared her. All that was left was to capture his prize and enjoy it . . . and that he intended to do.

"You know," he said smoothly. "You're really one of the most attractive women I've ever met."

"Thank you," she said politely, struggling to put a little distance between Phillip's chest and hers.

"Yes, you really are . . ." His gaze lingered hungrily on the soft mounds of her exposed flesh. "I think," and he licked his lips, "I think I would like to take you driving. You know, somewhere where we can get better acquainted, somewhere . . . quiet and remote." He punctuated his words by letting his hand dangle a little too low past her waist. She was getting angry. She wanted to please Gannon, but this man was going too far. She started to pull away in earnest, and was just about to tell him what she thought of his suggestion, when he continued, so sure that he had captured her and she couldn't escape from his charm. "You know, the moon is awfully lovely this time of the year. We can take a carriage tonight . . . some wine . . . a *blanket* . . . yes . . . I *really* would like to take you for a *ride*." His hand continued to drop.

"You *would?*" an icy voice growled. They both stopped dancing, though Jenny would have called it more of a wrestling match than a dance. She turned and stared into Gannon's glittering, dangerous eyes.

Phillip nearly had a coronary and silently cursed himself, wishing that he had heard Gannon coming. Instead he had been too busy scheming.

"Riding, Phillip? You were saying how you would *like* to take Jenny *riding.* Did I hear correctly?"

"As a matter of fact you did . . . and I would," he explained nervously, pulling back as far away from Jenny as was possible. "With your kind permission, that is." He smiled as innocently as he could. He had no wish to tangle with Gannon. At least not one-on-one, because he knew he could never win.

Gannon laughed when he saw the innocent mask Phillip slipped on. It was a hard, cold laugh, like the sound of brittle glass. Jenny had never seen eyes which burned so fiercely and looked so dangerous before.

"You want *my permission?"* he sarcastically asked.

"Why, yes . . . yes, I do." Phillip was terrified. He had seen Gannon's temper in action before, and knew that beneath the civilized polish of satin suits and starched white shirts a savage streak existed in Gannon, held coolly in check by his iron will. It was this inner strength which made him indomitable, and his control of it that gave him his power. No one had ever stood against him and won . . . no one. Phillip wasn't in any mood to try his luck.

"Well, then, Phillip . . . you have it." Gannon smiled, but the smile didn't reach his eyes. They only flashed hard and cold in the candles' light.

Jenny heard his words and her heart sank at the thought of driving with Phillip. Gannon must really want to be rid of me, she thought. She looked up sadly just in time to see Phillip positively beaming at her.

"Old boy, that is wonderful! Thank you!" he enthused, extending his hand toward Gannon.

"Yes," Gannon quietly repeated, ignoring the offered arm, "you . . . have . . . my . . . *permission,* my *permission* to *drop dead,* that is. I suggest that you move your arm before I decide to do something *more* than *shake* it."

Without another word Gannon took Jen's hand and began to dance her away from Phillip, who stood staring dumbfounded after them. The men who had been waiting to dance with her only laughed.

Gannon held her lightly and refused to look at her. Silently they danced, until the music ended briefly. He paused, still keeping his hand possessively about her waist as he waited for the next song to begin.

His face looked rugged and hard, with no trace of emotion showing, except for the glittering lights in his eyes. She felt the tension between them, and wondered what she had done until, unable to bear the silence any longer, she spoke.

"Mr. Gannon . . . Aaron," she stumbled. "Have *I* done something wrong?" she asked.

His gaze only flickered to her momentarily before the first strains of the next set began. Without a word, he began to whirl her a bit too roughly around the room.

She had only tried to do what he had wanted. Now it appeared as if he were angry with her. She was so bewildered.

"Please," she implored softly, "please tell me if I've done something wrong. I've been trying to do as you wanted. It isn't easy for me to get someone interested as you asked me to do. I'm ignorant and not very good at it yet. But I'll keep trying!"

Her voice was pleading and anxious. His eyes softened and found hers, reading the confusion in them. He knew it was because of him. She looked as though she were ready to cry and he found himself longing to pull her close.

"Phillip and Roger have asked me if they might call . . ." she ventured, still wanting his approval and not sure what she had done to make him mad.

"I told them," she continued hurriedly, trying to sound bright and cheerful, "that if I have your permission . . . that it would be fine . . ."

Anger flickered in his eyes. "Hah! No doubt!" he spat scornfully. "One a letch, and the other a stumbling incompetent. You have the nerve to ask *me* for permission so that they might call on *you?*"

"Well, then . . . what would you have me do?" She began to feel angry as well. "You *tell* me to find a suitable match because you're sick to death of taking care of me . . . even though I work *very* hard every day . . . and when I *do* what you ask, you treat me . . . terribly!"

"I never said I was sick to death of taking care of you!" he roared, and nearly stopped dancing. "I *said* that the situation at the hotel cannot continue as it is . . . for *your* sake!"

"Then it won't continue!" she flared angrily. "I'll leave first thing in the morning."

They both stopped dancing, each staring hard at the other. Gannon couldn't hear the music anymore, and didn't see all the eyes which watched them. He only saw Jenny. Her eyes were blazing at him, and her cheeks were flushed crimson. Her soft pink lips trembled ever so slightly.

Half mad with wanting, he took her, knowing only that he needed her, as he gathered her into his arms, and claimed her lips with his. She stiffened in surprise, until slowly, the flame from his kiss melted her neatly against him and her thoughts drifted away, leaving only the burning heat of his touch.

There was a fire in him too, as he drew away, breathless, and so hungry for her he ached. Her eyes were still closed, and her lips half parted, which only made him groan and pull her close again. She was an enchantress, a fairy princess, a witch all in white, who had cast a spell over him these past few months. He knew by the power of that one kiss, that no other woman could satisfy him now.

The hall was perfectly quiet, and the musicians had ceased to play. Slowly, as if from a dream, he became aware of his surroundings, but his arms still refused to let her go. He held her tightly to him as he looked around the room. Every eye was on them. He knew that soon every tongue would begin to wag. He understood the consequences of what he had done, but for the moment, he didn't care.

Taking Jenny by the hand, he walked her through the room, ignoring everyone, sealed from their words and eyes by the power of the tiny hand held so trustingly in his own. Quietly he led her outside, to the waiting carriage.

Outside, in the coach, the horses pulled away, heading for the hotel, taking a silent Gannon and a very confused Jenny home.

The night was still beautiful, and the moon still full, but for Jenny, it had become extremely strange. She was still dizzy from his kiss, and a warm, curling fire had blossomed inside of her which made her weak, filling her with a sweet sadness . . . a longing for something she did not understand . . . something she had no name for.

Shyly, she turned to look at Gannon. The moonlight

setting his face in shadow, while illuminating hers, told her nothing. He felt her looking at him, and turned. Her face was filled with simple wonder and trust, and an innocence he found irresistible. He watched as her eyes traveled searchingly along his face, as if by studying each line, this mystery she felt inside of her could be solved. Once again her gaze rested upon his lips.

"Jenny," he warned thickly, "don't look at me that way."

"Why?" she asked, and held his eyes so openly and innocently with her own, that a feeling of responsibility and guilt arose within him. He struggled with the powerful urges he could barely control.

Strangely out of place in August, the night had turned cool. The humidity, which had plagued the city constantly and caused fine silks to be ruined and stick like second skins to one's body, had melted away with the heat of the day, leaving only a barely perceptible breeze which whispered in and out of the carriage windows and touched intimately against their skins. Even so, there were tiny beads of sweat on Gannon's brow that caught and glistened in the moonlight. His skin was flushed and painful . . . every nerve in his body acutely aware that she was beside him. Sitting next to her was the sweetest torture he had ever known. Barely able to stifle the flames which roared out of control inside of him, he closed his eyes and shook his head slowly from side to side, half sick with wanting and unable to answer the simple question she had asked.

"Aaron, are you ill?" Worried that he had caught some disease which caused his body to tremble and burn with fever, she reached out and touched his forehead gently. He felt hot against her skin, and he flinched when he felt her. A deep, powerful groan escaped his lips. With his eyes still closed, he captured her hand by the wrist, kissing her opened palm, and then the tip of each, tiny finger . . . tasting her sweetness . . . wanting so much more.

Her eyes flew open in surprise. Wherever he touched made her tingle and grow warm. When he turned toward her, she saw a dark hunger in his eyes burning with an intensity that nearly frightened her. As he stared at her, her heart began to race and a curious warmth rushed through her body.

"Driver!" Gannon shouted hoarsely. "Stop!" The driver did as ordered. With one long, last smoldering look, he opened the door and jumped outside. "I'll be riding home with you," he stated roughly. Jenny heard him climb on top, followed by the creak of the seat as he sat down and the crack of the whip as the carriage lurched forward. She was left all alone inside the coach with her thoughts.

Later that night, when everyone had gone to bed, Jenny lay awake, thinking. The last few months had been an emotional roller coaster ride for her. She had been hurtled into the deepest valleys of despair by her parents' deaths, then lifted to the highest peaks of happiness by Gannon, sometimes all within the space of a single day.

Tonight had been more of the same. A few hours before the dance, she had looked forward to this night, and then, when Joshua had been beaten because of her, all of her happiness had evaporated. She had been certain it wouldn't return for quite a while. But she had been wrong. Tonight Gannon had made her feel happy and confused. He had taken her someplace she had never been before . . . to a height that left her dizzy and shaken, filled with a feeling that was more than addictive . . . a feeling she wanted to have over and over again.

She wanted to talk to him about it, to ask him how he felt, and to tell him how confused she was. He had barely said two words to her when they had come home and he had left her at the door without so much as a backward glance, saying only, "Goodnight." There was no emotion in his voice that she could read, and he carried himself with such a stiff formality that it made her feel angry, although she wasn't sure why.

Mrs. Merit had been waiting up for her, eager to hear all the details. Jenny had pretended to be very sleepy and told her that they would talk in the morning. She had lain down, closing her eyes, trying to sleep. But her thoughts wouldn't let her. They all revolved around Gannon. He totally confused her. One minute he was yelling at her and treating her as if she were a child and a nuisance, and the next, he was holding her, murmuring softly in her ear, and kissing her. Restlessly she tossed about in her bed, with only the faintest sound of Mrs. Merit's breathing to keep her company, until a familiar noise from outside caused her to sit up. It sounded like someone was outside her window, down below on the street. She slipped out of bed and walked toward the window.

The moon, which was now setting, shined through it, casting its silvery light and deep shadows everywhere. She hadn't pulled her wrap on, as she meant only to peek outside, but when she came to the opened window, and looked out, her heart began to beat rapidly. It was Gannon. He had saddled his gray and was preparing to leave. He pulled his cloak around him and jumped easily into the saddle, and not knowing that she watched, turned as if to say goodbye, toward her window. Her hair was unbound. She had left it unbraided, cascading down her shoulders like liquid moonlight. Her flannel gown was thick. As she leaned forward, the movement pulled it tightly against her, outlining her form in every detail.

When Gannon saw her he drew in his breath sharply and stopped. She wanted to say something to him, to tell him not to leave. Instead, she only gazed silently at him, until with a sharp kick to his horse's flank, he spun around and bolted noisely away.

Jenny watched him ride down the empty street until the sound of the horse's hooves melted steadily away. He became nothing more than a dark blur in the moonlit night and then was gone.

CHAPTER

9

Clackity-clack, clackity-clack . . .

The rhythm of the train was as comforting as the ticktocking of an old clock. It measured the days and miles in precise beats and the starts and stops in altered tempos. After a while, one didn't seem to hear its beating. Like the pumping of one's heart, it was just there.

John watched the morning slide by his window, the scenery magically changing each day, bringing him closer to Kansas City and closer to the end of his journey.

A loud wailing cry, winding down into a tremulous sob, drew his attention from the outside of the car into its smoky interior. A baby's cry. The mother tiredly wrapped her shawl around it, bringing it closer to her breast. She spoke softly to the child, rocking it back and forth on the hard wooden bench. The baby's contented murmurs were barely noticed by the other passengers.

The car was a dismal brown and gray rectangular box filled with people crowded closely together. Babies and bundles littered the floor. Human smells hung heavily in the air. Entire families traveled together, eating and sleeping, living in these cars, huddled close, their languages and cultures the walls that separated them, but their dreams had been the same. To prosper. To grow fat on the lands the Union Pacific advertised as the most fertile soil in the world. And so it had been, the lands out west, but these people had not prospered. It wasn't for lack of trying. The people who had sold them the land had not told them all that they would face. To the Indians who were native to this soil, they were intruders. To the cattlemen who grazed the lands unhampered by fence lines, they were a nuisance and pestilence to be driven away. The very trains that had brought them here and opened the lands robbed them of their profits. All grain and all produce had to be shipped by them. Their prices had not been negotiable. Tired and weary, too whipped to fight, these people came back to the cities. Defeat showed clearly on their faces and John felt sorry for them.

His toes ached and he longed to stretch and move, but there was no room. Sighing deeply, he rummaged through his bag and drew out a small piece of cheese and slice of bread. The bread had grown hard, but he ate it anyway. The growling of his stomach was loud enough to provoke a few raised eyebrows from some of the other people on the train.

He nibbled at the bread, avoiding the eyes of the others by pretending to gaze with great interest at the dry, flat desert passing by his window. Beige sand, flat and endless, filled his view. Occasionally, fireweed, burnt brown, rolled past, or a tall cactus would stand at attention and salute. But nothing moved out there, nothing could. The sand, bleached white by the blazing sun, went on forever under the pale sky. So blue, he thought, blue and pale and almost gray . . . like his brother Stephen's eyes.

He started to itch. He was uncomfortably hot, even though he had pealed most of his gear off by now, rolling it into his pack. Another day or two and he'd be in Kansas City. With any luck at all, he'd be back at his mine in two months' time . . . with Jenny. And by spring, they'd be working his claim, getting richer every day. He smiled to himself and closed his eyes, letting the soothing clackity-clack of the old steam engine sing him to sleep.

* * *

All was quiet at the hotel. Nearly four weeks had passed since Jenny watched Gannon ride away. He had left written instructions as before about what needed to be done. During his absence, Dugan had received more letters, but nothing had been written to Jenny and Gannon had left no word for Jenny in any of the letters that Dugan had received.

The day after he had left, several stout young men came to the hotel, telling Dugan that Gannon had instructed them to watch his place, and more specifically, to watch Jenny. Since the night of the mayor's ball, no one had seen nor heard from Kevin, but Gannon didn't want to take the chance that he might come back while he was gone. In one of his letters, he told Dugan that he needed some time alone, to think, but he wouldn't say what about. In every letter that followed the first one, there was a different postmark. He was moving around quite a bit, away from the source of his trouble and pain, but never too far . . . because his pain had also become his most treasured pleasure.

Mrs. Merit had questioned Jenny nonstop the next morning after the ball, but she was so upset at what had happened, that she wouldn't speak about it. Mrs. Merit and Dugan sensed a mystery, and were just that much more curious when Gannon left unexpectedly, and didn't return.

Jenny imagined all sorts of horrible things. She blamed herself for his absence, believing that if she had been someone else . . . someone who had money and power and came from the "right" family, Gannon would never have left. But she couldn't bring herself to ask Dugan if that was why he was gone, so these thoughts haunted her, even as she worked. She waited patiently every day for word of him. Each time a door would open she would look, hoping it was him . . . but it never was. Nights became eternities as sleep eluded her . . . and her dreams, when she did sleep, became fragmented nightmares which lingered long after she awoke. Mrs. Merit begged her to eat more, and clucked after her like an old hen as her appearance became more thin daily and her eyes haunted and lost, with deep, purple shadows growing ominously beneath them. Jenny tried to explain to the older woman that she couldn't eat and she couldn't sleep. Not until she saw him again. And she knew at that moment, as everyone else had known all along, that she loved him and needed him to hold her again.

She sighed heavily, lifting the pan of dough she'd mixed and carrying it to the stove to warm. Every day the pans became heavier; the work, more of a chore.

"Here, Jenny . . . let me do that," Joshua kindly offered. He took the pan from her. She didn't object and she gave him a sad smile, turning back to her table to make more.

Joshua felt so sorry for her. He understood what she was going through. He was back working now in the kitchen, and had recovered so fast that even the doctor had been amazed. Even when he couldn't work for the first few days, he would drag himself to the kitchen to check and see that everything was running smoothly, only returning to his bed when he was satisfied that they could manage on their own. But now he was back, giving orders, cooking, and making the kitchen run as smoothly as a well-oiled clock. He was all healed now except that when he walked too fast he winced. The bruises were still far from gone, but were beginning to fade.

He and Dugan and Mrs. Merit watched in silence as Jenny waited. Their soft hearts ached to see her pain. Unknown to her, a week ago, Dugan had written a letter to Gannon. He sent it with a sturdy young lad on a very fast horse, telling the boy to find Gannon, no matter where he was. They were all afraid for Jenny and knew her only cure was Gannon.

CHAPTER

10

The sun had set hours ago and the drapes had been drawn. Clouds, black and fierce, had been building all through the day. Now that the light was gone, lightning sparked erratically overhead, crackling and casting purple shadows over the land. Thunder boomed and the wind began to roar. A late summer storm was fast approaching and Gannon had barely beat it home. He leaned wearily against the window frame and pulled the drape back so that he could watch the lightning as it played across the sky.

The air felt heavy and charged with electricity. His shirt clung wetly to him. He had discarded his jacket hours ago, carefully placing the letter he had received from Dugan in his shirt pocket. Dugan had said that Jenny needed him. Since he had left she had barely eaten and Mrs. Merit had caught her many times, in the early, dark hours of morning, sitting by the window, peering out into the shadows. Once she had even caught her sleeping there, shivering in only her nightdress. She had awakened her, leading her quietly back to bed. When Gannon had read this, he hadn't bothered to change his clothes or write to announce that he was coming home. He had saddled his gray and ridden as if the devil himself were chasing him. In a way, he was. His conscience accused him better than any devil of the wrong he had done to her. He knew it was his fault for causing all of her misery. If she became sick because of him, he would never forgive himself. So he had ridden hard, stopping only long enough to buy or trade for a new mount, and to hurry on home . . . hurry back to Jenny.

The lightning flashed sharply, illuminating the sky and him. He was tired and rough looking, with two days' growth covering his face. His eyes burned with a feverish intensity.

"Well . . . so there you are . . . come at last!" Dugan greeted happily as he walked into the room. Gannon was too tired to speak, so he just nodded. "Can I bring you something to eat, lad? You look like you could use it . . . and a bath too, if I'm not mistaken." Obviously, Jenny wasn't the only one who had been in a bad way. Perhaps now that each one knew how the other felt, things would change around here . . . for the better.

"I don't want anything," he tiredly refused. "Just ask Jenny to come here, please."

"Well . . . it's about time!" A very happy Dugan left the room with wedding bells sounding gaily in his head to search for her.

Gannon had thought of nothing else these past weeks, except Jenny. Apparently his conscience could make him feel guilt in a variety of ways. His heart ached and he couldn't sleep, but even when he did, the shadowy figures in his dreams accused him of doing wrong. It seemed his conscience not only had power over all of his thoughts, but his heart and mind as well. Everywhere, that is, except below his belt. That "thing" seemed to have a mind of its own and a will for doing exactly what it wanted, when it wanted, wherever it wanted, at all costs. That night, at the Mayor's ball, his willpower had been pleasantly sedated by at least a quart of the finest brandy he couldn't remember drinking. The taboos he had carefully placed on their relationship were gone, and whatever morality he possessed had been neatly numbed by the alcohol. All that was left in his mind was sweeping, raw passion and the desire to possess Jenny's body and soul with every indrawn breath.

When Phillip had touched her, bells had sounded in his brain and he had seen red. Six thousand years of carefully polished, civilized veneer vanished from his consciousness and the man in the cave took over. She was his, he knew that, and he didn't give a damn what anyone else thought. First he intended to punch Phillip squarely in the nose. He hoped he would be foolish enough to punch back, and then . . . then, oh then, what would he do? Pick her up? Yes . . . pick her up, and toss her over his shoulder and run until he found some green, moonlit meadow to lay her down in, with only a starry blanket to cover them, and the moon to stand guard, and then . . . oh, then!

But the night had not ended with her in his arms. It had ended with him riding away in the cold dark hours before dawn. He had held her in the weeks he had been away. Every night she came to him in his dreams. He would awake feverish and aching, with the sheets tangled roughly around him. And he knew, as everyone else had known all along, that he loved her and needed to be with her. But he also understood what his conduct that night had caused them. He had allowed his passion for her to overwhelm him. In doing so, he knew that he had ruined any chance she might have had of finding a decent husband in Kansas City. He knew Mrs. Kenton, and others like her, would never leave the situation alone or let it die a natural death. If he made any attempt to reintroduce Jenny to society, they would stop him, making a scandal so large and dirty that they would never be able to be seen in public again without someone pointing a finger, or making a petty remark . . . not to his face . . . no, never so honorable . . . but in the corners of rooms, behind cupped hands, whispering to one another. For himself, he didn't care. But for what his clever scheme had done to Jenny, he couldn't forgive himself. She was innocent.

Her only crime had been placing her trust in him.

He had even thought about leaving. Taking Jenny and starting over again, maybe someplace further west . . . but, he had worked so damned hard and long for this place. The thought of giving it up nearly made him sick. Before he would do this he had to know if she really loved him, and not his money and power, like all the rest.

The door clicked softly and he turned. The rumbling of the storm outside was getting closer. The lightning grew bolder by the minute, but he didn't pay any attention to it as he saw Jenny walk through the door.

When Dugan had told her that he had returned and wanted to see her, she had run toward the study, not even bothering to check her hair. And when she saw him standing there, his face so drawn and haggard, she rushed into his waiting arms, not caring who saw.

"Jenny," he murmured huskily. He gathered her to him, until she could hear the sweet, thundering beat of his heart against her. She felt his breath, warm and soft in her hair. He was filled with a fire that had begun in his heart on the day he had first seen her . . . a fire that made him feel warm and alive and good, a fire that belonged only to her. Tenderly, he lifted her face toward him and kissed her. It was a hungry touch. He was starving for her and she returned his kiss so passionately that it only made him want her more. Instinctively she moved against him, drawing him nearer, wanting him to be a part of her. His body automatically reacted to her touch and the feel of her against him. His hands and lips could not remain still, as he caressed and kissed her more times within the space of a few minutes then she had ever known in her entire life.

It would be easy to love her now . . . easy and so right. He knew he could lift her up at this moment and carry her upstairs to his bed, and love her willingly all through the night. But he wanted it to be her decision too, because mornings always followed nights, and sometimes brought regrets. He wanted her to understand what it would mean, to both of them. So with all the willpower his poor, tortured body had left, he drew away, holding her quietly at arm's length. She was so pitifully thin and white. A pale, fragile, ghost-child who made him half mad with desire. Quietly he moved away from her, knowing that distance helped a little. She watched as he stood with his back toward her, resting his arm on the mantel.

"I never intended to hurt you, Jenny . . . you must believe that . . ." His words fell softly away, followed by a sigh. He spoke so quietly, that she had to move nearer, to be sure she understood what he had said.

"I never . . . never . . . wanted to hurt you."

A loud, thundering boom shook the hotel, and caused her to jump. She could hear the first few splatters of rain as they hit the window, and knew it wouldn't be long before it was pouring. Gannon didn't seem to notice as he stared moodily into the darkened hearth. She could see his face, cast sharply in profile by the room's oil lights, and she didn't understand why he looked so sad. Suddenly she felt a chill that wasn't connected to the wind or the storm's building fury. If premonitions came like tiny black birds, one had just roosted painfully close to her heart. She could feel its sad, little presence, and knew without being told, that something was wrong.

He turned to face her, raking back his hair roughly with his hand. He was searching for the right words; the words that would make her see how he felt. But he was afraid of giving away too much of himself . . . too soon. She made him feel vulnerable and raw, and he was afraid of the power her kisses had over him. He *wanted* to know . . . *needed* to know, if she felt the same, and would feel the same if he were covered with coal dust, instead of fine silk, and was a common man with callused hands whose only power was in the love he had for her. He didn't want to be hurt.

"Jenny," he started. "These past months, since you've been here . . . would you say, in spite of everything . . . that you've been happy?"

"Happy?" she asked, feeling that the words were somehow inadequate. Yes, she would have to say that she had been happy, even with the specter of her parents' death lingering constantly in her mind. These months had flown by, and she had been happy. Except on the night she had watched him ride away and on the long, gray days which followed.

He watched her face as confusion gave way to sad and thoughtful expression. He took her silence to mean no. A cynical look quickly replaced the searching light in his eyes. It was somehow just too much to ask . . . that she love him. He wondered how he could possibly continue without her.

Silently he moved away from the hearth and pulled back the drapes. His back was to her as he stared at the blackness outside. Jenny could hear the rain beat steadily on the window. The wind, filled with moisture, went whistling furiously now past the eaves, trying to enter the room by going down the chimney. Tiny whirlpools of ash and blackened embers danced wildly with each moaning gust before disappearing silently into the corners of the room. The storm was growing progressively worse. She could hear the lightning as it crackled and popped all around the hotel.

"Aaron," she began. He stiffened at the sound of his name but refused to turn until he felt a small hand touch his shoulder briefly. "I *have* been happy here . . . you, and Mrs. Merit, Joshua, Dugan . . . you've all been so kind to me . . ."

Gratitude, he thought darkly. The hope that had been harboring inside began to evaporate. He checked his movement to turn toward her and stubbornly refused to even acknowledge what she had been trying to say.

His back looked immense to her and his shirt, dampened by the heat, molded against him. She watched the slow and rhythmic movement of his breathing and felt the tautness of his muscles when she touched him. How could she explain what she felt? How could she tell him of the emptiness inside of her when he wasn't near? Or the longing she had when he was? How could she find the words to tell him how he made her feel . . . how he made her burn?

"I have been happy, Aaron," she whispered. "Until . . ." She paused, leaving a silence so heavy, and so expectant between them, that he had no choice but to turn and look at her.

"Go on," he coaxed, boring holes into her with his eyes. "Until when?"

His gaze was a magician's magic, conjuring up images from her memory and playing them back to her in her mind's eye. She vividly recalled the night of the Mayor's ball . . . the music and dancing, the men who were a blur and left no impression, their hands, useless hands, hands that meant nothing to her until *he* had touched her . . . his hands, so strong and sure, and his lips which kissed and drew fire. The searching, famished way he looked at her. The feelings he aroused, so intense, so sweet, and so very, very bitter as she had watched him ride away, listening to the hollow sounds of his horse's hooves, as it carried him away into the moonlit night . . . away from her . . .

"Until you left," she softly confessed. "Until I watched you ride away."

Relief washed over him, drugging him with a kind of happiness and peace he had very seldom felt. He smiled happily and pulled her close.

"You love me, lass . . . is that what you've been trying to say?" He tangled his free hand gently into her hair and held her face away from him, just for a second, just long enough to see what she would say.

"Yes," she breathed. "Yes . . . I love you." She felt the color rise to her cheeks and a wave of searing heat wash over her.

He laughed quietly and immediately began to kiss her face, her eyes, her hair. The weight he had been carrying seemed to have been magically lifted. He felt relieved and happy as she returned his kisses.

"You love *me* then?" she managed breathlessly, between kisses, while his hands roamed as freely as his lips had over her aching skin.

"Yes, lass," he whispered. "From the first moment I saw you . . ." He groaned aloud as her lips, urged only by instinct, reached upward to nuzzle an ear.

"Jenny . . ." he said hoarsely, and lifted her up, never allowing his lips to be too far from her skin as he carried her through the door and up the winding stairs to his room.

Dugan had laid a fire in the hearth and turned down the quilts of his bed. Food, for one, had been prepared and left waiting on the table beside his chair, and clean clothes and warm water placed side by side for his bath. The rain had stopped outside and now only the last few drops trickled quietly down the roof and trailed to the ground below. The air was soft and clean. A light breeze, touched with the sweet scent of late flowers, filled his room through the opened window. Gannon didn't see all these things and even less did he care. For the first time in his life, the painful longing of his loneliness had left him, his memories, even though still there, had receded into the far, dark territories of his mind and he was happy.

He roughly kicked the door shut, impatient to shut out the world as he held her in his arms. His eyes, so dark and hungry, frightened and pleased her at the same time. His very nearness excited the beating of her own heart, sending the blood soaring through her veins until she felt giddy and light-headed.

His passion for her was a great thing—no stallion could equal the fire in his veins, or the throbbing strength between his legs. She was his, for now and forever, and he was hers.

He was trembling as he laid her down, never letting his eyes leave her face as he loosened his shirt and quickly pulled it over his head. He made no move to extinguish the lights in the room. He wanted to see her as he loved her, to know it was really her and not a dream he held in his arms. He quickly finished removing his clothes and stood before her, naked and unashamed in his love.

Her cheeks were crimson roses and her breath came ragged and sharp. She had never before seen a man without his clothes. Her eyes were drawn hypnotically to the fine, corded muscles of chest and the rippling strength of his immense shoulders. Every inch of him was beautiful. She watched, mesmerized, as he came to her, noticing how the light caught and glittered darkly gold in the curling hair of his chest and the mysterious patch below his waist. The fire inside of her, long since banked, smoldered and burst forth, burning brightly at the sight of his enormous masculinity. She longed for him to quench the fierce heat inside of her.

Gently he laid down beside her, kissing her as tenderly as he could. Never had he felt such desire for a woman or such love. Her lips were warm and moist, and parted as naturally as the petals of a ripe flower for his curious tongue. He wanted to be gentle and kind, to make this first time for her good and sweet, a lasting memory and a promise of a new beginning for them. But he burned so fiercely that he could barely control himself as his hands found the buttons of her dress and clumsily began to undo them. The fabric loosened and opened slowly. The full, soft mounds of her breasts were exposed to his touch. Warm and white . . . the nipples the palest shade of pink . . . so sensitive to his touch . . . became erect as his hand slowly teased her skin.

She was tingling all over and she arched forward, wanting him to touch her and hold her closer, needing him inside of her. He responded to the yearning in her eyes, and the thrusting movement of her breasts, by kissing her lips, her chin, inching closer and closer to her breast, leaving a bright flaming trail wherever his mouth touched. "Aaron . . . please!" she moaned, begging for a release from the sweet torture of his mouth, and hands.

"Lie still . . ." he commanded roughly through gritted teeth. His hands, so expert and loving, removed her dress with a speed and economy of movement that was surprising. The breeze from the opened window touched them, bringing the fragrance of the night with it . . . newly washed and sweet. It lingered briefly, cooling the heat of their bodies and sending shivers along bared flesh.

Aaron touched her gently, encircling her and bringing her closer with one large arm, as his other hand impatiently removed what was left of her clothes. All was fire and longing . . . bright desire that moved her hips instinctively against his. Her thighs, milk white, pressed against his shaft. No longer able to control himself, he pressed his knee deftly between her legs and rolled her roughly onto her back. He wanted to plunge deep inside of her now . . . to release the taut steel of his throbbing flesh, but he held back, not wanting to hurt, as he gently stroked the soft, velvet folds beneath him. She cried out in delight, all movement and wiggling flesh, until he could hold back no longer. She gasped as he lowered his body over hers, and he felt her shudder as she opened willingly to him. A soft moan escaped her lips, as he parted her slowly. She felt the pain, but only for a second, before deep, shuddering tremors coursed through her body.

"Aaron!" she cried, as she surrendered herself to him, and wrapped her arms tightly around him, bringing him closer, pulling him deeper into her, until the sweet, rocking motion they shared became one long, lasting embrace and they lay spent and happy in each others arms, floating on a cloud of feeling, unwilling to let go.

CHAPTER

11

John stood on the platform and stared in disbelief. His solitary Alaskan life hadn't prepared him for this! Kansas City was overflowing with people of every imaginable color, size, and shape. Even though night had fallen hours ago, they were still here, in front of the railway station, waiting for trains, or people on them . . . talking, arguing, selling goods. He was just one old, weary man among them.

He sighed tiredly, slinging his pack over his back. His backside was sore as hell from sitting. He reached up absently and rubbed it. "Oooh . . . I sure ain't made for trains," he muttered. He walked stiffly off the platform, heading in what he hoped was the general direction of Main Street.

He had watched the rain for the past hour, cringing each time lightning cracked the sky in pieces and glad when the clouds had moved away. He didn't like storms. The only good thing about them was the fresh way everything smelled when it was over. He sniffed the air, wrinkling his nose. This city stank. Here, on the street, with the houses all piled up together, reaching higher than the trees, it smelled. The clouds had begun to blow away and starlight poked feebly between the cracks, dimmed into obscurity by the many street lamps. If this is what it smells like after a rain, he thought, I sure don't want to be around when it ain't been washed clean for a while. He shook his head as he walked gingerly past piles of garbage left to rot in the street, remembering the cool, clean Alaskan air, touched by the scent of ancient pines.

Since the storm had passed, people inside the buildings opened their windows and doors wide to sniff a few, appreciative breaths and let the cleansing air into their homes. Somewhere, down a darkened alley, he heard a dog bark and the clattering of crates as they fell against the stones. John didn't know where to go; there had been no directions given in the letter, only an address, and it was late. It wouldn't look too good, showing up at this time of night and getting everyone out of bed. He started to hunt for a place, halfway dry and out of the wind, to sleep. A doorway up ahead looked promising. The building was old and broken down. Blackened cavities yawned darkly out at him where windows used to be, their shapes distorted by the crumbing walls and rotting timbers. No light burned within.

"No lights . . . no people . . . good enough for me," he said, heading straight for it. The doorway gaped crookedly and had long since lost its door. He cautiously poked his head inside, looking around. His eyes, used to the inky blackness of northern nights, made out the shadows of crates and litter in the large, empty room inside . . . but nothing else . . . no people, just the scratching sound of rats in the walls and the yowling of cats searching for them. He pulled his coat out of his pack and sat down with his back against the jamb. His stomach began to growl menacingly, but he had eaten the last of his cheese yesterday and he hadn't bought anything else since then. He had counted what was left of his money on the train and knew there wouldn't be enough to feed Jenny on the way back if he gave into the weakness in his belly just now. So he hadn't eaten, distracting himself from his hunger by thinking other thoughts . . . thinking about home and his mountain cabin.

The doorway was hard, the air, damp . . . but he was tired and could've just as easily slept on a bed of broken glass. He absently wondered if Kaiuga had checked their traps. He knew the moment he had thought the question, what the answer would be . . . that he had. Kaiuga was not only his friend, but his partner and teacher as well, as had been Kaiuga's father. He smiled to himself as he remembered the day his ship had docked in Anchorage. He was so green . . . and so young that his hair had been black as pitch, with dreams of gold filling his head and not the least bit of knowledge as to what it would take to fulfill his plans. He half expected to see the yellow metal laying on the streets and in the creeks, visible to the eye and easily accessible to his hand. But that hadn't been the case. Some men searched their whole lives and never found more than a mere handful for their trouble, while others seemed to know instinctively where the huge veins of yellow lay. Was it dumb luck or the mumbo jumbo magic the Eskimos had taught him? Perhaps he would never know. For him, his dream was about to be fulfilled because he had found the motherlode, laying deep and hidden in the heart of the Alaskan earth. It was pulsating and alive . . . filled to overflowing with gleaming, yellow gold. His life's ambition had finally materialized, and now because of Jenny, he even had someone to share it with.

Sleep weighed heavily on his eyes. He yawned wide enough to hear and feel his jaw crack in protest as he started to drift off. His last, waking thoughts were of lush, green meadows, filled with bright, yellow butterflies and multitudes of wild flowers where he walked under an eternally bright sun, all alone.

Kaiuga walked silently on a carpet of thick pine needles, beneath a blanket of heavy boughs. The air was sharp and moist, and a light ground fog had begun to develop. He sensed many eyes watching him through the heavy silence as he made his way to the traps . . . but he was not afraid. All were brothers in this land. How many seal had he taken in his life, or rabbit? How many foxes had searched out his traps and given themselves to him so that he might cover his body and protect it from the cold? It was only right. In the end, his body would feed them and nourish the green grass. When his life had gone his spirit would then be set free and he would become one with them all.

The land was beginning to change. The days were growing shorter and the light was weak and tired sooner than in the early spring. Soon the snows would come and the great sleep would begin. But not for his people. They must live through the hard, white world. If they did not lay aside enough food for all the long, dark days ahead, they would never live to see the next great thaw.

Soon he must return to his people by the sea. Since the white men had come, they had bought many great things with them, one of which was the rifle that he now proudly owned. He was considered a man of property, with many fine dogs, a metal file, and knives made of the sharpest steel. John had even promised him half of the traps they used when he was ready to return to his village. This made him smile greatly. The steel traps had very sharp teeth and were far superior to the old, stone snares he and his ancestors had always used. The white men loved the blue and silver fox furs and trapping the wily creatures had fallen into the men's hands now. Before, only women trapped them, as they were small, and not very fierce . . . not considered worthy of a man's attention . . . not until they became so valuable. The skins could be traded for many things in the white man's store . . . more things than a man could wish for. He nearly smiled as he remembered how much smarter and more dangerous the little foxes became after the traders had shown how desirable they were.

He was an important man now, a man of means. When he returned to his settlement he planned to take a wife . . . maybe two. A rash of warmth enveloped him as he thought of fat little Narvaranna, who was all curves and flashing, white teeth. Her eyes were tiny black rocks which sparkled prettily, and her cheeks were so broad and flat that her nose positively disappeared! She was one desired by many. He would be an envied man if he could steal her away. But now it was time to check the traps he and John had laid out before he had left. Kaiuga could sense that John's dream time was not far away. Many times, when the old man was stiff and sore, and walked painfully in the snow, he would tell Kaiuga that his life was becoming heavier than death. Kaiuga understood his need to have someone of his blood near, to see that his spirit was properly sent off. He and John had trapped these woods many times. They knew all the secret places where the foxes lived and played, and he knew, without a doubt, when he rounded the tree up ahead, that another brother had willingly given himself to him and his family.

The path narrowed and curved harshly to the right. He made no sound as he moved along it. The pines were thicker here, and the branches denser, hanging almost to the ground. The light was mute and nearly opaque as it filtered in from above. No breeze stirred the trees, and the fog, impenetrable and white, moved only as he walked through it, swirling quickly back, eager to cover the exposed ground he left in his wake.

He rounded the tree and bent down, unable to see the trap from above the fog. He groped blindly, sure where he had staked it, until he felt soft, cold fur and icy metal beneath his hand. Quickly he lifted it, not surprised to see a fox, newly turned silver-white, caught securely in its savage teeth.

"Thank you, brother," he whispered. His senses, sharpened to a hunter's perfection, felt something else in the fog. He turned slowly, searching the knee-level cloud of white, until he spotted a large, gray wolf, with pale, amber eyes of fire, looking at him.

"Hello, old hunter," he said quietly. He watched as the wolf blinked slowly, as if in greeting. "This is a fine fox, do you not agree?" The wolf's nostril's quivered slightly, and his ears pricked sharply forward in response. "I cannot share this with you, brother . . . it does not belong to me . . ." Before Kaiuga could continue, the old wolf rumbled deep in his throat and opened his jaws wide, revealing rows of strong, yellowed teeth, as sharp as any knife. Quietly, Kaiuga lowered the fox and reached behind him for

129

the rifle he had slung over his back. As if the wolf had read his thoughts, he snarled savagely and took one, bold step forward. "No . . . old one . . . it is not my day to die . . ."

Kaiuga swung the barrel upward, aiming directly between the eyes which glared so balefully at him. Before he could fire, a twig snapped behind him. He whirled instinctively, squeezing the trigger as he did so. The others had circled around him, and a large, rough-looking male yelped as the bullet burned hotly into his flank. He flailed the air wildly for a moment before crashing loudly to the ground below. Kaiuga pivoted to face the leader, determined to finish him off . . . but he was gone, as were the others, fading like the ghostly gray smoke from a campfire. They had vanished into the forest, leaving their wounded friend to his fate. Kaiuga knew that this was the pack the elders had told him about . . . the pack who hunted men.

He grabbed the trap and with one mighty pull, heaved it out of the ground. He slung it, fox and all, over his shoulder. Calculating the amount of light left, he figured he would have just enough time to reach the sod house before darkness closed in around him. With his rifle held securely in his hand, he started to walk back along the path he'd come on, until the high, solitary cry of a wolf rang out and filled the air. He was somewhere behind him, hiding in the dense cover of the trees. Kaiuga walked faster as the single cry faded and began again, only to be joined now by many others, on all sides. Their mournful cries echoed around him, building, and coming closer . . . and then . . . he ran.

CHAPTER

12

They lay in a tangle of brightly colored sheets, their legs entwined. The fire had burned low in the hearth and the room was set in soft, glowing shadows of yellow-gold.

The storm was gone and the clouds had drifted away. Crickets measured the peaceful silence with their tiny, rhythmic beats, and the frogs boasted loudly in their throaty, croaking way.

She lay sleeping, curled snugly against his shoulder. Her body was warm and soft. Even now, after a very brief interlude of rest, he wanted her. His hand absently stroked her silky hair.

She had given him all of herself, without asking for anything in return. And that was precisely why he felt like giving her everything he had . . . even his name. She filled the dark, empty places in him with sunshine and sweet desire. His body ached to take her to him again.

With his arm still curled protectively around her, he half turned and kissed her, barely touching the soft, pink lips with his own, while his free hand caressed her, molding her to him. Her eyelids flickered open slowly, a golden Snow White awakened to love by the kiss of her prince. She smiled warmly and sleepy-eyed as her own arm curled slowly upward around his neck, drawing him to her again. In the glowing, golden light he loved her, sure in the knowledge that each time, though superbly satisfying, would never be enough. Her love was addicting and mystically strange in its depth. He longed desperately for her touch to quench the deep hunger inside. His body trembled as he mounted higher to the precipice of his desire and she rode with him. Together they reached an ecstasy beyond words, swimming through feelings of pure delight and love, holding snugly to one another and needing nothing else.

"Stay with me always, Jenny . . ." he breathed softly into her ear. "Never leave me." He groaned aloud as the sweet waves rocked him nearly senseless. He held her tight.

"Never . . ." she murmured huskily, floating with him on a calm and tranquil sea.

Spent and shaken, he reached for her, pulling the quilt up over them. Together they began to drift.

"Never . . . leave . . . me . . ." he sighed. From somewhere, far, far away, she spoke, not a question, but a statement, confirming what she thought she already knew.

"You're asking me to marry you . . ." she said sleepily, softly. She felt him stiffen beside her. Her body, so tuned into his, became fully awake, as she sensed the difference in him.

When he spoke, his voice was cold and held a bitter edge she knew all too well. Now, he too, was fully awake, an ugly feeling growing in him.

"Do you *require* a sheet of paper to compensate you for loving me?" he asked icily.

Now it was her turn to stiffen. Slowly, she sat up, dragging the quilt up over her breasts. She stared at him softly. Suddenly, she heard Angie's voice in her head and saw her sneering face, poking up angrily at her in the kitchen . . . "He won't never *marry* no *poor* girl . . . he'll just *use* you, like he done all the rest! *Use* you . . . *Use* you . . ." singsonged in her mind. The happiness she had felt inside of her melted away, along with her innocence. She stared, for a very long moment, into his hard and angry eyes. If her heart had been made of glass, it would have shattered. She felt the tears rise uncontrollably to her eyes. She struggled to maintain some dignity, as she realized what she had given away . . . all to a man who obviously didn't want to marry her.

He didn't trust himself to look at her and stared hard at an unseen spot someplace across the room.

"I said I would take *care* of you, *always* . . ." he continued pointedly. "Give you *everything* you need . . . why do you think it is necessary to be *married* to me? You can have everything *without* that!"

Everything *without* that? she thought darkly. Everything, yes, except the dignity and respect and public acknowledgment of his love. Anger burned fiercely in her, drying her tears before they had a chance to show themselves. Perhaps, she thought, if I were rich, a mayor's daughter, or English . . . perhaps then I would be good enough . . .

"I misunderstood," she said quietly, a steely edge to her voice. He heard the rustle of blankets, and felt her get up from his bed. She would never give him the satisfaction of seeing or knowing what his words had done to her.

Ignoring her nakedness, she dropped the quilt on the floor. She began to pick up her clothes and put them on. Her movements were mechanical and stiff. It took all of her willpower to keep from throwing something at him, or rushing over to the bed and slapping him for what he had done to her. All the weeks he had been gone she had longed for him, neither sleeping nor eating as she waited. Now, after everything that happened, she felt cheated, nothing more than a monumental fool.

He watched her dress, and sat up. So . . . he thought bitterly, he had been wrong about her, too. That damned paper was all-important . . . love meant nothing to women . . . nothing! But even in his anger, he couldn't keep his eyes from moving restlessly over her form. Even knowing that she was no different than the rest, he still wanted to carry her back to his bed, and hold her there, never letting her out of his sight.

"Where are you going?" he asked harshly.

She was lacing her dress when he spoke. When she looked

at him, he could see the coldness in her eyes, and the anger flushing her cheeks crimson.

"Aren't you *finished* with me, Mr. Gannon?" she asked pointedly. Her eyes flashed blue ice, crystal barbs that would surely have impaled him if she had had the power to throw them like daggers.

"Finished with you!" he bellowed. He sprang out of bed and came toward her, towering menacingly above her like some bright and angry god of war. "What in the *hell* do you mean by that?"

"Finished," she repeated evenly, and even managed a sweet, acid smile. "You know, *sir . . . done, complete, through* with me . . ." she explained as though he were an idiot child. "Have I not *paid* my debt?" Her voice was lyrical and low. He stared incredulously at the softly dimpled, beautifully curved young woman before him. Her voice had not risen, yet he could see the tornado brewing inside of her. He grabbed her roughly by the shoulders, but she didn't even flinch as she just continued to stare coolly at him. His face was livid and his eyes crackled and sparked as he glowered at her, a flaming Mars and a marble, cold Venus, neither one giving an inch.

"Paid your debt?!" he growled. "What do you *mean!"*

"I told you earlier . . . I was *grateful* . . . Mr. Gannon . . . and since, as you know, I am a girl of no particular means . . . I *paid* you with the only thing I had of any value. Was it not enough?" Her words were calculated and measured, each one aimed directly at his heart with deadly accuracy.

"You *love* me!" he hissed. "You *said* that you did. What we had was not playacting. I won't believe that!" But his eyes began to carry the cast of one bitterly disillusioned. "All those weeks I was away from you . . . Dugan's letter, saying how you pined . . . nearly to *death,* I might add . . . for *me!* And now you claim that you only repaid a *debt?"*

He released her and walked toward the open window. She was quite shaken but she refused to give in, knowing that the consequences would be bitterly sweet. She wanted his arms to hold her and his lips to urge her on. She needed his love, but what a price there would be to pay! And what if there were children? His anger seemed to be melting away. Now he only looked like a confused little boy as he stared outside.

"Then what," he asked quietly, "made you so ill?"

She had reached the door as her resolve to be loved *and* respected by him had begun to crumble. She bravely turned the latch before she stopped and answered him, but she could hardly bear to see his face.

"I have been nervous, sir . . ." She swallowed a painful lump which had been growing progressively larger by the moment. "Waiting for my uncle . . . and the sadness of my parents' death still causes me to grieve . . ." She struggled to rekindle her anger against him, or else, she knew, all would be lost, so her words continued, in a biting and hurtful way. "And I suppose now, sir, when my uncle does come . . . that you and I are settled on *all* accounts." She wanted to provoke him, so it would be easier for her to leave. But she was surprised to see the sad and sardonic smile which spread over his face, instead of the angry one she had anticipated.

"Settled?" he said softly. "Aye, lass . . . we're settled . . . on *all* accounts."

"May I leave, sir? Mrs. Merit is probably worrying about me."

"Of course," he said bitterly. "By all means."

And she did, entering the hall and closing the door securely behind her before the first traitorous tear fell.

Inside, Gannon had pulled his robe on, grabbing the closest bottle of alcohol he could find. He intended to get drunk . . . very drunk. "Maybe I should've been a priest," he muttered, slumping down in his chair, moodily staring at the blackened embers in the fireplace.

The light had been left on low for her. Mrs. Merit was luckily snoring away, deep in her own dreams as Jenny climbed quietly into her own bed, not even bothering to shed her clothes.

She let the tears fall freely now, feeling shattered and

more alone than she ever had in her life. She hated him . . . and loved him . . . all at the same moment. She blamed him for what he had done to her, and herself for allowing it. Nevermore would she be the same, and always, always, she would long for him. She muffled a sob against her pillow, tucking it securely beside her. She couldn't keep from wishing it were him, warm and alive, against her, instead of goose-down feathers, and cold, cotton cloth. "Aaron . . ." she wept quietly, and knew that people did indeed die from broken hearts. She could never stay here now. Even if she could keep herself from his arms, his constant nearness would be a never-ending torture. Quietly she prayed that her uncle would come. Maybe being two thousand miles away from him would quench the heat, if not quell the love she felt inside. She began to cry, fresh and hard, the tears springing from the deepest cellar of her soul, so profound was the pain.

How long she lay there, suffering and wounded, she didn't know or care, until her ears picked up the unsteady tread of footsteps in the hall. Quietly she lifted her head and stared at the crack beneath her door. The lamps were always lit in the hall, and yellow light cut across the floor at a long, obtuse angle. The footsteps were growing louder and drawing nearer, until they stopped in front of the door. For a second, she feared it was Kevin. Talk had been circulating in the kitchen that he was around. He intended to get even with Gannon for firing him, and with Jenny for being the cause of it all. She thought about waking Mrs. Merit, but before she could react, the door burst inward. She sat up in bed, and so did Mrs. Merit, uttering a startled cry. They both stared fearfully at the large, swaying figure in the doorway.

"Mr. Gannon . . ." Mrs. Merit declared in surprise, clutching her nightgown closely at her throat. "What on earth . . ."

"Out!" he bellowed at her before she had a chance to finish.

"What?!" she cried indignantly.

"Ooutt! Now! Mrs. Merit . . . unless, of course, you would like some help!"

"Well!" she snorted, grabbing her robe as she headed for the door.

Gannon's shouting had woken the entire household staff. Dugan and Joshua stood out in the corridor, bleary-eyed, wondering what all the fuss was about, when Mrs. Merit joined them.

"What's the lad up to *now?*" Dugan asked grouchily, wishing this whole business would settle itself so he could get some sleep.

"I don't know," she said excitedly. "He just rushed into our room, and demanded . . . *demanded,* mind you . . . that I leave!"

"Oh . . ." Dugan groaned. "'Tis the lass again, I might've known . . . she makes him quite mad, she does."

They all nodded their heads and stared with renewed interest at the opened, now empty doorway.

Jenny was half-scared and half-pleased at seeing him. He was totally drunk, wavering slightly from side to side. His robe was half open, revealing his massive chest to her as he came forward, barely concealing his lower half. She felt a surge of heat rush through her and her stomach did a neat little cartwheel, which left her quite dizzy.

She was half-kneeling on the bed when he caught her arm and pulled her against him. Her hair was loose and billowed down her back. He wound his hand into its mass and brought her mouth up to meet his. His kiss was hard, not asking for her touch, but demanding it. The strong smell of brandy was overpowering as she tried vainly to push him away. She was determined not to be made a fool of again and willed her thundering heart to be still, chaining her desire, afraid to let it go.

His hands were like steel bands upon her shoulders. She fought the anger in his eyes by letting it build in her own.

When his lips failed to get the response he wanted, anger replaced his hurt and need. He drew away, knowing that even if she didn't love him, he could never let her leave.

"You are mine, lass . . . mine! Everything you see around you belongs to me! This hotel, the walls, this room, that bed . . . it *all* belongs to me . . . and I do not let go of what is mine!" he warned.

"I do not belong to you . . . or anyone!" she hotly retorted. "I've told you before, I am not a piece of furniture or a side of beef to be bought or sold! When my uncle comes, I *will* leave . . . and even if he never comes . . . I will still leave, I have paid my *debt* to you!" She pulled away, staring defiantly into his fiercely burning eyes.

"I could make you stay," he vowed softly, dangerously. "I could bolt your door and hold you captive." He studied her silently. "I could make you do as I wish . . . I could *love* you as I will . . . I could bend you with one hand and love you here and now. You're nothing but a fragile reed . . ." His words became soft and the hard light died in his eyes. "Look how she defies me . . . the tiny, little thing . . . look how her eyes threaten, and her lips tremble in anger . . ." He took a step nearer to her, but she didn't move. Tenderly he tipped her face upward and she felt her anger being drawn away in the cooling, green waters of his eyes. She longed to dive deep inside, to quench the thirst of her burning heart, but she couldn't allow that. She wouldn't allow him to see how he affected her. Anger was her only shield against the overpowering waves of love she felt for him.

"You're no better than Kevin . . ." she whispered softly. "You have manners and charm . . . all the right words . . . but you're no better. I was nothing more to you than a . . . a . . ." She couldn't bring herself to say what she was thinking as she waited for her words to start a new torrent or rage. But they didn't. Instead, he gave her that funny, half-smile again, which always seemed ironic and bitter at the same time.

"Aye, you're right, Jenny . . . no better, no different." With the same half-smile, his eyes wandered to her lips and she saw the hunger flicker briefly across his face, drawing her in.

"Your lips throw daggers, lass . . . sharper than any I've ever felt before . . ." He closed his eyes and sighed wearily, deeply. "Your lips could give me heaven . . . but your eyes guarantee me hell." With a polite, albeit shaky bow, he turned and strode out into the hall, narrowly missing the wall.

Dugan, Joshua, and Mrs. Merit watched as he staggered toward them. Dugan was ready to scold him, but before he could, Gannon bent over and shook his finger in Mrs. Merit's face in mock anger. "You best go back into your room, Mrs. Merit. Go into it and lock and bolt the door. Shove a good solid chair beneath the latch. You never know what sort of ruffians are lingering about these days." He hiccupped softly. "Shooo . . . Shooo . . ." he said, and walked past the trio in a crooked line, heading for his room.

"I better go after him," Dugan said and trailed quickly behind, while Mrs. Merit hurried into her room, eager to hear what had happened, leaving Joshua standing there silently by himself, wondering at the colossal foolishness of his boss. No woman was as sweet and good as Jenny, at least, not in his book. He shook his head in disbelief before turning to the rest of the staff, gossiping at the end of the hall.

"What're you lookin' at!" he bellowed. "Mind your own business. And get yourselves back to bed. There's work to be done in the morning!" Everyone obeyed, including him.

Dugan had followed Gannon into his room, where he had toppled unceremoniously onto his bed.

"What have you done, boy?" Dugan asked quietly, a trace of sadness in his voice as he tried to pull the blanket up around him.

"Done? *I've* done nothing, Dugan . . . nothing . . . but I think I'm bleeding to death."

"You . . . what!" he exclaimed, looking down in startlement as Aaron pointed in what he thought was the general vicinity of his heart. "Don't you see?" he said through hiccups. "I'm bleeding . . . right here . . ." He squinted his eyes and peered through the fog in his brain, jabbing his finger at his stomach. "She's torn my heart to pieces . . ." He closed his eyes against the rapidly spinning room.

"You're not bleeding to death, lad . . . and that's not your heart, I might add. But what I'd like to know is what'd you do to Jenny in the first place?"

"Do? To *her?!*" His eyes flared brightly. *"She* can do more with her mouth than ten men with pistols . . . Good Lord didn't need to make 'um stronger than men, no . . . he gave them tongues more lethal than swords and ice cold stones where hearts should've been!" he yelled, trying to rise. Dugan shoved him easily back onto his pillow. "All I did was offer her my heart and soul . . . that's all! And now . . . now . . . I'm dying . . ."

"You're not *dying* . . . you're drunk!" Dugan informed him in an amused voice, still not sure what the problem was. It sounded as if he had proclaimed his love for her loud and clear. What could have possibly gone amiss? "You mean, you proposed to her . . . and she refused?" he asked.

"Proposed? Who the hell said anything about being married!" he bellowed, grabbing the mattress as the room turned upside down.

"You didn't ask her to *marry* you?" Dugan asked incredulously.

"No . . ." groaned a dizzy Aaron, petulant as a little boy. I offered her my *love* . . . what's that got to do with a piece of paper?"

"Oh, lad . . ." sighed Dugan. "You offer a whore a dollar, and your mother a rose . . . but you offer your *love* your name . . . as it means everything to them."

But Aaron was beyond hearing.

"We have to have us a serious talk, boy . . . first thing in the morning . . . if your head'll allow it . . ." The old man mussed the copper curls he'd come to love and smiled at the unconscious man sprawled on the bed before him.

Down the hall, Mrs. Merit had tried all her best methods to elicit information from Jenny, but she just wasn't talking. She said she was tired just so Mrs. Merit would be quiet.

Their door had been bolted, and a chair—the stoutest, most solid chair available—had been pushed up against it, too. Every time Jenny looked at it, she thought of him.

Tomorrow she would get together her few belongings and leave. The certainty of this threatened to send her into fresh gales of tears at the thought of leaving him . . . but it was obvious that he lacked respect for her . . . and that she could not tolerate.

She dreamt of going on to Alaska and finding the gold her uncle had spoken about. In the smugness of all dreams, she saw herself as rich as a queen, coming back here and showing him and Mrs. Kenton and all the others . . . showing them all. Sleep finally claimed her exhausted body and she dreamt no dreams she would remember, so black and deep was her rest.

CHAPTER

13

The kettles of water were already boiling on the stove when Jenny finally came down. Joshua was nowhere in sight. Her life had been changed last night, transformed by a simple and natural act. It would never be the same again. Just like the black, stark dots of music written on a page, nothing more than ink marks until the right eyes read them and the right hands played them . . . then they became music. Her feelings were the black ink dots he had read so well, and their bodies had been the hands that made the music. It was something at once terrible and beautiful, and something she would not soon forget, she thought bitterly. She wrapped a towel around her hand and went to the stove to get some water to wash the dishes that had been left over from the night before.

The wind had begun to whine a little under the eaves. Last night's storm had circled back around, lazily emptying its contents on the already soggy ground outside. One brief glance at the window showed her that the weather mirrored her own mood quite well. Gray skies and bleak, water-logged trees. She sighed. She still planned to leave, but her anger had been replaced by a modicum of caution. She knew she must have at least enough money and clothing to last her through the trip. Tiredly, she picked up the boiling kettle and walked back to the tub, spilling as little as possible on the way. The kettles were made of seasoned, black cast iron and extremely heavy. She was glad when the weight of the water tipped from the kettle in her hands, sloshing into the huge basin below. Putting the pot down beside her, she started to wash a plate when the sound of the door opening slowly behind her made her turn with a start. Cool air swirled into the kitchen and she uttered a little cry. A hand, old and gnarled, rested on the latch. A man, whose rough and craggy face matched the hand, poked his head inside. He cautiously began to peer around. His hair was stiff and winter white, framing his face in shaggy locks which flowed and finally meshed into his long, unkempt beard.

"Sorry, Missy . . . I sure didn't want to scare nobody," he apologized. Jenny began to breathe again, her heart slowing to its regular pace. She smiled weakly, glad it wasn't Kevin who had come to call.

"It's all right, sir. You just startled me, that's all. Can I help you?"

He looked around the room nervously and wouldn't come in. He just held onto the door with one hand, and leaned across the threshold. That seemed about as far as he was willing to go.

"That big fella . . . is *he* around?"

"Do you mean Joshua?" she asked, puzzled as to why anyone would be afraid of him.

"I don't know what you call that big ol' walrus . . . but if'n you mean the one what run me out this morning . . . hollerin' to wake the dead . . . I reckon he is one in the same."

"No," she smiled, and couldn't keep from conjuring up an image of a huge walrus tucked neatly into a white apron, surprised that it did sort of resemble him. "I think he's in the bar, sir."

Now it was his turn to look a little puzzled. "Why you keep calling an old rock hound like me 'sir' for? I been called a lot of things, Missy, but 'sir' ain't been one of them!" He managed a brilliant smile showing a lot of surprisingly white teeth. He looked a little less nervous now. She couldn't help but notice the startling clarity of the blue eyes which twinkled merrily at her . . . eyes which looked for all the world like her father's.

"Is something the matter, Missy?" he asked, as he noticed her frown.

"No . . . you just reminded me of someone . . . that's all. And as far as why I call you 'sir,'" she added, "my parents always taught me to respect those older then I am." She paused, looking down at the puddle of water that was quickly forming on the floor. The rich, dark furs he wore were acting like a gigantic sponge, soaking up as much rain as possible on the surface, before dumping it all on Joshua's floor. "Do you think you could come in and shut the door?" she asked. "The floor is getting awfully wet . . . and I'm sure, so are you."

He looked down, and smiled sheepishly, but he made no move to come in. It was easy to see he was still afraid of Joshua. "Sorry 'bout yer floor there, Missy . . . these furs are like that . . . I be done dry underneath, 'cept just a might cold from lack of food, that's all." His eyes wandered over the kitchen until they came to rest on the kettle of leftover beef stew from the night before. It had been a long time since his last meal, and his mouth began to water. "Are you gonna eat that?" he asked hopefully, the puddle, now forgotten, growing rapidly beneath his feet.

Jenny realized why he had come . . . he was hungry. She smiled softly and went over to him. It hadn't been so very long ago when she had understood all too well what that felt like. Taking him gently by the arm, she brought him reluctantly into the kitchen, closing the door behind him and shutting out the rain.

"I jest as soon eat it out there . . ." he said anxiously. "You could just sort of throw it to me . . . a little water never hurt nobody."

"Don't worry," she reassured him. "The bar was quite full last night. I'm sure Joshua has plenty to keep him busy for a while." She went to the kettle and scooped up the last of the cold stew, heaping it high onto a plate. The old man leaned against the door, his eyes bright in anticipation.

"You sure that Josh fella won't come back here?"

"Even if he did," Jenny said calmly, "I don't think he'd mind if I gave you this stew. I was told to toss it out anyway." She handed him the plate. He didn't question her anymore, he just ate. In a remarkably short time the plate was clean. He licked the last few drops of gravy appreciatively with his tongue before wiping the plate courteously on his sleeve and handing it back. His eyelids began to droop automatically and a little color had returned to his cheeks, which now glowed a bright, apple-red. "Thank you, Missy. It was awful kind of you." He smiled tiredly. "What's your name? Mine's Joh . . ."

Before he could finish, Joshua burst through the kitchen door, a look of utter amazement settling on his large features when he saw the old man resting idly against the jamb.

"What in thunder!" he yelled. "I thought I throwed you out once already this morning!" He moved forward quickly, grabbing the old man by the coat.

"Let go of me, you ol' walrus! I'm a rich man! Let go of me, I say!" He wind-milled his arms wildly, striking only thin air as Joshua held him up nearly half a foot off the floor.

"Joshua! Stop!" she screamed. "It wasn't his fault. I told him to come in—the rain—can't you see . . . he's soaked!"

"*You* let him in?" he shouted, unable to believe his little idol had such poor judgment. He temporarily forgot about the bedraggled old man twisting frantically at the end of his arm. His grasp loosened momentarily, and that's all that was needed as John bolted for the back door. "What? . . ." Joshua said in surprise as he looked at his now empty hand. Then he was after him.

John had reached the latch. He began to pull, but Joshua used his huge bulk and threw his weight against the door before it could be pulled open.

"Joshua! Joshua! Please!" Jenny begged. "He was hungry. I would've thrown the stew to the dogs anyway!"

Joshua stopped in midstride, his eyes wide and unbelieving. "You gave him *my* stew?" he yelled. "This ain't no charity institute, girl!" Then he remembered John and made a frantic grab for him. But it was too late. He had just cleared the door and was heading straight for the bar. "Damn that crazy old fool!" Joshua muttered, running after him.

Jenny followed quickly. She couldn't let the old man take a beating because of her. Silently she prayed that Gannon was still asleep.

They had made the bar. She could hear Joshua's loud, excited voice, and the old man's frightened one . . . only he didn't sound all that scared.

When she entered the room, she noticed that the old man had taken refuge behind the huge bar and was pelting Joshua with shot glasses. "Hee! Heeee!" he cackled. She saw that Joshua had hidden under a table. His huge body was scrunched awkwardly between its spindly legs, spilling out comically on nearly all sides. She had to giggle.

"You old dirt ball!" Joshua roared. "When you run out of shot glasses . . . I'm comin' for you!"

"That so?" he answered smartly. Another shot glass whizzed past. "There's always beer mugs, ya know, an' if'n they run out . . . I reckon I can still heave a bottle or two!" He chuckled gleefully.

Jenny didn't know what to do. They might kill each other at the rate they were going . . . and if they didn't, Gannon would when he saw this mess. She couldn't help but think who would be to blame for the entire thing.

"Please," she begged. "Please, stop! Please, sir . . . don't throw anymore glasses. Joshua won't hurt you!" she promised.

"Like hell, I won't!" Joshua bellowed, covering his face as a shot glass flew past. "I'm gonna truss you up, just like a Thanksgiving turkey, you crazy old son of a bitch!"

"Gotta catch me first . . ." Whiz! A beer stein flew past Joshua's head, nearly grazing an ear before crashing to the floor. "Do ya hear, you ol' walrus? You got to get your hands on me and I don't think ya will! Hee, heee!" He was having fun!

"What in heaven's name is going on in here!" An incredulous Mrs. Merit stood gaping at the mess before her. Since she was the official housekeeper, she would be the one forced to clean it up. Her usually mild manner and docile temper were kindled to a frenzied degree at the prospect.

"It's my fault, ma'm," Jenny stated. "I . . . I let the old man in!" Whiz! Crash! A beer mug nearly made the door. Jenny jumped back, more out of reflex than fear, but an infuriated Mrs. Merit didn't budge an inch. "He was so wet . . . I just wanted him to dry off a little . . . and he was hungry . . . so I gave him the rest of the stew . . ." Joshua gave Jenny a scathing look at the mention of his cherished stew, but he didn't move, knowing that his safety depended on staying firmly entrenched beneath the table. "I would've thrown it out anyway!" she retorted in her defense, but her words were wasted on him. "Please, Mrs. Merit . . . make them stop before Mr. Gannon comes down. It's all my fault!"

Mrs. Merit understood the problem now. Joshua would rather bury his food in the mud than give it away free . . . and Jenny, tenderhearted child, could not stand to see the old man go hungry.

"Don't come in here, Mrs. Merit. He's crazy!" Joshua yelled, covering his head with his hands as another shot glass flew by, followed by crazy laughter, as if to confirm what he had said. But Mrs. Merit ignored the warning, walking straight into the room. She looked for all the world like a giant warship under full sail, with her skirts swirling grandly around her and her ample breasts jutting out like dual cannons in front.

"I got no quarrel with you, ma'am." John said. "Just that *big* tub o' lard hiding under the table over yonder like some *sissy girl!*" he sneered and fired another well aimed glass squarely into its center where it pinged loudly before rolling harmlessly away.

"Then your quarrel must be with me," a quiet voice said. Jenny turned with a sinking feeling in her stomach to see Gannon standing directly behind her. "Those are *my* glasses you're breaking." He strode confidently into the room without even so much as a nod in her direction.

He wore his riding clothes. For a moment she was afraid he would ride away again and not come back. Her heart gave a painful tug as she watched the tall figure move so gracefully ahead of her. His trousers were as black as a moonless night and hugged his long, lean legs well before disappearing into shiny, knee-high boots of the same sooty color. A white silk shirt, hastily put on, and left wide open, revealed his massive chest and rippling muscles. She closed her eyes against the unbearable longing she felt inside, simply at the sight of him.

"You the owner?" John asked cautiously, keeping one eye focused on Joshua while he spoke.

"Yes, I am. Just what in the hell do you think you're doing with *my* glasses?"

"I wasn't tryin' to do nothin'!" the old man snorted resentfully. "I jest asked that ol' walrus over there fer some work, so's I could eat a little, and maybe get me a dry place to sleep . . . and he throw'd me out!" He puffed up his chest indignantly, looking for all the world like a ragged old Santa Claus who had fallen on hard times, in his soggy fox furs, with his cherry cheeks, and full, white beard.

"If he threw you *out* . . . how is it that you just *happen* to be standing behind *my* bar, breaking up all *my* glasses?" Gannon was fast running out of patience.

It was right about then that Jenny was hoping a hole would open in the floor and swallow her. She spoke up, somewhat timidly, in the old man's defense. "I let him in, Mr. Gannon . . . he was wet, and hungry . . ." Her voice trailed away as he turned to look at her for the first time since he'd come down. His eyes flared briefly as they swept over her face and form, before lingering for a moment on her lips. She felt the color rise uncontrollably to her face.

"That's right!" piped in the old man. "If'n it weren't for Missy there, I'd not had a drop to eat now going on three days!"

Joshua crawled out clumsily from beneath the table and stood up, cramped and angry. "You can't blame it all on her, you old bum!" he said hotly. "If you hadn't been begging around here, in the first place, she would never have given you *my* stew!"

"I ain't no beggar! I said I'd work . . . and I would'a too! Only you wouldn't let me work . . . and I couldn't get no directions out'a ya neither!"

"Directions?" Gannon asked softly, the pain in his skull threatening to split it in two any moment. Being hung over was beginning to be a regular experience since he'd met Jenny. He wished someone would draw the drapes and shut out the sun for just a little while.

"Yessir. All's I wanted to know is where this here hotel me niece wrote me about is. S'pose to be something pretty special. He wouldn't even look at my letter to help a fella out!"

Hotel? Niece? The fog in his brain began to clear as he looked at the old man perched behind the bar. For the first time that morning, he noticed the furs he wore and the bright blue eyes that peered out from beneath his bushy brows. Eyes, as bright and blue, as penetrating and clear as Jenny's. As if their thoughts had been the same, Gannon and she looked at each other in surprise, at almost exactly the same instant. His amazed expression quickly gave way to bold triumph, while hers reflected only shock, and disbelief.

"And just who might your niece *be?*" he asked, a mischievous grin curling the edges of his mouth as he spoke. Jenny just held her breath.

"Be? Oh . . . her name is Jenny, Jenny Bydalek," he stated matter-of-factly. "Do you know her?"

Gannon broke into a full smile. "Maybe." He turned slightly and spoke to her under his breath, so that only she could hear what he said. "I might've known *he'd* be a relative of *yours.*" He grinned like the devil himself, believing that one of his fears had been permanently put to rest. Feisty though the old gentleman was, he didn't look too rich. He doubted that even Jenny, with her muleheaded stubbornness, would want to run off to some wilderness now.

"You're my uncle?" she skeptically asked, staring at the old man swaddled from head to toe in furs.

"Not unless you're Jenny," he said. His eyes, bright enough before, positively glowed with interest now.

"I am . . . Jenny . . ." Her words were watered-down and weak, and her dreams, so fresh and fierce last night, evaporated in the glaring reality of the morning light. Her savior had come to rescue her from Gannon and herself. She had fed him leftover stew because he didn't even have enough to eat. She had saved her savior and there was no humor for her in the irony of it.

"Well!" John proclaimed delightedly. "I might've known!" With a speed and agility surprising for one so old, he hoisted himself up on the bar and propelled himself easily over it, walking toward her.

Gannon watched the pair with an amused grin on his face. His headache had long been forgotten.

When the two faced each other, toe to toe, neither one spoke. John beamed at the beautiful young girl before him, letting old memories of Stephen slip happily through his mind. She was like him in every way, except for her diminutive size. Suddenly he was very, very glad he'd come.

Jenny, however, didn't look all that thrilled. Perhaps if her expectations hadn't been so high, and if all her hopes hadn't rested so heavily on the man in front of her, the part of her which was secretly very happy to see him, might have come to the surface. Instead, she didn't know what to say. How in the world could she ever leave the safety and security of the hotel and go away with him? But when her eyes happened to rest on Gannon, who stood leaning insolently against the wall, with his arms folded confidently across his chest, and an arrogant, amused, "I told you so" expression on his face, taking on the unknown seemed far better than the humiliation of giving in to him!

John didn't know whether to hug her or shake her hand. Then he remembered his wet furs and decided the hug was definitely out as he extended his arm toward her. Reluctantly she took it, feeling the coarse, dry skin of his palm, solid as a rock, with the texture of dried leather, against her own. It spoke of a man who worked hard and battled daily against the elements. It was a good hand, but she was so caught up in her own thoughts that she didn't care. She let him shake her hand woodenly up and down without too much enthusiasm of her own.

John saw the troubled look in her eyes and felt the coolness of her grip. His happiness at finally seeing her began to be replaced by acute embarrassment. Her clothes were finely made, and she was as pale and as fragile as a rose. It slowly dawned on him just how he must look to her. He took a halting step backward, clearing his throat nervously.

Gannon watched as the reunion turned sour and the awkward silence grew more intense. He could give John a job. Of that he had no doubt. The man looked as if an honest day's work wouldn't frighten him. He pushed himself away from the wall and walked toward him.

"You said you'd be willing to work for your keep, John. I'd be more then willing to hire you, if you want a job."

"I reckon I would'a," John quietly answered. "But I guess I don't need to now. I done found my niece and that's what I came here for. We'll be leaving first thing in the morning," he added.

"Leaving?" Jenny said, shocked. The old man cocked one eyebrow and squinted at her. This wasn't turning out the way he had expected at all. "Yep . . . the train is leaving for Seattle around ten in the morning . . . I plan to be on it." He left an unasked question hanging in the air and Jenny didn't know how to answer him.

"But, Uncle John . . . in your letters, you said you were rich . . . that the gold in Alaska littered the streets and flowed like dark honey down the rivers from the mountains. I memorized that, Uncle John. Father read it so often!"

"I am rich, Jenny. Now that I done seen you, my old heart don't hurt so much anymore, 'cause I know your pa ain't gone—I can see him real clear in your eyes . . ." he said softly. "And I didn't lie to you neither, not in none of my letters. There is plenty of gold in Alaska, and other things too—all a person could want. I got us a mine there, Missy. A million-dollar mine. It's up high, way past Anchorage. Your nearest neighbors be the Eskimos—good folks they are too. And the mine, she sits right in the middle of the prettiest mountain range you ever seen, come winter or spring, and she's filled plum full with gold too, jest ripe fer the pickin'. *My* gold . . . and yours, too . . . if'n you'll go with me."

That was as close to begging as the old man had ever come. His life had been spent searching for just this one spot. And now, his old bones told him, when they creaked loudly and failed to bend, and his heart, with its painful little jumps and the dreadful weight he sometimes felt on his chest at night, that his time was nearly over. It was only natural that he wanted to give away what he had sweated blood for to someone he truly cared about. But, it appeared as if she didn't want what he had left to offer.

Her eyes wandered from Gannon's face, which had lost its grin, to the weatherworn features of the stranger in front of her. For a moment, she took comfort in his gaze, seeing what her father would have looked like in another twenty years. But it was there that the resemblance ended. His dialect was as hard and chiseled as he was. She wondered at how the often beautiful and poetic letters they had received over the years could've come from this man. Now he was asking her to decide. She felt as if she were backed into a corner, caught unmercifully between the devil in Gannon's green eyes and the deep blue sea of her uncle's, with nowhere left to turn.

"I don't know . . ." she said hesitantly. "It's so very, very far away . . ."

The old man nodded and seemed to accept that as her answer. Quietly, he reached deep inside his jacket, pulling out a leather thong which he had tied around his neck. He lifted it up over his shaggy hair and Jenny saw what appeared to be a rock, about the size of an apple, hanging from the end. Its surface was not smooth and polished, but when the morning light touched it, she gasped. It was as if someone had captured a handful of sunlight and pressed it together so its rays wouldn't try to stray too far. It glowed and glimmered and pulsed, seeming to have a secret life all of its own.

John sensed her misgivings were more in him than in the trip itself. He ruefully had to admit that he must seem a pretty rough old bird. Without looking her directly in the eye, he placed the thong around her neck, letting the gold dangle heavily down on her breasts. Its weight surprised her, and she didn't know what to say.

"I guess I don't hardly blame you none for not wantin' to go traipsing off with an ol' dog like me . . . but I can't stay here, neither. The snows . . . they come early, and I got traps to tend. I can't afford to be cooped up all winter in town—so's I got to go back tomorrow. I'll understand if you don't come along, but I don't reckon we'll see each other again. You take this. It's all I kin give you now. In the spring, after I start working the claim, I'll send you back a good portion, so's you kin keep yerself in them pretty, yellow dresses." He smiled softly. "But if you change yer mind, the train don't leave till ten. I'll wait, Missy, jest as long as I kin." He reached out his old gnarled hand to touch her face, sheepishly stopping before he did. "Well . . . I best be gettin'." He turned and walked jauntily toward the door, leaving Jenny and the others staring after him, long after he'd gone.

Outside, the rain had stopped and the trees looked a somber gray-green against an even grayer sky. The wind was moist and felt good on his skin. He wished for a moment that the rain would come back. That way he could pretend the water on his face fell from the skies above and not from his tired, old eyes. He coughed loudly to cover his feeling as he rounded a corner, just in time to run smack dab into a large and burly young man.

"Are you blind, old man?" he growled, shoving him cruelly away.

"Oh, sorry 'bout that, sonny . . . didn't see ya." He righted himself without another word, heading down the street toward the train station.

"Drunk old bastard!" Kevin snorted contemptuously. He resumed his discussion with Bloyd. "Like I was *sayin'* . . . you and them river rats you run with, meet me here tonight, around eight or so. We'll take care of Gannon but good!"

"I don't know," whined a terrified Bloyd. "He ain't like a regular guy. He's got connections, ya know? He's even friends with the mayor, fer crissakes!"

Kevin laughed. "You don't keep up, Bloydy, old boy. He ain't friends no more! Ever since the mayor's wife found out about little 'Miss-High-and-Mighty' in there—she ain't exactly been on the best of terms with old Gannon! Figured that washed-out rag of a daughter of hers would latch on to him . . ." He laughed again. "Don't worry about no *high* connections, just do like I say!" He grabbed him roughly by the collar and slammed him up against the brick wall for emphasis. "Because if you don't . . ." he warned. "My little sister is gonna hear all about some things that you been doin'—and I don't think she's gonna like it too good. Got that?"

Bloyd mechanically shook his head up and down, scared of his brother-in-law, but more terrified of what would happen if his wife found out.

Kevin seemed satisfied, and dropped him carelessly to the ground.

"Yessir . . . yessir!" he vowed out loud, rubbing his palms together greedily. "Tonight's the night, Jenny . . . you and me, whether you want to or not." He secretly hoped she'd fight like hell . . . and laughed at the thought of what he'd do if she did.

CHAPTER

14

The storm had subsided hours ago. The wind, still blowing strongly from the southwest, had chased the fierce, gray thunderheads before it, sweeping the skies clean. Once, very briefly, before the sun had bid "adieu" for the night, it had forced its powerful yellow rays from beneath the last of the shadow-blackened clouds, to show itself triumphantly over the gloom. Its golden light had pierced the cheerless sky, penetrating for an instant every window and door and crevice in town. The clean, whitewashed walls of the kitchen reflected its light for a moment and Jenny looked up, startled by its brilliance.

The evening meal was over and most of the help had left for the night. She had felt their eyes on her all day. She knew the gossip was flying fast and free all around her. Whenever she entered a room it became inordinately quiet, but as soon as she left she could hear the buzz of conversation start up. Gannon didn't help matters either. This afternoon, while she was preparing a salad, he had come into the kitchen, still wearing his riding breeches and billowing white shirt. If the silence had been loud before, it was positively deafening now. Jenny knew by the way they acted that everyone must have heard about what had happened between them last night, and were breathlessly waiting for more. It was unnerving. Yet Gannon didn't seem affected by it, as he casually asked her to accompany him to his study. Reluctantly she obeyed, knowing her willpower to resist him was decidedly lacking, especially when they were alone.

He hadn't spoken a word to her since her uncle had left. As he ushered her into the study with a sweeping gesture of his arm, he still was as silent as before. His face was a mask made of stone, where no emotion, of any kind, showed.

He shut the door quietly and turned to face her. Her heart skipped a beat. If someone had told her of the wanton creature which lurked inside of her whenever he was around, she wouldn't have believed it. But it was there, deep and powerful and as old as time itself. She remembered the long winter evenings when her father would read from his aged and well-worn Bible. She would sit by his knee and beg to hear the Creation story and the Fall, secretly amused at the antics of the wily serpent. Over and over again, he would read it. As she looked at Gannon, with his beautiful face, powerful, manly build, and catlike grace, a verse from Genesis, obscurely buried in her mind, came to her. "Thy desire shall be to thy husband, and he shall rule over thee." She knew that it was true. Her desire was for this man, even though no paper or wedding band had been exchanged. He did rule over her heart, and always would. And this knowledge caused her pain, as she silently damned the evil snake who had started it all.

"I thought you might want to put your gold in my safe, Jenny. It will be much safer there," he added innocently.

"No," she flatly refused, shaking her head at his colossal gall. "I wouldn't dare put it in your safe."

"I don't need your *money*, Jenny, if that's what you're worried about," he said slyly. "I have plenty of my own." He stopped, eyeing her and the door. "Or is it that you think I'll keep it there, just so you won't get any foolish notions about leaving?" He took another tentative step forward, his eyes not leaving her face for an instant.

She was hypnotized by him. She could neither speak nor move as he came toward her. Coming in here had been a dreadful mistake, but it was too late to do anything about it now, as she felt his practiced arms slide around her and pull her close. Her heart raced and her pulse throbbed, but she was powerless to resist him. He shattered her senses with a hungry kiss. When his tongue parted her lips, she clung to him, weak and wanting, knowing no end to the burning heat inside.

"Jenny," he murmured huskily, crushing her desperately to him. She felt his hardness against her soft and yielding curves. Breathless, he pulled away and stood looking down into her face. "Tell me," he said, with a mocking smile. "Tell me you don't love me *now.*" He traced her lips with the tip of his finger, his insolent, self-assured gaze never leaving her eyes. "I want to hear *again* how you're going to run away from me." She struggled to free herself from his iron grip, and he laughed softly. "No, little bird . . . you belong to *me . . .*" His eyes were dark with passion, as he lowered his head to reclaim her lips. But when he touched her, the heat was gone, and bright anger flushed her pale cheeks scarlet. He tried to rekindle the passion he had felt only moments ago, letting his lips roam and plunder at will . . . but no results. She refused to be made a fool of again!

"Kiss me!" he demanded, forcing his mouth to cover hers. She promptly bit him . . . hard!

"Ouch!" he cried. "Why you little . . ." He drew back, more out of surprise than pain.

"Little *what?*" she demanded coldly, staring hard at him. He brought out the best in her and the worst, never allowing her feelings to be dull and mediocre. Hot or cold, feast or famine, Eden's cool bliss or Hell's raging inferno, never solid, safe earth beneath her feet when he was around! With fierce determination, she set her will against his, allowing no tenderness to fill her thoughts. "You're such an arrogant . . . bastard!" she breathed. The new word she used so easily, shocked her. Gannon went white.

"What did you call me?" he said softly. A savage light shone in his glittering eyes.

"You heard me," she answered a trifle haughtily, with a toss of her head. "You are an arrogant, conceited *bastard!*

But, you were right about one thing," she conceded, her voice as melodious and quiet as if she were reciting poetry instead of waging war. "I *do* love you—but then again— you're wrong about another. I *can* leave you . . . and I *will!*" With one last, venomous look, she turned and opened the door, leaving the room without another glance at his livid features.

And now, hours later, it was evening. She was in the kitchen, all alone, except for a mountain of dirty dishes piled high in front of her, wondering if she really had the courage to go, knowing that her time to decide was fast coming to an end.

Joshua came into the kitchen, tired from a long day's work. He made no mention of last night or today, treating her as he always did. For that she was grateful.

"Go ahead, Jen . . . sweep up a bit, then take your supper and go on to bed."

That was always his last order of the day.

"Right away," she promised tiredly, reaching for the broom, the final ritual of an already long day. She began to sweep. Carefully she picked up any vegetable peels on the floor, placing them on the table. These were used in soups and stews, which as Joshua claimed, "you couldn't make a decent stock without 'um." Jenny knew that was partly true, but was also due to the fact that Joshua believed in wasting nothing (so long as that particular stock didn't find its way into anything *he* ate). But it was quite all right and sanitary for the hotel's stews and soups.

With a sweep of her broom a potato peel peeked out from under a counter. With Joshua's dogma of proper soup base firmly entrenched in her mind, she bent over to retrieve the shy vegetable. She was so engrossed in her own thoughts that she never heard the door open, or the quiet tread of footsteps fast approaching.

"Whoops, darlin'! You ought not to be bendin' so far over like that. Why you just might fall!"

So saying, rough hands grabbed her from behind, sliding deftly up to form tight circles around her ample breasts, pulling her savagely backward.

"Hello, Jenny. Guess who?" Kevin laughed cruelly as his arms tightened around her.

Still grasping the broom, she moved more by reflex than thought, thrusting it backward with all her might, while twisting her body away from him.

"Leave me alone, Kevin!" she breathed. The broom connected with the hard stomach muscles pressed against her back. "Just leave me alone!"

He groaned, reluctantly releasing her as he fell back against the wall.

"You bitch!" he cried through clenched teeth. "I'll get you for that! Always thinkin' yer too good to be seen with the likes of me. Yer nothing but a kitchen maid. I'll have you yet! Aye, tonight y'll be beggin' for me . . . you and them great tits of yours!" he hissed.

Poised lightly, ready to fight or run, she watched him. He lay between her and the door. She silently prayed that Gannon would come. Slowly, she brought the broom around in front of her, and waited, forcing a smile to her lips.

"If you touch me again I'll take great pleasure in splitting that thick skull of yours into a hundred pieces."

It was a bluff. She didn't know what she would do if he actually came toward her, but she had learned one thing since she'd come here. She mustn't show any fear, because if she did, she wouldn't have a chance. Only those not willing to back down in this part of the city survived, and she would survive. She wouldn't allow Kevin, this kitchen, or this city beat her. She would survive because she had a dream.

His eyes narrowed, a speculative gleam in them. Was this the timid little beauty he ached for? Then he remembered her fight with Angie in the kitchen and the vicious slap he'd received over a month ago. So, she was a fighter after all! He grinned. That only made it that much more fun! Slowly he stretched out his hand, grasping the counter to pull himself forward, his gaze never leaving her face.

"I don't see your *protectors,* Jenny . . . and besides," he soothingly drawled, "can't you see, I only want to be your *friend?*"

He began to move slowly toward her. For every step he took, she took one backward.

"A young girl, like yourself . . . *orphaned* so recently—God rest their souls—needs someone to talk to . . . someone who can look after them a bit. This here is a wicked city, girl. A lot can happen to an unprotected woman, 'specially one as *pretty* as yourself."

Each word was emphasized with a measured movement toward her. But her attention had faltered for a moment at the mention of her parents' death. That moment was all that he needed. He quickly stepped forward, knocking the broom down with one hand and sinking the other into her stomach. A sharp pain made her gasp for breath and double over. But before she had a chance to recover, he had grabbed both of her hands in one of his large ones, jerking them high above her head in a rapid, violent movement. His other hand grasped her hair at the nape of her neck, pulling her head roughly back, as he pushed against her, grinding his lips into her own. The pain in her stomach and arms had been great, but nothing compared to the revulsion she felt at the touch of his lips. She tried to turn her head, to keep his mouth and probing tongue away, but it was no use! He was much too strong for her. Tears flowed from her eyes. They were not tears of fear, but of anger and frustration. To be so helpless and alone seemed more than she could bear.

"Please," she begged. "Please don't hurt me . . ."

He laughed cruelly in her ear. "I ain't gonna hurt you, Jen . . . leastways, *not just yet.*"

To her surprise, he pulled away, still keeping her pinned with one hand. He looked amused, and a sadistic smile curved the thin, cruel line of his lips into a caricature of a smile. She could imagine him as a young boy who took great pleasure in pulling wings off flies and torturing cats. She fearfully wondered just what he had in store for her.

"What's the matter, Jen? Your uppity ways getting you a little more *man* than you can handle?" He let loose a short, malicious laugh as his free hand trailed slowly down her neck, resting lightly on the bare skin above her breast.

"Tonight, I'm gonna show you what a *real* man is like. Yer gonna *love* it when I do. But not right now. You see, I need your help . . . you will *help* me, won't ya, Jenny?" She struggled vainly to free herself and was rewarded with a vicious slap. "Shhh . . . now, don't fight it. I don't want to hurt you just yet . . . and don't you say a word either . . . not till I tell you to." He caressed her reddened cheek before letting his hand wander again to her breast. He teased her flesh, till she thought she would die, before grabbing the fabric of her bodice and ripping it straight down the front. She cried out, and tried to pull her arms away to cover herself. Her white lace camisole was all that stood between her flesh and his. He laughed.

"I'm gonna let you go now, Jenny. There's the door. I want you to run, just like a rabbit, right through it . . . and scream too . . . real loud!" He released her and shoved her hard toward the door. "Run, Jenny, run!" he shouted. "I'm coming for you!" She didn't wait for more. Quickly lifting her skirts, she bolted from the room, followed by his howling laughter as he started after her.

The connecting door, which led from the kitchen to the main serving hall, burst outward as she rushed through it. Diners, old men, gray and bent, and younger men, showing signs of becoming old long before their time, looked up. Some were startled by the interruption while others, hardened by life's experiences, barely noticed the young girl, out of breath, eyes slightly wild, and skirts pulled up nearly past her knees. Her feet felt as though huge lead weights had been tied to them, and the floor had become a bog laden with molasses as she ran. Some of the men taunted her as she passed, while others reached out to try and pull her down. Through it all, she could hear Kevin's voice. "I'm coming, Jenny . . . run!" His sick laughter kept following her.

She searched the crowd for Gannon . . . Dugan . . . anyone who could stop the monster chasing her. But they were nowhere in sight.

Kevin stood watching the crowd, patiently waiting for Gannon. He knew that he was here because his men had watched the place the entire day. Gannon hadn't left. Maybe if he'd liven things up a bit, it would flush the bastard out. Kevin grinned.

"Hey, you men!" he yelled good-naturedly. "Stop that girl! Stole me money, she did! A dollar for the man what stops the dirty thief!"

"A dollar? A dollar!" jovially rang out. "Well . . . stop her, boys! Stop the dirty little thief!"

She was like fresh meat in front of a pack of hungry dogs. Out of sport and lust, they tried to capture her. She ignored their calls, shoving their greedy hands away, desperately propelling herself toward the door, afraid she'd never make it. A large, shadowed figure loomed beside her. She knew it was already too late as he pulled her roughly around. She looked up fearfully into the face of the man that held her . . . and breathed a sigh of relief.

"Aaron," she whispered, collapsing gratefully into his arms.

The room was suddenly very, very quiet. The only sound was the steady ticktocking of the old grandfather clock in the hall. All the workers stood poised like frozen statues in their places, eagerly wondering what was next.

Gannon was trembling as he looked at her loose hair and torn dress. With shaking fingers, and eyes burning with rage, he unbuttoned his shirt, placing it gently around her shoulders. He softly touched her hair for a moment, letting his fingers linger lovingly on the silken strands, before handing her into Dugan's waiting arms. Slowly, with the turbulent waters of his Nile-green eyes gleaming and filled with deadly intent, he turned around.

"No, Aaron! You mustn't! It's a trap!" She tried to free herself long enough to stop him, the certainty burning in her mind that he was doing exactly what Kevin wanted.

"Easy, lass . . ." soothed Dugan. "He can take care of himself. Besides," he said scornfully, "it's about time that scoundrel got his medicine!" There was deep conviction in his voice and thoughts. No one could beat Gannon in a fair fight—no one. He looked forward to seeing that scurvy rat

Kevin pay for all that he had done with a great deal of pleasure.

"No, Dugan! You don't understand!" she pleaded, a terrible feeling, deep inside, growing ominously larger by the minute. "It's a *trap!* I know it is!"

"We've got an army of men around this place, Jenny," Dugan explained patiently. "I'm surprised the devil even made it through the door! He's foolish, lass . . . I've never seen Aaron so worked up. *You* can't stop him now—*no one can*—from wanting to revenge himself on that *scum*—and you shouldn't! Let him be a *man,* Jenny, and protect what is *his!*"

Dugan emphasized the "his," and Jenny knew she could do no more than stand mutely by, watching as the two men approached each other. One, loathsome to her sight, with a malicious sneer carved into his coarse features; the other, much loved, bared to the waist, ready to kill for her honor.

"Gannon!" she whispered helplessly. She cried softly as they started to circle.

The crowd of men had given up their chairs. They lined the walls, making a ring for the two combatants. The air was tense, and Jenny could see the bloodlust glow dully in their eyes as they waited eagerly to see who would win . . . and who would die.

"What's the matter, Gannon?" Kevin taunted. "Afraid I might damage the goods? After all . . . it ain't like the package has never been *opened* before . . . now is it?"

A lightning-quick, crashing, right hand blow to the side of his face was the answer. Kevin spun to the left, careening drunkenly off the wall before crashing loudly to the floor, where he lay quiet and dazed.

"Get up!" Gannon ordered with quiet menace. "Or I'll take you where you lie!"

"It's always the answer, isn't it, Gannon? I can still smell the streets on you—you're just another brawlin' shanty mick!" He wiped his fist across his bleeding mouth. "But you've come up in the world, haven't you? Why, you're a *big man* now! Hmph! If ya can't buy 'um with your dirty whiskey money . . . then you beat them with your fists, or any way you can . . . but you *always* have to *win!* Well . . . not this time, boy-o, not this time!" He didn't try to get up, he just looked around at the circle of men, waving his blood-smeared hands in their direction.

Slowly, in answer to his signal, five burly men hesitantly peeled away from the walls, bringing forward the weapons they had carefully concealed, walking toward Gannon.

Gannon turned around slowly, eyeing each man who approached. His powerful muscles, taut and rippling, were amplified by the slightest movement, looking like molten gold in the flickering gas lights. He was cornered, outnumbered, the odds against him. But he meant to fight. A reckless, dangerous light filled his eyes. The men looked at each other nervously.

"If you're wondering," Kevin said softly as he got to his feet, "where all *your* men are . . . I may be mistaken, but my brother-in-law tells me that most of them are locked up tonight. Somethin' about littering or spittin' on the sidewalk, or some other such heinous crime. But don't worry—I don't plan to kill you, *not just yet.* I want to see you suffer for a while . . . maybe for days. Bloydy there," he pointed to a nervous, ferret-faced man, clutching a two-foot club in his hand, "has a room all ready for you at his jail . . . and I plan to visit you there *every day.* You needn't puzzle yourself as to how Jenny is gonna get through all them long nights while yer away. I'm gonna see she doesn't get *lonely* . . . personally!" He grinned lewdly in her direction, as he made his way toward her.

Gannon roared in rage, letting loose the sleeping lion that lived inside of him. He sprang after Kevin, intent on killing him. But the others, their confidence increased by his turned back, fell on him like a pack of hounds.

"Let go of me, you bastards!" he bellowed, swinging wildly in all directions, dealing out pain with every blow, as he tried to make his way to her. But they kept hitting him from all sides. He didn't have a chance, as they knocked him off balance and he fell forward with a curse.

Dugan saw the mass of men, rolling and twisting frantically on the floor in front of him, watching helplessly as Kevin made his way unerringly toward them.

"Go, lassie—go!" he urged, pushing her behind him, toward the door. "Don't let that animal get his hands on you—I'll help Aaron. Just go!" He shoved her as near to the door as he could, without taking his eyes off Kevin. Helplessly she watched as he approached. Dugan turned to face him. He was old and weak, no match for the younger man, but he was determined to protect Jenny with his life.

Beneath all the men, she couldn't see Aaron anymore. The other diners, too eager to watch the fight, had all but forgotten about her, as she moved cautiously backward, rounding a table, inching closer to the door.

Dugan bravely strode forward, directly toward Kevin. He held up his hands, to fight and fend off the blows. But he was no match for the younger man. Kevin regarded him as nothing more then a nuisance. With one well aimed punch, he sent him sprawling, unconscious to the floor.

"Dugan!" Jenny screamed.

He was very still and white. She couldn't see Gannon for the crowd of men swarming over him. But she could see Kevin, and he was coming toward her, with a triumphant smile spread over his broken mouth.

The big door was behind her. She groped blindly, until she felt the brass doorknob resting against her palm. It was cool and welcome to her touch. She gave it a yank and the door swung wide. With one helpless glance at the brawling men, she ran, hearing Kevin cursing angrily as she did.

The night was welcome and cool. She didn't have her wrap on, but it didn't matter. He hadn't caught her—and she swore under her breath that he never would. She hugged Gannon's shirt closely, his sweet, spicy scent all around her, as she ran along the darkened lanes, not sure where to go. Every part of her wanted to return to the hotel, but she knew she couldn't; he would catch her. All of Gannon's bravery and Dugan's futile courage would have been for nothing, because Kevin would have won.

Her thoughts were whirling crazily ahead of her. She remembered Kevin saying that Bloyd intended to put

Gannon in jail. She could see the weasel-faced man with the nervous, narrow eyes, and wondered what it would take to get him to free Gannon. In her pocket, she felt the chunk of gold her uncle had given her, bouncing roughly against her thigh with each step she took. Would it be enough? How could she approach him without Kevin knowing? Could she trust him, even if he agreed to free Gannon? She doubted it, but what choice did she have?

"Gannon . . ." she sobbed. The wind caught his name as she cursed herself for being such a coward and leaving him.

She gulped for air. Her throat was parched, and her lungs burned with every indrawn breath. Still she ran blindly down the deserted street, away from the hotel, not sure if Kevin followed.

Up ahead an old stone stairway rose dimly in the gloom. She ducked beneath it, sitting down in the farthest corner, near the old building, drawing her legs up as close to her chest as she could and wrapping her arms around them.

She could see the lane she'd come on, stretching back between rows of crowded brownstones, until the night devoured it. A man with a lumbering and clumsy gait was approaching. His shadowed form was blacker than the surrounding night. His coat flapped like raven's wings as he stirred the air with his passing. She could hear footsteps now, slapping the bricks with a fast, irregular rhythm, coming toward her.

"No . . ." she whispered, and held her breath, praying that it wasn't Kevin, as he clopped methodically in her direction.

A street lamp stood directly in front of the tenement, reflecting only a weak and glittering yellow light which the fragile breeze broke and tore to pieces with each passing breath. She knew he would have to be nearly on top of her before she could see who it was. His height was the same as Kevin's, and his girth matched as well. Yet there was something different about him. She held her breath as he came closer, fearful as a rabbit caught in a snare.

"Jenny?" he called softly, peering into the blackened

cavity beneath the stair. She started breathing again. Joshua had found her! Jumping up, she ran toward him, grateful for the massive arms which wrapped protectively around her.

"Girl . . . you gave me a fright!" he said, and unwound himself, happy he had found her in one piece. These were dangerous streets and times. Certainly no place for a lady.

"Is Aaron all right?" she asked breathlessly, wanting to hear the best, but fearing the worst.

"As far as I can tell. Those river rats hauled him down to the jail . . . but not before they laid him out cold."

There was a small silence, as he watched the hope fade from her eyes.

"It's all my fault . . ." she said bleakly. She tried desperately to think of a way to get his release.

"It ain't your fault, Jen. It's that damned Kevin! By the time I got back to the hotel, it was all over. Me and Mrs. Merit hauled Dugan up to bed. The doc's with him now. I think he's going to be all right, but Gannon was gone."

A muscle in his jaw worked, as he recalled the scene when he entered the dining room. When Mrs. Merit had told him about the cowardly way they had ambushed his boss, on top of beating poor old Dugan, he had felt a vengeful rage boiling in him that reached a peak he hadn't felt in years, especially after he had learned what Kevin had planned to do to Jenny.

"All's I know is, when Mr. Gannon gets out . . . there's gonna be hell to pay!" He planned on being there when it was dished out.

"Gets out? Joshua, how can he possibly get out? Kevin's brother-in-law is the sheriff!"

"Gannon's not without friends, girl," he sniffed indignantly. "Why, even the may—"

He cut himself off, leaving the word dangling in midair. The words of the only person in Kansas City with the power to free Gannon.

"The mayor," Jenny said dismally, supplying the word that he was hesitant to speak.

His heart went out to her. She looked so sad and helpless,

with her long hair falling loosely around her shoulders, and the white, oversize shirt draped over her, hanging nearly to her knees.

"He has other friends, too, Jenny," he added softly, wanting to spare her feelings as much as possible. "That fella out east, the politician who's always cookin' up those deals—why, he's got plenty of connections!" He started to sound a little more optimistic. "We can telegraph him first thing in the morning. I bet he'll be here in no time!"

"We don't have *any* time, Josh! Those men are planning to *kill* him!" Her voice broke and she choked back a sob.

"We gotta try, Jenny!"

His words were spoken in deadly earnest. Jenny could hear the rest of his thoughts as though he had spoken them aloud. "We gotta try, 'cause it's his only chance!"

"It's all my fault," she said quietly. "I've been nothing but trouble ever since I've come. He would still be friends with the mayor . . . if it hadn't been for me!" In a flash, she knew what she had to do.

"Joshua," she said, with grim determination etched in every line of her face, "take me to the mayor's house."

"What . . . *now?* Are you crazy?" he asked incredulously. "The butler'll take one look at us . . . especially at this ungodly hour of the night . . . and slam the damn door in our faces!"

The tears, which had rolled like crystal drops freely down her cheeks until now, were gone. One hung precariously from an eyelash, but stubbornly refused to fall. He could see that her mind was made up. With or without him, she would go . . . for what good it would do, he didn't know. With a sigh of resolution and a shrug of his massive shoulders, he agreed.

"They'll turn us away, Jen," he warned.

"I won't let them," she firmly resolved, her voice trembling with emotion. Her eyes, bright with the residue of tears, flashed in the street lamp's glow. "They *have* to help him. They just have to!"

Together, arm and arm, they started down the street, on the long walk that would take them to the mayor's mansion. One an awkward giant, still in his apron, the other a tiny, porcelain doll in a flowing white shirt—a woodlands troll and a flaxen-haired fairy, setting off to save a courageous prince.

CHAPTER

15

Let go of the bars, you dirty Irish bastard!"

The deputy smashed his club against the rusted, iron bars of the cell, nearly hitting the fingers which curled around them.

"Now get back, if ya want anything to eat," he warned.

Gannon's hands tingled as he stepped away from the doors. He longed to wrap his fingers around the thick throat of the swaggering deputy.

Nearly an hour ago he had come to, and found himself thrown on a hard, concrete floor, with Kevin leering at him from the other side of the bars.

"Where's Jenny?" he had groaned. "If you've hurt her, I swear, I'll kill you!" He had tried to push himself up, while every muscle in his body screamed in protest.

"No, I haven't hurt her . . . not yet." Then he grinned evilly. "Seems your little dolly has run away . . . but don't worry, I'll find her, and when I do, she'll be real sorry she made me come lookin'!" He laughed. "See you later, Gannon! That's a promise!" He left the room.

Now this deputy had him caged like an animal, with iron bars the only thing keeping him from finding Jenny.

It was totally dark outside. The one light burning on the wall, outside of his cell, gave only a feeble glow.

Gannon looked at the tray in the deputy's hands suspiciously.

"What are you trying to do?" he asked. "Poison me?"

"If Kevin had wanted you dead, mick . . . you wouldn't be talking *now,*" he sneered. "He just wants you to stay healthy so he can have some fun with you. Now . . . move away . . ." He slammed the club against the bars.

Gannon had seen his type many times before. Every word was yelled at the top of their voices; every word a threat intended to intimidate. Little men with big ideas, afraid of their own shadows, trying desperately to prove to the world and themselves that they were men.

"Why don't you put that stick aside, there, lad, and come in here and face me—man to man?" he said softly, slipping as easily into the soft rolling burr characteristic of his people, as into a well-worn pair of shoes. He challenged the deputy, keeping his voice calm and only slightly above a whisper. If he could get him to come in and he could overpower him, he might have a chance to escape.

The deputy, his key in the lock, stopped and glanced up uneasily.

A slow, deadly smile spread across Gannon's face and into his eyes, turning their mischievous twinkling green orbs into gleaming crystals of jade.

The key didn't turn, but stayed in the lock as both men eyed each other. The deputy, his bowels turning to jelly as he stared anxiously at the smiling Irishman, wanted desperately to run away from his steady, unwavering gaze. He knew he was no match for this man, but he couldn't let the others see how afraid he was.

"Bloyd!" he shouted nervously, causing Gannon's hope to disappear. "Hey, Bloyd! Come give me a hand with this mick—got a right smart mouth on him yet!"

"Be right there, Dean."

Gannon heard a chair squeak, and the scraping sounds of the legs, as it was pushed backward.

"It'll take more than two of you to bring me down, lad,"

he said softly. "But of course, you already know that. How many of you were there tonight? Three? Four? Seven?"

Sneering, the guard pulled the key from the lock and took one small step backward.

"You're gonna get it, Gannon! You're gonna get it good!"

Gannon could see right through him. He saw his fear. He grinned, stepping closer to the bars.

"Tell me, Deputy," he asked conversationally. "Did your Mum mistakenly cut off your balls when she circumcised you? Is *that* why you're such a bloated sack of cowardly shit?"

His voice never rose as he continued walking closer to the bars.

"Bloyd!" the deputy screamed in rage. "Bloyd . . . you get in here—NOW—I mean it!! This here big-shot, fancy-pants hotel owner's been saying some awful nasty things 'bout you . . . saying you ain't no man and all!"

A wicked look mixed with fear filled the deputy's young face.

"A liar, too," Gannon said. "A coward and a liar—makes you about worth spit, the way I see it."

Gannon was up to the bars now. Slowly he wrapped his fingers around them, his eyes never leaving the face of the quaking man on the other side. A look of mock sympathy replaced his grin as he slowly shook his head.

"Deputy?"

The deputy, the thick iron bars replacing his backbone, looked defiantly into his face. He suddenly wondered who was the prisoner and who was the jailer.

"You're no man, Deputy . . . none of you are. Just a pack of stinking dogs," he said. "You're not even worth the effort." Gannon spit on him.

Impotent rage boiled up in the deputy, as he rolled his arm across his face.

"You bastard!" he screamed. "We're gonna wrap your potato eating balls around your ears!"

"Come on, then," Gannon challenged defiantly. "I'm waiting!"

172

Two guards had come in; one was Kevin's brother-in-law, Bloyd. He searched the younger man's red face, trying to make some sense out of his anger.

"Dean?"

"I'm all right!" he hissed. "Come on—let's get him!"

He unlocked the door and the three of them marched through, slapping their clubs against their hands and cracking their leathers.

Gannon watched them come. He knew he was going to have to take a beating, but he was going to make them hurt too, hurt real bad.

They tried to circle around him, but he backed slowly away, wanting to keep the wall behind him. Then, eyeing each other, the guards waited for the first move.

Gannon smiled, watching the fear pop out of them like beads of sweat.

"What's the matter, boys?" he asked in a friendly voice. "Do you need a few more of you to make it even?" He laughed softly.

The guards looked at each other nervously. Their fingers clenched their weapons so tightly that their knuckles turned white. No one moved.

"Here, boys, let me make it easier for you," he said. He turned quickly, grabbing the fat deputy who had tried to hit his hand, and slammed his face hard against the old brick wall.

"You dirty, cowardly bastards!" roared Gannon. His iron fists began beating bloody paths wherever they landed.

More had come. More deputies into his cell. They used their sticks and leathers, their boots and fists. Gannon's head ached in a thousand places, as blood flowed like a curtain across his eyes. Still he fought. They were kicking him, the pointy toes of their boots gouging deep holes in his legs. Higher and higher they kicked as down to the floor he went. Still he fought, swinging his powerful hands, making the deputies hurt, until he couldn't feel anything anymore and he began to sink onto the cold, hard floor.

It should've been hard, he thought dreamily, and cold, but

it wasn't. With every ounce of strength he had left, he pushed with his legs and moved his arms, not sure he was hitting anything, but not willing to give in.

He felt that he was floating in a sea of bright, red pain. He knew that they were still kicking and beating him with their sticks, but it didn't matter anymore. His head had touched the floor. Its cold, white softness turning into a black wall that rushed toward him.

"Jen," he whispered softly, as the darkness enveloped him and he knew no more.

CHAPTER

16

They stayed off the main roads, taking the narrow, winding lanes that led like a maze toward the mayor's mansion. The streets were deserted and still, and even the breeze had ceased to blow. One set of stars had moved, and another had taken its place. The night was tired and nearly worn through, and dawn was quickly approaching.

Slowly, the houses had changed, going from towering old brownstone tenements to small, clapboard-sided homes, placed so closely the windows nearly touched. Some were decorated with porches and bric-a-brac sidewalks. Others sprouted round medieval towers, with cone-shaped roofs and elaborate stained glass windows. The further away from the center of town they walked, the more beautiful and ornate the houses became, until they sprawled on mani-cured acres, all alone, with odd-shaped hedges, and filigreed, wrought iron gates surrounded by stone fences, higher than a man could look over. The mayor's house was the last of these, sitting haughtily and aloof at the end of a circular drive. No golden lights warmed its chilly facade tonight, and no music spilled out gaily into the hushed night air. The only light which shone issued from a lower window, in what Jenny knew to be the hall.

"They're all sleepin'," Joshua whispered. The quiet was beginning to get on his nerves.

"Then we'll wake them," she announced, walking straight up the winding front stairs and pounding loudly on the huge, double doors.

"Jen! Jen! Take it easy—we want their help, don't make them mad!"

But it was too late. Her fists, though small, had hit the wood as hard as she could. The sound had echoed and reverberated nearly two stories up in the empty foyer, until it sounded like thunder.

A light up above snapped on, and one further toward the east end followed. Joshua felt like a schoolboy who had just pulled a prank and was about to get caught. His body was all geared to run like hell, until he looked at her face.

Quiet determination showed in every line. Gannon had said she was stubborn, mule-headed, and willful. With a sinking feeling in his stomach as the sound of shuffling footsteps came nearer, he knew it was true. She had no intention of leaving till she got what she wanted.

The bolts slid back, and the door opened with a barely audible squeak to reveal a man, still in his nightcap, holding a lamp and peering through barely opened eyes.

Joshua sighed. It was too late to run now.

"Yes?" the butler asked. He couldn't hide the irritation in his voice, or the snobbishness of his gaze when he looked at their rough attire.

"I want to see the mayor, please," Jenny said firmly.

His eyebrows nearly disappeared beneath his cap. "Really? Well, I hardly think that's possible." He started to close the door, but Jenny pushed against it, running inside.

"Now, see here, miss!" he spluttered. Joshua, worried about Jenny, shoved his way past him as well.

"This is most irregular . . . most irregular!"

"I need to see the mayor, sir. It's a matter of life and death!"

"It always is, you little vagabond. You'll not see our mayor, or anyone else in this house for that matter. I must *insist* that you leave this house *immediately*, before I am

176

forced to take action!" He stamped his slippered foot for emphasis.

Joshua hid a smile on his face when the little butler, in his matching, pin-striped nightshirt and cap, said this. He knew what an idle threat it was. The butler, flushing with embarrassment, did too. But there were other men here. The gardener, for example . . . a large, swarthy man of questionable reputation. The butler was getting ready to call on him when a soft light fell on them from above. Turning, they all saw Penelope on the open stairway. She was dressed in a satin pink wrap and matching slippers, with ribbons of the same hue tied charmingly in her hair. Her lips, however, did not look charming, or sweet. They were curled into a sneer when she recognized who stood in her hall.

Jenny rushed to her immediately. Penelope backed away, as though the thought of Jenny touching her was too repugnant.

"Please, Penelope . . . I must see your father! It's . . . it's a matter of life and death!"

"Ohhh . . . rea-lly!" She laughed a little at the bedraggled girl standing before her, not one bit concerned as to how she had come to look that way. Then her laughter died. She stared hard at Jenny's disheveled appearance, angry that even dressed as she was, she was still fetchingly attractive. "My name is *Miss Kenton* to *you,*" she ordered harshly. "My father isn't here, but even if he was, I doubt that he'd see you . . . that is, unless you happen to be soliciting *his* favors as well. I've heard from my mother that he isn't above *coarse* amusements."

"Why you . . ." Joshua stepped angrily forward, ready to give Penelope a piece of his mind, when Jenny stopped him with a look. She turned to face Penelope again.

"It doesn't matter what you think of me, Penelope," she said quietly. "Gannon is in terrible danger. He needs your father's help."

"Gannon? Nonsense! That *man* has more lives than a cat—an *alley* cat that is—who could possibly do *him* harm? What's more, after he made such a fool of *me* in front of all my *friends,* at my *own* father's party, I might add—why would I, or any member of my family lift a finger to help him?"

"Because," Jenny pointed out flatly, *"you* want *him."*

"Well," she sniffed petulantly, *"you've* taken care of that, now—haven't you?"

Jenny saw a spoiled brat, pouting in front of her, because her pride had been injured. She didn't love him, Jenny knew that. He was just something to parade up and down in front of her friends, a trophy she could escort to her different parties. He was just something she could add to herself, because there was so little there.

"Please, Pen . . . Miss Kenton . . . I'm begging you! Kevin and his brother-in-law, the sheriff, are holding him at the jail, and beating him senseless . . ."

"On what charge?" she asked haughtily, starting to feel the power she had over Jenny.

"There isn't any charge. Kevin and his men ambushed him at the hotel and dragged him off. They thought that since your family and he weren't getting along, he wouldn't have anyone powerful enough to help him."

Penelope frowned. "Why would they go to all this trouble in the first place? What did Aaron ever do to this man?"

She searched Jenny's face for a clue, but she remained totally quiet, not wanting to go into detail. All she wanted was for someone to help Gannon . . . no matter what it cost.

"It doesn't matter, Miss Kenton." Jenny rummaged inside of her pocket and brought out the chunk of gold. "Take this . . ." she offered, extending her hand.

"A rock?" Penelope asked, looking puzzled.

"Gold," Jenny said quietly. "All that I have."

"Pooh!" Penelope said. "What do I need with that? We have more money than anyone. Besides, how do I know that isn't just a filthy old rock and you're trying to trick me?"

Jenny looked helplessly from Joshua to Penelope. She was desperate.

"Penelope, *please* . . . I'll do anything you ask . . . anything! You must help Gannon!"

Penelope's eyes lit up. "You'll do whatever I *want?"* she

asked slyly, not able to believe her good fortune. Jenny nodded her head.

"Don't, Jenny . . ." warned Josh, seeing Penelope for the scheming bitch she really was. "The little tart is laying for you."

Penelope threw Joshua a scathing look, but seemed unaffected by the word he had called her.

"Anything?" she repeated, a little louder, and more demanding.

"Yes . . . anything!"

"Hmmm . . ." She tapped her finger thoughtfully against her lips. "They're beating him you say? Down at the jail?" But she wasn't really listening for a reply, as she became agitated and began pacing back and forth on the stair. "And only *my* father can help him? Is that correct?"

Jenny nodded her head, and Penelope smiled brightly.

"And you'll do *anything* I ask if we free Gannon?"

"How many times you gotta ask her?" growled Joshua.

"I just want to get the rules straight. Don't interrupt me again, or I'll have my men toss you out. *Anything*, Jenny?"

Jenny nodded her head mutely, and her shoulders sagged. Anything . . . she'd do absolutely anything for him.

"Leave," Penelope said simply.

Jenny looked up, puzzled. Did she mean now? Wasn't she going to help Gannon?

"I want you to leave Kansas City, Jenny, and never come back. That's the price I'm asking for Gannon's life. Do we have a deal?" She smiled sweetly.

Jenny was reeling. It was one thing to be angry at him and plot revenge by running away, but it was quite another to actually *leave* him, never to look upon his face, or hear his quiet laughter, or feel the strength of his arms around her again. How could she stand it? How could she possibly live? But what alternatives did she have? If she stayed Penelope would never ask her father to help him. Kevin would almost certainly kill him before she could get help. It was a devil's bargain she was forced to make, but one she had no choice in.

"Yes," she whispered. "We have a deal."

"Wonderful!" Penelope clapped her hands together excitedly.

"Jenny! Do you know what you're saying?" Joshua exclaimed. "How can you leave Gannon? You love him! Besides, where would you go? You've got no money . . . nothing!"

"I've got my gold, Josh. I'll go to Alaska with my uncle. He said he would wait for me as long as he could. Maybe you could go back to the hotel and pick up my belongings, and tell everyone . . . tell everyone . . ." A single tear worked its way out from inside. "No . . . Josh, don't tell them anything. I'll wait for you at the station. My uncle should be there, somewhere."

Joshua shook his head. "I think you're making a mistake, Jenny."

"It's the only way, Joshua. Don't you see?"

What he saw was her heart breaking in her eyes, and he envied Gannon the love this girl felt for him.

Penelope was delighted. This was better than Christmas morning! She had Gannon all to herself! Jenny had practically gift-wrapped him, and made him ready for her bed. She couldn't be happier.

Jenny, on the other hand, felt as though a part of her were dying.

"Arthur, you can show these . . . people . . . out now. And remember, Jenny," Penelope warned. "If he finds out about this, or you come back, I'll make sure he pays as well as you. My father can ruin him. My father does whatever I ask!"

She giggled as she turned and rushed up the stairs, her head full of Florence Nightingale and grateful patients who had been half beaten to death and whom she had so carefully nursed back to health.

The door was opened and the two were ushered out. Dawn's pale pink fingers had stretched upward from the horizon.

"So little time," Jenny whispered. Joshua knew she meant the time she had spent with Gannon.

Quietly they walked down the stairway, heading west, where the sun's light had not yet reached. The late September breeze had awakened and begun to stir the nearly naked branches of the trees, sending wispy black shadows dancing against the lighted brick pavement. Their sibilant movements were applauded by the few remaining leaves. Circumstances beyond her control had flung her into Gannon's world and into his arms. Their destinies had met and meshed, and they had become one, if only for a little while. Fate had again destroyed what she loved, not by death—although it might as well have been—but by the miles she was forced to put between them. Her dreams were shattered, her future unknown, as she took her first few steps in a journey that would lead her toward a land she had only read about . . . a land of crystal ice and blinding white snow. A land without Gannon.

CHAPTER

17

Pain filled his mind as he struggled to wake up. One eye refused to open, and his head felt as if it were about to explode.

He was still on the floor. He felt the cold bricks beneath his face and sensed that the light had changed. How long had he been out? He tried to push up with his hands, and winced again. Better not try that again, he thought. Better see if anything's been broken first.

He clenched the fingers of his hands, scraping something hard and crusty underneath. Mud? he thought dully. Slowly he opened his eyes and tried to focus, ignoring the pain. It wasn't mud he was lying in, but a thin pool of his own blood, dried to a crust. Nausea washed over him and he closed his eyes against it.

Thoughts flooded his brain. The memories of the fights, the one in the hotel and the other in the jail. He could see the deputies with their clubs, and the railway workers' staring faces. A composite of the last few days danced through his mind. Behind it all he could see Jenny leaving, running through the door of the hotel, out into the night. Running away from Kevin. And him.

"Jenny," he whispered. The longing made him weak. He

didn't know where she had gone, or if Kevin had found her. He pushed up again, ignoring the pain and trying to stand up. He swayed slightly and walked toward the bars.

"Deputy," he called. "Deputy . . . would you be willing to let me out of here, for, say, a small fee?"

"I wouldn't let you outta there if you gave me the keys to the bank!" he growled, rubbing the swollen purple skin over his eyes.

"Then perhaps you'd let Mr. Gannon out in lieu of losing your position with our fine city, Deputy."

The deputy jumped to his feet, letting the chair he'd been resting on clatter noisily to the ground. He hadn't heard anyone come in.

"Mayor Kenton!" he said in surprise. He tried to smooth the rumpled uniform he was wearing.

"Can you tell me on what charges you're holding Mr. Gannon, Deputy?"

"Charges?" the deputy asked nervously, praying that Bloyd would come in. "Well . . . uh, Bloyd says we should, on account of . . . on account of . . ." His eyes darted around the room as he wracked his brain for a reason. "Well, he just said we should. He's our *sheriff!"*

"And I'm your *mayor,* and I'm telling you to release Mr. Gannon immediately!"

The mayor's expression of pompous authority was not wasted on the deputy.

"Yes, sir, Mr. Mayor. Right away, sir!" The deputy hastily obeyed, dragging out a set of jangling keys from his pocket.

The mayor looked at Gannon, expecting a torrent of gratitude, but received only a cool stare as Gannon wondered what this favor was going to cost him.

"Well," he blustered, "you needn't *thank* me, Gannon!" he said, lacing his voice with as much sarcasm as he could. "After all, getting you out of jail was nothing . . . I've only just returned from Boston this very morning. I've neither eaten nor slept all night!"

Gannon let him rattle on for another five minutes, while the deputy fumbled with the lock. When there was a temporary lull in his speech, Gannon spoke up.

"Where *is* the sheriff?" he asked quietly, aching to get his hands on him.

"The *former* sheriff," he said, emphasizing "former" with a sneer, "is being held in custody, until I can get to the bottom of this whole affair. I don't mind telling you . . ."

"And Kevin?" interrupted Gannon.

Not used to being stopped in the middle of what he was saying, the mayor looked slightly taken aback.

"Oh . . . uh, Kevin . . ." He frowned. "Do you mean that rough Irish lugger who used to run your, uh, products?"

The mayor was trying hard to refer to Gannon's illegal whiskey trade without coming right out into the open and saying it. Gannon would have smiled if his jaw hadn't ached so, because the mayor was one of his biggest customers. Instead, he just nodded his head, not letting his face show the turmoil he felt inside. Wherever Kevin was, he prayed it wasn't near Jenny.

"Oh, sad situation, that one . . . found him in the water this morning, down by the wharf, belly-up. Must've tied on a good one, and lost his footing or something. There was a rather nasty looking gash on the back of his head when they fished him out."

"Was there anyone else?" Gannon held his breath.

"Else? You mean floating in the water?" he asked in surprise. "Why would there be?"

The rest of what the mayor said was lost on Gannon as he ignored the pain in his head. He walked through the cell, out of the building, and down to the street. He could hear the mayor talking as he walked along beside him, but he wasn't paying any attention to what he said. He had other things on his mind.

"Here, Gannon . . . here's my carriage."

Gannon looked where the mayor had pointed. He could see his buggy parked alongside the curb, and he nearly groaned out loud. Sitting side by side, dressed in yards of ruffles, with their parasols opened above their heads, were Mrs. Kenton and Penelope, beaming at him with tender, motherly concern and . . . triumph?

"Oh, *poor* Aaron!" Penelope gushed, doing her best to exude just the right degree of shock and concern. "What have those evil, evil men done to you?!" She extended her delicately white, gloved hand, hoping that he would take it, even if it meant ruining a brand new pair of France's finest imported gloves. "We must get you to a doctor!" she exclaimed.

This was absolutely the last thing he needed today. Sighing, he took her hand, and climbed into the coach.

"Now . . ." she said confidently, secretly delighting at what an angel of mercy this would make her seem to all her friends. "You just come along home with us! Mama and I will see that you're properly taken care of. Won't we, Mama?"

"Of course we will, my dear!" She reached across and patted his hand with one of hers, already picking out the silver patterns and china for their wedding, mentally running through the list of all the "right" people she intended to invite.

Gannon noted without amusement that she wore one of her ridiculous hats again, only this one had pendulous globes of fruit hanging from it instead of feathers. He wordlessly resigned himself to less than a pleasant drive, as he settled back against the seat while the mayor sat down beside him.

The driver turned expectantly, and before anyone else could utter a word, Gannon spoke.

"The hotel, driver," he ordered. It was little more than a growl. The driver, not one to argue, especially with someone notorious for his right crosses, gave a curt nod. Turning, he clucked softly to his horses, snapping their behinds lightly with his whip, and the carriage lurched forward.

The patronizingly sweet smile Penelope had worn was now edged with acid. Her eyes had lost their confident gleam, becoming hard and scheming. This was not turning out the way she wanted at all!

"But, Mr. Gannon . . ." she protested. "You can't possibly go home! You need attention, and tender *loving* care . . .

which Mama and I are quite ready to provide!" She was starting to pout again, unable to believe he would turn down so wonderful an offer.

Gannon wondered if he would last the ride, as he pretended not to notice the slippered foot which inched its way over to his leg and began to rub against his calf. Mama had noticed, smiling with satisfaction, sure that her darling Penelope had him now. Papa cleared his throat, pretending not to see.

"We'd take *very* good care of you," she murmured huskily, in what she thought was a breathlessly sexy voice.

"I'm sure you *would,* Penelope." He wondered if she had ever had an honest emotion in her life. He watched her face and hands and voice fall easily into the roles she wanted to portray as any veteran actress playing a part would do. "It isn't that I don't appreciate everything you and your family have done for me this morning. . . ." He nodded in the mayor's direction. "Because I do, and I will never forget it. But there are things I need to take care of at the hotel. They cannot wait." He winced as the carriage hit a bump.

"No doubt," Penelope said spitefully, unable to hide the malicious smile on her face. "Business must be run . . . 'things' taken care of." She pulled her foot away from his leg, staring angrily out the window. Maybe when he found out that the "things" he needed to take care of had left him, running off to Alaska, or some other godforsaken wilderness, well . . . maybe *then* he'd come to his senses! She shook her head slightly, causing her bonny golden curls to bounce, unable to imagine, outside of a few obvious physical attractions, how he could possibly prefer Jenny to her.

The drive was nearly over, ending in an awkward silence as the carriage pulled up in front of the hotel. Before it had even come to a full stop, Gannon was bounding out of it, running to the door. All was strangely quiet. No ladies strolled the sidewalk, or workers eager to get a decent meal stood outside. The bright blue sky and lemon-yellow sun, so happily shining, seemed like an illusion as he stared at his hotel. The shades were drawn and the door stood silent and shut. Scrawled in an irregular script, a sign stood resting against the front window. "Closed for Repairs" it read. Gannon barely noticed it as he rushed through the door and into the hallway.

It was dark inside and it took a moment for his eyes to adjust to the comparative gloom after the glaringly bright light of the morning outside. The drapes had not been opened and everywhere he looked was a mess. Chairs were tipped and broken, and tables were strewn about. The air was heavy and still, no breeze freshened or stirred it. All was nervously quiet. It looked as if a tornado had built up within the hotel, wreaking havoc with everything, leaving nothing except the windows intact.

"Jenny!" he shouted, at the top of his voice. Her name echoed loudly.

There were no sounds coming from anywhere, no people talking, or clattering of pots and pans. Nothing but silence.

He ran to the study and flung open the door. It was just as silent, and just as empty as the hall. Without pausing, he turned and headed for the stairs, taking them two at a time, calling her name all the way up.

The mayor and his wife stood watching him from the doorway. She was glaring at him, feeling that he was being insulting again. The mayor just sighed and looked extremely tired. Penelope had followed Gannon into the hallway. What a fool he was making of himself over the little slut, she thought angrily, and in front of *her!* Hands on hips, her foot tapping furiously, she waited for him to come to his senses.

Up above, out of their sight, Gannon had come to Jenny's room. He knocked with such force, it threatened to split the wood, and entered even before his fist had stopped striking the door. He called her name softly, his heart beating furiously in his chest as he looked around the room. It was as it always was, clean and neat as a pin. But empty as well.

Slowly he turned and walked to the landing, uneasy thoughts forming in his mind. She wasn't here. Thankfully, she wasn't at the wharf, floating in the dirty, black waters beside Kevin. Feelings he had not allowed himself to feel since he was a child began to surface. He remembered his beautiful mother and their last days together in the run-down shantytown. How they had existed from day to day, beneath the crumbling ruin of an old brownstone, with no heat or food, no comfort except each other. She had lain in a filthy hole, until her body, tortured by the twin demons of hunger and numbing cold, had finally succumbed to the shadowy death which lurked in every alley and corner of that part of town. Even his small hands, rubbing her limbs as furiously as he could, would not bring back their warmth, or the fire of her life. He was powerless to save her. She had died and it had hurt so bad that he vowed, even then, to never let anyone that close again. But he hadn't known about Jenny. Her existence, miles away, across stormy seas, in lands he'd only read about, he hadn't foreseen. And when they met, he'd forgotten about his childhood oath and fallen desperately in love with her.

Now he stood in his hotel, wondering where she was, while the same feelings of helplessness and fear he'd known as a boy came back to haunt him, twining together like an icy braid that wound itself around his heart and threatened to choke the life from him.

"Where are you, Jenny?" he whispered to the silent room.

Maybe the kitchen, or out back, his mind hastened to reply. But the part of him that sensed things that his logical mind would never accept, knew she wouldn't be in either place. One day last month, an odd notion had entered his thoughts as he watched her work. He felt as if he were looking at his twin, even though her coloring and size were nearly opposite to his. It was as if he had found a piece of himself that was missing, like the last part of a jigsaw puzzle, that made him complete. They were linked, tied together by a cord of magically woven light that reached between walls and miles, binding them together, making them one. He had to find her. His own life and sanity depended on it.

Below the landing, gazing up at him, stood Mrs. Merit and the others, watching him as he approached the staircase. Like a man caught in a dream, he barely noticed them.

"Where is she?" he asked softly, directing his question to

Mrs. Merit. A dull throbbing pain had begun at the back of his head.

Mrs. Merit, her old heart filled with pity as she looked at his lost and battered face, searched her mind for the right words—the words that would take the razor sharp edge off the painful truth—that she was gone, running off to Alaska with Joshua, and even she didn't know why.

He took a step forward and placed his hand on the railing.

"Where?" he demanded, his voice regaining some of the force it usually carried.

"Gone, sir . . ." She stopped, unable to finish.

"Gone? Gone *where?* To the market? Shopping? *Where?"*

"Alaska, Mr. Gannon . . . with . . ." She hesitated, not wanting to add the rest. "Joshua."

"Alaska . . . with Joshua!?" He tried not to believe what he was hearing. "I don't understand . . . what did she say?"

"I didn't talk to her, sir. Joshua came back early this morning to get his things and hers. I asked him where Jenny was, and why he was taking them. He said he couldn't tell me! Then he asked how Dugan was, and I told him he'd be fine. He just nodded his head and started for the door . . ." Color was flushing Mrs. Merit's cheeks as she relived the incident in her mind. She was getting worked up and angry all over again. "It was right about then that I started getting pretty upset. He'd worked for you all those years, Mr. Gannon, and he didn't even ask how you were! So I said, 'Joshua, don't you and Jenny even care about poor Mr. Gannon? How can you leave him when he needs you, especially as kind and good as he's always been to the *both* of you!' And then he said to me, with kind of a funny look on his face, that you didn't need anyone, because you had an angel looking out for you . . . and then he left." She frowned and bit her lip, remembering how confused she was. It was so hard for her to believe that Jenny could actually leave, and not say a word, or leave a message . . . and why should an old man like Joshua forfeit the security of a good job to run off to some wilderness? It just didn't make any sense. None at all.

Gannon struggled with the same questions. Like Mrs. Merit, he failed to understand what had happened or why Jenny had left. Mrs. Merit saw pain in his eyes, a deep hurt that didn't have anything to do with his bruised body.

Quietly, guarding his every word, he spoke, still unable to accept that she had gone.

"Is there a *note,* Mrs. Merit? *Anything* that might explain *why* she went?"

His voice started to rise. Anger, born of betrayal, had begun to build inside of him, replacing his hurt. He had been beaten half to death trying to protect her, and she had run out on him, not even bothering to find out if he were dead or alive.

"Nothing, sir . . ." Mrs. Merit said softly, looking at him sadly.

A shaft of light had snuck between the pleated folds of the drapes, illuminating his face. Cuts covered his lips, and his cheeks were swollen black and blue. But worse than all the physical wounds he had suffered was the way his eyes looked. Lost and haunted, staring at nothing, slowly beginning to fill with tears. The small cord that he felt had bound them together in his mind was being stretched to an impossible limit. He was afraid that it would break and he would start to bleed inside, where no one could see except himself.

"Damn her!" he cried angrily, his voice trembling with rage. He gripped the railing so hard that his knuckles turned white. With eyes flashing, he started to turn toward his room.

"Pack my bags!" he growled. "And bring my horse around—I'll teach her to play games with me!"

"But, sir . . . where are you going? What about the hotel?"

"You can run the hotel, Mrs. Merit . . . and Dugan will help when he is better. By then I should be back."

"Back, sir? Where are *you* going?"

"Alaska!" he shouted. "To find that little Judas!"

Mrs. Merit was instantly all smiles. "You're going to bring Jenny home, sir?" she asked hopefully.

He nodded his head, knowing that what he was doing was totally insane and damning himself for his own weakness.

"If I don't kill her first," he muttered under his breath. He turned, stalking angrily down the hall until he entered his room, slamming the door shut with a resounding whack.

"Well!" huffed Mrs. Kenton, pivoting on one of her delicately shod heels. "Come, Penelope! There is no point in waiting any longer . . . that ungrateful wretch!" Without so much as a backward glance, she left the hotel.

Mayor Kenton sighed wearily. "Come along, dear . . . it's time to leave."

"But, Daddy!" Penelope protested loudly. "He can't go to Alaska . . . it's all been planned . . . I've even told my friends that we are *unofficially* engaged! Make him stay, Daddy!" she demanded, stamping her foot.

"I couldn't make that man stay if I held a gun to his head! Now, please, *dear* . . . let us leave him in peace!"

She was so like her mother, he thought sadly, taking a firm hold on her arm, knowing that when Penelope finally *did* land a man, he, too, would spend an awful lot of time away from home.

"But, Daddy! Ouch, Daddy . . . don't pull! Da-ad-yeee!"

The mayor urged her forward, deaf to her pleas, shutting the door behind them and leaving Mrs. Merit standing all alone in the empty foyer, wondering what could possibly happen next.

CHAPTER

18

The ship had rocked and pitched for days. It hadn't taken her long before she became used to its rolling motion and could walk about freely, preferring this method of travel over the chugging, bumpy, stifling train ride she had endured weeks ago.

Joshua had found her uncle resting as comfortably on the platform of the railway station as if he were lying in his own bed. He seemed surprised and happy when he saw her. But when he noticed her appearance and the redness of her eyes, his smile had faded, and he demanded to know what had happened. She told him very briefly about that night, omitting nothing, ending with her decision to accompany him to Alaska.

He had shaken his head, tugging thoughtfully at his beard.

"You shouldn't give in to her, Missy," he said. "As much as I want you with me . . . that there Penelope ain't got no right pullin' such an ornery trick!"

He was all fired up. Ready to go back and do battle against the conniving Penelope, and the crooked and cowardly sheriff.

"No, John . . . it wouldn't work," she said tiredly. "All of

Aaron's men are either in jail, or gone. Without Penelope's help, he wouldn't last till morning. It's the only way."

"Well, then, you let him know when we gets to Alaska. Write him, same as you did me. Don't leave him thinkin' you done run out on him."

"I can't, John . . . I promised."

"Promised . . . promises . . . they's fer honorable people. The way that young girl acted, I don't reckon she's none too straight. Let her get him out . . . then let him know what happened. Don't let that boy think you done him dirt!"

Too tired to fight with him, she just sighed, sitting down at the edge of the platform and letting her head sink into her lap. Leaving Gannon was the hardest thing she had ever done. It left her feeling weak and drained.

She heard a crinkling, rustling sound, and felt something heavy and soft fall across her shoulders. Looking up, she noticed that John had taken his heavy coat of fox furs off and draped that around her. He grinned sheepishly.

"That's my new one. You won't be sharing it with nothing else but yourself!"

"Sharing it?" she asked in confusion, her weary brain refusing to think.

"Yup . . . it's new. It ain't had enough time for those little white critters you call 'lice' to set up house."

She jumped to her feet, letting the coat slide to the ground.

"Lice?" she asked in horror, wondering how many more terrors she would face tonight.

"Yeah . . . but like I told ya. This here coat is *new* . . . made it before I come down here. I ain't had to pick even *one* of them outta it!" he said proudly. "So, you jest snuggle yourself up in it, and get some rest, whilst your friend picks up your things. We got us a long journey to take." He reached over and handed her the coat, which she took and placed around her shoulders, sure that each time a silken piece of fur tickled her cheek, it was one of his "little critters" just being neighborly.

The sun was clearly visible now, and the platform crowded with people, before Joshua came back with her things. It was nearly 10:00 A.M. The train was taking on water and coal, and when John saw all the baggage piled on the loading platform, he frowned.

"I know women need a lot of gear . . ." he stated, "but, I never reckoned on *this* much!"

"It isn't all mine," she said quietly, not sure if this was the right time to tell her uncle about Joshua's plans. "Joshua has decided to go with us, too."

"What in thunderation would that ol' walrus want to trail after us fer?" he angrily asked. "I only got just enough money for the *two* of us . . . and that's all I booked passage fer on the ship!"

"I have my *own* money, you crazy old son of a bitch—and if the ship doesn't have enough room for me in the cabins, I'll sleep on deck!"

Joshua looked angry. His face was flushed and his eyes shone hard, glittering like dark topaz beneath his deep-set brows. He had thrust out his lower lip and chest, making him seem even larger than his already towering size.

"Besides, what would make you think I'd let a sweet girl like her run off without *some* protection!"

"Yer tellin' me, yer goin' all the way to Alaska jest so's you kin protect *my* niece?!" he asked skeptically. "What yer really sayin' then, is *you* don't trust me to take care of her!"

"You said it, old man!" he retorted. "I don't have no reason to trust you, and I don't want to see nothin' happen to her. She's been through enough!"

The two eyed each other tensely, one as gnarled and bent as a piece of driftwood, the other, massive as a bear.

"She's my kin," John stated evenly. "My only living flesh 'n blood. I'd sooner lose both my arms than let any harm come to her. Besides, just what do you think you'll *do* when you get there? It ain't like Kansas City with all its fancy folk and fine hotels!"

"They *eat*, don't they? Maybe I can get a job cooking for a while."

John eyed him suspiciously. "A while? You sound like a man that plans on doing *other* things."

"What if I am?" he retorted. "You think a man's gotta

cook all his life? I got dreams too!" he said defensively, puffing out his chest even further.

John was about to say more, when a loud, long blast shrieked through the air, followed by several shorter ones. It was time to board.

"John, Joshua . . . it's time to leave," Jenny piped in, grateful the departure whistle had ended their battle. But she knew by the hostile way the two men glared at each other while gathering the bags that their feud was far from being over. The three boarded the crowded train in utter silence, searching the benches till they found a place where they could sit together. They piled their luggage in every conceivable spot, beside them, around their feet, and even under them, trying hopelessly to find some measure of comfort in the mob of people who were all heading west.

The train ride was stifling and hot. She had barely noticed the landscape's changing faces, or heard the petty squabbles that had become a daily event between her uncle and Joshua. Babies cried, mothers soothed in strange tongues, and fathers stared, wondering what futures they had claimed for themselves and their families. Most were farmers, migrating from Europe, with the promise of free land spurring them on. Their faces read like diaries, where lines etched in furrowed brows of deep brown skin told stories more vivid than the written word. Hardships were common to their lives. But all these things were lost on her, as the realization began to dawn that with every chugging beat of the old steam engine's heart, she was being carried further away from Kansas City . . . further away from Gannon. The barren plains she stared at but didn't see could not have been more desolate than her soul. And the hunger she felt that made her ache and burn by dizzying turns could not be quenched with food or water. She knew she would write to him as soon as she could, knowing that even a page of words would soothe her jangled nerves, just as his shirt, tucked beneath her head at night like a pillow, or clasped to her breast in her sleep, gave her peace. It still carried the spicy clean smell he wore.

And now they were closer to Anchorage. Every day, the

rocking blue waters brought them nearer. She loved the ocean. Standing at the rail, she would stare into its gray-green depths or look out toward the horizon where water and sky merged. The colors fascinated her, changing without warning. Sunlight would paint the waves flaming oranges and reds, which the wind would whip into a wild dance, its white crested peaks pointing like pale fingers toward the heavens.

The farther north they went, the more turbulent the waters became. Cold, gray fog enveloped them in the mornings. Once at twilight, when the sun was just about to sink into the sea, she had watched a cloud bank scuttle across the surface of the water toward them. It had filled her with wonder, but also a little fear. Nature is a mystery, she thought, sighing as she watched pale Venus glow brighter by the moment as the last sliver of sun slipped away.

Today she would find out if Alaska was more than she had imagined, or less. The captain had said they would be docking by late afternoon. She watched eagerly for the coastline to appear.

The wind began to pick up, blowing the fog away in little pieces. The air was brisk, and the tang of salt spray fell on her face with each forward roll of the ship. She clung easily to the rail, anxious for her first glimpse of the Alaskan coastline.

"Land!" someone yelled. "Land, ho!"

A sailor, straddling the yardarm high above her head, had sighted the coast.

Clang-clang! Clang-clang! The bell began to peal and the activity aboard the ship increased.

She glanced from the sailor above her back toward the horizon, her eyes straining in the afternoon light. She couldn't see anything, just a rolling, gray expanse.

"Come on, lads. Trim her up a bit, and send her in!" shouted the captain from behind her. She turned and saw that he was standing beside her uncle, studying her. His face was stern and weatherworn, with wrinkled nut-brown wood that passed for skin, surrounded on all sides by a startling white beard and hair. Her uncle and he seemed to be cut from the same cloth, except where the captain's face appeared grave and austere, her uncle's showed good humor, and his eyes always seemed to twinkle.

A sudden pitching of the ship caused her to lose her balance. She started to fall forward.

"Easy, Missy—this here ain't no ballroom," John warned, catching her easily.

"Thanks," she said, smiling. He nodded his head and let go of her arm.

She was coming to like him very much, but still couldn't bring herself to call him "uncle." He was too much of a stranger to her yet, and it was hard for her to reconcile the image she had carried with her for so many years, because of his poetic and sensitive letters, with the crusty frontiersman standing in front of her.

"We need to set a spell and talk, Jenny. We're almost there."

"Of course, John."

He guided her to a pile of flour sacks stacked on the deck, covered with canvas to keep out the rain. The captain had returned to the wheel.

"What I got to say ain't gonna be easy, but it needs sayin'." He paused, sorting out the words he needed to use, delicate words. Words that he could write with pen and ink, but words that stuck like glue in his throat when he tried to speak. "Ya see . . . you're a white woman, Jenny, and there ain't many of them in these parts, 'specially *pretty* ones. The women what comes here, gets bought and sold . . . sorta' like cattle, from the mainland. 'Less, of course, they're already married afore they come."

He sat down heavily next to her, letting out a large sigh, and continued. "Alaska, Missy, is a place so beautiful it can clean take your breath from you. But she's untamed . . . hard times is common there. There's mining and logging startin' up, and it will be a while b'fore it gets goin' good. Alaska ain't like you suppose . . . it ain't no paradise, Jenny. It's a rugged land."

"But, John . . ." she started to protest, remembering all his letters, praising the country, its beauty, and its people.

He raised his hands to silence her.

"I know . . . my letters. Well, what I said was true . . . mostly. But you got to understand . . . it's *new* to the white man . . . some might even call it a savage place, dog-eat-dog, every man for hisself. Me, painting Alaska into a rosy picture and winter jest knockin' on the door . . . it weren't right. But all I want you to do is give it a fair chance. Maybe that fella you keep pining over these past weeks would like to give it a shot too. There'd be no limit what a man with some drive and a good head on his shoulders could accomplish. Besides, I'm getting on in years. I could use a strong partner with a good back at the mine."

He looked out toward the rugged coastline that had grown clearer by the minute, and thoughtfully pulled his beard. She was silent, wondering what he would say next.

"Seems I know a lady in Anchorage . . . tough as nails, she is, but I reckon if we play our cards right . . . she might let us stay on a while, till we get enough gear to go on. Maybe she'll even give us a little work."

Jenny looked doubtful. "Work? What kind of work?"

"She owns The Miner in Anchorage. It's the only hotel there is, not as elegant as your Mr. Gannon's, but the best one around. Me and her go way back. She'd probably do a favor for an old friend, and if I kin get Tanith on our side, I know she won't refuse!"

His eyes were twinkling, and he smiled.

"She's tough . . . like I said. Has a few girls besides, but I know she'd look out after you like you was her very own!"

"Girls?" Jenny repeated hopefully. "Oh, that's wonderful!" The thought of having female friends to talk to and share things with made her happy instantly. "How many daughters does she have?"

John nearly choked. "Daughters?!" he spluttered. "They, uh," he fumbled for the right words. She was so damned innocent! "They ain't *exactly* her daughters . . . they're more like, well . . . oh, you'll just have to wait and see when you get there!" He finished his explanation hurriedly and stood up. "Get yer things ready, Missy . . . there be Anchorage to yer left," he said, and pointed.

She looked and could make out the dim outline of a few buildings on the coastline, surrounded by a semicircle of towering peaks. Black, rocking, pencil-thin sticks of ships anchored in the harbor came into view. Her heart began to beat rapidly. Anchorage . . . at last!

CHAPTER

19

Alaskan night comes early in October and stays late. The sun was setting, and it was only 4:00 P.M. The temperature had begun to fall, while a wet blanket of fog rose slowly from the ocean to envelop the town.

There were no paved roads or slowly flickering street lights. Just wide, muddy tracks filled with water, slowly freezing. The harbor had wooden planks for loading and unloading, but sidewalks had been forgotten in this busy port town.

Dogs were everywhere, outnumbering the people by three to one. They were in cages and tethered by ropes, or they trotted freely together in small groups. Their yelping, howling cries filled the air, mixing with the steady banter of men. The atmosphere was loud and unruly. Fights would break out between the dogs, bringing their owners running, cursing and clubbing the animals until they stopped.

While Jenny waited for her things, she watched as a couple of black and gray, wolflike animals eyed each other, growling. A circle of men surrounded them and Jenny saw money being counted out between one large, dark-skinned man and another, who was much smaller. Their faces were broad and flat, with hawklike noses roosting in the center.

200

The smaller man's face was marred by dozens of pock marks, whether an act of birth or illness, she didn't know. But their clothing was the same, as were all the men's. Furs of every color and length were draped over them, and black boots, so shiny that they looked wet, totally encased their legs. Wherever fur failed to cover exposed skin, hair did— long, shaggy, unkempt hair, some curling, some straight, all colors, especially black, beginning under hoods and connecting without a break into their beards. No pin-striped suits in this mob of men, or double-breasted coats, or warm towels with heated shaves, just rugged men in rugged gear, surrounding two of the most savage animals she'd ever seen.

When the two men seemed satisfied with what they had collected, the bigger one reached down toward his animal and touched the back of his neck. The dog's hackles were up and his muzzle was drawn away from his teeth, exposing long, white fangs. He was drooling, growling deep in his throat. His master held him by a touch at the back of his neck, for only a fraction of a second, before a barely audible, "Sic 'um!" was heard. The big dogs lunged toward each other, enraged, leaping and tearing, slashing with their deadly teeth. The larger one was smarter. He had fought many battles and won, knowing that strength and speed were not always enough. There were places on his face and body that refused to grow hair—the scars were too deep. Backing away, he watched the other dog as he circled, looking for an opening. It came when the younger dog was distracted by a sneeze from his owner. That was all the older one needed. With lightning speed, he hurtled forward, his teeth ripping into the other dog's throat. A startled yip of pain came from the smaller animal as he tried to get away, but the other dog was too smart. He dug his back legs into the soft mud and savagely shook his head from side to side. Blood sprayed everywhere, shooting out in rhythm to the wounded dog's beating heart. His jugular vein had been severed and the smell of blood had caused the already excited strays roaming about to go into a frenzy, growling and slashing at each other, trying to shove between the men.

The big man moved forward, roughly pulling his dog away. The other dog fell to the ground with half his throat torn open. His owner waved his hand in the air and shook his head in disgust. When the circle of men trailed away the strays moved in, closing in on the fallen animal. She glimpsed it once, as it tried to raise its head. It saw the other dogs coming closer and knew that it was done. Quietly the animal laid its head on the ground and waited for the end.

"I told ya, Missy—it ain't no paradise here." John's voice, a little sad, reached her. She was still in shock, not wanting to believe what she had seen—it was just too cruel. No one had even tried to stop the dogs from fighting, they were even *betting* on which one would win. And when the dog who had fought so bravely at his master's command had fallen, no one, not even the owner, rushed to help him. The dog had seemed to know that if he went down, he was doomed. What kind of a savage world had she come to?

John waited patiently, beside an equally shocked Joshua. When she turned to face him, wanting an explanation, he just shook his head.

"The Miner ain't far, Missy—but I'm afraid yer gonna get yer shoes a might dirty," he said.

John offered her his arm, for which she was grateful, and Joshua, not one to be excluded, claimed the other. Into the crowd they went, pushing their way through the men who stood in front of them. Angry faces turned to see who was shoving through. When they saw Jenny, surprise replaced anger and they politely moved aside. She could feel them staring at her, hungry eyes, lonely eyes, eyes of men who had left wives and sweethearts to tame this rugged land. They followed her every step.

John could see that she was worried and scared, and patted her arm gently. "Jest keep to yer business here, Missy, and don't go out after dark by yerself. Emily and me will look out fer you . . . and when these here *coyotes,"* he said loud enough for all to hear, "and *varmints* come to call, which they will . . . we'll let 'um know yer *taken!"*

His words weren't very reassuring. She wished now that

she had never come. It was so strange here. She began to believe that she had made a terrible mistake. Perhaps the captain would be willing to take her back if she cooked and cleaned for the crew. Perhaps. Then she remembered that *those* men hadn't looked at her any differently than *these* men . . . and she would be all alone . . .

Her thinking was cut short by John's hearty voice.

"Kaiuga!" he exclaimed loudly. "It's good to see you!"

They had stopped in the middle of the muddy road, John and Joshua still holding her arms securely in theirs.

She looked where he looked, startled to see a giant of a man approaching them. He was dark as coffee, with spiky black hair protruding from beneath a large parka made from the same kind of fox furs her uncle wore. His breeches were white as snow, and his boots as black as ebony, matching exactly the color of the intelligent eyes which peered out from beneath his hood.

"John!" he greeted with a smile, revealing rows of perfect teeth, as white as his breeches. "It's good to see you, my old friend!"

A huge, fur-covered hand reached for his and was met and shook heartily.

"Yep, it's been a while, ain't it?" John laughed. "What brought you down from the mountains, Kaiuga? I always thought you hibernated in the winter like the other bears!"

A slow grin spread over his face.

"I've been checking our traps, John . . . just like we planned."

"I know, Kaiuga . . . I was just havin' a little fun, that's all. How are they runnin'?"

"Good," he said thoughtfully. "Enough for me to take little Narvaranna this winter to wife. Maybe even her sister, too!" he added happily.

"Well, I guess congratulations will be in order!" He grasped his friend's hand, pumping it up and down several times while slapping him on the back. "We'll have us the biggest wedding party anyone's ever seen. It'll be news all up and down the coast!"

"Take?" Jenny asked quietly, still thinking about what Kaiuga had said. "You *take* women here?" She wondered if that was a common fate for all females in these parts.

John started to laugh, and Kaiuga grinned.

"It ain't like you think, Jenny," John soothed. "It's their custom. Goes way back to when they crossed over the water from the west. Women were scarce. The harder the times got, the fewer and fewer there were."

"Why?" she asked, curiosity plainly showing on her face.

"Well . . ." he said carefully, thoughtfully pulling on his beard. "That one is sorta' hard fer people to understand, unless they've lived here a while. You see, boy babies is kept, always . . . mostly on account that they do the huntin' and trappin', while the women's job is mostly cookin' and sewin'. Girl babies ain't always as lucky as the boys. Their folks figure when they grow too old to take care of themselves their daughters'll belong to some other family and they won't have no one to look out fer them. So when winter comes, especially a hard one, followed by another jest as bad . . . girl babies are left out in the snow . . ."

"That's horrible!!" she exclaimed.

Kaiuga and John shared a look between them, which said the same thing.

"Not always, Jenny," he said softly. "There are worse things than freezin' to death. I've been so cold, I started thinkin' I was warm, and the snow looked jest like a feather bed, waitin' fer my head. 'Bout then, all's ya want to do is sleep . . . you jest want to sleep . . . that ain't so bad. But there's things that make you *wish* you would jest go to sleep . . . things like goin' hungry fer days, till ya start chewin' on yer furs, and yer dogs start disappearing, one by one. Yer mind gets weak, and you start thinkin' crazy things . . . things you'd never think otherwise, so layin' a baby out on the snow, so it won't suffer through a dark, cold winter filled with hunger, kin be a kindness. Do ya see?"

"No," she said softly, shaking her head slowly from side to side. A light, drizzling rain had begun to fall, and the gray world she'd come to became impossibly darker and gloomier than before. She shivered, hearing the ghostly wailing of hundreds of lost children in her mind.

Kaiuga sensed her horror and grief, and saw that John had no more words to make her see or understand. Harsh and cruel one minute, this Alaskan land could also be bountiful and kind. Through both extremes his people had learned to survive. They had stayed in the far northern regions because migration south had been prevented by the fierce Indian tribes who claimed those lands. Their customs were born from necessity. But since the coming of the white man and his guns and steel traps, hunting had been better. Food was gathered more easily, predators dealt with more swiftly, and winter's long dark and cold had become more bearable on a full stomach. But to someone who had never known a starvation so intense as to force people to take their beloved children and lay them out on the ice, or release the older ones with a noose about their neck, it was something you could not explain.

"Three days," Kaiuga said softly. Jenny looked at him and saw a great sadness in his eyes. "When the storms come in winter, and you must stay in your ice house . . . for the first three days, you do not eat . . . even if your racks are full of meat, because you do not know how long you will be *in there.* And when the storm passes, if you have food left, you invite all the people to *share* in what you have. You dance and rejoice, thankful that you may live yet another day."

"Savages and heathens!" Joshua spat out scornfully.

"Savages?!" John said angrily, "and heathens?! You don't know what yer talkin' about! Kaiuga's people live where no other men ever could . . . through storms and loneliness that'd drive others crazy, including you! Yet they live and smile and laugh, sharing *everything* they have right down to the last bit even if it means they'll be goin' hungry the next day. You call 'um savages? What right have *you* got to judge them? You don't even know them!"

Joshua just looked disgusted and refused to reply.

Jenny felt a pinch of conscience at his words. She, too, had judged them, without really trying to understand what their world was all about. Timidly, she reached out her hand.

"My name is Jenny, Kaiuga . . . and I'm pleased to meet you."

He smiled warmly and took her hand. Jenny was again amazed at the almost stonelike quality of the skin . . . a skin so tough as to endure temperatures cold enough to freeze an ordinary hand.

He looked over questioningly at Joshua. He didn't remember John ever mentioning a man like this before.

"Oh," John said, forgetting his anger. "Where's my manners gone now-a-days? You already met my niece, Jenny. This here is a friend of hers, Joshua, uh, er . . . what's yer last name?" he asked politely, unable to recall if he'd ever heard it.

Joshua, still angry, wouldn't answer. He just thrust out his lower lip a little farther, looking as belligerent as possible.

John's eyes narrowed slightly, wondering how a man got to be his age and still got away with acting like a pouting child.

"Well," he started innocently, "since he won't *say* . . . and I don't rightly know, I guess we can call him 'Walrus.' That'd be a fair name fer a man his size, wouldn't ya say?"

"Why you ol' . . ." Joshua came around with a wide right, which John ducked easily, laughing all the while.

Kaiuga grinned, and so did Jenny.

"We're going over to The Miner to see Emily . . . gonna get us some work for a while, so I kin get a few more dogs and supplies to take home. Don't ya think she'll brighten up the place a bit?" he said cheerfully, his brief argument with Joshua all but forgotten.

"Yes," Kaiuga agreed. "Very much!"

Jenny smiled graciously at the dusty-skinned giant who beamed so openly at her, while Joshua just continued to stare angrily at the three. He had expected John to make fun of him, and even the Indian . . . but Jenny? He had never thought it possible!

John gave her arm a reassuring squeeze, and looked back, as he saw the captain trailing up the road. He was whistling a merry tune, and his arms were swinging with the flow of his walk. Even the dreary afternoon rain didn't seem to dampen his spirits as he approached them.

"Hey, Cap . . . do you think Emily can use some help?" John asked and winked.

"I s'pose so!" the captain said brightly. He and John had talked it through earlier. She might even need a new cook as well. I get real tired of venison stew and fish!"

Joshua failed to respond to what he said, so the captain simply ignored him as he fell into step with Kaiuga. They all headed in the direction of town.

In a few minutes, The Miner loomed in front of them, poking through the fog like a great, gray monolith. Its squared and weathered sides made a simple, two-story, rectangular block against the sky. The only color besides gray was the words "The Miner," ornately drawn and vibrantly painted in red across the top, above the second story windows. More men and dogs tied to sleds clustered around the front. Jenny suddenly realized that the entire time she had been there she hadn't seen one woman.

Suddenly, the door burst open and a tall man shoved something through it. It bounced roughly and rolled over into the street looking for all the world like a large dark dog with shaggy fur.

"And stay out, ya old bum, until you can pay for your drinks!" The men scattered around the front door laughed, while the big man brushed his hands together and went back inside.

An old man, breathing deeply, lay on his back in the muddy water.

Kaiuga strode forward and easily lifted him with one hand.

"Are you all right, old man?" he asked.

"All right?!" he said excitedly, "All right?! I guess I'm just about the all-rightest a man can be!" He grabbed Kaiuga's parka and pulled him forward. "I'm rich," he whispered. "Rich!" His voice rose with the last word, as if he didn't quite believe it himself. "I ain't no beggar!"

Kaiuga nodded, gently freeing himself from the old man's

hand. He reached deeply into the folds of his coat and pulled out some coins. The old man was looking at him oddly, as Kaiuga took his hand and placed some coins in it, closing the fingers around them. "Just a loan, old man, for a while."

"A loan . . . is that what you said, boy?"

Kaiuga nodded.

"Well," he said smacking his lips together in anticipation, "I guess it'll be all right . . . long as it's just a loan . . . that ain't like charity!" He clenched the money tightly. He was beginning to shiver. The wet parka and cool, misty evening were having their effect. "I got to get in somewhere's warm," he muttered. Then his expression brightened. "I knows just the place." He winked at the four of them and grinned, as he turned around and headed for the door he'd just been thrown out of.

"We'd better follow him, Kaiuga," John said. "Could be trouble. Besides, he's goin' the same place we are!"

Kaiuga laughed softly and nodded. With Jenny tucked carefully between them, they walked toward the front door.

The old man had reached the door and some of the men out front looked at him curiously. "I wouldn't go back in there, old-timer," warned one of them. "He'll just throw you out again."

"He ain't a gonna throw me out again! See!" He stretched out his hand toward them, showing them the money. "I got money—a loan from that big S'kmo over yonder." He lowered his voice to a whisper. "It's just a loan, see, on account of I'm rich."

"Yer crazy, old man! The bottle's done used you up. You ain't rich . . . you're just an ol' drunk!"

"I ain't crazy!" he said indignantly. "And I ain't a used up, old drunk, neither . . . I'm rich, do ya hear? Rich!" He closed his hand over the money, licked his parched lips, and started for the door. "You'll all see," he muttered. "You'll all see . . . I'm rich . . ."

The other man shook his head and looked around at his friends. "Crazy old drunk," he said with a contemptuous sneer. "Just plain crazy!"

Everyone heard what he had said. Some felt a little sorry for the old man, while others didn't give it much thought at all.

"You could at least leave the old-timer with his dreams," Tanith said softly. "It don't cost you much except maybe silence."

The younger man started to say something when he and the rest of the men all noticed Jenny. The crazy old man was forgotten. Interest clearly showing on their faces, they all stood a little straighter, clearing a path for her. All their eyes were focused on her. Her cheeks, already pink, became crimson as they continued to stare. "It's all right, lass," Tanith said. He patted her arm lightly. "Is that all ya got to do?" he bellowed. "'Tis a good thing none of you works for me. I'd give you more to do than standing around gawking like a bunch of schoolboys at a lady!" Some of the men looked away, but most of them continued to gape hungrily at Jenny as she walked through the doors and past them. Low whistles of appreciation followed her. Unconsciously, she tightened her grip on John's arm as they entered The Miner.

The hall was warm and well lit. A stairway to her left disappeared into a shadowy hall, and a desk along half of the left wall held a book and a bell. A board rested against one wall with hooks protruding in a dozen places with half as many keys dangling beneath them. A wide doorway in front of the desk opened up into a large, smokey bar filled with men and a few women in exotic dresses of bright canary yellow, deepest crimson, and peacock blue. Their smiles were bright and their talk lively and animated as they flitted from one man to another. It was odd to see such bright and marvelous creatures against the dark, sparrow-brown men, who sat or stood like granite statues around the room. They looked like pagan gods of old, all mutable and dark, chiseled from the rocks and earth, while the women appeared nearly ethereal and fragile against them. The old man who had been thrown out earlier rested against the bar. He hadn't been noticed yet by the bartender, who was bent over, clearing a table full of empty dishes.

"Can't a body get something to drink around here?" he

demanded, pounding his still soaking wet arm against the bar.

The bartender turned and nearly dropped the dishes in his hands.

"How many times do I have to throw you out, old man? Like I told you before, no money, no booze!" He started to walk toward him when Kaiuga stepped forward, but before he could do anything the old man held out his hand showing the money.

"I got money, do ya see? I got enough money to buy me somethin' to drink and maybe," he added haughtily, "maybe even a warm place to sleep!" His old eyes, red-rimmed and yellowed, gleamed triumphantly.

"Give me whiskey!" he shouted. "And just keep it comin' till I say, 'no more'!"

The bartender shook his head and scooped out the money in his hand.

"Take a seat, old man. I'll bring you yer whiskey!"

The old man chuckled softly and rubbed his hands together, expectantly. He could almost taste the fiery brew as it burned its way down his throat. He shivered and started to look around for a place closer to the stove, when he noticed Kaiuga and the others by the door. "Thanks, sonny!" He waved happily. "'Member . . . it's jest a loan— I got millions!" He winked and walked over to a table next to the stove and took his coat and gloves off and laid them over a chair to dry. He pulled out another chair and cheerfully sat down, propping his feet up, and sighed contentedly.

"Well," Tanith grinned, "looks like the old fella can take care of himself." They all smiled in agreement. "Now, we best be seeing about ourselves."

He went to the desk and began ringing the bell. A high-pitched, slightly tinny, "ding-ding-ding" filled the hall. "Emily!" he shouted. "Where in thunder are you, woman! 'Tis me, Tanith McGee!"

The bell continued to ding until a large, dark-haired woman appeared on the second story landing. She placed her hands on the rail and peered down at the four standing there. The sun had set and the kerosene light flickered weakly, casting dim shadows around her face.

"Tanith? Is that you making all that racket down there?!" she shouted good-naturedly.

"Aye, darlin' . . . the very same." There was a smile on his face as he peered upward and a certain softness in his voice. "Come home at last."

Quickly, she brushed back a piece of graying hair and, picking up her skirts, came down the stairs as fast as she could.

"Tanith, darling . . . it really *is* you!" She smiled wistfully. "It's been a while."

"Em, I do believe you get prettier every time I see you!" he said happily.

"Humph! You old sea dog! Still as charming an old liar as ever!" She opened her arms and hugged him, quickly giving him a kiss on the cheek. Her eyes had grown soft and luminous when she looked at him, making her seem almost pretty.

He held her at arm's length and studied her face.

"How long have we known each other, Em?" he seriously asked. "Thirty years now?"

She pretended indignation, giving him a little shove. "Thirty-*two*," she pouted. "But who's counting?"

They laughed heartily and then she noticed the others. She knew Kaiuga and John, but she had never seen the girl beside him or the sour-faced man. She must be John's niece, she thought, marveling at her fragile beauty. "You must be Jenny!" she cheerfully welcomed. She took Jenny's hands in both of hers. "I'm so happy to meet you!"

"Thank you," Jenny murmured. She looked quickly from the captain to Emily, but before she could continue, he spoke up. "Well, Emily, old girl . . . Jenny, here, is the reason I wanted to talk to you . . ."

"Oh?" she said, a hurt expression on her face. Here I thought you came to see *me*, Tanith." She pretended to pout and the captain moved closer to her, placing his arm around her back. She was wide, and as to just where his arm reached, Jenny couldn't tell. A grin spread over his face as a sly look passed between them.

"To be sure, Madam, I've come *especially* to see you. But there is another matter I'd like to discuss first." He winked.

A quick nod of her head and Emily moved toward the back of the room. "Come with me. I'll get us some coffee and we'll talk in my rooms."

They followed her through a couple of corridors. The Miner was bigger than it appeared from the street. It held eight sleeping rooms, a large bar that boasted a stage, and a spacious eating room off the kitchen.

The evening meal was being prepared and the kitchen was a flurry of activity. Girls dressed in the same vibrant colored silks as the ones in the bar were laughing and talking, fixing food as fast as they could.

"Dolores, bring a pot of coffee and some cups to my rooms." As an afterthought she added, "Throw a few rolls on a plate, too, will you, dear?"

"Right away, Em," she promised.

"Come on," Emily said. "We'll take the back stairs." They trailed after her single-file, while the captain walked up ahead, joking easily with her.

"Here we are!" she announced, opening a door into a brightly lit room. A large, four-poster bed hung with plush red velvet drapes stood in the center. Its very size and brilliant color dominated the entire room. A sofa and two chairs surrounded a table in the corner, and a huge wooden dresser with a large oval glazed mirror sat on the opposite side.

"Just make yourselves at home, folks." She eased her girth onto the sofa. When they had all found a seat, Emily looked over at Tanith expectantly.

"Well, now, Captain . . . just what did you want to discuss with me?"

The captain took off his cap and rested it on his knee. He cleared his throat and appeared to study a spot on the wall, before he began.

"See, Em, it's this way. John and Jenny need a little work. Their supplies are pretty low and they need a few more things to see them through the winter. And Joshua, here," he pointed to the sour-faced man she didn't know, "came along with Jenny to look out for her and I hear tell he's a pretty fair cook."

Emily nodded, mentally placing them in what she considered the right jobs.

"Well," she began, "John would make a pretty fair bartender. Lord knows, the man I got now is overworked and I know you can handle the business end of a broom, too. And you . . . Josh, is it?" she asked, looking at him and he nodded. "You're a cook?"

"I've been a cook most of my life," he offered gravely, as though he were telling her about a terminal disease he suffered from instead of his life's work.

"Uh—hmmm . . ." She turned her attention to Jenny, tapping her finger thoughtfully against her lips. "But, what to do with you?" she pondered pensively.

Jenny was puzzled. She had seen all the girls and what they did. She wasn't afraid of work.

"Whatever you have, ma'am. I'll work hard for you. All I ask is a chance."

"I know you will, my dear." She patted her knee. "But you're not like my other girls."

Jenny's eyebrows shot up. "Ma'm, you have no need to worry about me. I don't want to be treated any differently than the others. I can do what they do. I've cooked and cleaned before!" She remembered seeing the girls waiting on tables, chatting with the customers, cooking, cleaning, doing things she knew she could do. She might have a little trouble getting used to the costumes they wore, but she would give it her best try. "I'll do my best," she offered, "right along with the other girls."

John went pale and the captain and Emily looked at each other helplessly. Tanith tried to make her understand. She was so damned innocent! "Jenny," he said in a pleading voice, "you don't know what you're saying. Her girls, though I love them everyone," and he looked quickly at

Emily, "her girls . . . well, they ain't what most people would call *good* girls." A blank, confused look continued to stay on Jenny's face. Tanith was getting desperate while John began to look very ill until even Jenny noticed his coloring.

"John," she asked quietly, "are you all right? You look kind of *green*. Did you eat something bad?"

"No, Jenny, I ain't ate nothin' bad." He sighed. Being a bachelor for sixty years had not prepared him for this. "What Tanith's tryin' to tell you is . . ." He stopped as he felt the color rush to his cheeks. "Damn it!" he muttered. It had been fifty years or better since anything had made him blush. "What he's been trying to tell you, is that you *can't* do what the other girls do . . ."

"Yes I can, John!" she argued. "It isn't much different than the work at the hotel. Maybe I won't be as good as they are at first . . . but I'll learn . . ."

"Oh, damn it all to hell and back!" thundered the captain. "You can't do what they do, because their job is to *bed* the men what comes here on a regular basis for pay. Now, can *you do that?*"

A startled, "Oh!" came from Jenny as she suddenly realized what they had been trying to say. Utter silence then filled the room. No one spoke, only the ticking of the clock on the dresser could be heard and the distant sounds of laughing and talking from below.

Emily decided it was all very funny and would have laughed; except when she looked at Jenny, her head hanging down and near to weeping, she knew she couldn't laugh. Suddenly she felt very sorry for the poor, motherless child. Awkwardly pushing her large form from the couch, she stood in front of her.

"Jenny," she said gently. But Jenny wouldn't look up and Emily watched as she swallowed back the tears. Gently, she lifted her face upward. "It's going to be all right—don't you worry." Her tone was kind and gentle and matched the expression in her eyes. "You can cook and clean for me. Maybe even do a little sewing for my girls. We'll work it out." She patted her kindly on the cheek. She turned to face the men. "So, it's a mother then you want for this little girl, boys?"

Tanith grinned. "Aye, Em . . . a mum and a watchdog to keep the men at bay . . . leastways till we get her married-up right and proper."

Emily nodded. "You can all start tomorrow."

Everything was happening so quickly. Memories whirled through Jenny's mind. The trip, the fighting dogs, the painful longing she felt for Gannon—it was just too much and she began to cry. John and Tanith stared, dumbfounded, and John wanted to rush over and put his arms around her, telling her it was going to be all right, but Emily got there first. The captain looked totally mystified.

"Lass! What is it? Are you in pain?" He was really worried.

The kindness of the captain and these people who barely knew her was overwhelming. She cried all the harder.

"There, there," crooned Emily, hugging her tight. "It'll be all right. Em's here, she'll look after you now."

She looked over toward the captain and John, still holding the girl close. "She's tired, boys . . . she needs rest." She drew away from Jenny just far enough to wipe a tear away with her hand. "You'll stay with me tonight, honey. I've plenty of room in that big ol' bed. Tomorrow you'll feel so much better."

Tanith moved forward, a frown settling on his face. "Stay with *you*, in *here*? But Em, what about . . . us?"

Emily carefully sat Jenny down and waved her arms frantically at the men. "Out! Out!" she cried. "Can't you see she needs some sleep?" They backed away from her waving arms toward the hall.

"But, Em," Tanith continued plaintively. He'd been aboard ship for twelve weeks, and that was a long time to go without a good woman. "Em, please . . ." A large hand shoved him through the door to join John and Joshua outside in the hall. The door slammed shut in their faces with a bang.

The men stood in silence. The captain pulled nervously on his cap, still looking longingly at the shut door.

"I need a drink," John said.

"My sentiments exactly," Tanith agreed, still mystified at the outcome of this evening. He'd had such a grand night planned!

They all looked at each other and wondered if *they* looked as confused as the faces they were staring at.

"Women!" they said in unison, slowly shaking their heads as they turned around and trudged down the hall toward the bar.

CHAPTER

20

The days passed quickly while she worked. Her mornings began before light, when she started the bread, and ended after dark, when the last pot and pan had been carefully scrubbed and put away.

Joshua helped her in the kitchen, but she could tell that his heart wasn't in it. He became impatient and irritated by even the most trivial things. And his food, instead of being his pride and passion, fell into the realm of mediocrity. As soon as the meals were over, he would scamper outside with his newfound friends, eager to hear all their stories of life in the wilderness and learn all that they could teach him. Dog sleds especially fascinated him. He marveled at the economy and swiftness with which runs were made. Sometimes Jenny would catch a glimpse of him through the window, standing behind the runners, with a full team ahead of him pulling like mad. He seemed gigantic behind the fragile looking sled and the dogs like toys, as they pulled with all their might. Daily he changed, shedding his past life as though it were a useless skin or a remnant of clothing he no longer wanted to wear. A frontiersman was evolving from the once somber kitchen cook, with no apparent regrets. She had never seen him look so wildly alive as when he ran with his dogs or so happy. And only one short week had passed since the first night they'd come.

Emily had given her a small room next to hers. It was comfortable with a large, brass bed and a rough-hewn wooden wardrobe. There were no doilies or homey scarfs adorning the walls as Mrs. Merit had done. Just warm, yellow and brown wood all around her and a braided rag rug for her feet. Emily had even scouted around until she had found a chair and a table for her to use, placing them near the one small window which overlooked the street. Jenny had settled in easily, but not before writing to Gannon. Paper was precious, so her words had been well chosen and few, but they carried her feelings well. She only hoped the letter would reach him before it was too late and Penelope had sunk her polished hooks too deep.

Sighing, she stared out of the small polished glass at the shadowy pearl-gray world around her. Anchorage was hauntingly beautiful even with its perpetual clouds and rain. Wind sang to her at night, and mist greeted her in the mornings, only to become rain again by the end of the day. Great pines, their trunks so straight they appeared like brown granite beneath crowns of emerald green, rose from the mists to encircle the town. Mountains—smoky plums and ice-cold blue-ridged peaks, frosted with sparkling white —stood behind them. The unapproachable settlement was open only to the sky and sea, and the harbor, which she could see from her room, rocked with ships, tied to the piers. The blue-gray waters slapped at their sides and tickled their bows as if teasing them to come and play in her yielding depths and ride her foam-crested waves. Only their moorings held them in place, as they danced and strained like sea stallions against their reins.

Tanith had come to inspect Jenny's room before he left, liking the idea that the only way you could get into it was through Emily's. He figured that would give some of the men a thing or two to think about if they thought about visiting her after dark. When he was satisfied that all was set in order and his friends were taken care of, he prepared to leave. Originally, he had planned only a three-day stayover. But he was still at The Miner along with the others and it was already going on a week. Sighing tiredly, he stuffed Jenny's letter into his inside coat pocket and headed for the dock.

He walked stiffly, shaking his leg occasionally or clenching his fingers tightly together and opening them wide. He ached in every part of his body. Arthritis had welded his joints together and become worse by the day, mostly because of the moist conditions he worked in. With some measure of relief, he knew that his seafaring days were fast drawing to a close. The seasons of his life had sped past, leaving all but one, to travel. Now, with his hair frosted as brilliantly white as the glittering ice caps he sailed past and his hands stiff from their own inner cold, he knew that winter had finally come and lodged itself deep inside his chest. His days of carefree joy and monotonous toil were nearly through. All he yearned for now was the quiet years with Emily by his side to help pass the time and reminisce about days gone by.

Another ship had come in during the night. It was smaller and sleeker than Tanith's. It was elegant compared to the bulky cargo vessel that rocked beside it and it had the look of speed about its slender body. Tanith recognized the captain of the other vessel and made his way toward him. He did not see Emily and the others who had trailed after him to say goodbye.

Jenny and Emily walked together in the center, flanked on both sides by Kaiuga and John. They could not protect them from the mud or the elements, but they could field the ragged strays or the newly docked seamen. They saw Tanith up ahead, talking to a small man, and headed toward him. A fragment of the conversation drifted their way.

". . . paid me more than a full cargo was worth jest to bring him here," he said.

"Yer pullin' my leg, Ned. Why would someone pay you *more* than a full cargo was worth just to get him here a few days earlier?" Tanith asked skeptically. He towered over the little man who stood like a shabby Napoleon, next to him, with his fist jammed into his dark blue seaman's coat and a perpetual squint in his right eye.

"Aye, Tanith. I told him we'd be leaving in a few days anyway, but he insisted on going now. A rich one, he is. Some of my men were in favor of knocking him in the head and taking a look-see in his bags . . ."

Tanith shook his head and started to say something when he noticed Emily and the others standing close by. "What brings you all the way down here, 'specially when it's starting to rain and all?"

As if on cue, Jenny felt the first large drops of water trail down her nose and wondered for a moment if the sun ever shone at all in this soggy place. Emily just smiled.

"Aren't you happy to see us, Tanith?" she asked, giving him what she hoped was a flirtatious smile.

"Happy? Why . . . sure I'm happy to see you! Did you come to wish me farewell?"

They nodded and smiled and Tanith positively beamed.

"Looks like you have some fine friends there, Tanith," Ned commented, smiling a bit enviously.

"Yes," he said. "That's a fact." He looked at Ned and back at the others. "This is Captain Ned McPherson . . . a lifelong friend and drinking buddy." He reached over and slapped him on the back, rocking the poor man nearly off his feet.

"How do?" Ned inquired politely, tipping his hat once he regained his footing.

Emily's curiosity had gotten the better of her as she looked at him.

"Captain . . . I don't mean to seem like a *busybody.*" She looked uncomfortably at Tanith who was about to say something, but thought better of it. "I couldn't help but overhear you saying to Tanith about how well-to-do your passenger is. Did he *really* pay *that* much money just to get here a few days earlier?" she asked. Having known Tanith all these years, she was well acquainted with the price of a full cargo.

"Aye, it's a fact. Took all my efforts just to keep my mates in line. 'Twould be easy to say a man fell over the railing during a sudden storm, ya know, 'specially when there wasn't any other passengers on board." He seemed to think about this a bit. "I'm not the type to allow such activities aboard my ship, you understand, but I *have heard* of such things occurring. Still," he mused, "I don't think my men would've had as easy of a time with him as they think . . . looked like a fighter to me . . . bruised and cut . . . and I swear he had murder in them green eyes . . ."

Before he could say any more, activity increased on the ship, drawing their attention. A tall man dressed all in gray appeared on deck. He seemed to blend into the fog and rain, while his cloak billowed around him in the breeze. Gray water, gray mist, all gray, except for the vibrant red flash of copper in his hair that not even the clouds could dim. Jenny caught her breath.

"Gannon!" she breathed.

Even though his features were indistinct in the swirling haze, she knew who it was.

John had heard her and peered hard at the figure.

"Speak o' the devil," Ned muttered, raising his eyebrows at Tanith. They all turned to face him.

If he was aware that they watched him, he paid them no mind as he walked slowly over the deck toward the boarding plank. His eyes were focused on only one face on the dock . . . a face which haunted and plagued him and drove him two thousand endless miles to find her.

But seeing her with the others dashed several of the speculations he had formed on his many long, sleepless nights. Weariness had set in, bringing with it a whole host of odd notions. He had imagined her an unwilling captive, abducted by her eccentric uncle with Joshua's unwilling aid. John must have tricked them, he mused one night in his rocking berth, using Jenny to blackmail Joshua into returning to the hotel for her things because he couldn't believe that his old friend would have been a part of this for any other reason. But obviously from watching them together talking easily with one another this simply wasn't so. He hadn't wanted to believe that she would willingly leave him, especially when she couldn't have possibly known if he were dead or alive . . . but the truth was she had abandoned him when he had needed her most and he felt like a fool. Reality has a bitter taste, he thought sardonically, but even now, knowing all these things, his body reacted strongly to the sight of her. He longed to wrap his arms around her, pulling her close.

Scowling, he came forward, walking down the boarding plank without so much as a glance at his footing.

Jenny stepped forward, also not sure if he were real or only another dream her obsession had formed from the very mist.

"Gannon?" she whispered again, reaching out a hand as if fearful that he might vanish. It was only then that she noticed he didn't smile. In all her dreams he had smiled and called for her. They had run toward each other in the molasses-slow atmosphere of her mind, making love the minute they had touched. In her dreams, he *always* smiled . . . but not this time. This time he scowled and his eyes glittered in that hard and deadly way she'd come to know. But they had never flashed at *her* that way. In her confusion she took a faltering step backward and then another and another after that. And still he scowled, looking like a snarling, spitting cat ready to pounce as he walked past the others. He didn't even bother to acknowledge Joshua when he spoke. He just kept walking straight toward her.

The wind had begun blowing in from the sea, charging the gently falling rain with the tang of salt spray. She could feel it hitting her head coldly in little, gusty breaths of ever increasing size before trailing down her neck to fill her soggy clothes. Her dress was dripping with water, trimmed in mud, and it clung heavily to her legs as she walked.

Behind and all around her the men on the docks openly stared, wondering why the furious red-haired stranger was chasing her. Urged by curiosity and boredom, they all moved closer to the pair to find out, forming lines on both sides of the road and behind them as they did. Even the strays with their acute sixth sense discreetly tucked their tails between their legs and scampered out of the way.

"Is he kidnapping Jenny?" Kaiuga asked calmly. Since stealing the woman of your choice had been the custom of his people for centuries and usually worked out quite well, he saw no wrong in it. Besides, he could see as all the men could, the twin demons as she pulled each foot loose from the slimy ooze with a loud sucking noise. Annoyed and confused, she pushed a clump of wet hair away from her eyes.

"This is insane!" she muttered. "I *wanted* him to come . . . and now I'm running *away* from him . . . why?"

Hands still holding her skirts up, she turned to face him. The rain had flattened her hair to her head and molded her clothes to her form. The people in the mob obligingly parted, forming a semicircle, so the two could face each other and *they* could hear every delicious word.

"Why?!" she demanded angrily. "Why are you acting this way?" She stared at his approaching figure. The rain had made his billowing gray cloak lifeless and soggy. His hair, though smoothed back from his face, was now totally wet with droplets of water flowing down it. Even his eyelashes held the rain, looking for all the world like glittering tears. But though he was as wet as she and his clothes were just as splattered and muddy, she marveled at his rugged beauty and the clear, clean lines of his face made her catch her breath.

"Why?" she asked again, though not so loud. "Gannon . . ." she pleaded. "What *is* the matter. What have *I* done?"

He paused for a second, oblivious to the crowds and rain. She felt his eyes, cold and hard, sweep over her, lingering on rounded hips and swelling breasts . . . lingering on every sensitive and sweet place on her body until the color rose to her cheeks and his bold gaze stopped on her mouth, wet with rain.

"Gannon . . ." she whispered. His eyes, blazing with an inner fire, found hers. "Why?" she asked, retreating once more from the anger and desire in Gannon's blazing eyes. Suddenly she knew that she was in no real danger.

"Could be," John mused happily, answering Kaiuga's

earlier question, as he watched the pair play an odd sort of tag down the middle of main street. "That's Gannon!" he added proudly. "I jest knew he'd be coming fer her . . ." Then he frowned and a worried expression replaced his smile. "Looks a might *mad* though, don't he?"

"I'd say!" Emily agreed enthusiastically. She was so excited that her pupils had totally dilated and her eyes looked almost black. In the last week she had heard so much about the famous Gannon from Jenny and John that she felt that he was more of a legend than an actual flesh and blood man . . . until now. With her experienced eyes she could see now why Jenny slept with his shirt tucked beneath her head at night and why she would catch her staring out toward the harbor with such heartbroken longing in her blue eyes. *He* had even caused *her* old heart to skip a beat or two. She smiled a bit ruefully. That powerfully built darling was all *too* real!

"Well?" she asked impatiently. She couldn't bear the thought that she might miss out on anything exciting. "What are we *waiting* for?"

They all turned . . . both captains, John, Kaiuga, and Emily, along with most of the men from the ships and any idle person who just happened to be standing close by. All walked eagerly toward The Miner, following the pair.

Up ahead, Jenny had nearly reached the hotel with half of the townspeople and most of the strays trailing behind her. The mud was getting impossibly deep and her legs were getting tired under that smoldering gaze backing her up the steps of the hotel . . . backing her toward the door with her heart thundering in her breast. A dizzying heat flowed through her, making her legs weak as she fumbled for the latch.

Inside, The Miner was filled to capacity. The traders had come down from the high places. They stood and sat and some laid at odd angles all around the room. The piano pounded out a tinny tune, and the raucous laughter of the trappers was joined by the murmuring voices of women and clinking of bottles and glasses on the bar. She stumbled inside, grateful for the solid floor, closing the door behind her. Brushing back a wet curl from her forehead, she thought about what to do. Gannon was barely a hundred yards behind her. She wanted to go to her room, to change her clothes and think . . . and to lock her door. But as she ran toward the stairs two burly men refused to let her pass. One of Emily's girls, Dolores, stood in front of them. The three were so engrossed in what they were talking about, that when she tried to go around them, they refused to move.

"Please!" she begged, glancing back over her shoulder, "Let me by!" She touched the largest man in front of her.

He turned slightly and frowned when he saw who stood there.

"It's the lil' Quaker gal . . . go away, lil' Quaker gal," he muttered drunkenly. "Go 'way . . . unless you'd like to join us fer a while upstairs!" He grinned lewdly at her as did his friend, while Dolores just laughed as she turned and headed quickly down the stairs.

The front door opened and Gannon walked through, not bothering to close it. She had reached the front desk and the only place left to go was into the bar. With as much speed as her wet clothing would allow, she darted into the room, determined to make her way toward the door that went into the kitchen. At first, she tried to be careful and not touch any of the customers as she wound her way around the tables or passed the jigging dancers on the floor. Most moved politely aside to let her pass, until one stout old man, saturated in corn whiskey and filled with good humor, grabbed her about her wet waist and spun her clumsily around the floor in the same thick, clogging manner as the others. "Buff-a-lo-ow gals . . . wo-n't ya come ou-ut ta'night . . . come ou-ut ta'night!" he bellowed gayly, "Come ou-ut ta'night!" He whirled her around a little *too* close to the door. "Buff-a-lo-ow gals . . . wo-n't ya come ou-ut ta'night . . . and dance by the light of the moo-ou-ooohhhnn!"

Suddenly he stopped and stood very, very still as he stared directly into a pair of furious green eyes. The song he had begun to sing again died in his throat. "Ahhmmm . . ." he said, clearing his throat loudly as he let go of Jenny's waist. "Sorry, Mister . . ." he muttered as he recognized *that particular look.* He raised his hands high above his head in surrender, as if Gannon had pointed a gun at him instead of his eyes. "Didn't know she *belonged* to somebody," he muttered. "Honest to BeeJesus . . . I didn't know she was yours!" Slowly, he started to back away with his arms still raised as if to say, "No harm done, honest!"

Jenny barely glanced over her shoulder. *"I don't belong to him!"* she spat angrily as she bolted for the door, weaving not so carefully this time between the tables. A few more feet and she would make the kitchen and then up the back stairs, down the hall, through Emily's room, and into the safety of her own . . . she hoped. She had long since stopped worrying about *why* he was acting so crazy. There would be plenty of time to figure that out later, after she was safely locked inside her room.

She started to round the last table by the corner, where all the serious card players were sitting. She had nearly made the kitchen entrance when Gannon, not willing to let her go, leapt out in front of her, barring her escape. With a little cry of surprise, she changed directions in midstride, pivoting sharply on her left foot. Keeping her back toward the wall and her eyes on him, she darted behind the table.

The card players, salty old miners and rugged trappers, barely noticed them. All the money that some had, a whole year's work, lay on the table. The stakes were high and the game was hot. No one paid Gannon and the girl any attention . . . too much was riding on this hand . . . until Gannon, bent on capturing her this time, shoved the table roughly back toward the wall. He didn't touch her, but the table effectively blocked her escape . . . as well as destroying one of the best card games these men had ever played.

"Hold on there!" one man shouted, who thought he'd won the pot. "What in the Sam Hill do you think yer doin'?"

The rest of the men grumbled and groaned and started to push away from their chairs. Money had been evenly spread between all the players, which meant that everybody had still had a chance to come out on top. But now the careful piles of chips, green money, silver and gold coin lay scattered around. One of the men looked not too happy with Gannon, who couldn't have cared less.

"What in thunder do you think yer doin', boy? It took me all summer jest to make that!"

With one hand still firmly holding the table, Gannon reached inside his wet coat and produced his wallet, letting several crisp twenties fall.

"Here," he offered calmly, keeping one eye on Jenny all the while. "I'll buy your table . . ."

The men, too practical to let such easy money slip through their fingers, scrambled to pick up their chips, money, and cards.

"Reckon that'll do it!" chuckled the man who thought he'd won the pot. He winked at Gannon as he tipped his hat to Jenny and they all moved away grinning, leaving her at the mercy of the wild-eyed Irishman.

The piano had ceased playing and the dancers had stopped gyrating. Drinks were ignored and talk dwindled away to silence. The steady popping and hissing of the old black potbellied stove behind them was the only sound. No one moved, not even Emily and John, who stood silently next to Kaiuga and Joshua in the doorway. Every eye of every person in the room was focused on them . . . waiting . . .

Jenny's heart was beating so fast she could barely breathe as she stared into Gannon's face. Instead of hundreds of miles, only a table's length separated them.

A while ago on the street, she had stopped retreating long enough to ask him what was wrong, why he was so angry at her . . . but now, with him so close, none of those questions seemed to matter . . . nothing seemed to matter, except him.

She could still make out the faded bruises on his cheeks and the not quite healed cut on his lips.

Her searching look caused his glittering eyes to suddenly flare and smolder and it filled her with such a desperate longing, a sympathetic ache deep within. She recognized where she had seen that expression before and a curling warmth began to grow in the junction between her legs in response. It was the same penetrating, hungry look that he had worn that night in the coach as they had traveled the moonlit road home from the mayor's ball. It had come before a kiss . . . the briefest, feathery-lightest touch she had ever felt on the tips of each of her fingers. A fragile caress, gentle and sweet, that contradicted the powerful storm that raged in his eyes . . . a storm that he held in check by the force of his will. Here it was again, the same bold, sensuous look etched in every line of his face and taut controlled movement of his body kindling a fire in her that made her feel vulnerable and raw. But there was more than restrained desire this time. There was anger, too, and she didn't know why. She had saved his life, making a devil's bargain with Penelope that had nearly broken her heart . . . surely he knew that. He must have found out somehow. Perhaps Penelope had told him herself. Why else would he have come so far? But her confusion was starting to give way to embarrassment and anger as she noticed all the people eagerly staring at them as if they were a circus act newly arrived in town.

Pushing a wet curl from her forehead, she pulled herself up as straight and tall as her five-and-a-half-foot frame would allow, defiantly meeting Gannon's gaze.

"Let me *out* of here!" she demanded. She was in no mood to entertain the population of Anchorage, especially at her expense.

"I *said,*" she repeated in a voice shaking with rage, *"let me out of here! NOW, Gannon!"* She stamped her foot for emphasis as she tried vainly to push the table away. Her attempt was utterly futile.

"By all means," he answered dryly. His expression was one of cynical amusement. She looked like a half-drowned kitten, complete with claws and needle-pointed fangs, who was spitting mad at him. Without another word, he jerked his head in the direction he wanted her to go, which was toward the wall, so that she must pass directly in front of him. Slowly, he eased back on the table, drawing it away a few inches at a time. But Jenny was determined not to be further humiliated by this arrogant Irishman whom she couldn't understand. The minute the table moved she tried to go the opposite way, still planning on making it through the kitchen and up to the safety of her own room.

"Tricks again?" he asked icily, shoving the table roughly back into place, trapping her once again behind it. "You're as untrustworthy as the rest of them, I see."

"Untrustworthy?! Tricks?! Who are *they?!*" she screamed furiously, nearly choking with rage. Her cheeks were as flushed as crimson rubies and her eyes sparkled dangerously like ice-blue diamonds. She searched for something to throw . . . anything, but there was nothing within reach. In frustration, she clenched her hands into tiny impotent fists, glaring at him.

He saw the nearly murderous gleam in her eyes and noted her ragged breathing. "What, Jenny . . . does the truth hurt?" he asked sarcastically, wanting to cause her as much pain as he had felt these past weeks.

"The truth . . ." she breathed softly, unable to comprehend why he was treating her so.

"Hold on there!" John shouted. He hitched up his trousers and came striding forward, looking oddly like a fur-clad Don Quixote ready to do battle against a windmill he couldn't possibly defeat. "You got no business callin' my niece names and treating her like a . . . like she weren't no lady!" he finished hurriedly. He knew he could never beat the man in a fight, but he thrust out his sagging old chest as far as he was able, knowing there were just some things a body had to do. Standing up for the honor of kin was one of them.

Gannon half turned and studied him coolly, while Jenny, seeing his attention focused on John, decided to make a run for it. Since she couldn't go around the table, as he had never lessened the pressure on it and she doubted her ability to jump on top and scamper away before he could reach her, she did the most logical thing she could think of. She ducked down, tucking her wet skirts beneath her, and crawled as quickly as possible under the table. Holding her breath so as not to make a sound, she easily avoided the thick pedestal

Victoria Morrow

base in the middle before veering sharply to the right in
order to dodge the pair of long, lean legs planted directly in
front of her. On hands and knees, with clumps of wet hair
trailing down her back and face, and her light blue dress of
soggy wool beginning to itch, she scurried underneath,
making her way inch by quiet inch toward the door.

John had seen what she was up to, as did all the people in
The Miner . . . except Gannon, and he was determined that
she should make it. He tried with all of his might to divert
Gannon's attention for as long as he could.

"You ain't got no call to treat her such!" he said loudly,
shaking his fist for emphasis as he watched Jenny's progress
with a great deal of interest out of the corner of one eye. "No
call!"

A few of the customers snickered and some turned their
backs so as not to give her away, but it was too late. Gannon,
sensing something was up, turned sharply around, only to
see an empty corner and hear a suspicious shuffling noise
from underneath the table.

"No call!" John exclaimed again, but he knew the jig was
up as the tip of Jenny's head came into view and Gannon's
eyes zeroed in on her, locking on target.

She had just reached the edge and thought she was home
free. Gathering her skirts around her, she started to stand
up, preparing to bolt until she felt a tug at the back of her
dress right where her bustle lay soggily against her wet back
end.

"Let go of me!" she cried.

"Yeah!" John agreed angrily. "Let her go!"

Gannon didn't listen. He had what he had come two
thousand miles for in his hand and he wasn't about to let go.

"Gannon . . . let me go!" she shouted, as she felt herself
being pulled upward and turned, *not too gently,* around to
face him. "Please let me go!" She struck at his large chest
with her tiny hands, but his hold only became that much
tighter.

"No, little one . . . not ever again!" he said harshly. He
glowered at her with something like triumph in his eyes . . .

mocking her. "I told you, I never let go of what belongs to me . . . and you *do* belong to *me.*"

"I do not!" she retorted. Unable to suppress her building rage, she struck him, as hard as possible on his cheek, leaving a perfectly red, perfectly visible handprint behind.

"I think," he said slowly, a savage gleam in his eyes as he touched the reddened skin, "that you need your claws trimmed, hellcat!" He grabbed her wrist before pulling a chair toward him, sitting down and easily tossing her over his lap, where she kicked and thrashed like a small child. "Gannon . . . let . . . go . . . of . . . me!"

Swat!

"Ouch!"

"Swat!

"Gannon . . . stop it! John . . . Emily . . . help me! Ouch!" she cried, as he began to issue a series of sharp swats right on her soggy bustle. "Gannon . . . stop!" she pleaded, so embarrassed she wanted to die.

"Hey, now . . . Gannon! You stop that!" shouted an angry John. He started to reach for his arm.

Gannon paused, but only for a second, giving John a look that said, "You'd better not interfere," before he began to spank her in earnest, hitting her wet bottom until her cheeks were warm and smarting and quite pink.

She was crying and still thrashing around more out of anger and indignation than any real pain. And just as suddenly as he had started, he stopped, flipping her over and bringing her into a sitting position in his lap. Possessively he circled her waist with one arm and held both her hands in his other.

"If marriage is what you want, my little beauty . . . then, marriage is what you'll get . . . although I wouldn't attest to the sanity of any man who'd make a wife of you!" He was staring hard at her and his breathing had become ragged. Whiskers shadowed his cheeks and weariness clouded his eyes. "And when we are married and you're not giving birth to our sons and daughters, you'll be flat on your back in our bed making more . . . and if children cannot curb your wandering spirit or being in my bed several times a day, sap your strength, then God help me . . . I'll burn your damn shoes and hide your clothes. Never . . . never again will you leave me and put me through hell . . . or practice your womanly tricks at my expense!"

"You think," she said slowly, starting to comprehend what he was saying, "that I left you in order to force you into *marrying* me? *Is that what you think?*"

He didn't answer, he just looked at her coolly and stood up, still holding her around the waist.

"I think," he said, this time so softly that she strained to hear him, the events of the past weeks beginning to catch up to him as he looked into her tear-stained face, "that you are a beguiling witch, a Judas, and a child . . ." He had stopped, sighing so deeply that everyone in the room heard him, closing his eyes, unable to tell her that *she* was the *only* woman he had ever truly loved, and that morning and night, he needed her . . . unable to tell her that he ached for her touch and awoke burning and lonely from dreams he couldn't forget . . . unable to tell her that her face went before him like a living flame in his mind every minute of every day . . . unable to tell her that he hoped someday, someday *soon*, she would come to love him as he . . . loved . . . her . . . Unable to tell her . . . His eyes opened slowly and he looked at her longingly . . .

She trembled, but not from the wet clothing as she felt his strong arms, like bands of steel, slide around her. Her lips, unknown to her, had parted slightly as if in invitation. He could feel every yielding curve or thrusting mound she possessed melting against him and he responded in the only way he could . . . he kissed her, claiming tantalizing flesh instead of illusive dreams. "Jenny . . ." he whispered, abandoning his anger and hurt for his need as he tasted her salty tears and felt her sweet breath in his mouth.

For a second, she had responded to him as though yielding to this man was as natural as breathing. But for only a second. He had called her a Judas—a betrayer—and he had chased her through Main Street while everyone watched with no regard for her feelings or respect for her worth.

"You think so little of me . . ." she cried softly. She pushed against him. He moved easily, made nearly senseless from the touch of her lips. "So little!" she repeated more vehemently. Her hand, moving without any conscious direction on her part, swung around and came up. She meant to hurt him as he had hurt her, but the streets gave him an awareness of such things most others didn't possess. He ducked easily beneath her blow, which was thrown with such force that it spun her all the way around and he caught her as she made a full circle.

He didn't try to argue with her as other thoughts too strong had claimed his mind. He simply sought her lips again, but this time with such force it nearly took her breath away. His hands moved across her back, molding her against him while his tongue teased and played with her, promising so much more.

Her anger began to dissolve as her arms, which had been held like a wedge between them, slid upward and curled around his neck. Breathlessly, her lips parted and she swam willingly into the dark green pools of jade which glowed at her with a savage inner fire. His stare was bold and slowly, seductively, his gaze slid downward, causing her to shiver in anticipation. "Gannon . . ." she moaned softly, all the weeks of want and need encased in a single word, as she wound her hands roughly into his still damp hair, pulling him forward seeking his moist lips with her own. Everyone, from the piano player to her uncle John, began to clap and whistle and pound their feet on the floor or their hands on the table in approval.

"By jiggety . . . that's the way, boy!" hooted one old-timer.

"Now, ya got her!" called another. "Go fer it, buckaroo!" The noisy din began to sink into the velvet warmth she had fallen into and scarlet stain colored her cheeks as she pushed him away. He had called her a betrayer . . . a Judas, and she had reacted by giving herself to him in a roomful of people, as though what he had said was a compliment.

His mouth curved into an arrogant smile as he reached forward to touch her hair.

Angrily she slapped at his hand.

"You're wrong, Gannon!" she declared, her voice shaking. "I didn't come to Alaska to force you into marriage . . . and neither did I come because I am a willful child . . . or a Judas!" A tear had worked itself out of the corner of her eye and fell quietly, followed by another. "And as far as me marrying you . . . I wouldn't marry you now if you were the last man on the face of the earth!" She turned and headed for the door.

"Jenny!" shouted John. "Wait . . . tell Gannon what happened!" he pleaded.

"No . . ." she replied in a low voice taut with anger. "And none of you will either!" Looking back over her shoulder her eyes found his. "If he doesn't know me by now . . . he never will. If he thinks I would stoop to such measures just to get my way . . . then let him think that . . . and be damned for it!"

"Jenny!" John called, but it was too late. With tears blinding her eyes and a pain in her heart that went past despair, she pushed her way through the rest of the crowd of people and ran sobbing to her room.

Quiet. Utter, total quiet. Not one sound was made or one person moved.

Gannon stood in the middle of the room with his eyes flashing like lightning from a late summer storm. "Well?" he demanded, wondering if this, too, was another trick. "What is she supposed to tell me, John?"

"I ain't gonna tell ya nothin!" he said angrily. "She's right, ya know . . . if you don't know what kind of a person she is by now . . . then you never will! You don't deserve my niece!" he added. He turned and stomped heavily up the stairs to try and see if he could comfort her.

Some of the customers had resumed talking in low whispers, and a few of them sipped their forgotten drinks, careful to avoid the eyes of the angry stranger. The captain and Emily stood in one corner talking quietly between themselves with their eyes focused on Gannon, until they seemed to reach an agreement about something. The captain straightened his coat and hat and walked over to Gannon.

Gannon regarded him coolly and didn't say a word.

"I'm Captain McGee . . . you can call me Tanith." He reached inside his breast pocket and produced the letter he was supposed to deliver to Gannon in Kansas City. "Jen's a good girl and I wouldn't want to do nothin' she didn't want me to . . . but this was supposed to be for you anyway . . . and she didn't *say* you couldn't *read* what happened."

So saying, he tipped his hat to Gannon and handed him the letter before he walked away, letting him read it all alone. The people in the room were kind enough to pretend he wasn't there.

Later, after he had read the page over, front and back, nearly twenty times, the full realization of what he had done sank in. She had left in order to save his life by going to the mayor's and bargaining with Penelope for his freedom. Penelope was the scheming witch . . . not Jenny. She had written that leaving him had been the hardest thing she had ever done and that was why she couldn't keep her word about not getting in touch with him. Twice now his hotheaded emotions had caused her pain. But it was just so damn difficult to think when she was near. It seemed he always ended up doing the wrong thing. "The road to hell is paved with good intentions," Dugan had always said, and Gannon had to admit that he could see the simple truth in that. If he had only given her the benefit of the doubt, she wouldn't be upstairs sobbing her eyes out and hating him for making a fool out of her.

"Jen," he said softly, folding the letter and placing it into his pocket as he walked through the room and made his way up the stairs.

Emily was on the landing talking to a pretty, blond-haired lady. When she saw him and the sad expression on his face she paused long enough to point to the door of her room. Gannon nodded his thanks and went to it, knocking softly.

"Jenny," he whispered hoarsely. "Jen . . . I'm sorry . . . I didn't know . . ." He could hear her inside, crying. But when he had spoken, the sobs became muffled, as though she were trying to conceal the fact that he had the power to hurt her so.

"Please, Jenny . . . I'm sorry. I was such a fool! Jen?" He tried the door and found that it was locked.

"Oh, Jenny . . ." he pleaded, laying his weary head against the door. She wouldn't answer. "I love you, Jenny . . . please forgive me . . ."

Quiet was all that he heard in return. Feeling more miserable than he ever had in his entire life, he walked toward the landing. Emily and Dolores were there. They had heard every word, but both pretended not to.

"Come on, son," Emily said kindly. "I've got a warm room and I'll have a hot bath made ready for you, too . . . she'll come around. Lord knows, she loves you, too!"

Gannon just sighed and followed her past the room. He was unaware that Jenny stood listening silently at the doorway as his footsteps slowly disappeared down the hall.

CHAPTER

21

The wind had picked up outside and set large drops of rain splattering against the windows. It was October and the sun's fire had grown dim. Weakly, it would rise at seven in the morning before making its feeble climb heavenward, only to tire and set by four in the afternoon. Darkness was winning and would rule unchallenged for over twenty hours in December.

But it was warm and cheerful in The Miner and if the people inside heard the wind rise and knew the freeze had begun, they pretended not to. They laughed and drank and ignored the frigid night spreading over the land.

It was nearly nine now and evening had settled in long ago, as Jenny cleared away the supper dishes. Her mind wasn't on her work, though. The events of the day paraded through in minute detail. Emily had coaxed her out of her room by telling her rather sternly that her work must be done. She had also added, though merely as an insignificant detail, that Gannon was in *his* room and hadn't peeped out all day . . . and judging from the way he looked, she doubted if he'd make an appearance much before night. So Jenny had conceded wordlessly and went about her work, acting as though nothing out of the ordinary had occurred today. The people, customers and workers alike, were kind enough to ignore her as she went about her business. Everyone, that is, except her uncle John. He just couldn't keep still.

". . . just grips 'um, like a fever, makes 'um do stuff they'd never do otherwise. Why, I remember on . . ."

Jenny cut him off before he could finish. "What you're saying, John, is that I shouldn't *blame* Gannon for what he did?" she asked incredulously. "That *he* isn't responsible for chasing me down Main Street, and, and . . . *beating me* in the tavern!?"

"He didn't *beat* ya, Missy . . . he just sorta *spanked* you a little, 'cause . . . 'cause . . . he was so glad to see you!"

"Oh, John!" she cried in exasperation. "You're all alike!"

Supper was over and they were in the kitchen, washing up the last pot and pan. Gannon had been noticeably absent for most of the day. Even though she couldn't see him, she could *feel* his presence and it created a nervous energy in her that was difficult to bear.

"No, Missy . . . you don't understand . . ." he started as she absentmindedly picked up a plate and began to dry it, not even aware that it had slipped through her fingers until she heard it crash to the floor.

"Wonderful . . ." she muttered, sighing as she knelt down and began to pick up the shards of white glass.

"Here, Missy . . ." John offered gently. "Let me help." He too began to pick up the broken pieces. "Why don't ya jest wash up a bit and fix us a couple of plates? I kin do the rest."

Jenny nodded in agreement, too preoccupied with her own thoughts to protest.

"Put lots of gravy on mine and biscuits, too . . . bunches of them!"

She smiled. "Would you like a glass of milk? There's half a pitcher left. I don't think it'll keep another day."

John visibly shivered in disgust. "Hay's fer horses and milk's fer cows," he recited earnestly. "I'll get myself a brew. Lord knows I earned it!"

Jenny laughed as she heaped his plate full, making sure the gravy spilled across his meat and potatoes and cascaded over his mountain of biscuits.

"Ready?" he asked. She nodded as the two of them headed silently for the bar.

The bar was noisy and crowded. People were packed into every corner, drinking or eating. A pair of singularly beautiful green eyes locked onto her as she entered the room and her heart skipped a beat.

Gannon sat at a table near the back of the room with Emily and Kaiuga, facing the door. He was cleaned and shaved and breathlessly handsome. He was waiting for her and she knew it.

For a moment she wondered what her hair looked like and chided herself for putting on her old, brown cotton dress before condemning such betraying thoughts to the cellar of her mind.

Grudgingly, she admitted that he looked wonderful. Then she saw the woman standing behind him with her hand curiously wound into his coppery locks. She was dark skinned with midnight hair and obsidian eyes and only a delicate little upturned bump that must have been her nose. She was dressed nearly the same as her male counterparts, with the exception that her boots of black sealskin stretched forever upward past her knees, darting beneath the folds of her white, fox skin parka. For a second, as Jenny stared at her, she wondered if there was anything *else* beneath the coat except boots. And that thought, with the image of her hand idly toying with his hair, caused her blood to boil. Gannon's smile broadened as he watched her, knowing full well what her reaction meant and apparently delighted by it.

"Ain't you set down yet?" John scolded. She jumped slightly at the sound of his voice.

"No," she apologized halfheartedly. "I guess I'm a little slow tonight." Pain filled her as her eyes were drawn like a magnet back to Gannon. The girl had looked up and seen her standing in the doorway, watching her. But idle curiosity and a beautiful innocence was all that shown on her dusky features.

Gannon just winked.

"What are ya waitin' fer? The food'll be cold by the time we eat it," John said impatiently.

He reached for the tray and started walking back . . . back toward the table where Gannon sat, near the old cast-iron stove. Swallowing hard, she followed him.

John avoided Gannon's table . . . no rudeness intended . . . preferring his favorite spot, which was as near to the stove as a human could possibly get. He always claimed he'd gotten frostbite clean down to his bones one winter and needed all the warmth he could get. Gannon's eyes flashed their displeasure, as Jenny breathed a sigh of relief. She still wasn't ready to talk to him . . . not just yet.

Behind their table, in the corner near the wall, a group of Eskimos sat together on some skins, a little bit away from the rest of the people. Some slept and others appeared to take little interest in the goings on of the others. They were here for the big trade. Determining what gifts they would require in exchange for their furs kept them occupied.

Jenny was having a hard time controlling her feelings and she hurriedly sat down. There was no way that she could turn her back on him because that would have meant moving closer to the stove and scorching her behind. But she moved as far as she was physically able to, which gave him only a profile view of her and made it easier for her to keep her restless eyes focused on her food. No, she couldn't see him, but she could hear quite well . . . every syllable of every word . . .

". . . are his people," Emily was explaining to Gannon. "They are a tribe known as the Nunivaks . . . a sea people from deep in the interior. They come about once a year to trade fox skins and such for things they can't make themselves."

Gannon had overheard some of the bargaining earlier. He was confused because it didn't sound as if the Eskimos thought very much of the product the white man seemed to want.

"This afternoon I heard you talking with a buyer, Kaiuga. I have to admit, I was a little confused at the way you do business." Kaiuga started to smile, knowing full well what was coming next. "You had a huge mound of skins laid out and every time he complimented you on your fine catch, all you would say was that they were not fit to wipe a nose with and that you were a 'worthless hunter.' Why? . . . Obviously he was willing to pay you a great deal."

Emily laughed and Kaiuga grinned, turning halfway around to explain to the woman who was still staring greedily at Gannon's hair, what had been said. She smiled too.

"That's just the way it's done," Emily explained. "It is the big social event of the season for the whole family! Everyone participates. It's something they look forward to all year. We, here in town, and those who come to buy the furs, have, out of respect for these people, learned to play by their rules. The pelts they bring in . . . the blue fox, bear, and such, are the finest in the world. But to these generous people who share everything, *selling* is foreign to them. So we all just kind of make a game out of it, kind of like a ritual of sorts, complete with rules. Besides," she added, "it is one of the best excuses I've ever seen for a party . . . we celebrate for days, feasting and drinking until everyone is clean wore out. Then, one day, one of the buyers will ask someone if he might *have* some of those fine skins be brought in. Mind you now, he says *have* . . . so that the hunter might have the honor of giving him a gift. That's when it gets to be real fun because then the hunter makes a great show of being embarrassed and unworthy, telling everyone as loud as he can what a worthless hunter he is and what a lazy, untalented wife he has who cannot even prepare a skin. On and on it goes, for hours, back and forth, until the family starts to name things they would like to have in return for their 'worthless skins,' as 'presents.' After a while, the 'presents' are added up and placed against the value of the skins and a bargain is reached. But it is never, never referred to as a trade, simply as the exchange of gifts between friends!"

Gannon shook his head. "Sounds pretty complicated to me. Why don't they just trade outright? It would save a lot of time."

Emily and Kaiuga exchanged a look and smiled. "That," Emily said, "would take all the fun out of it!"

Kaiuga nodded in agreement as his fat little wife, Narvaranna, with the bold, flat cheeks, picked up a lock of Gannon's hair, chattering excitedly to her husband.

Jenny just could not keep from looking.

"What is it?" he asked good-naturedly, especially after he saw Jenny turn around.

"My new wife has a question for you," Kaiuga said to Gannon, grinning broadly. Jenny, for reasons unknown, held her breath. "She would like to know if your hair is as red as fire *all over your body.*"

"Aye." He smiled mischievously, catching Jenny's eye. "Just as red . . . and twice as hot!"

Their table burst into laughter as Jenny turned and savagely thrust her fork into the now cold meat.

John had watched the entire proceedings with acute interest, even managing a grin at Gannon's reply, knowing full well what it was intended to provoke. His old eyes missed nothing. He shook his head as he looked at his niece with her head down, pretending to concentrate on her food so no one would see the feelings Gannon evoked in her.

"Jenny, I got something to say to you and you kin tell me to mind my own business if'n you want, but I'm gonna say it anyway!"

He sounded so cross that she looked up startled. She had never seen him mad at anyone with the exception of Joshua until now.

"What is it?" she asked.

"I'm an old man, Jenny . . . and sometimes that's better than being young and fresh, like you, ya know. All's I got to worry about now is whether or not I'm going to wake up tomorrow morning. But that ain't really much of a problem because I'd never know if I didn't." He sighed a long, deep sigh and adjusted the belt on his pants, letting it out a notch or two. He had eaten too much again and was afraid he'd be splitting out of his pants if he kept it up.

"But you know," he resumed, "that's a different matter altogether. Right over there where your eyes keep wanderin'

242

is a man that loves you." He held up his hand to silence her. "Before you go getting yourself all riled up again . . . let me finish. He *loves* you, Jenny . . . and *you* love him. Maybe me bringing you up here was a mistake. Maybe even thinking about the mine . . . is a mistake."

"No, John . . . it wasn't a mistake! I *had* to come!"

"That's right," he said quietly, studying her. "On account of Gannon."

"No . . ." She answered slowly and frowned while she trailed her fork through her gravy. "Not altogether. It was him . . . mostly . . . but that wasn't the only reason, John." She hesitated for a moment, as if searching for the right words to explain to him all her reasons for continuing. "It was Papa and Mama's dream . . . and now they aren't here anymore . . . there's only me and I feel that I have to do this . . . for them."

John nodded and seemed satisfied with her reply. But then, when he spoke, he dropped his voice so low and talked so softly, so conspiratorially . . . as if he were divulging a secret plot . . .

"If you're sure you got to do this thing . . . then we will. I done bought all the supplies we'll need and rounded me up the finest team of dogs I've ever seen. We'll have to leave before light . . . first thing in the morning before anyone else is around."

"Tomorrow?" she asked, startled. He hushed her with a finger to his lips and a curt shake of his head.

"If we kin leave tomorrow and get up to the mine, we'll be back here with a sack full of gold in about a month. By then, you'll have a better idea of what it is you really want."

"What about Aaron?" she asked softly. "What will he think?"

"I'll leave a note in the kitchen explainin' where we've gone, so's he won't worry too much. You kin leave him a note, too . . . if you want. I'll bring by the gear you'll have to wear out there. No dresses, unless you want the north wind riding beneath them the whole way."

Jenny didn't hear the rest of what he had said. All she could think of was leaving Gannon again, and not seeing him, wondering if she had the strength to do it a second time. Maybe her determination to see her parents' dream fulfilled would cause her to lose him for good and that was something she simply couldn't bear to think about. She shuddered.

"Remember, Missy," John said quietly, and the gravity of his words reached her as she looked into his eyes. His cackling, happy-go-lucky expression was gone along with the stern one he'd worn earlier. "Remember . . ." he said again. His face appeared ageless, momentarily changed into one of wisdom and intelligence, the mask he'd earned through countless long years and lonely nights of experience. Lightly he tapped his beer stein against the tabletop, apparently engrossed in his own thoughts.

"Remember *what*, John?" she asked, puzzled by his behavior.

"You think," he said, and peered out at her from under his bushy brows, "that money will buy you happiness . . . am I right? Is that what you think and your father thought, too?"

He had said it more as a statement of fact than a question. She hesitated for a moment, thinking back to all the evenings of fantasizing that her family had done before the fire. Rich, her father had said, they were going to be fantastically wealthy, never knowing want or sacrifice when they finally reached Alaska because of what her uncle John had promised in all of his letters. Her cheeks had flushed a rosy pink as pride welled up in her . . . after all, *he* was the one who had planted those ideas in her family's mind.

"Yes," she answered firmly. "I think it does. It must. Why else would everyone struggle so hard all their lives to attain it? Your dreams became *our* dreams. We lived to come here and build something we could call our own."

He nodded, understanding all too well that he had put those ideas in their heads. Suddenly his expression became vague and dreamy and he seemed far away.

"There's a place I know where the walls are painted yellow with gold," he said, this time forgetting to keep his voice down. "The purest, prettiest, brightest gold I've ever seen . . ." His voice had taken on a dreamy quality and she noticed that he had attracted a few listeners. No one at Gannon's table talked any longer and Narvaranna, no longer the center of attention and not knowing why, sat pouting in a chair behind Kaiuga. Even the other Nunivaks, those who could speak English fairly well, started to listen. "It's bright as day in that mine, and it goes on for miles . . . gold, miles and miles of yeller gold . . ." John continued his story, oblivious to his surroundings. His thoughts had taken him elsewhere, to a place far away. So engrossed were the people becoming in his tale that no one saw as Joshua, soaking wet, with large, lacy-shaped flakes of snow—the first of the season—clinging to his beard came in.

"Gold?" he said sarcastically, as he peeled off his coat. *"Walls* of gold? I think you've slipped into your dreams, old man. Where is this so-called mine of yours?" He shook his head in disbelief.

John snapped around quickly, his eyes narrowing when he saw who stood there. There was just no use trying to get along with this walrus. No use. "You think I'm crazy too, don't you?" Well, you just take a gander at this!" He reached inside his shirt and pulled at something which hung around his neck. His hand remained closed over it as he brought it forward, the leather straps which held it dangling limply down. The barroom full of people, sensing something exciting, became suddenly quiet. All were interested in what the old man possessed, and he, realizing he had an audience, exaggerated his movements, becoming more theatrical with each one. Standing up, he nearly tipped a chair over backward, as he turned full circle, his hand still clutched tightly around the object as he thrust it forward like an amulet.

"Gold!" he proclaimed. "Walls and miles of gold. I'm the only white man who knows where it is!" He stopped directly in front of Joshua, staring straight at him. The crazy expression was gone and with all the dignity and seriousness of a newly married groom showing off his bride, he slowly unclenched his fist. Lying in the center lay a large golden object, the giant twin to Jenny's lovely gift. The light from the kerosene lamps fairly danced on its surface and it appeared more like a live, warm thing than an inanimate, cold mass of stone. "Gold," he whispered. A collective sigh rose and echoed around the room, followed by appreciative "oohs" and "ahs" and shaking heads.

Joshua looked startled. So, he thought, there was more than one nugget in that mine. He looked at John with something like contempt or jealousy . . . or maybe even hunger. But he struggled to appear indifferent, shrugging his shoulders as he tried hard to conceal his greed. But John had seen it! Oh, yes! He knew that he'd been right about Joshua all along.

"Where'd you get that one, you old bum?" Joshua sneered. "You mean you could have paid your way around here instead of having you and her living off of charity?"

"Joshua!" Jenny shouted in surprise. What was happening to her old friend? "How can you talk to him that way?"

"He could've bought the best for you, Jenny . . . *should've* bought the best!" he said in defense of his actions. "But instead of letting you live like a lady . . . like you deserve . . . he's been keepin' it from you . . . wearing it around his neck like . . . like what he is . . . a crazy old bum!"

"I ain't an old bum!" John said indignantly. "And I don't want to hear you tell me we've been living off'n charity . . . I done work fer my keep and her as well. Same as you!" he added, straightening up. He looked him boldly in the eye, forgetting for a moment the chunk of gold glowing in his hand.

"He's right, Joshua," Emily broke in. She moved heavily from the now silent table toward the back of the bar. "They've *both* worked—and worked hard, I might add. But John, I have to tell you . . . you luggin' around that rock makes me a bit nervous. If I were you I'd get that gold over to the assayer first thing in the morning and the money in the bank as soon as possible."

"I agree," said Gannon, who'd been silent until now. "There are too many things that can happen to it, and *you*, so long as you're carrying it around." His eyes happened to focus on Jenny when he said this as if to let her know that "things" could happen to her as well, but she pretended not to comprehend his message.

"Naw!" John said defensively. "It's my lucky charm. I've carried it with me for quite a few years now and nothin's happened to me yet." He fingered the rock lovingly and looked long and hard at the roomful of staring and silent people. Joshua had totally divested himself of his wet furs and was nursing along a large glass of beer, deep in thought. "Besides," continued John, "nobody in their right mind would want it anyhow. It's supposed to be cursed!"

"Cursed!" laughed a man by the bar and nudged his friend. "Sure . . . it's cursed!" They both laughed along with quite a few other people.

Murmurs rose from the rest, some skeptical, some wary, some shaking with laughter. But a few of them, mostly those who had lived here as long as he had, and the Nunivaks resting in the corners, appeared a little uneasy at the mention of that particular word.

Joshua turned, resting one arm on the bar, yawning in apparent boredom. "Cursed, huh?" He yawned again, his gaze never moving from John's tired old face. "You're just plain crazy . . . from the first I met you I knew." Yet his eyes flickered slightly and rested on the gold still held out in John's hand. "What sort of a curse would there be on a piece of gold?" he asked, innocently challenging him to tell his story in front of everyone.

John knew if he didn't, they would all think he was nothing more then a daft old fool. *Them* he could tolerate, what they thought of him didn't matter . . . but Jenny, he just couldn't let her think that *everything,* the mine, the dream, *everything,* was nothing more than an elaborate lie told by a lonesome old miner.

"Well?" Joshua prompted, taking a slow draw of his beer. "Don't you have a story for us? My friends," and he pointed to a group of men by the door, "they told me that there wasn't a mine around these parts that hadn't been used up. Why don't you tell her the truth and let her get on with her life? You got no right keepin' her here just 'cause you ain't got no one else!"

John looked around slowly. Everyone, expecting something, had begun to move in closer, their faces showing a curious mixture of excitement and skepticism . . . all but the Eskimos, whose faces registered traces of fear. Some of them spoke English and were translating what they were hearing in whispers to the rest of their group. Curses were very real to them in this harsh land and they believed without question stories most white men would scoff at. It was not that they weren't civilized or what most whites would call "ignorant savages." It was just that living as they did, depending on the forces of nature to survive, they had learned to see and hear things no white man could even imagine, except in the confines of his dreams. Nature was not always kind. There were rules to be observed and penalties exacted when they were broken. So they listened, knowing already that a law had been broken.

John still hesitated. Being challenged to repeat what he knew made him nervous. It wasn't that he was superstitious. Some of the stories he had heard were downright funny, but not this one . . . this one made him nervous . . . even *thinking* about it.

The people in the bar had begun to crowd around him, eager for a story. Even drinking and making merry became boring after too many repetitions. The thought of an exciting story to break their monotony was inviting.

John looked around at their expectant faces and collapsed resignedly in his chair, sighing heavily. Gannon had moved his chair right beside Jenny, who didn't object, as the sound of the wind outside began to build, whistling mournfully around the eaves. A few more logs were shoved into the red heat of the stove and a few more drinks were poured as everyone settled in, waiting.

"Seems I ain't got no choice but to tell ya," he said quietly. "Mind ya now . . . I didn't make this up! It comes to me from a tribe of Nunivaks further north . . . some of the relatives of these very folks sitting here . . . one of *your* kin, Kaiuga, the man with the five names I never can remember . . ."

"Well," he began and everyone pulled together, forming a

tight ring around him . . . a primitive circle of magic drawn by people on a windy, wintry night; a circle of protection filled with eager faces ignorant of the figure they had formed.

"Seems there were these two friends, a long, long time ago . . . way after the people had crossed over the water and come to this land. One was of the Sea People and the other was an Angakok . . . a kind of an Eskimo sorcerer or medicine man, who lives far away, deep in the interior. They were thicker than thieves, these two. Got together regular every year to celebrate and brought gifts to each other just like they was brothers. Only one winter when the lights warned the medicine man of hard days ahead, he didn't show up on time. It was a real bad year for the reindeer and even with all his hunting spells and conjuring words, it seemed he just couldn't get one to bring to his friend. But he didn't give up, he just kept on searching, knowing he'd find one someday. While he was hunting for his reindeer, his friend, who always sat aside the biggest, fattest seal he could find, was doing just that, even filling it with some sort of bird . . . the best treat he knew how to make . . . just for his friend. But the days started to grow long and he never came until the Nunivak started to believe he'd forgotten all about him . . . like he wasn't important to him anymore. He started to get real mad, feeling worse and worse with every day that went past. Until one day, so fed up with anger and hurt, he took out his special seal and started eating it himself, silently cursin' his old friend with every mouthful . . ."

Jenny noticed that when a nervous-looking young Eskimo translated this last part of the story to the rest of his clan, the others began to look as uneasy as he did, glancing quickly at one another as if they already knew the rest. Especially Kaiuga, who had been John's friend and partner for many years and had known nothing of his visits to the mine. But John didn't seem to notice, he just stretched a little and looked out toward the window, contemplating the sleet that the wind had plastered to the fogged window for a second, before it tore it savagely away. "Like I said, he got mad, figured he'd been forgotten by the sorcerer. But what he didn't know was that his friend was still out on the frozen plains still hunting, looking for the finest reindeer he could find to bring him. Finally, after many days the Angakok did the grand-daddiest bit of conjuring he could and, lo and behold, he got one! A big buck, full of fat and tender meat!"

John reached for his beer and swallowed long and deep before he went on. His mouth had gone dry. All the Eskimos had backed away from him, breaking the circle that had clustered around him . . . all except Kaiuga, who stood and listened motionless with a sad expression on his face. John looked around at the eager faces and began again, choosing to ignore the frightened Eskimos and the somber-looking Kaiuga. "Well, after he had caught that big ol' buck, he packed him on his sled and journeyed many days over the ice toward the seas and his friend . . . only when he got there the other fella was still pretty mad, even after he told him how bad the huntin' had been and all that he had been through just to get this buck."

John sat up a little straighter and looked intensely at the people. His voice had fallen lower, barely above a whisper. "The Angakok didn't know that the man from the sea tribe was planning some mischief, wanting to get back at the ol' sorcerer for havin' come so late. So he tells his friend to take a seat, they're gonna have a great feast in his honor! The Sorcerer sits down, happy to be with him again . . . happy to be with his friend. But the man from the sea tribe is full of dark thoughts and dark magic is on his mind, but he keeps his intentions well hidden as he goes outside and sneaks around to the back where a small icehouse sits, its openings filled with snow and sealed with ice. It is the last dwelling place of a man who has just died, one of their own. The Nunivak commences diggin' . . ."

John's hand started to move mechanically through the air as if he were burrowing through hard, icy snow. His eyes stared hard and had taken on a feverish gleam, while his breathing was shallow and rapid as he pushed his arms stiffly against imaginary snow. "He keeps on a-diggin', diggin', in the hard white snow, till he breaks through the hard doors of ice and finds the man what was buried there . . . Then he looks all around to make sure nobody has seen him and he pulls out his knife . . ."

John produced an invisible knife from thin air and held it poised high above his head. "The knife, it's sharp, but the body, well . . . it's hard as a rock . . ." He began to make a sawing motion with his hand. "It's pretty rough goin', cutting past all the furs they buried him in, until finally he gets to the man's frozen meat and starts cutting off a piece of it!"

A startled "Oh!" rippled through the room, followed by uneasy silence as everyone listened with rapt attention. It was only a story to them and an interesting way to pass a winter's night, but for the Eskimos crowded together near the stove it was a terrifying truth and they were frightened. John liked having an audience and paused for effect, holding one hand in the air with an imaginary chunk of flesh dangling from it and a crazy grin on his face.

"When he gets himself a piece of it, he goes back to the seal he was carvin' up for supper and rubs the meat with the fat from the dead man. See," he explained, like a teacher giving A-B-C lessons to first graders, "the Eskimos believe if a man eats any part of another man—even by accident— he'll go crazy and start trying to carve up and eat anybody what comes around. That's what the fella from the sea wanted him to do, go crazy and do awful things because he had been so mad at him and it was the worse thing he could think of to do—worse than even killin' him."

There were nods and murmurs of understanding in the crowd, as if this story seemed believable to these people. And maybe, because it was dark, and the wind blew coldly and the first snow had started to fall . . . maybe it was *easy* to believe . . .

"But this fella from the interior, being he's a magic-man himself, has a guardian spirit that looks out for him. When his friend brought him the bad meat to eat, the spirit would tug a little at his leg . . . like this." He demonstrated, capturing his trousers at the bottom between two fingers and giving them a yank. "Just enough to make him put his food down. The Angakok was hungry and after a while he started to get a little mad at his spirit, thinking it was only having some fun with him and wishing it had picked a better time to play. Finally, too tired to put up with its tricks any longer, the magic-man excuses himself to go out back and when he does his spirit is there waiting for him and tells him what his friend is up to. At first, he doesn't believe it's true, mostly 'cause he don't want to. But the spirit convinces him, takin' him down to the center of the world, dragging him through the cold, hard snow and rocks, dragging him down . . . down . . . till he is in the Dream Place, far below, where time don't mean nothing and what's already gone by can be seen. The spirit does a little conjuring and pretty soon the magic-man sees his friend, all stooped over in a little ice house sawin' away on one of his own kin and his heart is black and filled with evil thoughts . . . evil thoughts against *him.*"

John stretched a little and took a sip of his beer. His joints seemed frozen from the inside out and he found it difficult to hold the mug. Ruefully, he stretched them open, ignoring the pain, gingerly rubbing the sore knuckles of his right hand with his other while he continued the story.

"The sorcerer gets mad . . . real mad, thinking to himself how his friend has done him dirty and he wants to get even real bad with him for what he had tried to do. But his spirit senses his thoughts and tells him to just let it lie. Just eat the other side of the meat and forget all about what he'd seen. If he could do that, then things would be just like they used to be before evil ideas had come to hide in his friend's heart.

"But the magic-man was smart. Quietly, so's his spirit couldn't hear, he does a little conjuring prayer and draws a shadow over *his* heart so his thoughts couldn't be known. Then he pretends that he was going to do just what it wanted . . . eat the other side of the meat . . . turn the other cheek . . . and jest let things be . . . even though, in his heart, he knew he couldn't. But his spirit didn't know this and was satisfied that it had done its job and things would be like they was. Together, the two of them made the hard climb back up into the world . . ."

The windows shook a little under the building fury of the storm outside, but no one seemed to notice. They were just like children telling ghost stories when the lights are low . . . so engrossed in the legend of the two friends—thrilling to the frantic beating of their hearts and the cold shivers of fear dancing against their spines like icy fingers—that they were oblivious to everything else, including the violently born arctic freeze which had just begun.

Gannon noticed with some amusement, and also a surge of pleasure, how Jenny had inched closer, leaning nearer, until their sides nearly touched. He could smell the faintest trace of rose and ambergris—the scent he had given her—in her hair, and restrained the desire to touch her ashen curls and kiss the wispy strands of silver that trailed so innocently down her neck. Ghost stories had their advantages, he mused, grinning, as John resumed his tale.

"Well . . ." he started, "hardly a minute or two had passed before he goes back into his friend's house, smiling all the while and playing games . . . like he don't know what is going on. They sit down together and start eating, but not until the magic-man flips his meat over when his friend ain't lookin'. Seems like his old spirit was right all along because the only thing the sorcerer got is a little stomachache. But that don't stay long, no, not too long, and he don't go crazy, neither."

A relieved sigh rose from the crowd, happy at his near escape. The Eskimos were the only ones in the group who didn't appear at ease, but John didn't notice as he took another sip of his beer, wiping away the last of the foam with the back of his hand.

"Kin you fill this up, Em?" he asked politely, as he squinted one eye and peered unhappily down the inside of the empty mug. "Seems my cup has a hole in the bottom . . . and maybe if it ain't too much trouble," he added, almost guiltily, "could you throw another log or two on the fire? I think my backside's startin' to ice up."

"Sure thing, John," she said, smiling in her good-humored way. "Wouldn't want icicles hanging from your rump!" Everyone laughed, including John, as she waddled toward the stove, where she picked up a couple of large pieces of old dried pine from the wood box and chucked them neatly into the stove. They sizzled and popped angrily, catching fire almost immediately as she swung the heavy door shut with a loud bang.

"Ahhh . . ." he said appreciatively, as he felt the first licking flame of warmth caress his back. "That ought to do just fine! Now . . . where was I? Oh, uh . . . thanks again, Em . . . story tellin' is mighty thirsty work!" He took the offered beer gratefully, nearly draining the entire glass in one long swallow, while a few onlookers giggled. "Now," he said, refreshed and warm, "this story should've ended right there . . . but it didn't, no sir . . . it didn't, 'cause the sorcerer, for all his magic ways, was just like most men. He couldn't forget what his friend had tried to do to him and he couldn't forgive him for being so weak and foolish. All the while they were eating, he was contemplating his revenge while the man from the sea was contemplating his guilt and was starting to hope that his foolish magic hadn't worked. He'd started to feel so bad for what he had done that he repented inside, wanting only for things to be like they was . . . wantin' only to be friends again. So, when the sorcerer seemed all right he became real happy, talkin' and swappin' lies just like in the old days, until the meal was over and it was time for the magic-man to go on home. He was a shrewd one, that old magic-man. With a big ol' grin on his face, he invited his friend to come over to his house, promising him a real good time and a big feast, too. Well, that sea fella became downright jolly, sayin' he'd be over straight away . . . and he was, too. Just as soon as he could pack a sled, he followed the sorcerer home."

A hush had fallen on the crowd as if they sensed the climax to the tale was not far off. They were sheltered in the wooden walls of The Miner, protected from the bitter night outside by only a few thick inches of pine, while Boreas, the cruel north wind, blew in from across the black waters, wailing like a banshee. Sleet and snow rode into town across its broad back, and driven by the galelike intensity of the storm, it wedged itself into every available crack and crevice, layer by subtle layer, until the muddy roads hardened and filled and every trace of man had been erased. The town looked both deserted and savagely new.

Inside, beneath the cheerful glow of the lamps and the pine-scented warmth coming from the stove, the people settled in eagerly, waiting for the rest of the story.

John stretched a little and yawned a little, staring absentmindedly across the room and not seeing the snow build on the windows, or the flushed faces of his friends. What he saw was in his mind and the words that came only described each scene. . . .

"When they got to the sorcerer's home, he makes a big to-do over him . . . makes him feel real welcome, setting out the best food he has. When his friend ain't lookin', he reaches inside his coat and brings out the piece of poisoned meat . . . the piece that was meant for him . . . and he rubs it real good all along the reindeer fat he had cut off. Then, sure of the justice of it all, he gives it to his friend to eat, knowing that it was the piece of meat he liked the best . . . And he ate it, every bite, even lickin' the juice from his fingers. You see, the Sea People, like most of the tribes, ain't like their magic-men. They don't have no guardian spirits lookin' out for them. After a while, when they're just loungin' back shootin' the breeze, his stomach starts to hurt real bad . . . and he starts getting queer thoughts in his head, bad thoughts . . . hungry thoughts . . . And he knew, at that moment, what had been done to him. Standing up as far as the icehouse would let him, he looked long and hard at his friend and then nearly falling to the ground in pain, he did one last noble thing . . . one act that showed how much he really cared about the old Angakok—he left . . . ."

Gannon's arm had stretched protectively across Jenny's chair, encircling her with his strength. With the wind lashing bitterly at the windows and exploding in little gusts down the flue of the stove, she didn't seem to mind, even allowing herself the pleasurably secure feeling of his touch along her back.

"Well, that tainted meat . . . it done its job all right!" John said forcefully. "'Cause when the sea fella returned home, he done lost his mind to the sickness in him and the pain of his awful want. He killed all the people in his house . . . his wife and kids and even his own ma, eating them up, before he started working his way through his dogs, one by one, and any passerby unlucky enough to stop over. Meanwhile, way up north the magic-man had started to feel pretty bad for what he'd done and decided to go and visit him, hoping his magic hadn't worked. But when he got there, he seen his friend had killed all his family and eaten them. He would've ate the magic-man too, 'cept the sickness was working on him and he was just too weak to catch him. That old magic-man turned tail and run like the red-eyed devil himself was after him, feeling both scared and sad about how things had turned out . . ."

John seemed to reflect for a moment until someone standing near Joshua cried out impatiently, "How'd it end? Was that it?"

He looked at the man who'd spoken up. His expression became impossibly old, as though he had aged fifty years in the space of a few seconds. "End?" he asked as if he didn't quite comprehend the meaning of the word. "Well . . . I guess you could say that the magic-man felt so bad on account of what he'd done he decided to take his best spells and charms and go on back and see what he could do. But when he got there, no one was around, nothin' . . . 'cept a lot of old bones and scraps of hair. But he searched around, not wanting to give up . . . going outside and looking in all the familiar places. He still caught no sight of him."

John's eyes began to take on a peculiar faraway look, as if he was not only telling a story but seeing it happen. People eager to hear the rest urged him to finish, and when he looked into their excited faces the weariness of all his long years seemed magnified . . . as if he had just seen too much . . . lived too long . . .

"You got to have the key to the cellar," he said quietly. "Is that it then? I know ya do," he said tiredly, the years weighing heavily on his mind. *"I* did, too . . ." In a low, calm voice, more like an echo from a dream, he continued. "Well then . . . that's the way it is and always will be . . . so, here she is . . . That ol' magic-man, he kept on searching till he came up to a cave in the side of a huge old mountain. The snow hadn't fallen for three days now, and a trail wide and unbroken led into it. There weren't no footprints—no, no footprints. It was more like somethin' had 'drug' itself there . . . lying down in the snow and pulling itself along . . . inch by inch . . . He followed that track right into the cave . . . Yes sir," he whispered, pausing for effect. "He done followed those tracks right into the very heart of that old mountain, thinking maybe his friend might have been hurt. But when he gets inside, he's mighty surprised because there ain't much light coming through the opening . . . hardly any at all . . . but it's bright in there, real bright . . . 'cause the walls and floors are made of gold . . . pure, yellow gold . . . And there, lying all curled up in a little ball on that cold floor in the middle of a great cavern of gold is his friend. He could see the blood dried on his face and hands, and there was still bits of skin clinging to his teeth. But he was dead . . . no doubt about that . . . at least his body was. This here magic-man believed that once a man died who'd eaten other men, he couldn't rest and his spirit was let loose on the world looking to eat again. So the sorcerer went outside and killed the biggest fattest dog he had, and 'drug' it inside to lay beside his friend. This way the sea fella's spirit would have a little meat to keep him busy while he boarded up the cave. After he was done and all the wood was in place and the snow piled high, the magic-man said a little prayer callin' on all five names of his friends hoping he could sleep now on account of he couldn't get out of the mine. And as long as nobody disturbs him . . . he would sleep on that cold, hard floor . . . as long as nobody wakes him up . . ."

John stared thoughtfully into their frightened faces, before catching Jenny's eye. He spoke directly to her, ignoring the others.

"A few years ago, I heard about the mine and I decided to go take a look-see. I'd been diggin' in these blasted hills for so long now without a lucky strike. I just wanted to hit it big . . . just once to make my life stand for something . . . and maybe leave a little behind when I'm gone. The cave was right where they said it was, beneath an old mountain, all closed up with trees and snow and such. I knew what lay in there, I *knew*, but I hungered too . . . for the gold and what it could get me. I pulled the wood away, piece by piece, and I dug through the snow till I made a hole just big enough to crawl through and I went on inside. It was just like they said too, rooms full of gold, like steppin' into the womb of the mother lode herself . . . And I seen *him*, too, in the great old cavern in the center, lying all alone in that cold grave. Old bones, lying there . . . human bones and a dog, side by side. I guess he ain't restin' no more. No, he ain't sleepin', 'cause I done woke him up!"

No one moved and not a sound was made. The wind began to pound its fist against the walls, wailing in misery around the eaves while the old black stove popped and hissed mechanically. Jenny felt her neck tingle as if a small electric current ran along her back. For a moment, she began to wonder if Joshua wasn't right about her uncle all along. Maybe he was crazy.

"Pretty darn good yarn, wasn't it?" John asked. He started to chuckle like he had really pulled a good one. "Hey, Kaiuga, why don't ya come on over here and tell them a few more. He knows some real good ones! Tell 'um about the lights, Kaiuga, and the wolves too!"

Kaiuga just shook his head slowly, a sober expression on his face. He made an attempt to move closer, shoving a little past his kin and the miners that flanked John on both sides.

Joshua had drained his third beer and was working on his fourth when he spoke up. "If this cave is haunted like you say it is . . . how come *you* weren't bothered?" he demanded skeptically.

John appeared to consider the question carefully before he answered, examining the cracks in the floorboards for quite a while, before he slid his gaze to the now nearly white, snow-packed window while he thoughtfully tugged at his beard.

"That there, Walrus, is a good question, on account of I don't rightly know," he confessed. "But I've carried these rocks around for quite a while—mine and the one I gave to

Jenny in Kansas City—and I never seem to have any trouble at all."

"My name ain't *Walrus!*" Joshua shouted angrily. He slammed down the rest of his beer. "It's Joshua, old man, Josh-u-ah! And if you're telling me that you really believe all that stuff, then I know I was right about you all along . . . you *are* crazy!"

John had felt a good many emotions in his long life, but none quite as strong as the dislike he felt for Joshua. He was good to Jenny . . . on that account he wouldn't argue, but for himself, he couldn't stand the sight of him.

"I never said I believe that story or ghosts or buggety-boos neither!" John retorted in self-defense. "But I've lived long enough to know there are things . . . evil things that live even if only in the hearts of some men!" The last statement was more like an accusation then a comment and a hard look fell on him from Joshua.

"I believe," came a soft voice from the back and everyone looked to see who had spoken. The words, so quiet and filled with authority, came from Kaiuga, whose manner was not fearful but somber. The other Eskimos stood together near the stove and nodded their heads in agreement. White men had always laughed at their stories, their beliefs, at first . . . until they lived out here a while and then they became less skeptical, more open-minded, more afraid.

"John speaks the truth," he added simply and walked toward them. "You shouldn't have let him loose, John," he scolded, wagging a finger in reproach. "But you are good, that's why he cannot live in you," he explained. "The evil one must find a dark heart to plant his seed. When he does, he will dwell there, growing stronger by the day, until the one he inhabits becomes wicked and loves wicked ways. Take the gold rocks back, John," he admonished sternly. "Bring a little food for the spirit, so that he may stay a while near his bones. Then you will have time to put the boards across the cave so that he may rest again . . . and things will be like they were before."

John was looking at Kaiuga with a hopeful gleam in his wide eyes. Jenny realized at that moment that deep down inside, he *believed* in the curse and that he had defied it in order to bring real all the dreams that he had written about to her and her family all these years. It was no wonder to her now why he had acted the way he did and she felt sorry for him.

"Ya mean, if I put 'um back and bring a little meat, everythin' will be like it was?" His face had brightened considerably as Kaiuga nodded.

"Yes, but," and there was an ominous tone in Kaiuga's voice, "if you do not . . . the evil one will come. And soon people will die because he is always hungry . . ."

Bang! A sudden, sharp gust of wind burst through the door, sweeping coldly into the room.

Jenny cried out and instinctively threw her arms around Gannon's neck, while everyone in the room looked around nervously, suddenly sober. Some hid behind embarrassed laughs, pretending not to be afraid, but the Eskimos were clearly terrified. The oldest ones began to murmur a chant in a singsong rhythm as old as time itself, while Joshua ran to shut the door.

Kaiuga motioned for his kin to follow and they all moved toward the hall. At the threshold, he stopped and turned around, looking for John. He wasn't calm anymore.

"John, you must hurry and return the gold . . . for I fear it is already too late!"

He turned and opened the door, letting in white swirling snow devils and icy cold air. Another loud bang and they were gone.

The silence was oppressive and Emily couldn't stand it. Ghost stories aside, it just wasn't *natural* for this many people all bunched up together to be so quiet!

"Joshua!" she hollered, breaking the silence with her throaty roar, "bring me a beer!" She waded through the people toward the piano. Pulling out the narrow bench, she sat her ample girth down, neatly spilling over the sides, and soon the walls and rafters were shaking with the music made by the agile probing of her large hands. Tiny notes rose into the air, creating a melody that was soon accompanied by the harmonic sounds of human voices. Some laughed, some whispered, but the noise was glorious and reassuring in its intensity.

It was then that Jenny became aware of the regular, strong beating of the heart that pumped beneath the chest her head rested against . . . and the firm arms that wound securely around her. She drew away just a little until her eyes met his and he smiled . . . not arrogantly or angrily, but sweetly and tenderly. It was as if the last few horrible weeks had not existed. All that there was in the world was the sight, the scent, the *feel* of him against her . . . no ghosts or dreadful lonely nights to bare, just him . . .

"Dag nabbit!" someone hollered, crashing drunkenly down in front of them on the table. The moment was gone, but not the feeling . . . the feeling that she had come home at last and that *home* was Gannon.

The room had become boisterous and loud, as if the patrons intended to ward off evil spirits and spooky thoughts with as much noise as they could make. But standing motionless in the center, all alone and so obvious because of his silence, was John, a quiet, somewhat crazy old miner with a headful of unfulfilled dreams and a lonely old heart. Jenny, in her happiness, ached for him. Gannon had followed her gaze and felt her attention, which for one brief wonderful moment had been focused solely on him, slip away. Softly, he let her go, carefully unwinding his arm before catching her eyes with his, an understanding look in them.

She hesitated for a moment before standing up, not wanting to relinquish the feel of his arms tucked so snugly around her. But she did, moving away, being drawn by the pain so visible on her uncle's face, his grief moving her more than she cared to admit. So like her father, he was—only older, more bent and used. But the same gentle spirit lingered in his sparkling blue eyes and the same sorrow, too—the sorrow of a life still unfulfilled and wanting.

"John?" she asked. "Are you all right?"

Her hand had touched his shoulder briefly. It was as if he were waking from a bad dream. He noticed her, not altogether at once, but in pieces, as if he were desperately trying to come back to focus on what was going on around him instead of what was in his head.

"Missy . . ." he murmured. "We got to go to the mine, Missy . . ." He grasped her hand, a wild, feverish light filling his eyes. "We'll get us a load on, a *big* one—as much as the dogs'll carry and bring it on back before the big snows come. We'll show 'um!" he said defiantly, shaking his fist at the empty air. "We'll show 'um all, Missy—jest like I promised!"

"John, you don't have to *prove* anything to me. The mine . . . it's not important any . . ."

"It is to *me!*" he shouted angrily. "It is to *me!* It's all I got left to give, Missy . . . all that's left . . . of *me!*"

She had become silent under his fierce gaze. A muscle worked reflexively in his jaw and she felt the tension in his words. The mine was everything to him. She could see that now. It was what his life had been all about, what he had dreamt of, yearned for. The searching for it had been his quest, his mission, like a rustic Don Quixote who fought the hardships of Alaska instead of imaginary windmills. It was his way of proving to all these people, to her, and most importantly to himself, that his life hadn't been lived in vain.

Sighing, she resigned herself to her fate, wondering if there ever were such things in life as choices or free will. She remembered the Greek Fates, the Three Sisters she had read about who sat and wove the threads of human life— weaving and clipping and deciding without ever considering what the puppets they controlled might want, might *feel*. Destiny, it seemed, had dealt all the cards and had saved the aces for itself. Jenny knew she had to finish what she had begun, what had begun nearly twenty-five years ago, before she was even born, and for a second she feared for her own sanity, feeling it leaving, being drawn away in the wild night winds of Alaska and the impossible dreams of a lonely old man.

"When are we going?" she asked.

"Morning . . . b'fore light," he whispered.

"In the *morning?!*" she sputtered, not caring who heard. "*Tomorrow* morning?"

"Shhh!" he hissed and drew her head close to his until she could feel his scratchy beard of wiry gray whiskers poking at her cheek and smell the faintly disagreeable odor of beer and biscuits on his breath. "Yesss," he hissed, "tomorrow morning—'fore light! I'll throw a few rocks at yer window to wake you. When I do, you get up right away and put on the clothes I'm gonna bring you tonight. Don't wake Em up! Her nose is longer than most men's legs—she won't let ya leave till she knows everythin', and maybe not even then!"

He paused for a second, studying her intently. She was quite sure what little color she did possess had drained away and she felt a little dizzy. "And don't say nothin' to *him* neither." He jerked his head in Gannon's direction. Jenny started to protest and he shushed her for the second time that night. "No, Missy . . ." he warned. "He'll try and stop you . . . and I'm thinking if he tries hard enough he will. Just remember your folks if you start to feel weak. Just remember what they worked so hard for . . . what they came here for . . . it can be for you, too . . . all of it!"

"Gannon . . ." she whispered softly, one word that encased a thousand emotions. "What will he think? I don't want to lose him."

"Don't go troubling your mind about *him,* Missy. He won't leave, not till he has you! Now, you best get some sleep. Tomorrow is going to be a long day."

Everything that her parents had worked for, dreamed of, planned for, had finally reached its climax. And so, too, was the desperate need of her uncle to prove that his words had been true and his mind was sound. All *this,* she mused, to fulfill others' dreams, her dream too at one time, but now . . . she was not so sure.

Without another word, John turned and walked jauntily out of the bar. She watched him leave with a sinking feeling in her stomach as she turned to face Gannon, wondering how she was to keep from telling him, secretly hoping that

263

maybe, just *maybe,* he might convince her to stay . . . and found that he wasn't there anymore. Her heart skipped a beat as she saw the empty chair before she hastily began to scan the room. She searched for him through the tangled mass of dancers, serious card players, and pretty professional women. No flash of copper, only garish red skirts. No eyes of searing, clever green . . . No Gannon.

Sighing and damning her luck all in a single breath, she started to think that perhaps it was better this way, better to take the coward's way out and leave with only a note to hold him here, a slip of paper to keep him from thinking that she had fled again . . . Besides, it would be easier because her resistance to him was notoriously low. Even a glance at his broad, sweeping shoulders or the tight curved thighs she'd come to know so intimately—even a *word,* or worse yet, his *touch,* would cause her resolve to melt like a snowflake in summer's heat. One last look, hoping and dreading at the same time, feeling a little angry and a lot frustrated, she turned and headed for her room.

The steps were dimly lit as she climbed them, following the corridor to her door. The sounds from the bar were slowly receding with each step, but silence didn't claim the empty space. The wind moaned forlornly around the wooden building, begging to be let in. She shivered involuntarily as she reached for the doorknob to Emily's room. The wind whistled shrilly and she felt cold air pushing through the cracks around the door. Turning the knob, she opened it and was about to enter when a delicate touch at the back of her neck made her jump and turn with a startled "Oh!" on her lips.

Gannon laughed quietly, a devilish light shining in his eyes.

"I didn't mean to startle you, Jen," he stated teasingly.

"Oh?" she answered tartly, a little sarcasm lacing her words. "I think you did!" She gave a nervous laugh.

He grinned broadly, while the golden glow of the lamps cast dark shadows all around his face. Still, she could see the nearly perfect whiteness of his teeth and the firm sensuous curve of his mouth. All the emotions he felt were shown in his eyes this time. He hid nothing from her—delight, amusement, mischievousness, desire . . . everything he felt or thought was registered plainly for her to see, finally emerging from the arrogant, self-assurance she had come to know so well. He leaned against the wall, jamming his hands into his pockets to keep them from straying.

"What were you and your uncle John discussing so intensely down below?" he asked in an off-handed manner as though he really wasn't interested at all . . . but he was, painfully so. Their conversation had seemed all absorbing and far too secretive with all the shushing going on.

"Nothing special," she quipped, feeling guilty the moment the lie had escaped her lips. Then she caught her breath, as she watched the slow knowing smile start to form on his face as if he had read her mind. He had such power over her, evoked such passion! It was at once a curse and the profoundest blessing, but nothing she could control, no switch to regulate the flow or stop the current of attraction she felt whenever he was near.

"Uh-hmmmm . . ." he murmured, as if he didn't believe her. "Whatever you say, Jenny." He turned fully toward her, standing quite still, framed in the light of the lamps. He was so tall and masculine, a stark solid shadow outlined in golden fire.

Slowly he brought his hand out of its hiding place, touching her lips gently, tracing the outline with the tip of his finger. His eyes had transferred their gaze to her mouth and a slow sensuous warmth began to curl around her middle, inching upward, making her legs tremble and go weak. In a moment not touched by time, she was stepping into his arms of steel, the music from the tinny piano fading away as Gannon held her close. His hands, strong and powerful, played lightly over her back, her hair, the sensations incredible, the abandonment complete . . . the wet heat of her loins testifying that she wanted him, needed him, now . . .

"Hey, Missy . . ." John called as he cleared the landing, his arms filled to overflowing with furry things of every color. Then he stopped, as what he had thought was a single shadow, paused and separated. He saw his niece in the obscure light, her cheeks pink with acute embarrassment, and Gannon looking slightly frustrated and a trifle mad.

"Oh . . ." he said, knowing his ears had turned a glowing apple red. "I didn't mean to, ah . . ." He stopped, unable to complete the sentence.

"It's all right, John," Jenny said quietly. "I was just getting ready to go to bed and a-h-h-m, Aaron stopped by to say goodnight."

"Well, uh, sure," he said, fidgeting for the words to cover his discomfort. "These," and he thrust the furry clothes toward her, "are for you."

She took them from him while the three of them stood together in the most uncomfortable silence Jenny could ever remember.

"Well," John interjected, wanting to fill the void with something, *anything* . . . "I best be getting on to bed, too . . . got a lot to do tomorrow . . ." He caught her eyes as best he could.

Silently she nodded, taking the armful of furs inside the room while Gannon and her uncle stood outside. It seemed for a moment as if John waited there, waited until Gannon was ready to leave himself.

"I'll talk to you in the morning, Jen," Gannon said tersely. "We have a lot to discuss. Goodnight John." He turned and started to walk down the corridor.

"Aaron?" Jenny called and peered out toward him. He stopped and turned. She could just make out his features in the dim light. "I . . . I . . ." she started, uncomfortable in what she wanted to say because John was still standing at her door. Swallowing a painful lump that was beginning to form, she mustered up her courage and threw propriety to the wind as she dropped the furs and ran to him.

His arms were open and waiting as he caught her and crushed her to his chest.

"I love you!" she whispered fervently. "Remember that, Aaron! I love yo . . ." but her words were never completed as his mouth covered hers in a fiercely possessive kiss.

John silently watched the two with something like sadness

and a sense of loss, but not without a trace of pleasure. Their love was sweet and so beautiful . . . so *new*. It was the kind of love that transcended time and circumstances, that braved all odds and won. It tugged guiltily at his heart as he wondered if what he was doing were right. He knew he had practically blackmailed her into going on with him. But he had told himself it was for her, too . . . for her own good and the good of her future. He had told himself many things, but now he wondered if what he had told her had been the real reason behind what he was asking her to do.

"Stuff and nonsense!" he snorted. "Don't even think about it, John . . . don't even think . . ."

He watched as the two held each other for another long moment, before Jenny reluctantly pulled away and walked heavily back toward her room, looking like a doomed prisoner on her way to the gallows . . . all to fulfill a promise she had made to him.

"Till morning, Jen . . ." Gannon called, his heart as light as the air itself. "We've much to talk about."

CHAPTER

22

Jenny woke with a start. Something had frightened her—
something in her dreams, but she couldn't remember what.
She sat up, her eyes straining against the darkened room,
and remembered running. Something had been chasing her
and . . . it was hazy. Every time she'd reach for a fragment
of the dream, it would disappear from her mind like smoke.

Her eyes had become accustomed to the dark and the
room was not totally without light. It was still; the wind had
stopped blowing and the sleet and snow weren't pattering
against the roof anymore. Maybe the quiet had awakened
her. She slipped out of bed and pulled her nightgown down
over her legs. Flannel always had a bad habit of rolling
up when you slept, she thought crossly. The floor was
cold beneath her feet. The temperature had dropped. Quietly she walked to the window, afraid she would wake
Emily, and looked outside. Frost had formed on the edges
of the glass and her breath appeared silvery in the cold.
It wasn't cloudy anymore and the stars sparkled coldly
in the black velvet sky. A thin, wicked-looking crescent
moon smiled crookedly at her. Down below along the
street nothing stirred.

She shivered, never having imagined a more primitive,

desolate scene than the miles of untouched snow and acres of dark forest that spread out before her in the half light. The cold had penetrated her nightgown. It was time to return to bed because in only a few short hours, John would be tossing stones at these panes of glass and it would be time to go.

Looking once more at the empty street, she padded lightly back to her bed. The covers had chilled by now and were cold to the touch. Gingerly she climbed in between them and pulled until they were all the way up to her nose. "Brr!" She shivered. So cold! she thought, hoping they'd warm soon so she could go back to sleep. She snuggled deeper into the pile of quilts, curling up into the tightest circle she could make.

She wasn't afraid anymore and laughed at her foolishness. It had only been a dream. She was safe, at least for tonight, in Emily's Miner, and down the hall, barely three doors away, lay Gannon. She was beginning to feel warm and drowsy and she let her mind drift free. Where are you? she asked herself as she felt herself floating high above the clouds. People and scenes and snatches of tinny music danced in her mind. A face, a beautiful face, a face with eyes the color of jade. She whispered "Aaron" in her half sleep, concentrating on his face, bringing him closer, studying him, wanting him . . . He smiled in her dream and came to her, stirring passion deep inside. But her body, frozen in sleep, could not respond. Closer, closer he came, touching her, smiling, wanting her, his eyes bright, warm pools of light coming nearer . . .

"AW-OOO-O-OO-O!" crashed through her mind and she sat bolt upright in bed. What was that, she thought? A dog? Another dream? "AW-OOO-O-OO-O!" Then another being joined by others. A plaintive wailing that belonged in the dark hours and trailed away into the night.

Throwing back the covers, she ran for the door. Her heart was thundering in her chest. It sounded like they were right under her window! Opening the door wide, she ran through it, not bothering to shut it as she flew into Emily's wide bed, landing nearly on top of her.

"Em! Em!" she cried. "What is *that?*"

"What . . . ? Jen? Is that you?" Emily's voice was full of sleep and sounded surprised as she cleared her throat loudly.

"Yes, it's me!" she said excitedly, her hands going to Em's broad shoulders. "I heard something . . . something *awful,* like dogs, only *worse!*"

As if on cue, the howling began again and Emily understood what was wrong. Jenny had never heard a wolf before. Poor child, she thought. She put out her massive arm and held her close.

"It's the wolves, Jenny, that's all. Nothing to be afraid of, at least not in here." Her voice was gentle and quiet as she tried to reassure her. "I haven't heard them this close for a long time, but it be a hard winter coming. You don't need to be afraid though, child, they'll be gone by morning. Now lie down here and get some sleep . . ." She pulled the covers around her. "I think we've had enough excitement for one night."

Jenny obeyed quietly. Lying down beside Emily she felt a little better. Wolves! They must be horrible creatures, she thought, and shivered, not wanting to go back to her own room, now confident that she would hear John, confident that sleep was gone at least for tonight. . . .

Emily lay down beside Jenny, tucking the covers up under her neck. The wolves continued their mournful cries, moving farther away, by their sound. Soon the bed became warm and as Emily listened, Jenny's breathing became soft and regular. She smiled a little sadly, remembering her own youth and innocence so long ago, so far away, and she whispered for no one else's ears but her own, "Sleep well little girl . . . little girl, wheeeeeeerever you are . . ." A quiet tear rolled slowly down her cheek, as she remembered another baby girl, years ago, born wailing and afraid in the middle of the night aboard a rocking ship with a much younger Tanith acting as midwife, and a much younger Emily cradling the infant until its tiny bud of a mouth puckered instinctively, searching for her warm milk while the sea, benevolent that night, rocked them both to sleep

. . . long, long ago before the fever had taken the only child she had ever had. "Sleep well . . ." she murmured and was lost in her dreams once again aboard a rocking ship . . . in a midnight sea . . .

Tap! Tap! A couple of rocks were pelted against her window and then a few more. Jenny awoke slowly from her sleep, knowing before she was even fully awake that it was John.

Careful not to wake Em, she tiptoed to the casement in her room and waved her bedside light back and forth. The night was still and the stars plainly visible and twinkling. The moon's silver crescent had nearly vanished into the mountains, leaving only black sky and deep shadow all around.

John raised his hand. He'd seen her light. It was time to leave.

Quickly, picking up the few things she would take with her, she hurried to the door, dressing as she went. She liked wearing the soft, white bearskin trousers and the warm, fur-lined shirts and parka. It was very comfortable and she looked like a petite Nordic Eskimo, as she quietly let herself out, moving discreetly in the shadows like a thief in Emily's large room.

The door had been bolted, just as it was on all the other nights. She worked as quickly and quietly as she could, sliding back the heavy lock with a minimum of sound.

Opening the door a crack, just wide enough to fit through, she placed her letter to Gannon on the dresser and entered the hall. Not one sound came from any of the rooms. She felt as if she were totally alone except for . . . ghosts? She shivered as the story of the Two Friends decided to take this particularly forlorn moment to pop into her head. Were they real or only myth? Did they soar, unhappy and lost, high above the frozen plains or walk deserted halls at night . . . searching . . . waiting . . . waiting *patiently* . . .

Fear crept through her thoughts, icy tendrils as cold as death, nearly paralyzing her. She wanted to turn and run back into Em's room, back into bed with the covers pulled up to her nose and the bolt securely in place to wait for the rising sun . . .

"She pounds her fist against the post, and still insists she sees the ghost . . ." she recited quietly. "And still insists . . ."

Stop it! she screamed to herself. You gave your word.

"My word," she said softly. With fear threatening to choke her, she walked quickly down the distance of the dark corridor, cringing at every squeak of the floorboards beneath her feet.

"My word . . ." she repeated nervously. "But why am I so *afraid?*"

The stairway stretched down ahead of her, black shadows crowding every corner and pooling at the bottom until she could not see the floor. She half expected a dark form to pull out of the walls and reach for her. This new horror gave her quite a chill and with one foot perched over the first step, she looked fearfully back over her shoulder. Could a hallway become darker in a matter of seconds, she wondered, or had the light only gone out?

"She pounds her fist against the post . . ." Jenny swallowed hard as another light darkened momentarily and winked dimly before going out. "And still insists . . . she see's a . . . a . . ." She tried to focus on the inky black hole behind her. It was as if someone had stood between it and her, blocking the light . . . someone or *something* . . .

". . . ghost . . ."

Someone was there, in the corridor, coming slowly toward her. She could just make out a shape larger and darker than the blackness of the surrounding hall.

Run! Her mind screamed and she did, taking the stairs two at a time until she reached the door. The handle felt good in her hands and she was trembling. She looked behind her before she opened it and saw a shadow, a large, black shadow standing at the top of the stairs. It was even darker than the now totally darkened hallway.

A scream caught in her throat as the door she held onto burst inward.

"Missy!" John hissed. "What in thunders . . ." His words died in his throat as he saw what she stared at.

"Run, Missy, run! We gots to get out of here—NOW!"

He pulled her toward the waiting sled.

She heard the snow crunch beneath her feet and felt the cold air on her face. John was practically dragging her along. When they reached the sled he roughly pushed her down on top of their provisions. "Hang on, Missy, jest hang on." With whip in hand he yelled "Mush!" at the dogs and cracked his whip over them. Some had been sleeping, but at the sound of his voice they came instantly to life. "Mush, boys!" John yelled. The lead dog, growling deep in his throat, sprang forward, jerking up and pulling even before the other dogs had gained their feet. There were nine of them, a mixture of native sled dogs, more wolflike than domestic dogs, and a few dogs who were imported. Their fur was not nearly as dense, and their wits not nearly as keen as the others. But they would learn to pull or die.

John started to run with them, heading them out of town. They were going north. "Mush!" he shouted again and encouraged them with his whip. He never looked back.

Jenny had held on as he had told her. The sled had jerked rapidly to life and had nearly thrown her off, but she had found part of the sled that had been built up to create a sort of rail and hung on. The cold air was exhilarating as it rushed past her face and her reason was returning. Still breathing hard, she tried to look back.

The town was receding. The darkened shops and houses became rectangular boxes, darker then the darkened sky. Smoke curled gray and ghostlike up into the frozen air and nothing moved except them.

She could not see anyone coming. It had not followed them. Relief washed over her and she let out a long breath, the tightness in her arms and shoulders leaving her. It hadn't followed . . . it was back there, at The Miner. Back at The Miner, her mind repeated and suddenly she thought of Emily lying helpless and asleep in her bed, her door un-locked, unlocked by *her*. Panic seized her.

"Oh God," she whispered. "John!" She tried to turn as far around as she could. "We have to go back! We have to warn the others!"

He didn't say a word. His face was set, filled with a half-mad purpose.

"John, stop!!" she screamed and started to pull on the traces from where she sat.

"Stop that, Missy. We still can make good progress tonight," he said sharply.

She only pulled harder. "John, we left Emily and Aaron back there—we have to go back and warn them!"

He sighed deeply and glanced furtively over his shoulder, convincing himself he had put enough distance between him and the village. Satisfied, he pulled back hard on the lines. "Ho, Duke! Ho, boys!" The dogs obediently stopped, looking back and wagging their tails.

Jenny climbed clumsily off of the sled and stood facing him.

"We have to go back, John. Emily, Aaron, they're in danger!" She had reached forward and tugged on his coat. He had lost so much weight that another tug would have sent him sprawling in the snow.

"He ain't gonna hurt them," he said patiently. He reached inside his parka for the rock. "He wants this," he explained. His voice was slow, measured and very tired. "He wants our gold and the mine. That's why we got to put as much distance between us and him as we kin."

Jenny was bewildered. Here she had been near to believing that ghosts and "buggety-boos," as John called them, were chasing her, and now, John just called it "him."

"John, how can you know who it is and that it's not back there right now . . ."

"Because," he said quietly, "I seen the other sled set to go out back tonight. He ain't back there, 'cause he's after us . . . that's how I know."

A shudder ran through her.

"Who is it, John?" she asked quietly.

"I'd rather not say just yet, Missy. Not just yet."

Silence filled the moment and the distant hooting of an

owl, as they stood and measured the moment with the beating of their hearts.

Logically it just didn't make any sense, none at all, but she knew deep down that what he said was true and that he would tell who it was in his own good time.

"We better hurry, John," she said. Somewhere inside of her, where logic falls apart, she knew he was right. He was following them because he wanted the gold and the information as to where it had come from.

She climbed back onto the sled without so much as a backward glance because she knew, too, that Emily and Aaron were fine, because he was chasing them.

"Mush, Duke!" John yelled, and the big curly dog seemed to laugh at them before it turned and hurled its weight against the traces. The sled jerked ahead, squealing as the runners cut the ice, while John ran beside it. Soon it settled into a smooth run, gliding easily over the hard snow, and John hopped onto the back of the runners. He was out of breath.

Jenny just stared straight ahead while the dogs pulled, quickly heading further north.

CHAPTER

23

Hours had passed and the stars had moved, but there was no more light than before. Both were absorbed in their own thoughts, the sounds of the runners in the snow and the panting dogs the only accompaniment.

The landscape was changing. There were more trees here. Great scented pines stood like sentinels guarding their journey north. The forest had been getting progressively thicker, blotting out the speckled stars now and then. She wasn't sure but they seemed to be climbing. She wondered if you could go so high traveling north that you'd eventually touch the stars. The thought made her dizzy and she smiled a little sadly to herself.

The night pressed in around them like thick cotton and made it easy to believe that you were dreaming. She stared straight ahead, feeling the rush of cold air peel back away from her face. She didn't want to think about the reason she was here because when she did, pictures and fragmented scenes vividly played across her mind, making her hurt inside.

A sudden shift in the wind brought her sharply back. The dogs were breathing harder, not pulling as fast. She knew they were tired. They had pulled for many hours and now their strength was spent.

Some of the dogs, those closer to the back, would jerk against the traces, trying to stop the lead dog. Whining petulantly, they would brace their front legs, rearing back as hard as they could. The lead dog—Duke, John had called him—growled menacingly each time, hurtling his weight roughly against the lines, yanking the lagging dogs ahead. He was a strong animal with muscles that stood out in sharp relief under his shaggy coat. But he too was tired, white froth lined his jaws and he pulled now, not with ease, but by painful determination. He lived to pull.

John knew he could run them like this no longer. "Ho, Duke! Ease up now." He tugged firmly on the lines.

The big dog halted immediately, not slowing down and stopping; just stopping. The others behind him were not as adept and ran pell-mell into each other. One unlucky fellow rammed his snout rather ungently into Duke's powerful hindquarters, and was rewarded immediately with a viscious bite on his tender snout. The offender yelped painfully and lay down whimpering, not wanting to tangle with him, while many of the other dogs just dropped to the snow ready to relax, but not Duke. He was all duty, standing proudly at attention, waiting for the next command.

John walked around the sled and straight to him.

"Good ol' fella." He mussed the fur on the huge dog's head. Duke wagged his tail appreciatively as John bent over and began to unsnap his traces. Some dogs would lick their masters' faces when the lines were taken off, but Duke didn't. He waited with quiet dignity until John was all done. "There you go, big fella." John laid the lines down straight in the snow to avoid any tangles in the morning. "Go on now, boy—you can rest." Duke understood but instead of lying down, as his tired body demanded, he ran sniffing the ground around him. Periodically, he would lift his leg, marking the boundary of his territory, growling at shadows, head lowered and hackles raised. There was much of the wolf still in him. No amount of domestic breeding can take away a dog's true nature, that of the pack. In this primitive forest ancient blood cried out.

The other dogs whimpered and whined, licking John's hands and face while he untied them. He gave them neither praise nor pat on the head.

Jenny stretched her legs, and moved off the pile of their provisions. She ached from sitting so long, and felt little needles prick her toes when she stood up.

She watched John expectantly, wondering what to do next. He looked up quickly as if he knew she had been watching him.

"Go ahead there and untie the ropes around the top. We'll make camp here for a spell," he said.

She nodded in reply. The lines were heavy, the knots a little wild. They had been tied with great haste, so now she spent several minutes working on each one. Without saying a word, John joined her, working determinedly at the rope. The hemp was coarse, pieces of it stuck out like quills on a porcupine, which had a way of getting stuck in your fingers. Jenny had tried to untie them with gloved hands, but it just hadn't worked. Finally, after a multitude of pricks and pokes, the lines became loose. John pulled the tarp off the top and laid it to one side. He tried to explain to her what he was doing every step of the way.

"We'll use this here piece like a tent. It'll keep some of the wind off'n our backsides."

Jenny nodded and helped him find a likely spot to make camp. John selected a place inside a circle of pines. He looked around until he found a low branch on one of the trees and pulled it down. Jenny didn't know how to help him because she didn't know what to do. "Bring me that rope there, Missy," John patiently said, grunting a little from the strain of holding the branch down. She obeyed quickly and handed him the rope. "Hold onto this branch whilst I tie the rope around it." Jenny did. John made a loop much like the knot cowboys make for roping calves, and slipped it over a part of the branch that forked out. He pulled it taut and began to look for a likely tree behind him. A huge old pine was directly in back of him, and John

walked backward, pulling the rope and the branch with him.
He made it to the tree and walked in a circle around it twice.
When he met the line again in the front, he secured the loose
end to it. The branch was now pulled down high enough off
the ground to throw the tarp over. Jenny smiled. "For the
tent?" she asked.

"Yep," John answered, and walked to the tarp which lay
on the ground. He picked it up and threw it over the branch.
"Come along, now—you can help with this."

Jenny followed him to the side of the tent. John knelt
down and began tucking the edge under the snow. When he
had pushed it down hard enough, he began to scoop up great
piles of snow and heap it on top. When he was satisfied that
they had heaped up enough snow, he went around to the
other side and pulled it out, creating an A-frame shelter big
enough to sit or lie in and airy enough for a fire. Jenny
helped him pack the snow around the other side. When they
were through, John sighed heavily and stretched his aching
limbs. "Well, I guess I better build us a fire so we kin eat."
But before he could start, the dogs started barking and
fighting with each other.

"What's the matter with them?" Jenny asked, startled at
their sudden change in behavior.

"They's hungry, that's all. Should've taken care of them
right off," he mumbled, trudging wearily toward the sled.
Jenny watched him go. He looked so tired, so *old,* that she
wondered if he could survive this trip.

When he had reached the sled, the dogs started to
surround him, their hungry yips and yaps filling the air.
Duke didn't whimper; he just walked right through the
crowd of dogs, snapping at the few who didn't move fast
enough. Most of the others parted quickly because they were
smart enough to be afraid of him.

He marched straight to John, looking at him expectantly.
He didn't yip or wag his tail or lie on his back in the snow,
begging. He simply waited for what he had earned.

John grinned. Duke was one fine dog! He couldn't imagine what fool would've given up such a fine animal, then he
remembered the man he'd bought him from. He had the

diseases the white men bring to the Indians. He was all liquored up and didn't have money for more. John had gotten Duke for a fraction of his real value.

"Here ya go, boy," he said with affection, handing him the frozen meat. Duke opened his mouth politely and took the bulk of fish from John. He wagged his tail once, like a salute, and turned round. The other dogs parted to let him pass and not one of them attempted to touch his food.

John started to dole out the rest of the fish, while the dogs yipped and yapped and jumped in the air trying to get a piece of meat. Some of them started to fight, the bigger, more aggressive ones trying to steal from the smaller ones. John settled the arguments with a well aimed boot. Eventually they all wandered off to find a place to eat their meal and it was quiet again.

Jenny went to the sled and began to take their food out. There was some cornmeal and coffee and strips of deer jerky. John had gone ahead and started to build a fire within their tent. Pine needles made good tinder, and he blew softly on them to encourage a blaze. Jenny brought their blankets in and tried to get organized. She needed water to make a paste for the cornmeal, and realized they hadn't brought any.

"John, we need water," she said.

"Jest a minute now, soon as we get a fire going here, you can melt down some of that snow—takes a lot of snow to make a decent cup of coffee, but that's the only way."

Jenny nodded and went outside to find some clean snow. She stayed away from footprints, both theirs and the dogs', and steered clear of any recently darkened areas.

John had poked his head outside the tent. "You don't have to be so particular, jest fill the can and come on." He sounded irritated, but Jenny knew he was just tired. She bent down and scooped as much snow into the container as possible, wondering at how much water it would make, as she hurried back to the tent.

John had a fine fire burning, and he stood up when she entered. "I gots to get us some more wood—maybe you can rustle us up somethin' to eat."

"Right away, John." She bent over, placing the can of snow on top of the iron grill John had bought. There was a dull ache in the pit of her stomach. She translated it to mean she was hungry. It was different than the other kind of ache she'd been feeling lately.

John left the tent, and Jenny left it two times to gather snow before he came back. His arms were filled with wood and some of it was off balance, skittering over the other sticks and falling to the snow. He was slightly overloaded.

She ran to help him, catching an armful just as it toppled from the top of his pile. They walked to the tent and dropped the wood just inside the door. Coffee was boiling in one can, and she nearly had enough water to make the cakes out of the cornmeal. John smiled sheepishly. "I guess I could've made two trips, but I'm so darned tired today."

Jenny just smiled—she was, too. The coffee smelled good. The water in the can had turned a deep black, and most of the grounds had settled to the bottom. Jenny's mouth watered. She could hardly wait for something to eat.

John began to stack the wood in a neat pile and Jenny went outside for one final can of snow. The wind had changed again, and now, instead of blowing from one direction it gusted in small breaths from all sides. She stopped. It was so quiet here, even with the gusting of the wind. So still. A small, involuntary shudder ran through her. She hurriedly filled her can, and walked back to the tent. Inside she felt safe, and nearly smiled at how a thin piece of tarp could cut off the view of the outdoors and thereby make one feel secure. She knew it was a false feeling of security, but didn't care. She needed it.

She knelt down and let the snow melt. It amazed her that a full can only produced an inch of water. Still, she was glad for even that. She picked up the can with her glove because it was now quite hot, and poured the water into another. Cornmeal, still sticky and not quite mixed, rested on the bottom. The water from the melted snow blended with the cornmeal and made it smooth. She mixed it well and poured the batter on the flat iron griddle. It popped and sizzled and the edges started to turn brown immediately. She waited a minute and turned them with a stick she had. They tore slightly, and almost broke apart. She let them cook. John poured half the coffee into another can, and kept the other half with the grounds. Jenny scooped up the cornmeal cake with her wooden spatula and flipped them onto a tin plate. There was no butter or syrup, but when she tasted the cake, it seemed like the best thing she had ever eaten. John pulled strips of jerky out and handed some to her. It was tough and nearly broke her teeth, but the piece would soon soften in her mouth and send its delicious smokey flavor trickling down her throat. Her stomach growled in appreciation.

John had finished his meal before her. He was already yawning and stretching, ready to sleep. "I got to go look in on the dogs—be right back." He headed out the opening. Jenny finished her meal and dumped the grounds outside the tent. She tried to wash the cans and griddle with snow, drying them by the fire. She was yawning now, too.

John came in and sat down. He threw some of the bigger logs on the fire, and quietly began to roll himself into his blanket. Jenny did the same. There were no words, just the popping of the fire and the sound of the wind picking up. Her body yielded to the food and warmth and began to relax. Somewhere, deep in the woods, the wolves were hungry and began to cry. The dogs barked uneasily while John slept, his snores mixing with all the other night sounds. She looked at him, drowsiness washing over her in great, huge waves . . . rocking her, lulling her to sleep. Soon she was dreaming, hearing the wolves coming closer, but thinking they were only part of her dream. The dogs whimpered fearfully and growled outside, but she was too tired to hear them, and her limbs locked in sleep, refusing to move. She only dreamed.

CHAPTER

24

"What in thunder!" John yelled. He was sitting up, trying to unwind the blanket that held him.

Jenny was awake immediately. Something was wrong. She sensed it even before she awoke, but didn't know what it was.

The dogs were barking frantically, growling and snarling, and one was . . . screaming! Yes, it was a howling scream of pain.

She stood up, totally awake, and John, rifle in hand, was already outside.

In the starlight, a faint gray glow washed over everything. Daylight was fast approaching. The dogs were clustered together, hackles up, growling and terribly afraid.

John and Jenny ran into the clearing where the dogs had slept, and there, in the center, fighting for his life, was Duke. Four large, gray wolves surrounded him, their eyes glowing an eerie yellow in this queer half light. He was torn, a wide gash running down his shoulder to his leg. He tottered slightly before regaining his balance, growling savagely at the wolf in front of him.

"You git outta here!" John yelled, waving his rifle high in the air. "Git!" He started to approach the circle of wolves.

They looked at him; so did Duke. When he turned to see him approach, the big female Duke had been facing sprang forward, fastening her huge yellow fangs into the soft curly fur of his neck. He yelped in pain, and blood, black as the night, pulsed outward, spraying the female and speckling the white snow with crimson drops.

The others, the smell of blood sending them into a frenzy, forgot about John, closing in on Duke. He tried bravely to fight, but his strength was ebbing, flowing away with the loss of his blood. He started to go down while the big female closed in on his airway, suffocating him.

"You damned wolves!" John shouted, aiming his rifle at the mass of twisting bodies. He couldn't see Duke now, just the wolves who had driven him down to the ground. Desperate to save the animal, he fired straight into them.

Bang! And a yelp of pain. He fired again. Bang! Bang! He cursed beneath his breath. "You good-for-nothing bastards!" He unloaded another round into them.

They started to separate, leaving the torn body and running for the cover of the trees. John had gotten the big female. She lay in a heap beside Duke. All the others had disappeared into the forest. As soon as they were out of distance of the gun, they began to howl. John shook his head in disgust and went to Duke. There was little life left in him. His throat had been torn and lay open in a mangled mess, and they had broken his legs in their powerful jaws. He didn't look at John when he bent over him; his eyes were beginning to glaze over already.

"Good boy," John crooned softly. "Yer a real good boy." He reached out and stroked the dog's soft forehead. Something seemed to flicker in Duke's eyes when John called him a "good boy" and Duke, not yet gone, reached out his tongue, torn and bloody, licking John's hand goodbye.

There was a catch in John's throat and he had to swallow hard. Jenny was crying already, the cool wind chilling her skin. A fine mist covered John's eyes as he reached over and patted Duke on the head. "Yer a fine boy, you are—one in a million . . ." He stood up slowly. "Good ol' boy . . ." he whispered.

The other dogs had come toward them, the smell of blood heavy in the air. John kicked snow angrily at them. "Get outta here, you vultures! Get!" he yelled.

Jenny watched the dogs cringe and retreat until a slight movement in the corner of her eye made her turn. The she-wolf had lifted her head. Even now, closer to death than life, she forced her lips back from her snout and growled. "John—look out!" she screamed.

He turned instinctively, raising the rifle he had been loading, and saw the wolf snarl. He pulled the trigger, squeezing gently, aiming straight for her. The bullet hit her squarely in the head. Her body jumped convulsively and then she laid still, adding her blood to the scarlet snow.

John couldn't control his anger, and gave her a savage kick for what she had done.

Jenny put her hand reassuringly on his shoulder, and he turned. He looked totally bewildered. "Never seen 'um come in so close—'taint even winter yet—gots to be lots of food left . . ."

"You've never seen them do something like this before?" she asked, trying to keep the fear from showing in her voice.

"No, can't say as I have." He seemed to think about this a bit before he continued. "I done heard some rumors that there's been a renegade pack—a pack what finds it easier to kill sled dogs instead of deer—but I just thought it was a rumor, leastways until now."

In the distance the wolves began to howl. John and Jenny looked at each other, uneasy at the sound.

"Let's give Duke here a proper burial and move on. I don't think I could go back to sleep anyhow."

Jenny agreed, and working together, they made a basket of pine boughs and placed Duke's body in it. John found an extra piece of rope and tied it to the basket, throwing the loose end over a tree. Together they pulled and the makeshift coffin rose into the air. They hauled it up until it was nearly level with the branches, securing the loose end of the rope around the tree, satisfied now that the wolves couldn't get to him.

"I don't much care if the birds feed off'n him, they's

honorable creatures, but I don't like the idea of leaving him on the ground for the wolves!"

Jenny agreed, and with Duke laid safely to rest in the secluded branches of the ancient pine, they broke camp.

John had to select a new dog for the lead. He chose Amber, a large, good-natured Newfoundland, a gentle dog who would never be able to pull as well as Duke. John hitched him into the traces along with the others, and with the sled loaded, snapped his whip and yelled, "Mush, Amber, Mush!" and headed them north.

The weather was changing, and the snow swirled in little whirlwinds ahead. "It's coming," he said softly. A storm was brewing and the thought made him scared. "Mush, boy, mush!" he yelled, urging them on with his voice and whip. Amber, wanting only to please and sensing the urgency in his voice, threw all his 120 pounds against the traces with all his might.

With the clearing empty, and the sound of the sled growing dimmer by the minute, the pack silently approached the mangled body of the dead she-wolf. A large male, stouter than the rest of his pack, separated himself from the rest and trotted forward. He was powerfully built, and long, shaggy gray fur covered his sleek muscular form. He was the lead male, the head of the pack, and the female had been his mate.

Pausing a foot or so from her, his nostrils flared slightly and his ears stood stiffly upright, sorting out the sounds. He tasted the air, smelling the blood, the man-smells and the dogs. His fine senses were able to separate each one, reading them like a book which humans could never understand. The man-smell was strong, but he knew that they had gone, taking the deadly, loud stick with them. Bolder, he approached his mate, sniffing and whining deep in his throat. He nuzzled her, but she didn't respond. The smell of death was all over her.

Some of the other wolves began to whimper, the hunger in their bellies and the smell of blood making them reckless. A young male, small and with a slight limp, lowered his head and began to creep across the snow toward her. He had nearly closed the distance between them when the lead male, aware of his presence from the beginning, whirled savagely around, baring his fangs and growling loudly. The younger one knew he could not survive a challenge with him, especially after the elk he'd chased that spring had crippled him. So he quickly rolled over on his back, exposing his throat. It was a sign of submission, and the lead wolf, torn between a longing for his mate and this small triumph, began to howl. It was a long, low wail, an undulating song of grief, filling the clearing and being carried away by the wind.

His pack sat down on their haunches, a semicircle of gray shapes surrounding him, and joined in his mournful cry.

The lead wolf knew he would follow the man-smell. They were far easier prey than elks and not as swift as the deer. He didn't understand the loud stick, but he knew enough to fear it. Without it the pale, two-legged animals were easy prey. But not now. Now was the time to mourn the passing of his mate. He knew he would find another, but in the peculiar way of his kind, he had loved her, and would miss her trotting by his side. Pointing his muzzle skyward, in a ritual as old as time itself, he sang her a sad farewell.

A few miles away, in a sled skimming rapidly over the frozen ice, heading north, Jenny and John heard the wolves' cries. A shiver of dread passed through her and she wondered if John felt it too. Snuggling deeper into the robes of fur, she watched the snow coming down, heavier by the moment. It landed on her eyelashes and face, stinging slightly, but staying only a second before it melted away.

John listened to the wolves and watched apprehensively as the snow fell. He wondered how long they'd be able to go on in this. He'd seen storms start up just like this one before. Great heavy flakes, picked up and swirled into whirlpools all around him, going first clockwise, then reversing the direction. The wind was just as confused, not content to blow from one particular place, but coming from all four sides, in a little spasm, and the temperature was dropping. He looked down and saw Jenny's blond head buried deep in the piled furs. He wished to God he'd never brought her along. It would take another four days to reach the mine, and that was only if the weather stayed halfway decent. He didn't think it would. Mentally, he calculated the miles between here and his cabin. Two days, maybe three. But at least it was a better bet than going straight to the mine. He pulled back sharply on the traces. "Whoa, Amber. Whoa!"

Amber obeyed immediately, stopping and looking back at John expectantly.

"Missy," John said. She turned around as far as she could in the sled. "We're gonna take a little detour—my cabin's 'bout two or three days northwest of here." He paused and scanned the area head of them. A slight powder was already beginning to cover the ground, and the snow was now almost a curtain of swirling white. He only hoped they could reach the cabin before the worst of it set in. "This here storm's acooking up something a whole lot fiercer than this. I don't wanna take no chance of getting stuck too far out. We best find a place to hole up—that's what those ol' wolves are doing about now, before this gets much worse."

Jenny nodded, then turned around quickly. She didn't want John to see the expression on her face. He thought it was going to get worse than it already was, and she couldn't understand how. It was so cold that by now her feet felt numb, and wherever the snow touched her face, she felt a burning sensation like a match had been held there for seconds to torture her. But John said it might get worse, and she'd come to learn to believe in what he said.

John pulled the traces tight. "Mush, boys, mush!" The dogs obeyed. He wanted them to go to the northwest, so he pulled smartly back with his left hand. Amber pointed her nose in that direction and trotted steadily against the swirling wind and snow.

CHAPTER
25

"Mr. Gannon!!" an indignant Emily shouted, rapping not too gently on his door. The hall was dark, but her insistent knocking had aroused enough of the occupants to hear them softly milling around, opening their doors slowly —just a bit, small enough to appear inconspicuous, but wide enough to place either an eager eye or a straining ear over the crack.

Gannon reacted by jumping to his feet, fully awake and alert the moment he touched the cold wooden floor, but not quite quick enough to cover himself before Emily let herself in.

"What the devil!" he growled, reaching for the sheet.

"Don't bother!" She waved her arm indifferently. "I've seen enough of them in my day to know they all look pretty much alike, it's *technique,* not *length*—although I'm quite sure you have *both!"* she added sarcastically. "Now, where is she?" she demanded imperiously, taking her responsibility as surrogate mother quite seriously. She surveyed the room with hands soldered to her wide hips, looking oddly humorous in spite of her angry stare.

"Who?" he demanded furiously, as he watched the doorway fill with curious guests and giggling employees.

"Hmmph! As if you didn't know!" she shot back indignantly. Her curlers were pretty red and white silk ribbons tied at odd angles all over her head, and every time she sucked in air or spoke, they would bounce merrily here and there. "Jenny, of course!" She trounced across the floor, curlers bobbing, to look behind the bed and beneath it, while Gannon hastened to protect his flank with a flimsy sheet.

"Come out of there, Jenny!" she scolded as she peered beneath the bed. Then she frowned as she realized nothing hid there except dust bunnies long forgotten by a broom.

"Jenny?" Gannon asked, a suddenly inexplicable tightness gripping the muscles of his stomach. "She isn't here . . ."

Now it was Emily's turn to look confused, so righteously sure that when she had awoke, and found neither hide nor hair of her, that the two were snuggled together, beneath his quilts, enjoying each other without the benefits of a preacher first.

"I thought she was with you," she said softly. "I was sure . . ."

"She isn't, and she hasn't been," he said flatly. "I haven't seen her since last night when I left her at her door—so just where the hell has she gone *this* time?" Anger and fear fought each other inside of him for dominance, neither one winning, but neither one giving an inch.

"I don't know . . . The wolves frightened her last night so I let her sleep in my bed. When it was time to get up, she wasn't there. So I looked in her room, and the kitchen, out back, and everywhere . . ."

"They've gone to the mine," a quiet voice stated from the door. Gannon looked to see Kaiuga standing there, an unreadable expression on his face.

His arms were full of furs. He walked through the crowd of people and dropped them at Gannon's feet.

"You will need these," he said calmly. "I'll take you, but we must hurry. He has good dogs, and has a night's lead on us. The storm has erased his tracks, but I saw *two* sets of runner's in the snow before the wind buried them."

"You mean someone else is going with them?" asked Gannon.

Kaiuga became thoughtful. "Maybe—or maybe someone *follows.*"

A quiet moment fell between the two as they exchanged a meaningful look before Gannon bent forward, letting the sheet slide and not caring who looked as he picked up the furs and began to dress.

It was getting darker and colder by the minute. John didn't know how far they had come but he knew they would have to make camp soon. There wasn't much light left and they would need a fire tonight. He strained his ears, listening for the sound of wolves. Outside of the low moaning of the wind and the rhythmic padding of the dogs' feet, all was still.

He gave a sigh of relief. Those wolves had come directly into their camp. They weren't afraid of men. John had heard stories about a renegade pack of wolves in these parts from some Eskimos he had stayed with. They had said the male was very large and very smart. He had taken to hunting men when they were around because they were easy. Some of the Eskimos believed they were a pack of demons and wouldn't even try to hunt them down for fear of bringing a curse upon themselves or their village.

John used to laugh at such superstitious nonsense, but not anymore. He didn't doubt that a pack of demons was chasing them, part of the curse he'd brought on himself and those around him.

The snow was falling harder, making it nearly impossible to continue. John peered into the swirling darkness, trying to find a grove of trees to camp in, someplace where the wind wouldn't be quite so severe.

He turned the dogs from the path and directed them into the forest. An opening between some pines yawned out at him, blacker than a cave. He steered the dogs for it. Deeper into the grove he went, carefully guiding the dogs around the trees. They were thicker here, clumped tightly together in clusters, their low branches swishing against his clothing and occasionally slapping him in the face. He moved more slowly. The wind was less obvious in here. Little gusts would trickle by, but it was quieter and more protected. The last of the light was going, whether because of the dense forest or because night was close at hand, John couldn't tell.

They were in a small clearing now, surrounded on all sides by tremendous pines. There was no wind here, just calm white snow and branches bent nearly to the ground beneath it.

John pulled his traces tight. "Ho! Amber, ho!" The big dog stopped so abruptly that the dogs behind him ran into each other, tangling the lines. "Damn!" John exclaimed. The words hadn't come out right. His jaw felt nearly frozen and his tongue was thick and useless in his mouth. The tangled lines meant more work and he didn't need that now. Now he needed rest.

Jenny climbed stiffly from the sled. A slow, tingling sensation ran along her legs and arms; she knew in a few minutes they would be hurting when the warm blood pushed its way back into her veins. Her face was numb and her stomach churned and growled hungrily. She had not eaten since the night before.

The small clearing was now nearly devoid of light, and when her feet touched the ground, her boots sank into the soft white powder.

Her toes began to burn—painful little prickles, as if someone were sticking hot pins into them.

She tried to ignore her body and walked stiff-legged toward John. He was bent over, slowly pulling the traces apart.

"Can I help?" she asked, the words barely making it past the chunk of wood in her mouth that used to be her tongue.

John didn't turn around or look up, he just kept working on the lines.

"John?" Jenny asked. She started to bend forward, wondering if he had heard her.

He turned his head to look at her, and she couldn't help but see the tiredness in his eyes. They were flat, no sparkle, twin marbles peering out of an old, gray face.

"Jest start unloading the sled—it'll be faster that-a-way," he explained. "As soon as I get these lines straight, I'll build us a fire, before it gets too black in here."

She nodded and he turned back to the lines.

The shadows in the clearing were darker now and larger, as if they were absorbing everything in it. Something flickered briefly in the corner of her eye. She turned her head toward it, straining her eyes against the gathering gloom. Whatever it was, it was gone. She couldn't see anything now.

She turned and walked back toward the sled. Her limbs were nimble now, warm and pliant, and she quickly forgot about their frozen pain earlier.

The sled was loaded high, and the ropes had been crisscrossed several times and pulled tightly in order to keep their provisions safe. She grabbed a knot and started working it with her gloved hands. Try as she might she couldn't loosen it. She went to another, but the bulky gloves made it impossible to untie them. Impatiently she pulled them off, putting the tip of her right hand into her mouth and tugging. It came off reluctantly, exposing the soft, white flesh to the bitter cold. She dropped them to the ground, and went back to working the stubborn knots.

Her hands were cold and the rope was coarse with tiny strands sticking up like messy hairs all along it. They poked her hands and the feeling was intensified by the cold. She kept working, tugging and pushing pieces in and out and around each other until it finally loosened.

When she was finished, she laid the lines limply on top of the sled. By this time John had straightened the traces, but instead of letting the dogs loose, he only separated them and staked them to the ground. He wanted to make sure they would be there in the morning.

Jenny pulled most of the gear onto the ground, laying the tent out and separating the food and utensils.

John had spotted a dead tree not far from their camp and went to the sled for the ax.

"Got to get us a good supply of wood, Missy. I seen an old, dead pine not too far from here." He looked around and spotted a low hanging branch. "Jest see if'n you kin throw that old rag over that branch." He pointed to the spot. "I'll help you as soon as I get some wood." He slung the ax over his shoulder and walked into the woods.

She pulled the tent toward the tree. The branch was low enough for her to lift an edge of the tent and lay it over it. She ducked beneath the branch and pulled it over until it hung evenly on both sides. She was tired and the urge to lie down was strong. She remembered her room in Kansas City and the soft, white bed. Somehow that room and the one at Emily's blended together in her mind and she could almost feel the soft feather stick beneath her head.

A sharp bark aroused her. The dogs were whining and acting nervous, and she realized she had been dozing on her feet, her head resting against the branch. It would have seemed comical any other time, but not now. She straightened up and looked around. It was so dark by now that not even the dogs, who were only a few feet away, were visible. She wished John would hurry.

A twig snapped somewhere in front of her, and her heartbeat quickened. "John?" she asked, praying a little.

"Yep, it's me," he answered tiredly. In a few seconds he stood before her, a huge pile of wood in his arms.

"Better get this fire going—we're going to need a lot more wood than this." He dropped the wood on the ground.

He knelt down, piling the wood. "You better stretch that out a bit, and open up one side toward the fire—pack some snow along the bottom real good in case it starts to blow a little in here."

She obeyed him quickly. John might seem like a crazy old man to some, but he knew what he was doing out here.

She pulled the edge out and pushed it down into the snow as far as she could. Then she began to scoop more snow toward it, packing it down with her hands as she went.

She did the same to the other side, leaving a couple of feet in the back. When she was done packing that side, she went around to the open end and pulled the tent together until only a small hole was at the top. She pushed the tarp down in the snow, past the powdery surface, and into the hard crust below, packing it up and around the back. Now they had a shelter open only on one end where their fire blazed brightly.

She walked around to the front of the tent and gazed happily at the dancing yellow-orange flames, feeling the warmth touch her face and light up the clearing.

"We need more wood," John said, taking a brightly lit torch from the fire.

Jenny started to walk with him into the woods and he stopped her. He could see the dark circles around her eyes and knew she was tired. She was a good girl and he wished to Almighty God he'd never gotten her into this mess. "Jen, just go get us something to eat—there's jerky in one of them packets, and maybe some coffee to burn out the chill," he said quietly. "It won't take me long." He turned around and walked into the clump of trees. His light seemed to bounce around in the darkness, making the pines seem ominous and close, and then it stopped, not far from the camp.

She turned and headed toward the fire. Something moved in the trees; she could hear the "wooshing" sounds of moving branches. She stopped and stared into the dark forest ahead of her. For a second, something flickered and glowed yellow, like two candles in the dark. She gasped in surprise, and then they were gone. Wolves? she thought. Had they come this far? She didn't want to believe it. Jenny hurried toward the fire, reaching for the packet of jerky and the sack of coffee. The dogs whimpered, and she knew they were hungry too. John kept their food on the sled. She walked toward it, and the dogs, as if reading her mind, began to dance around happily, yipping and whining in the peculiar talk of their kind.

She found the fish and counted out seven large ones and carried them to the dogs. John had staked them far enough away from each other to keep them from fighting and stealing each other's food. Jenny gave them the fish and each dog fell to his eating ravenously.

The bobbing light was coming closer and Jenny hurried to the fire. She melted the snow for the coffee and filled the can full, placing it across two stones over the fire. It sizzled and popped and the snow began to fall in the can almost immediately, while Jenny kept heaping more on.

John entered the clearing with another pile of sticks and laid them near the others. He glanced at the dogs and saw she had fed them. That was good because he was really tired.

Jenny filled the can full and stood up. "I'll help you carry some more, while the water melts."

John nodded his head, and they left for the camp for more wood. They made several trips, each carrying as much as they could until the pile was nearly as high as the peak of their tent. Each time they came back, Jen would fill the can with snow, and each time they left, she wanted to lie down.

When the can was full of water merrily boiling and the wood had been brought and piled high, they stopped. Jenny scooped a cup of coffee grounds into the water and was immediately rewarded by its smokey aroma.

John sat wearily down, cross-legged like an Indian, in front of the fire. Jenny handed him the pack of jerky and John smiled wryly. "I don't know if I got the energy to chew." Jenny laughed in agreement.

The coffee was done, deep black and steaming. She picked up the can and poured the coffee into two tin mugs.

John pulled his gloves off and wrapped his cold fingers around the cup. The coffee had warmed it already, and his face filled with pleasure at the warmth.

They drank the coffee until it was gone, throwing the grounds into the fire. John was still chewing a piece of the jerky as his eyes began to close sleepily.

"We'd best get some rest—it's still two days to the cabin." With that he threw more logs onto the fire, piling them high, so they'd burn through the night.

Jenny climbed wearily back into the tent, pulling the warm skins around her. John did the same.

She faced the fire, taking comfort in it. Slowly the warmth of the skins and the food made her drowsy. John was sleeping already, his snoring fast and regular. She thought of Emily and her mother, and wished for their comfort now. She imagined looking down on their camp from a place high in the sky, and seeing a small glowing circle surrounded by miles and miles of dark forest. The thought made her shudder, and she forced her mind to think of other things, happy things. When she was younger, she had always dreamt of the house she would have someday, all the rooms and the way they would look. She began to build her house in her mind, one bright, cheerful room after another, and somewhere, between sleep and waking thought, the house became real and filled with the happy sounds of children. She was slipping away, falling deeper and deeper into sleep, walking through her house, filled with children, and a man stood there, tall and broad of shoulder, with gleaming copper hair and a soft gentle voice. She walked toward him, and he reached out his arms for her. She smiled, and spoke softly in her sleep, for only the dogs to hear. "Aaron," she whispered, and her dreams claimed her.

CHAPTER

26

Kaiuga and Gannon had run with the storm, taking turns riding the runners or breaking the trail, but night was settling in, and they could go no further.

"There is a cave up ahead where my people stay!" Kaiuga shouted. "We will stop there!"

Gannon was running ahead, packing the snow with his feet, struggling against the brutal wind. He didn't want to stop, even though his body demanded it of him. He had changed his white man's cotton and wool for the Eskimo's fur, feeling relaxed and comfortably warm in the bearskin trousers and fur-lined parka.

Kaiuga had watched him, wondering if he could take the cold or learn to guide the dogs as swiftly as was needed. He was pleasantly surprised, learning to respect the brawny Irishman for his drive and courage after only a few hours of this Arctic winter. Gannon's stamina and quickness impressed him, but he knew that it was love for his woman that drove this fiery-haired man on, understanding all too well the fear that he must surely be feeling.

Hauling back sharply on the lines, he brought the dogs to an abrupt halt before an opening, no bigger than about four feet high, in the side of a mountain. It was totally black inside.

Staking the dogs, he motioned for Gannon to unload the sled and carry the packs inside. He fed the dogs frozen fish faster then they could eat them. Then he turned and followed Gannon inside.

There was a natural room carved out of the massive, gray stones. No animals lurked inside, which surprised the wary Eskimo, and no wind to chill one's bones, either.

Their eyes, accustomed to the brilliant white world outside, ached a little, feeling almost comfortable in this semidark cave.

"We must build a fire," Kaiuga said. "Our furs must be dry before we begin again."

Gannon nodded and followed him outside for wood. Between the two of them, they had a cheery blaze started and meat thawing within a very short time. Gannon watched somewhat surprised as his companion began to undress. Not just his parka, but the sleek, feather-lined shirt beneath, followed by the warm kamiks and white bearskin breeches. He then motioned for Gannon to do the same. Curious, but trusting his guide, he did the same, until he stood just as naked as Kaiuga, shivering at the touch of the cold stones on his bare feet, in the middle of the cave. The firelight, glowing yellow bands of color, illuminated the pair—one dark and dusky as twilight, while the other's skin glowed with almost an inner light, like polished marble.

Kaiuga picked up the clothes and laid them out so they would dry, before he crawled between the furs of his bedroll. Gannon did the same. With his teeth clenched tight, sure that his skin was turning blue, he didn't have to be told what to do as he dived between his own, feeling the tickling fur all along his length.

They ate from where they lay, ripping the still frozen meat with their teeth, while the juices of their mouths unleashed the smokey flavor. Sated and warm, Kaiuga slept, while Gannon, head resting on his arm, stared at the flickering flames, wondering where Jenny was and praying she was safe. His business in Kansas City now seemed like no more than a dream. Indeed, everything that had happened, his whole life before he had met Jenny, seemed somehow irrelevant, as if his entire existence depended on her. He knew he would dream tonight, hold her, love her, only to wake to the reality of empty, aching arms in the morning. He swallowed hard, feeling a terrible pain and a desperate longing in his heart.

The wolves circled the camp. The leader had watched as the dogs had been fed, and seen and smelled what the two-legged ones ate. His stomach growled in sympathy, and saliva ran dripping into the snow. Some of the others had signaled to him that they wished to attack now, the smell of food making them reckless. But the leader, older and wiser than the rest, had waited, fearing the fire and the loud stick which had taken his mate.

Soon he knew they would sleep, and then they would attack.

He raised his large head and pricked his ears forward, listening. Sounds of sleeping came to him, in the rustling kick of a dog dreaming and the snores of the old man.

He looked back and the others immediately fell in line, running low and silent to the edge of the camp. Another signal and they fanned out, encircling the camp, hidden just out of sight, in the trees.

The leader raised his head, ears cupped forward, nostrils flaring. He was still afraid of the brightly burning fire.

Lowering his body to the ground, with most of his weight resting on his back haunches, he crept forward. The others followed silently.

He smelled everything, sorting out the food smells from the burning wood and odor of coffee still lingering in the air. He was near Amber, the big, good-natured dog whom John had chosen to lead. He was sleeping in a tight little ball with his bushy tail covering his face. Only his sleeping eyes were exposed.

The wolf could smell him so strongly that he began to drool. The dog was covered with odors, leather from the traces, a fishy smell from his supper, and even the now-familiar smell of the man. But under all of these the wolf smelled blood, warm and pumping, and it excited him.

Somewhere in his dream, Amber ran in the sun chasing rabbits across a lush green meadow, unaware of the gigantic gray wolf ready to attack.

The others, pulling themselves forward toward the sleeping dogs, were not as wise as their leader. He was silent, even in his intense excitement.

A young male growled softly. It had been brief, only a momentary lapse in his self-control, but it had been enough. The sleeping dogs heard them, their eyes snapping open in unison. The young male leaped and fell short of his mark. It was something he would be severely punished for later, for it was not his place to start the attack. The leader had taken note of this, and growled his displeasure, leaping a fraction of a second later toward Amber, but he had been alerted. He jumped to his feet and growled. The wolf didn't hesitate. Amber was staked to the ground and was easy prey. He lunged forward, trying to knock the dog off balance, to get at his throat. Amber moved quickly, but not far enough, the traces making it impossible to move as far away as he needed to. The wolf had missed knocking him over, and in an angry rage, charged, sinking his great fangs into the side of the poor dog's face. Amber yowled, a loud and painful cry, and pulled away from the jaws of the wolf, jerking nearly half his face away. Blood was everywhere. The other wolves had started to attack the rest of the dogs. It had all happened within a few seconds. John woke up and grabbed his gun. He pulled himself out of the tent, cocking the rifle as he did so.

It was a slaughter. The dogs could neither fight nor run. "You sons of bitches!" John screamed. He pulled the trigger, sending a bullet into the nearest wolf. It yelped in pain and all the wolves stopped and scattered, running into the forest.

Jenny stared around her in disbelief. Amber lay torn and bleeding in the snow along with two others. John walked toward them and stopped by Amber. He was lying in the snow, mangled, and half hidden by it. He was still breathing.

"Damn!" John said. There was real sorrow in his voice.

He knelt down and stroked the fur gently, but he knew there was no hope for the dog.

Standing up, he pointed his rifle at the dog's forehead. As if Amber knew what John was going to do, he closed his eyes. John pulled the trigger. Amber jerked once and lay still.

"Damn wolves!" he hissed savagely, and his voice trembled and broke.

Jenny went to the few dogs who were not hurt and stood beside them. Like frightened children, they clustered around her legs.

John had to shoot the other two dogs. Their wounds were bad, and every time he pulled the trigger, the other dogs yipped in terror while Jenny cringed.

When he was done, he went to the others who were left and untied them, careful to hold their lines tightly. He led them closer to the fire. The dogs hurried forward, eager to be protected. After he had staked them next to the tent, John threw more wood on the fire.

"How much longer till light?" Jenny asked.

"I don't know, a couple hours anyway." He sat down next to her.

"I ain't never seen nothin' like it," he said. "Wolves come right into a man's camp." He shook his head in disbelief.

"Why do you think they did, John? Were they just hungry?"

"Hungry? Yeah, I reckon they were hungry—but it ain't ordinary." He went on to explain, pointing to the half circle of dark trees in front of them. "There's plenty of food out there, the winter's just begun. I've heard of wolves coming into town when their game's scarce, but not like these, not coming into a man's camp where a fire's lit and just commence to eat up a man's dog whilst he's laying there." He hesitated and stared hard into the fire. "It ain't natural."

Jenny had been watching his face while he talked. When he looked down, she turned her gaze to the circle of dark trees, hoping to see a faint gray, glimmer of light, which meant dawn had come. But there was nothing, only black trees and blacker backgrounds. Something glittered gold, like a match struck in the dark. She sucked in her breath in a gasp as she watched more flickering yellow lights, pairs of them staring out at her from the dark forest.

"John . . ." she whispered, reaching over to touch his arm. He looked at her before following her gaze. "Devils!" he hissed, as he saw the many pairs of golden eyes. They stood like guards just out of range of the light, in between the trees. Jenny and John were their prisoners.

"John, what will we do?" The dogs began to whine nervously.

"Wait," he said with finality. "That's all we kin do, till light, then maybe they'll go away. I can't shoot at 'um,' cause I can't see nothing but their eyes, and I don't want to use up all our bullets." He continued to stare at the eyes.

One of the dogs whimpered and strained his line enough to lie at her feet. Absentmindedly, she stroked his head, as she watched the hungry, yellow eyes blink and flicker as the wolf pack settled in, waiting.

CHAPTER

27

With the coming of the gray light of dawn, the wolves had slunk away. The snow had stopped, but the clouds were so distended Jenny thought that they would burst any minute.

"Let's get going," John said. "If the weather holds, we might make the cabin by tomorrow."

Jenny was relieved. She wanted walls, solid walls surrounding her, and a dry place to sleep. She hurried and helped John load the sled. He took only the food, leaving the tent and clothes behind. There were only four dogs left and he knew they couldn't pull a full load.

"I'll walk, John," Jenny offered. He smiled a little.

"The sled ain't full. I think we can add another ninety pounds to it without too much bother. Later, if it looks like we're playing the dogs out, we'll both walk. All right?"

Jenny nodded and settled onto the sled. John shouted the command for "go" to the dog in the lead, and he started running with the sled. The dogs finally gained some speed and he hopped onto the runners for a rest.

Jenny tried to relax, but couldn't. She had a tight feeling in the pit of her stomach, a premonition that bad luck wasn't through with them yet.

It was calm enough during the day, and they made good

time. The forest had thinned a little here, and they traveled down a wide path through the center.

Occasionally, something would move in the trees. She would notice it at the corner of her eye. When she turned, she would see nothing, nothing but tall pines frosted with snow.

The light was changing again, becoming dimmer, and a breeze had begun to stir the fresh snow.

Something moved again just outside the range of her vision. She turned instinctively toward it, expecting to see nothing again, but this time she was surprised. A great, gray wolf stood stiffly on her right side, just outside the cover of trees. It was staring directly at her.

"John!" she cried, and he looked where she pointed.

"Oh God," he whispered in surprise, staring at the wolf, fear crawling up from his belly.

The wolf didn't turn and run or try to hide. As the sled started to pull past him, he raised his muzzle toward the sky and howled. "OWWW-oooo-ooo!" rode on the wind and was soon joined by the others. It reminded Jenny of the rounds she used to sing in school. When one verse was nearly over, before it ended its lines were picked up by the next group, repeating it, over and over again. The wolves began to sing their rounds—long, low and somehow melancholy cries that echoed in the empty valley.

She stretched to turn around and look back. He was still there, trotting now, arrogantly running outside the cover of the trees, following them.

Others, like gray arrows, shot out of the trees, loping along behind their leader, confident and unafraid.

"Kinda' sure of their supper, ain't they?" John shouted. He began to search for a place to stop. "We'll see," he said. "We'll see. I don't reckon I like the idea of being the main course."

He sighted a clump of pines up ahead, long dead, and he steered toward them. The lead wolf paused, lifting his head. He watched everything John did.

John pushed the dogs harder and when he had made the

deadfall, he pulled back roughly on the lines. "Ho, boy, ho!" he commanded, and the dogs obeyed.

Jenny sensed they wanted to run. They had seen the wolves, too. But she knew that alone and without them, they were no match for the pack.

"We'll set up camp here," John instructed. "We'd better hurry."

Jenny jumped up and began loosening the lines before John got there.

"We ain't got no tent, and I know it's still light, but the way these crazy wolves act, we're going to need a lot of firewood."

Jenny agreed. "How much longer is it till we get to the cabin?"

John looked around him, checking for familiar landmarks. "By tomorrow, 'for dark, if we make good time."

"Good," she said, looking around.

"This here trail between the trees takes you right there; it's as good as a road." He looked toward the forest across the path. A brash, young male wolf was approaching, while the leader hung back. A shudder ran through Jenny. The leader was *letting* him come toward them, of that she was certain. He wanted to see if it was safe! She stared incredulously at the fast approaching wolf.

John didn't hesitate. He raised his rifle and aimed it at the wolf. The wolf stopped and started to turn and run, but John was too quick. He pulled the trigger, squeezing off one bullet directly into the side of the male. The wolf yelped, springing into the air and flailing his legs like a swimmer in the air before falling to the ground.

John quickly turned the rifle on the leader, knowing he was too far away to do any damage, but all he saw was forest. The leader had vanished like a puff of gray smoke in the wind. He shook his head. "I never seen the likes of this," he murmured. "Never! They're just like a pack of ghosts!"

Jenny could see how upset John was. His face was drawn and haggard; a haunted, doomed light filled his eyes. She had to make him see that these were flesh and blood creatures, not some demons haunting him. "John," she called, going toward him. He turned quickly, a cold look on his face. She wondered just how far he actually was from madness, and guessed by his shallow breathing and trembling hands, that he was very close to entering its gates.

"John," she repeated, forcing her voice to become strong and calm. "They're not ghosts, they're just wolves."

"Wolves!" He laughed hysterically. "Wolves! You think them's just wolves!" He leaned toward her, thrusting his head to within an inch of her face. "Let me tell you a thing or two—I been in these parts most of my life—I seen crazy things, crazy things, but I could always explain them. But not this—ain't nothin', NOTHIN' like them damned wolves! They're after me." His voice became a whisper as if he were afraid someone was listening. "They's after me, ME!" he hissed. He backed away, clutching at the golden rock around his neck like a talisman.

Jenny was afraid—of him, for him, of the wolves and of this place. She willed herself to be calm, searching for a way to make John realize that the biggest danger they were facing was his own fear. It was paralyzing him, and she didn't know what chance they had of making it to the cabin alive with the way he was now. Suddenly, an idea occurred to her. She looked at the dead wolf and walked toward it. John's eyes grew wider with every step she took.

When she reached it, John began to twist his hands convulsively together. "Don't touch it!" he warned. "Missy, jest don't touch it—it's me they want!" She knew she had to show him it was real, a large gray wolf, dead from a bullet he'd leveled into it. She licked her lips, her stomach filling with butterflies and her mind with doubt as she bent over and grasped the rough, gray pelt in her hand. It was still warm. A feeling of nausea made her swallow hard and she started to tug the wolf backward. The pelt gave a little, as if his skin was a size too large, before she could move the wolf. His body spilled scarlet blood on the white snow and his head rolled lifelessly to one side. Jenny pulled and walked backward a few steps, dragging the carcass with her. John gasped loudly as she dragged it toward him.

"Get away," he murmured. "Get away from me!" But he

didn't move, only his eyes darted quickly from side to side trying to escape.

Jenny pulled it to his feet and let it drop to the ground, before she turned to face him. She looked deeply into his eyes, locking them to hers. She saw the fear there and something else too. Was it hope? she wondered. "It's a wolf, John. A *dead* wolf." Her voice remained calm and measured. Somehow between that and the dead ball of fur at his feet, he started to believe. Slowly the madness left his eyes, and a grim and weary tiredness replaced it.

"We best get camp made," he said briskly. He looked away quickly, embarrassed. What's happening to me? he thought. A wisp of a girl has to prove to her old uncle that there ain't no such things as ghosts. But deep inside, he still feared the wolves. They were real flesh and blood but unnatural in their actions, and he dreaded the coming of night.

"We better get a good supply of wood—we'll be able to get to the cabin by tomorrow, 'fore dark," he said.

He sounded more hopeful, and for that Jenny was grateful. But she knew his resolve was fragile, and she prayed for strength to continue.

They set up camp much the same way as they had the nights before, except John built a large circle of wood, and told her they and the dogs would sit in it tonight. They had to gather enough wood to last, so they hurried with their task.

They attacked the deadfall of pines. Most of the wood was rotted, but at least it would burn, and they piled it high in the center of their circle.

John had seen another old pine not too far away, but darkness had come, making it too dangerous to go for more wood. He only prayed that what they had would last the night.

They brought the dogs inside, leaving the sled staked to a tree nearby, and closed up any gaps with wood. John began to systematically light the fire. A blaze was started on each compass point, north, east, west, and south, like a ritual.

The flames built and joined, creating a living yellow flower of warmth around them.

They did not talk. They ate the rest of the jerky and melted snow for coffee.

The fire made Jenny feel safe and she allowed herself the luxury of relaxing. One of the dogs, a female, black and silver with blue eyes, crawled next to her for comfort and warmth. Jenny didn't mind, as she stroked its silky fur, lost in her own thoughts.

The night was cold, but the wind had ceased to blow. Looking up, she could not see any stars. The clouds had never left.

Absorbed in her own thoughts, John nudged her gently. She had been nearly asleep.

He was staring hard ahead of him, his hand grasping the rifle so tightly, his knuckles bulged white in the firelight.

"Lookee," he said. Even the dogs appeared to obey his soft command, looking where he stared. It was the wolf. The great, gray leader of the pack. He trotted toward them, some sixth sense telling him how close he could go and not be shot with the gun.

Jenny sat up straight, every nerve in her body tingling, as she watched him watching *them*.

He looked briefly back into the forest, and as if by some silent signal, the rest of his pack trailed out behind him.

Jenny could not see him command the others, but as if of one mind, they began to fan out, walking just out of range of John's rifle, surrounding them.

The lead wolf sat down and so did the others, their golden eyes reflecting the fire's glow in silent circles of gray shapes.

He raised his muzzle and sniffed the air. As if he had all the time in the world, he laid down on the snow, his snout resting comfortably on his paws, as he waited.

Gannon and Kaiuga had pushed the dogs to their limits, quickly narrowing the distance between them and John and Jenny, especially after they had come upon their first campsite. The bloody snow read like a diary where a battle had been fought. The female wolf had been left untouched, but the scene around her was horrible.

"These are wolf tracks," Kaiuga explained, showing him the clearly distinctive paw prints in the snow. "They are following them."

Walking around the camp, he began to frown, bending down to peer closer to something that had caught his attention on the ground.

"What is it?" Gannon asked.

"The other sled. A much lighter one, with many dogs— see how much smaller the tracks are?"

Gannon nodded. "I don't like it. It doesn't feel right."

Kaiuga agreed.

"Let's push on," Gannon insisted.

The two of them, with a team of weary dogs, headed further north, driving themselves on with a feeling of impending doom settling over their minds.

CHAPTER

28

The night was an eternity. Seconds flowed into minutes, and minutes seemed like days.

They had kept their fire burning brightly throughout the night, each taking turns dozing while the other watched.

The wolves were patient and silent, almost seeming to enjoy the warmth of the fire, each resting comfortably on the snow like domestic dogs around a campfire.

When Jenny would look directly into their eyes, they would close them, leaving only slits which appeared not to focus on her. But when she looked away, they would spring open, wide and shining, staring at them.

She was slowly becoming attuned to the conditions of the north, even becoming aware of the subtle changes that announced the coming of dawn. She sensed it was nearly light. There was a quiet expectancy in the air, a shift from night to the breaking of day. The wolves seemed to know it too, looking up expectantly at the sky and casting uneasy glances from it to their leader. But he didn't seem to notice or care that day was fast approaching. He didn't move any part of his body except for an occasional blinking of his eyes. He was waiting.

"They're not gonna leave," John said. His voice was flat

and resigned as he threw another log into the fire. "They're waiting us out—when the fire goes, they'll come." He didn't know how he knew this but he did. Maybe the wolves knew that in another day, John and she would have reached the line cabin, and been safe. He didn't know what they thought, only what he feared, and the supply of logs was getting desperately low.

Jenny was tired, but she wouldn't give in to sleep. She, too, had noticed that the wood was nearly gone. As if reading their thoughts the lead wolf looked up, staring directly into her eyes. She imagined a look of triumph in them, and tried to shake the feeling.

John started to stand up. Dawn had come and the wolves gave no sign of retreating. "I gots to get more wood." He stretched his aching body. The leader never took his eyes off John, watching every move he made, his long ears cupped forward, listening to what he said.

"John! You can't leave here—the wolves!" She could see in her mind what would happen if he did. He'd leave to get the wood and the big wolf would run toward him, leaping . . . She shuddered, and looked hopefully toward the weak, gray light. "It'll be day soon," she said eagerly. "They always leave when the light comes."

He shook his head and stared at the pack. "No, not this time." He smiled sadly at her. He had a few bullets left and if it looked as if they had no chance, he'd use them—one for her, and then one for the big male. And maybe, just maybe, he'd have time to squeeze one off right between his own eyes, too.

He reached down and picked up a larger stick; one end was flaming a bright yellow. He grabbed the rifle with the other hand.

The wolves were inching toward them; the fire was burning low. John looked from the hungry wolves to the fragile girl-woman and stooped down. He picked her hands up and wrapped her fingers around the rifle. She looked puzzled and anxious and a pang of guilt flowed through the old man. "Use it," he said gruffly.

"John," she pleaded, "you might need it!"

He sighed wearily. He didn't want to have to explain, but he owed her at least a quick death.

As he looked toward the ground and started to tell her, he kept his words gentle and soft. "There's only a couple of bullets left," he explained, "and there's a whole lot of wolves." His tongue felt thick with emotion and he struggled hard not to cry. He didn't give a damn about himself now. He was old and spent, but she, so young and beautiful . . . She had trusted him, too, and somehow in the last few weeks, he had grown to love her. "You gots to use it, when they come and I don't get back, you gots to use it." Then, unable to tell her what she had to do, he turned the muzzle toward her, resting the cold barrel between her eyes. "Here," he whispered. "Here." He choked back a sob.

She was trembling. She understood what he meant now, looking with dread at the approaching wolves. You couldn't tell they were moving, so quiet and slow, but they were.

Looking at them, she struggled against the panic rising in her. She turned to look at the old man who was now weeping uncontrollably, realizing how like her father he was. In that moment, she knew she loved him.

"My fault, Jen! God, I'm so sorry . . ." His sobs cut off his words.

"Go on, John," she said softly, "go for the wood." She licked her lips. They had gone dry and she searched for something more to say. "We'll make it, John. I know we will." She really didn't believe that. She saw her death creeping silently toward her, but she couldn't blame John. She had wanted to come, to fulfill her parents' dream—her dream. Now her dream was over, and the reality of its failure was stalking them.

He straightened up. Jenny still gripped the rifle in her hands, and stared vacantly at the wolves.

"Jen." She looked up hopelessly into his face. "Don't do it till you know you got to. All right?"

She licked her lips and nodded, irresistibly drawn to watch the pack.

John picked up his torch and a few more burning sticks and crossed over the fire barrier, heading for the dead pine.

The leader's ears pricked forward, as he watched John walk toward the tree.

Silently, they all rose, and in single file followed their leader, who was trotting after him.

Jenny stood up. "John!" she screamed. "They're coming! John!" But she couldn't see him anymore. He was hidden by the trees. Her heart was beating furiously, and her head was swimming. What should I do? she thought. Oh God, John— what should I do?!

The clearing was not totally light and she couldn't hear any sounds. She strained her ears, cocking her head slightly to one side without realizing it. Nothing. She heard nothing.

The minutes passed, and still no John. The fire around her feet dwindled, more black ashes than orange flames now, and still she waited.

He had told her to wait, but in her mind she could see John, lying in the snow, helpless and bleeding, being ripped apart by the wolves. She knew she must follow and help him if she could.

She sniffed a little and realized she was crying as she followed his tracks in the snow. She hadn't taken a torch, just the rifle. As she moved into the denser growth, movements just outside her range of vision caused her to turn her head sharply. Nothing. She saw nothing, but she knew the shadows were wolves, slipping through the trees, flanking her, waiting. The rifle clutched in her hand was keeping them at bay. She came to the deadfall and heard a low wail. Wolves! But she couldn't see them.

John's tracks led around the point, and she followed them. Clutching the rifle to her breast, she rounded the trees.

"Oh God! No!" she cried. There, next to the dead tree was her dear old friend Joshua, swathed head to heel in furs. He was holding John, brutally bending his arm behind his back so that he couldn't move. Horror stricken, she watched as he continued to push his knife deeper into John's chest, unaware that she stood there.

A look of intense pain shot across John's face, while his hands clawed helplessly at the one that held him. John's face was distorted in a mad rage, his eyes ablaze. He slumped forward in Joshua's arms. Joshua let the old man go, pulling out the knife, now crimson with blood.

Jenny screamed and dropped the rifle to the ground.

Joshua had started to bend over, but quickly turned toward her at the sound of her voice. His eyes, which had held such a wickedly determined gleam only moments before, appeared to shift at the sight of her, becoming both guilty and somehow lost.

"Jen . . ." he whispered, starting to rise. But she was running, thinking only of the poor old man lying on the ground, with his life oozing darkly out of him.

"Uncle John!" she cried. Her heart began to break as she knelt beside him. He opened his eyes at the sound of her voice, and tried to speak, but before he could, Joshua grabbed her arm and hauled her roughly to her feet. His eyes were pleading and desperate.

"He wouldn't listen, Jenny! I tried to make him listen . . . but he wouldn't! All I wanted was to be his partner . . . I even told him I'd take just a *small* share . . . but he wouldn't listen!"

His voice had risen to a petulant whine. "I didn't want to . . . hurt him, but he wouldn't listen!"

Frost had formed on his new beard, even tinting his eyebrows a crystalline white. His cheeks were ashen and deadly pale as though no blood flowed beneath them. He had not fared too well in the chill Arctic storm.

"Joshua!" She started to cry, remembering how he had bravely defended her in the kitchen so long ago, and then looked for her on the night Gannon was beaten. She cared about him, but it didn't erase the fact that he had just murdered her only remaining kin. "Let me go!" She struggled against his viselike grip. "Joshua, *please* . . . let me go . . ." There was no fight left in her, only sorrow over what had happened. He saw the look of defeat in her eyes, and mistook it for contempt. He saw in her what he felt about himself, and so he let her go, thinking it was useless to explain how the years of servitude and nonexistence had taken their toll on him. He knew, or thought he did, that she would never understand that the mine was his one chance—the brass ring—to finally be somebody.

In the distance, the wolves began to cry. Blood had seeped into the snow and their sensitive nostrils flared in anticipation.

Joshua paid them no mind as he walked toward his own sled. The last thread which had bound him to reality had snapped. His single thought was not for the dying man or the shattered girl who knelt beside him. He was not concerned about the voracious wolves clustered together in a deadly circle around the clearing. He heard a soft, feminine voice drifting up like a demon in the misty memories of his mind. High, tinkling laughter that thrilled him and caused him to shudder, and tiny fists which struck his chest, but left no mark that one could see . . . and the words, spoken so long ago, which had wounded him and caused his soul to crumble, "Marry *you?*" More laughter, soft, insinuating barbs that tore at his heart. "I could never *marry* you! You're nothing but a *cook!*" A tear, fluid until a sharp gust of wind began to slow it and freeze it before it entered his beard, slid from his eye. "You're *nothing* . . ." echoing, echoing, forever in his mind . . . damning him . . .

The wolves were more excited now, whimpering and growling in turn. The leader stood boldly in front, not bothering to follow the big man to his sled. He carried another loud stick, and the wolf knew enough to be cautious. Besides, he could smell the blood, taste it on the air. The old one would be easy, and his stomach was empty . . .

Jenny cradled John's head on her lap, lost in her grief, unaware of the danger which took quiet, sure steps forward. John's eyes flickered open, and she nearly jumped out of her skin.

"Uncle John!"

"Shhh, Missy . . . it's all right." But John had heard the crunching of the pads in the hardened snow, and had glimpsed gray shapes coming closer. "Pick up that big stick, Missy," he ordered. The leader, nervous now that the other had spoken, drew back. "They'll think it's a gun," he explained weakly. It was only then that her tears had subsided enough for her to see the wolves. She drew in a sharp breath, drawing the stick toward her, holding it protectively against her breast like a small child, her fingers and every part of her body trembling.

"Uncle John," she said, and even her words shook. He had closed his eyes momentarily, but when she had said his name, they had opened slowly.

She searched his face. "Uncle John," she begged, "how can I help you?" Tears were falling again from her already swollen eyes. He looked so much like her father!

"You can't," he said simply, and swallowed, closing his eyes again. He didn't want to see anymore, not ever again. "But I might be able to help you." He opened his eyes just a crack. "Take that stick," he said, "and *leave* . . . go the way we was going, and run with all yer might. You just might make it."

"No!" By now she was crying hard. "I can't leave you, Uncle John . . . not now." She stroked his old face with her trembling hand. "Yes, you kin," he said tiredly. "You kin, and you *will!*" He was looking at something she couldn't see. "I got one foot in the gate now, and it's just a short step over." He was so tired, he just wanted to sleep, but every time he closed his eyes, a light glowed, brighter and brighter with each passing second. Somehow, he wasn't afraid to die; he was happier now than he had been for many years. She had claimed him, calling him "Uncle" for the first time since they'd met, and her tears said how she felt plainer than any words. Sighing, he knew he could die now, because somebody would be left to grieve . . . somebody loved him. "Listen to me, Missy," he whispered. The words were getting harder and harder to say. He had to save her if he could . . . she must live! "The wolves will be content with me a little while—it'll give you a chance." He saw the look of horror on her face, and tried to smile. "Don't you worry none, I'll be long gone 'fore they ever get here—now *go!*" With what little strength he had left, he shoved her away from him.

"Uncle John!" she cried in protest, not wanting to leave him to the wolves . . . not wanting to leave him at all.

"Go on now, Mis . . . Jennifer," he commanded, smiling because she had called him "Uncle." "Go . . ." He closed his eyes, letting the light wash over him, and he was gone.

Jenny touched his chest, but he didn't move. No breath stirred the air above his lips, and his skin was already cooling to her touch. "I love you, Uncle John!" she whispered fervently, placing a soft farewell kiss on his wrinkled brow. Sobbing, she stumbled to her feet, seeing him as clearly in her mind as if he stood before her. "Go, Jenny . . . run with all yer might!" And she did.

The wolves were closer now and she held her stick toward them like a gun. They flinched and backed away. She passed them, and circled backward, pointing her stick all the while.

The leader growled in annoyance, but the cooling carcass of John sent messages to his hungry brain. As if as one animal instead of many, the group of wolves padded silently toward him, ignoring Jenny.

She couldn't watch. "Run, Jenny, run." John spoke to her in her mind, urging her on.

She heard a growl and a yip of pain and turned to see the leader with his snout buried in John's stomach.

"No-oo-o," she moaned, as bitter bile and acid arose in her throat. "Run, Jenny, run!" John's voice was urgent and commanding. She started to run, shutting out the sounds behind her, concentrating only on the path ahead of her. She had to make it to the cabin. She had to! For John, for Gannon, for herself. So she ran, her feet crunching rhythmically through the hard crust of snow, remembering John's voice telling her how to reach the cabin.

Fear drove Gannon on, making him relentless and hard in his pursuit of Jenny. The miles between them continued to grow smaller, but the dogs, pushed past their levels of endurance, were quickly losing speed. He growled harshly at them when he rode behind the runners, punctuating his commands with vicious stabs of the whip. He ran untiringly ahead of them, breaking the ever deepening snow with his feet, pushing himself, until the muscles in his legs screamed in white-hot agony, cramping and making him stumble, but he wouldn't quit. He'd just force himself up, and push on, ignoring the wracking pain of his body, and the sleep-deprived torture of his mind.

Kaiuga knew it was useless to argue with him, useless to tell him that they would lose dogs and time at this speed, because he knew, that should all the dogs fall and the sled pull apart and the wind blow like a nightmare, Gannon would still continue on, never stopping till he held his woman in his arms.

It was maybe an hour later when exhaustion and burning lungs made her pause. She didn't know how far she had come, or even how far she had left to go. Her mind refused to even think about the possibility that she may be going the wrong way.

The air had changed. Before it had been cold, but it had ceased to be windy. She could now feel short, cold breezes crossing her face, and she knew the weak Alaskan day was beginning to turn. Panic gripped her. She had to find shelter, a safe place to sleep. Maybe the wolves were after her now. She started to run, gulping in cold mouthfuls of burning air.

The rest of the day she spent alternately running and walking, never stopping. She was hungry, her throat was raw, and her hands and feet burned. Strangely she wasn't cold anymore, and the forest had taken on a dreamy cast. She was sweating beneath her furs. Small beads popped out and froze on her face as fast as they came. She wondered if she had a fever and then she wondered how long she could last.

"Must try," she breathed, forcing her legs to pump up and down. She was getting clumsy now, and her legs hit each other. The path she made wavered and was no longer straight.

The wind came faster now, swirling the snow into whirlpools before her eyes. "Stay to the clearing, it's a regular pathway between the trees. Follow it, and you'll find the cabin." "Yes John," she breathed, "I'll follow it."

Her mind began to play tricks on her. She heard crunching sounds like twigs breaking in the forest that rose up around her, and she could hear voices and music all mixed up together. She wasn't sure if it was inside her head or all around her.

Her feet were heavy, and when she picked one up to place ahead of the other, it fell drunkenly on top of it. She stumbled and fell, her face hitting the snow hard, but not hurting. She wanted to cry, but she couldn't. "Aaron," she pleaded, "I need you." She prayed for the shelter of his arms. Digging into the frozen crust with her hands, she pushed up. The world spun crazily before her eyes before settling down. "I must try." The words were barely a croak out of her tortured throat. She stood up, swaying slowly to the music in her head. Waves of warmth flowing over her made her sway unsteadily.

A loud cry filled the air. She stopped and stood very still. It took her mind a few minutes to register the sound. It was a wolf.

"No," she whispered. "No." She willed her frozen legs to run, not sure she was because she couldn't feel anything, but the forest was moving backward. She must be moving.

She was running against time as well as the wolves. It didn't turn dark gently here. Night came suddenly and completely and she knew in the dark she would have no chance.

She heard something behind her. A part of her screamed for her not to look back—just run—but she couldn't obey. Her head turned as her body staggered forward. They were there, loping easily along, following her.

"Oh, God," she thought. "Please help me." She tried to push her numb legs to run harder, to run faster. Her death was fast approaching.

The lead wolf saw his prey stagger and knew it was nearly spent. Triumphantly he gave way to his desolate cry. The others, sensing his excitement, joined in. It was a crazy round of savage voices, each picking up on the song of the others. Jenny started crying when she heard them howl. There was nowhere to run, nothing to protect herself with. She was going to die and she was afraid. Stark terror drove her frozen body on. How close? she wondered. How close?

She couldn't keep her head from turning like a puppet being pulled by a string from an unseen hand. They were closer now. She could make out each individual wolf and see its gaping mouth and hungry eyes.

Too late she turned, mesmerized by their presence. She stumbled and fell, whimpering like a child into the snow.

There was no energy left in her. Her mind continued to work, ordering the body to flee. But she couldn't move or even raise her head. Her fingers clawed convulsively into the snow as she waited.

The lead wolf saw her fall. It was time for the kill. Saliva dripped from his tongue and he increased his speed. He was full of the lust of the kill and his feet struck the snow with an increasing rhythm as he ran toward the girl.

Jenny closed her eyes. She could hear them coming, but she couldn't move. She prayed for the sweet oblivion of unconsciousness, but it did not come.

Her head was swimming, sounds all around her. She started to sink into blessed darkness. A loud cracking sound registered briefly in her dull mind and she thought of a twig snapping. Warm breath touched the back of her neck and she heard excited whimpering. Crunching snow was all around her. There was no more fear. She felt something brush against the back of her neck and braced herself for the killing blow. Silence. Seconds passed. Suddenly, over she went, over and up, an arm supporting her legs and shoulders. Not a wolf, her mind told her as she pulled herself out of the dark pool, long enough to open her eyes, but Gannon. He was holding her. She could feel his massive chest pressed against her, the steel of his arms encircling her. "Aaron." She formed the name of the one she loved and sank back into blessed darkness.

They had come upon the clearing before dark, and Gannon had nearly stopped breathing as he recognized the lumpy object in the snow.

Earlier they had followed the trail, both wolf's and man's, which had led them to the ruined campsite and John's pitiful remains.

Gannon had frantically searched the area, expecting to find Jenny at any moment.

"Here!" Kaiuga called. He had found her tiny tracks leading away from the area, and hurried to show the heartsick lover the trail. Impossible hope had urged them on as they prayed, each in their own way, to find her alive and safe. And now, with the wolf only inches from her head, they might be too late.

With trembling hands, Gannon raised his loaded rifle. The leader was snapping viciously at the others to wait their turn, as Gannon locked in on his big head. Carefully so the rifle wouldn't buck, he squeezed the trigger slowly. It jumped a little against his shoulder, but he didn't move or even breathe. He had hunted a good many pheasant and quail in his day, but no shot he had ever made could compare with this one. It must be perfect. From a distance, he saw the wolf. Suddenly he yipped and whirled into the air as if he'd been struck by an invisible giant. The others yelped in surprise, and scattered under Kaiuga's next shot.

Gannon didn't wait for more. Dropping the rifle to the snow he ran to her. She was lying so still! Trembling, he tried to say her name, but only choked back a sob as he lifted her to him. He thought she was dead, and remembered another cold day, many years ago, when someone else he loved had perished, leaving him alone. The idea of continuing without Jenny seemed so senseless, so lonely.

"Jen . . ." he whispered softly, his tears running unashamedly down her still, upturned face, as he hugged her to him.

She felt as though she were spinning in a black whirlpool that was drawing her down, farther and farther into its vortex. There was no pain or hunger or cold. No memories to haunt her, just a vast oblivion drawing her in, until *he* spoke her name and splintered the darkness like a jagged bolt of lightning ripping through her mind. The light hurt. The cold and the fear came crowding back as she opened her eyes . . .

"Aaron . . ." She tried to say his name, but her tongue was still a prisoner to the ice, as she slipped back into unconsciousness once again, knowing he held her, knowing she was safe.

Kaiuga was beside him with the sled, and together they laid her on the robes, pulling them up securely around her.

The cabin Jenny had run for was only a short distance ahead, and Gannon knew she would need a fire if she were to survive.

"Mush, Search!" he shouted. It was barely more than a growl, as he didn't trust himself to speak. The dogs, so weary and worn, sensed the urgency in his voice. With Kaiuga hauling the lead dog to his feet and pulling, the sled made its way in almost total darkness to the line shack.

CHAPTER

29

As she slept, her mind was filled with dreams. For two endless days and a night a fever gripped her, making her delirious, while memories, nightmarish and distorted, paraded grotesquely before her. She saw her uncle die over and over again, his clear blue eyes pleading and surprised, while buildings burned all around him. She heard her parents cry out. All the hateful, horrid events of the past year that she had endured—Kevin's greedy hands, and Gannon's moonlit ride away from her—had come back to haunt her now. Somehow she was transported to Em's, and then she wasn't. There were no wooden walls around her, or people laughing and talking. Everything seemed to dissolve like shadows cast into the light. She was left all alone in a dark pine forest crying and running for her life in painful, slow motion. Pale yellow eyes were everywhere, with nowhere left to turn. Dozens of golden flickering lights, drawing closer, becoming one great light, shifting and coming into focus until her dear old friend Joshua materialized out of the center, and reached out for her with his blood-stained hands. "He wouldn't listen, Jen!" he pleaded. "I tried . . . but he wouldn't listen!" Then he touched her arm, and she thought she'd go mad as she tried to scream but couldn't. Something glinted, silver and cold in the eerie light of her vision . . . closer, and closer, till she recognized his knife, rust-brown to the hilt . . .

"Joshua . . ." she moaned, as she struggled with his ghost. Please, Joshua . . . No—oo-o!" She twisted violently in the arms that held her.

"Jenny . . . shhh, lass . . . I'm here," Gannon soothed. But his words hardly touched her as he took her poor, trembling shoulders in his hands and drew her close.

Kaiuga had left yesterday to tend to John's remains, vowing that he could not rest until John did. He had left provisions enough for a week, assuring Gannon that Jenny would make it if the fever would break.

"You're safe, Jenny . . . I won't let anyone hurt you . . . I'm here," he whispered softly as he stroked her silky hair.

He pulled her head against his shoulder, trying to comfort her, making soft sounds deep in his throat as he rocked her gently back and forth in his arms.

She was still crying, sobbing hysterically, but he could feel that the fever had left her body, as her skin was cool to the touch.

The air in the cabin was cold, except for a semicircle of light around the fire. Though not beautiful, the cabin was sturdy, with thick, whole hewn pines, cut and braced for walls. There were only the most spartan of furnishings— pine posts lashed together for a bed, a table which tipped at an odd angle because one leg had been cut too short, solid, dark carved walls and an earthen floor and a tiny stone hearth. But the cruel north wind couldn't touch the pair, and the snow only gathered harmlessly around their door. Even the night sounds, prey and predator, creaking branches and hooting owls, seemed insignificant here. Secluded and sheltered, cut off from the rest of the world by the weather, wind, and walls, it was as if they were the only two people in the world.

"Joshua killed John!" Jenny sobbed, and Gannon pulled away enough to look into her face.

"Joshua?" he asked skeptically, unable to believe that his

325

old friend could be capable of such an act. But the truth was in Jenny's eyes, which looked at him wide-eyed and tearful, doelike in the flickering firelight, their innocence forever shattered.

"Where did he go?" he asked, remembering the second set of runners in the snow.

Jenny shook her head. "I don't know . . . He kept talking about the mine, saying he had tried to talk to Uncle John about working with him . . . he just kept saying, "he wouldn't listen," and then he left, and the wolves . . ." she shuddered and Gannon pulled her close.

"I doubt if he got too far in this. Cooking doesn't exactly prepare you for this kind of life." Pity touched his voice, as he pictured Joshua lost and wandering in the freezing cold. He may have killed John, but Gannon could hardly believe he had planned to.

It was only then that Jenny became aware that the robes which had covered her had fallen to her waist. She was naked. She gasped in surprise, as she reached down and started to pull the robe upward. Gannon's hand met hers, and he held it for just a second, the distraction of her breasts sending sensuous messages to his brain and the blood pounding through his veins. With his eyes locked on hers, he pulled the robe up, covering her, and then he placed a gentle kiss on her forehead.

"You need something to eat." He moved toward the hearth, where broth had been made and was still warm. Pouring it into a cup, he brought it back, letting her drain it thoroughly while he heaped several solid logs onto the fire.

He watched the fire catch, sending orange and yellow flames upward, and a sense of peace washed over him. Here he had nothing. Not reputation, honor, or distinction. All he had was himself, his two hands, and Jenny. No lavish balls or sweet debutantes. Nothing but wilderness, a raw land he could see that was full of wealth for the taking. A land where a man could dream, build, raise a family. The trappers had told him of the few ranchers there were, the mines, logging . . . words which had filled his mind with visions—dreams of stature where he could start anew. Not just an Irishman, or an orphan street fighter, but a man.

"Aaron," Jenny whispered.

He turned to look at her. The firelight had cast her silhouette against the wall, where it wavered and danced magically.

"Sleep with me," she said quietly. "I don't want to sleep alone." With those words, she drew the stiff, brown bear robe away, inviting him to join her on the rickety pine bed and lie down beside her. Even her shadow twin had done the same. He could see soft full mounds of pale cream, mirrored darkly on the wall behind her.

He would have been content tonight to hold her, reining in the passion he always felt when she was near. He reasoned that she was weak, in need of rest, and to feel her cradled against him—sweet torture that would have been was enough. But not now, though.

On legs as weak and slender as a new foal, she stood and walked toward him, yearning in her eyes and heart. She needed no more dark dreams or golden eyes tonight—she needed him.

His mouth had gone dry as he watched her walk toward him, with a throbbing ache he knew he could hardly control.

Her beauty kept him welded to the spot, a prisoner of his eyes and love, until she stood before him, both facing each other on the bearskin rug which had served as Aaron's bed. Timidly, not sure if what she wanted to do was what she should, she moved her hands slowly upward cupping her breasts, offering them to him. "Please . . ." she whispered.

With trembling arms, he encircled her waist, a deep groan escaping from his mouth as he bent forward. He lightly brushed his lips across the rosy tips, which were taut and straining and full. Shudders of delight coursed through her, the cool air and his mouth sensuously touching and caressing, making her tremble as she slid her hands along his arms to capture and hold his bowed head as close to her as possible.

"I love you . . ." she whispered, the words seeming so

inadequate to describe how she felt, as she pulled him closer, burying her face in his coppery curls, twining her fingers through them, losing the gentleness of her touch to the overpowering urgency of her need.

Gannon's clothes felt like a vise encasing his body, as though ready to explode any minute. Pulling back long enough to tug his shirt over his head and peel the white trousers from his thighs, he reached for her again, perspiration dampening his hair, while his breath quickened. She felt his need pressed between them. A rod of fierce, hot steel that she longed for deep inside.

"Aaron . . ." The word was full of want, barely more than a hoarse whisper.

The two sank down together on the rug, firelight playing with their flesh, shadows imitating their movement on the walls, as he parted her and entered in one swift movement. Crying out, she rode with him, wrapping her slender legs around his back, finding the rhythm that matched his own effortlessly as they danced out their love in the firelight's glow. And somewhere, in the midst of their lovemaking, the boundaries between their bodies melted away—wherever breasts, bellies, thighs touched and rubbed—the two came together in white hot flames of love, and became one.

They loved many more times that night, taking pleasure and giving it, expressing their feelings with actions and words, until near dawn, resting spoon-fashion with her small bottom and back pressed tightly against his stomach and chest, the two drifted into sleep.

Kaiuga woke them with a banging door, and a hearty greeting.

"Ho, Gannon! I see everything is as it should be!"

Gannon raised himself on one elbow while keeping a protective arm around Jenny, who tried to snuggle as deep under the bearskin as she could.

"How'd it go?" he asked nonchalantly.

"Good," he offered. "I built him an icehouse, and closed up the openings—but there is one thing we must take care of."

"What is it?"

Kaiuga brought out the large gold rock which had hung around John's neck.

"We must put these back, so that John can rest."

"Put it back?" Gannon asked crossly. "There isn't any need to go on to the mine now. Jenny's been through enough."

Kaiuga's dark eyes found hers. "John won't rest," he said quietly.

Jenny felt a superstitious tug on her mind. Ghosts and ghoulies—spirits that could not rest, wolves—smart as men. All these things had no place in Kansas City, but here, where time had surrendered itself to the past, all these things seemed possible. Besides, she felt a sense of responsibility toward John. He had been her last remaining kin, and he had lost his life in trying to give something of value to her. He had succeeded, though Jenny doubted that he had known. He had given her an uncle who used to be only words on paper. He had given her a sense of herself, a feeling that in some way, no matter what obstacles she would have to face in life, she would overcome them.

"We have to go to the mine, Aaron . . . for John."

She had turned over, lying on her back, so that she could gaze up at his face.

"Jenny, that old mine is at least a day's ride from here."

"We *have* to go! I don't know why exactly . . . I just know we have to!"

He stared at her for a long moment, wondering what to do. Joshua was out there, still roaming around, his mind unbalanced and dangerous . . . and the weather might change. He didn't want to put her through any more.

"No, lass," he said firmly. "It's too dangerous. I won't risk it."

"If you don't take me, Aaron—I'll go alone—I'll walk if I have to!"

There was a finality and desperation in her voice. Deep inside, he knew she meant it.

"Jen . . . I said no, and I mean it."

He tried to pull her close, hoping his body might convince her if his words wouldn't. But her eyes glinted stubbornly, and he knew it wouldn't work. There was something driving her to do this, with or without him. "All right," he growled. "We'll go to the damned mine in the morning!"

She smiled and looked relieved, snuggling close to him. She had to finish what was started—for her parents, for her uncle John, for herself.

He shook his head, immediately intoxicated by her nearness. He was putty in her hands.

His stomach growled, and she laughed softly. "Shouldn't we get something to eat?" she asked.

"Later," he growled. "Much later." He pulled her roughly to him while Kaiuga discreetly went for a walk.

CHAPTER
30

The next day was clear and bright. Breakfast, consisting of hard biscuits and stiff black coffee, was eaten hurriedly. A sense of urgency had overtaken the trio—a feeling that time was against them on these short, weak days. Without speaking, they knew they must hurry if they expected to reach the mine before dark.

While Jenny straightened the room, Gannon and Kaiuga cut wood and hauled it back to the cabin. They were careful in their choice of trees, looking for aged hardwoods, which would burn slow and evenly, and thin, flaked, soft pine to use for kindling, filling the cabin with more wood than they had taken, wood ready to burn for the next weary traveler.

Jenny had loaded the sled with the few items they had, laying the skins on top to protect the food. The dogs had been fed and were eager to run.

"Ready?" Aaron asked. She nodded, glancing once more at the squat old cabin, with its sod roof and dirt floor, knowing that she would always remember it with sweetness, as she turned and shut the door.

"We'll be there before dark," Kaiuga reassured, as she climbed onto the sled. Then he cracked the whip. The dogs jumped and barked and pulled gladly ahead, while Gannon trotted easily along beside them. North they went, always north, closer to the dark, rushing waters of the sea, and the barren, inhospitable coast. North, toward the mine.

The morning had been an easy run, the sled gliding swiftly along corridors of lustrous ice between giant columns of ancient spruce. An uncanny silence seemed to shadow them, filling the void behind the whooshing of the sled's runners and the dogs' hot, panting breath as completely as water fills the trail of a finger through a pond. They hadn't stopped except to eat some cold jerky and rest the dogs. Kaiuga faced west, calculating the shadows, scanning the distant horizon with eyes perfectly adapted by thousands of years of evolution, eyes as glowing black as anthracite, as keen and predatory as an eagle's.

A raised eyebrow from Gannon and a muffled "Will we make it?" was answered with a nod before they resumed their run. This time, with Kaiuga loping along beside the sled while Gannon cracked the whip and shouted "Mush!", the dogs sprang instantly to life and began to pull.

Farther along the trail, the landscape began to change. The endless sea of pines which had shielded them for so long began to thin, and the void surrounding them to fill with shrieking winds of almost hurricane intensity. The few spruce which clung stubbornly to the barren rocks were squat, tortured things, nearly devoid of needles, tenaciously reaching toward the bleak, gray sky like black, accusing fingers. It was colder here, and the light had steadily become weaker, diffuse, without power. Great, granite slabs of rock projected chaotically from the snow, polished smooth by the fierce, howling western winds blowing in from the Chukchi Sea.

Hell, Jenny thought, was not an inferno, but a frozen rock; its boundaries not flowing rivers of lava, but walls of brittle ice, filled with demonic winds. She was scared. It felt as if a chunk of ice lay in her stomach, growing larger with each passing moment.

The eastern horizon turned a bruised shade of purple, while the shadows around them darkened. She watched theirs as she went. They had become long, and spidery thin;

the outline of the sled and dogs undulating in the passing drifts of snow like cresting waves before becoming flat. How much longer, she wondered? As if in answer to her thoughts, Kaiuga shouted against the wind.

"There!" He pointed triumphantly with one hand.

Automatically their eyes followed his movements. For a second it seemed that nothing existed in this landscape except endless wind and biting cold. Squinting, she tried to shield her eyes with her hand, still not seeing what he saw, until a ridge seemed to materialize out of the swirling snow. Slabs of stone, heaped high, one on top of the other. In the very center, yawning darkly, was an immense black hole . . . a gaping mouth. They headed toward it.

The environment held all the elements of a nightmare: descending darkness; twisting, mad winds; and a chasm, sinister and brooding, that seemed to be waiting . . . Her heart began to beat a little wildly as they neared the entrance and Gannon reined in the dogs. There was a feeling deep inside her soul, a soft, sibilant, still voice warning her, but she ignored it as she stood up, stretching stiffly, staring at the entrance now with open curiosity.

"No one's been here," Kaiuga said, who was bent forward, studying the ground around the entrance. "There are no tracks." Jenny looked down to inspect the snow. All she saw was white, unbroken patches of powder. Occasionally the wind would gust low, blowing like a breath across the ground, and the snow would stir lethargically, lifting and swirling into the air, before coming to rest once again.

"Let's light the torches," Gannon suggested. "If nothing else, we can camp in there tonight and be out of this wind." Kaiuga nodded. Jenny liked the idea of torches very much, but as she peered into the gloomy hole, the thought of sleeping in there made her shudder. It was so *still*, so *large*—the opening nearly fifteen feet in height and twice that in length—and dark as a proverbial tomb.

"Sleep?" she nearly squeaked, unable to get the full word out because her hood was crusted over with ice. "In *there?*"

"Aye," Gannon smiled mischievously. "Either in there with all the ghosties and ghouls, or out *here* with those fierce ice bears Kaiuga was telling me about!" He winked at Kaiuga, who grinned broadly as he rummaged through the sled, bringing out two lengths of oilcloth and the branches he had carefully cut this morning. Jenny looked at him for confirmation, and he nodded, looking as serious as possible.

"*Big* ice bears!" he added, stretching his arms out as far as he could. "Always hungry, too!" He laughed as he watched her pale skin turn ashen.

"Stop it!" she said crossly, stamping her little foot so that her parka shook. The men continued to laugh at her as they entered the mine. No sound greeted them, the rock walls effectively blocking out the wind. But there was no light, either. Gannon helped Kaiuga wrap the oilcloth around the ends of the torches, using the weak light issuing from the door. Then he struck a match. The sulfur flared instantly to life, and he touched it to the torches. Within minutes they were burning brightly, and he smiled at Jenny, holding one out for her to take.

The shadows outside deepened in protest, and the walls danced happily in the flames of the torches, but not as brilliantly as she had expected, not with golden fire.

They moved farther into the room. The torches flared brightly, sputtered and kicked brilliantly. She looked at the two men, a question in her eyes. There was another breeze in here, and it wasn't coming from the entrance.

"Must be another entrance somewhere," Gannon suggested. Kaiuga nodded in agreement.

There was nothing in this cavernous room, except cold gray stones and cross-braced beams which looked relatively new. Myriad cracks lined the walls and ceiling. Gannon didn't think it looked too safe. He watched Jenny as she looked around and saw the disappointment register on her face. So, John had been spinning yarns all along, he thought wryly. He could see no walls of gold, or even a tiny glimmer. Nothing but rocks and dirt and a girl's dying dreams.

"Enough?" he asked quietly.

"No," she said firmly, shaking her head and holding her torch high. "Uncle John said there was a room with walls and ceilings of gold—and I still believe him." She refused to accept the idea that he had lied to her. He had gone through too much, waited too long. She just knew he had told her the truth. "Look!" she shouted, pointing excitedly to the far side of the room where two tunnels had been carved out of the stone. The larger one was fairly clear, while the smaller one was littered with debris and looked almost impassable. She started to cross the room, intent on proving her uncle right, when a firm hand spun her sharply around, nearly knocking the torch from her hand.

"*You* stay here!" Gannon ordered, "We'll look in there if it'll put your mind at ease—but you *wait here!*"

"Why don't you look in one, and I in the other?" she argued prettily, her curiosity dying to be satisfied. "It will save us both a lot of time, and I . . ." She stopped in midsentence as she felt his eyes boring into her.

"*You . . . wait . . . here!*" he warned, his fear for her giving his voice almost a harsh quality.

"But . . ."

A raised eyebrow and a firmly placed finger over her protesting mouth silenced her.

"Wait!" he ordered, kissing the tip of her nose before he and Kaiuga disappeared down the larger tunnel, leaving Jenny alone. She watched their light until it became no more than a glow and was suddenly gone. The tunnel must curve, she thought, and wondered about the other one. Perhaps the two met somewhere back there. Maybe she ought to just peek into the other one. She didn't think she could fit through it anyway, not with all those rocks, but, maybe . . . if she turned *sideways,* and pushed a little . . . Before she knew it she was midway through the narrow shaft, with her torch held high. It was getting colder in here. She felt a stiff breeze stir against her cheek as the passage began to widen. Her torchlight had fallen ahead, catching something which glimmered, throwing back her light, and she caught her breath.

The narrow passageway had widened until it opened into a small room where the timbers had partially fallen in. As she stepped into its center, her heart began to beat wildly. The room was literally ablaze with light, ablaze with gold!

"It's true!" she whispered, holding her torch aloft. She spun slowly, highlighting each corner and crevice of the little room. "A roomful of gold . . ." She lowered her torch, watching as a curiously luminous blue fog rolled only inches above the ground, flowing slowly as a current of air pulsed through it.

Marveling at the rich veins of gold throbbing like the hidden life of a mountain, she took a tentative step forward, until she felt something strike against her foot. Frowning, she bent down, waving away the blue mist from the floor. Then she screamed.

On the other side of the mine, Gannon and Kaiuga had come to the end of the tunnel. It had led nowhere. They were turning around to make their way back, when Jenny's cry pierced the air around them, echoing wildly until the dust began to fall from the ceiling above. They didn't wait for a second one, but ran, Gannon in the lead with Kaiuga trailing close behind.

In the little room of gold, Jenny backed away, peering hard at the swirling fog. What she had taken for broken timbers were bones . . . human bones stretched out in a mad design. One long, skeletal arm seemed to be reaching for something, clutching a smaller set of bones in its knobby hand.

This must be the sea man, she thought, who had cursed his friend and been cursed in return. He must have died here all alone, crawling back into this tiny room.

It was then that she noticed movement directly in front of her. What she had taken for shadowed rock slowly unfolded and stood up.

"Oh!" A startled cry escaped her lips as she took a fearful step backward, feeling the rough wall behind her. There was no place left to go; nowhere to hide from the hulking shadow coming slowly toward her. It was then that she recognized the tortured form of her old friend, Joshua. He stumbled forward, a moronic grin on his face. She saw with a pang of sorrow that the elements had not been kind to him. His cheeks and nose and the right hand he held out imploringly toward her were ashen in hue.

"Joshua . . ." she said softly, her pity making new tears appear on her cheeks. "It's me . . . Jenny."

He didn't appear to hear her, lost in a world she couldn't possibly understand. Pain had built his world, loneliness supplying the bricks, self-hatred the mortar. He didn't see Jenny swathed head to heel in furs standing sadly in front of him. He saw the blond, honey-eyed merchant's wife in pale pink silks that he had loved so earnestly so many years ago.

"I'm rich now . . ." he offered. "I'm somebody you can be proud of . . . not . . . not just a cook." His words were barely audible because his tongue had long since given part of itself to the cold. "Everything I have . . ." He gestured at the walls of gleaming gold with his tortured hand, "is for you!" Then he smiled and reached for her, the gnarled, blackened hand resembling more the claw of a bird than anything human. He touched her hair, his eyes dreamy, hopeful, and so lost . . .

"No!" she shouted in disgust, slapping instinctively at his hand; it was then that the soft light left his eyes and they blazed insanely as he wrapped his hand around her throat and began to squeeze.

She struggled like a rag doll in his grip, scratching and hitting him. But it was useless, he was so strong!

"I loved you . . ." he whispered hoarsely. Tears flowed down his cheeks. "I'd done anything . . . *anything* for you!" The pressure of his hand increased with his tears until the room began to grow dim. The shimmering gold, and the pitiful, tear-stained face of Joshua began to blur . . .

Gannon and Kaiuga were struggling to push their way through the last of the narrow passage, their shoulders making it nearly impossible as they moved along. Dust, thicker now, and small bits of rock continued to filter down in ever increasing amounts from above. Up ahead, Gannon felt the pressure lessening as the passage began to widen. Gold momentarily dazzled his eyes, obscuring the two struggling forms on the other side of the room.

"I loved you!" Joshua cried.

Gannon whirled at the sound of Joshua's voice. "Let go of her!" he bellowed.

The pressure, which had deprived Jenny of air and caused her neck to ache, lessened.

Gannon started to move forward when Joshua, seeing only the timid, spectacle-wearing merchant from long ago, pulled the revolver from his coat with his one good hand. He pulled the trigger.

Jenny had crumpled to the ground at Joshua's feet, drawing in painful breaths while the shot had gone wide and the two men had taken cover in the tunnel.

"Let her go, Joshua! She's done you no harm!" Gannon shouted. "Jenny . . . are you all right? Can you hear me?"

She struggled to concentrate as Gannon looked out to see her.

Joshua was standing absolutely still, the gun pointed exactly in the same place. He looked catatonic, as though not even aware of what he'd done.

"Stay down, Jenny," Gannon called softly. "Come to me . . . slowly. Don't get up!" She heard him, and with an apprehensive glance at the giant towering above her, she began to move very slowly toward the tunnel.

The shot had vibrated the interior so badly that the air was thick with dust and crumbling stone.

"Hurry, Jenny!" Gannon urged softly. She did as he commanded, crawling as quietly as she could.

But the stressed timbers wouldn't wait. With a groan, the beams began to crack and split, sounding like gunfire all along the room.

The sounds seemed to draw Joshua back. As confused as a man waking from a nightmare, he both remembered and wanted to forget everything that had happened. But it all came back to him as he saw Jenny inching toward the tunnel.

A cracking noise right above her head made her look up. She cried out in alarm as she brought her arm around in a futile attempt to shield her face as the beam began to fall.

"Jen!" Joshua bellowed, recognition dawning on his face. He stumbled toward her, catching the falling timber over his broad back. Like dominoes, one had fallen and the rest had begun to follow.

Gannon rushed forward, grabbing Jenny's arm and pulling her backward. Meanwhile the entire weight of the huge timber rested squarely on Joshua's shoulders. Groaning, he used what little strength he had left, locking his knees and pushing up as hard as he could, letting his huge frame act like a living brace, holding up the other beams.

"Go!" he growled, sweat lining his brow and his cheeks, still wet from his tears.

"No, Joshua!" Jenny cried, not wanting to leave him. She reached for his hand . . . and for a moment, their eyes met, the princess and the troll, his pleading for forgiveness, and hers granting it. The tips of their fingers touched for one last time. Suddenly, the walls gave a mighty roar, cracked, and started crumbling inward . . .

"Run!" Gannon commanded, shoving her roughly through the narrow passage while he and Kaiuga followed as quickly as they could, a single torch lighting their way.

Jenny gained the main room first and waited bravely for the others. Their parkas were nearly in shreds when they joined her, having had most of the fur stripped from the lining by the walls of rock. But the cold they would feel was the least of their concerns as they rushed forward, each one taking one of her hands in his as they ran for the opening.

The mountain, unable to stand the strain any longer, gave one last horrific groan, rumbled and fell inward, belching great clouds of dust into the night.

They had barely escaped and stood gazing in horror at the sealed mine.

"Joshua," she whispered, feeling love and pity and sadness for her poor, lost friend, unable now to even blame him for the death of her uncle, knowing he had not been responsible for his actions.

The stars were shining as Aaron wrapped his arms about her. He didn't speak, he just held her, his own tears making her hair wet.

EPILOGUE

It was late summer and the droning of bees filled the fragrant air. She sat in front of their cabin, holding their newborn son to her breast.

Gannon stood nearby, talking to a group of engineers from Seattle about how he wanted the flues constructed on his new mining and logging operation.

John Aaron Gannon pulled his tiny, perfect pink mouth away from her breast and studied his mother seriously with his newly opened eyes. They were bright and clear and as jade green as his father's, with tufts of burnished copper hair framing his face.

He had come before the preacher, but that hadn't mattered. Winter had not allowed much travel, and they had spent a good portion of it in the line shack planning their future.

They had both wanted to stay in Alaska, to build a life tied closely to this beautiful land. Arrangements with lawyers had been made, and Gannon's hotel had been given to Dugan's family in appreciation for all they had done for him. Jenny learned that Anna had passed away last winter. They had found her with a sweet smile on her face and her music box silent and open. In her mind, Jenny could picture her and her Glenn dancing gaily among the stars, happy again in each other's arms.

News from home also included some interesting gossip about Penelope. It seemed her father caught her and the rogue Phillip in a rather compromising position. All turned out fairly well in the end, as the mayor *persuaded* Phillip with the business end of a rifle to propose to his daughter. Jenny couldn't imagine a more suitable pair.

After leaving Gannon and Jenny at the line shack, Kaiuga went to fetch his wives. He and his pretty, fat little Narvaranna, with the obsidian eyes and broad, flat cheeks and her diligent, hard working sister, all lived together happily by the sea. The captain and Emily finally tied the knot as well, he claiming that the only ship he intended to sail was the small one he'd saved for his bathtub.

All things had come full circle, falling into place as they always did. She and Gannon had selected a beautiful, grassy hillside, placing crosses of oak and wreaths of wildflowers to honor both John and Joshua, though they were careful not to place the two too close together. Dugan had told Jenny the story behind Joshua's lost love, explaining his betrayal and hurt as well as an old man could, asking her to forgive him. Dugan didn't have to ask her to forgive Joshua because she already had. Sometimes, in the clear long afternoons beneath the sounds of wind and trickling brook, she could hear them, her wily old uncle John and her lost friend Joshua. Like echoes from the past, they drifted through her mind.

"You ol' Walrus!"

"My name ain't 'Walrus' . . . you old bum! It's Joshua! Josh-u-ah!" Then she would sigh, missing them.

Now, as she was sitting here, content in this beautiful, strange land, her past seemed like a dream.

She had come to Alaska to find her life and had nearly lost it. Instead of gold and furs and fancy words, she had this, her home, her child, her man. It was only the beginning of her life—the first pages of her story.

The engineers had left. She watched them as they wound

their way down the twisting, brown mountain path, looking like tiny toys in the distance.

Gannon, finished with his business, turned toward her. His expression was no longer guarded or lonely. No ghosts haunted his nights, but his arrogance—the tip of his head, the haughty smile—still remained. His cheeks were rosy in the afternoon light, and his glossy copper hair was tousled by the soft, August breeze. A mischievous glint lit his sparkling green eyes as he walked toward her. The wind tugged teasingly at his open shirt, causing the "V" of its neck to deepen, revealing the finely corded muscles of his chest.

A sympathetic yearning began to grow in her, a warmth deep in the golden valley between her thighs, simply at the sight of him. He took her hand in his. She knew that look, and she blushed in pleasure. "Love me . . ." he whispered and she saw the hunger welling up in his eyes.

Carefully she placed their son in his cradle, covering him with linen to protect him from the wind and sun before she and Gannon walked away together into the tall, swaying grasses.

Together they lay down in the soft green meadow that seemed to sit on top of the world, with valleys of dark green pine surrounding them and rivers of cold, sapphire water cascading beneath them. He cradled her head in his hands, and gazed long and deeply into her eyes.

"Love me, Jenny . . ." he whispered, softer than a sigh.

"Always . . ." she promised, sealing her vow with a kiss.

He loved her gently, and he loved her well, all the long afternoon, beneath the golden sun, covered only by a blanket of the bluest sky Jenny had ever seen.

Paradise is Alaska
Eternal is her night
Chill winds whisper warnings
While my lover holds me
Tight . . .